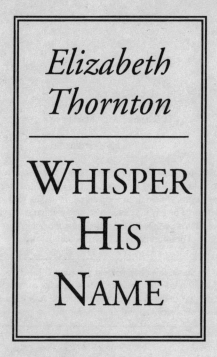

Elizabeth Thornton

WHISPER HIS NAME

BANTAM BOOKS

NEW YORK · TORONTO LONDON

SYDNEY AUCKLAND

WHISPER HIS NAME

A Bantam Book / March 1999

ISBN 0-553-57427-2

Published simultaneously in the United States and Canada

Bantam Books are published by Bantam Books, a division of
Random House, Inc. Its trademark, consisting of the words "Bantam
Books" and the portrayal of a rooster, is Registered in U.S. Patent
and Trademark Office and in other countries. Marca Registrada.
Random House, Inc., New York, New York.

PRINTED IN THE UNITED STATES OF AMERICA
OPM 10 9 8 7 6 5 4

WHISPER
HIS
NAME

PROLOGUE

The man who was after her didn't look like a killer. He was young and handsome and dressed in the blue uniform of King Louis's Lifeguards. The English ladies who were shopping in the bustling galleries of the Palais Royal could hardly take their eyes off the blond-haired Adonis. A short while ago, they would have spat on a French soldier, but now that the war was over, the past was forgotten and the English were finding a warm welcome in France.

No one knew this man's nationality. His facility with languages made it impossible to place him. He had many names and no name. He was a master of disguise. To her, he was simply Nemo, Napoleon's most feared and fanatical agent.

And he was supposed to be dead.

Murderer! she wanted to scream. It wouldn't do her any good. She would only give her position away, and Nemo would get to her before she could say her own name.

She stood stock-still, trying to even her breathing, pretending an interest in the window display of a milliner's shop in one of the arcades. But she wasn't interested in bonnets. She was intent on the reflection of the man who was idling his way through the stream of shoppers outside the café Very. When he became lost to view behind one of the stone arches, she attached herself to a group of strollers and moved on to the next arcade.

It took every ounce of willpower not to look over her shoulder to see if he had spotted her. She kept her face averted by pretending an interest in all the shopwindows she passed on the way. When she came to Dessene's, the bookseller's, she halted.

This wasn't how it was supposed to be. Her contact was waiting for her at a bookshop in the rue de Rivoli, but she would never make it that far. She was desperate. She'd had to improvise, and her one hope was that she could persuade old Dessene to deliver the book for her. Then she would draw Nemo off.

The chase was something he could not resist. He was a hunter. He didn't want an easy kill. He'd allowed her to escape with the book; he'd told her he would give her a sporting chance. Cat and mouse—it was all a game to him, and when he got tired of it, he would kill her.

A year ago, such thoughts would have sent her into a panic. Now, she felt curiously detached. With Jerome gone, nothing mattered anymore except to avenge his death. She wasn't putting her life in danger for love of country. That was something she'd learned about herself. She wasn't a true patriot like Jerome. She was driven by hatred of the man who had killed him.

When she entered the shop, a bell over the door rang, and the young woman who was at the counter paying for her purchases gave her a cursory glance. On the floor by her feet was a basket brimming with books. Dessene was not behind the counter, but a man she had never seen before. She tensed when a customer moved by her to stand beside the young woman with the basket of books. She wasn't surprised when they spoke in English. They had that look about them. With the man, it was his dark coat and impeccable tailoring; with the girl it was small things— a hemline that was too long, a neckline that was too high. The man was younger than the woman, and there was a strong resemblance between them. Brother and sister, she decided. Jerome had taught her to observe these small details. He'd also taught her to trust her instincts. She didn't know why, but she liked the look of this fair-haired English girl. But she didn't like the look of the clerk behind the counter.

A confusion of thoughts raced through her mind. The only reason she had chosen Dessene to pass on the book was because he knew her and Jerome, knew that Jerome was a penniless student, and he'd been kind to them both. But Dessene wasn't here. She had to do something. At any moment she could be discovered. She had to act quickly. She could hide the book and come back for it later. But if she couldn't come back, what then?

Her brain worked like lightning. She looked at the English couple and made her decision. With her own volume in her hand, she went to stand beside them and "inadvertently" jostled the basket on the floor. When the basket tipped over, spilling the books, she exclaimed over her clumsiness, quickly stooped down, and exchanged her own book for one from the basket.

She completed the transaction not a moment too soon, for the English girl bent down to help. Their hands met on the handle of the basket.

"It's my fault," said the English girl in slow but precise

French. "I should not have left my basket on the floor for someone to trip over."

She had kind eyes and a kind smile.

And all unknowingly she had just become involved in something that was supremely dangerous.

There was nothing she could say to warn the English girl without provoking a spate of questions. With a smile and a nod she straightened, then casually moved to the back of the shop. When the bell over the door rang, she turned slowly. Nemo wasn't alone. He was accompanied by two other Lifeguards. He said something to the English girl. When she blushed, the Lifeguards laughed. Her own heart had stopped beating. Had Nemo seen her pass the book to the English girl? She let out a soft sigh when he stood aside to allow the English couple to leave the shop. Then she slipped behind the last stack of books and made for the back door.

Before she opened the door, she felt in her coat pocket for her pistol. It should have been primed and ready for use, but she'd grown careless of late. The war was over, she'd reasoned. Napoleon was exiled on Elba. Nemo was supposed to be dead. It was time to enjoy the fruits of their labors. Jerome was more cautious than she. She should have listened to him, and now it was too late.

As she pushed through the door into rue de Montpensier, an ice-cold rage possessed her. It wasn't too late. She had another mission now. She had to give the English girl time to get away. If she, herself, escaped, she would track the girl down and retrieve the book. If not, she had to believe that the girl would work out the significance of what she'd been given and get it to the right people.

She darted between two stationary horse-drawn wagons and crossed to the other side of the street. At the corner of the alley, she halted and glanced over her shoulder. Nemo was framed in the bookshop's doorway. He had a gun in his hand. She wasn't afraid of the gun; she was afraid of being taken alive.

He gave a shout when he saw her. She wanted him to see her, wanted to draw him off. Jerome had trained her for this work, but she'd never been tested until now. This was one test she would not fail.

He was smiling that superior smile of his that she detested. No one ever got the better of Nemo. He was arrogant; he was pitiless. One day, she prayed God, he would meet his match.

She let the rage take her. *Come on you murdering swine! Come and get me!*

As they started after her, she dashed into the alley and began to run. The few people who were in her way took one look at the pistol in her hand and cleared a path for her. Her pursuers were gaining on her, but no shots rang out. It was just as she thought; Nemo would want to make the kill by himself.

She saw her target halfway along the alley—the brazier of the street seller, Thibeault. The aroma of hot pies and buns made her heart wrench. A memory came sharply into focus—she and Jerome stopping for a hot pie on their way home from the theater.

In a last burst of speed, she gained the brazier. She knew then that this was the end for her. Her lungs were burning, her legs were cramping, her stamina was gone. But her rage had not diminished. And it was rage that conquered all her fears.

She pointed her pistol at Thibeault's head. "Open the door of the brazier," she snapped out.

When the street seller hastened to obey, she thrust the

book into the hot coals. "Now get out of here," she said harshly. "Save yourself," and she quickly spun around to face her assailants.

As her pistol came up, they fanned out. Her eyes went to Nemo. A slow smile spread across his face. He'd seen her burn the book and thought he'd won. She'd bought the English girl some time after all.

Everything was now in the hands of God.

She leveled her pistol at Nemo and thought of Jerome. The first shot flung her back against the terrified street seller. They died in a hail of bullets.

CHAPTER I

The gloves were about to come off. That was the thought that flashed through Abbie's mind when her brother-in-law rose from the table and, on the flimsiest pretext, led Miss Fairbairn, her paid companion, from the room. Her suspicions were confirmed shortly after when her older brother, Daniel, signaled the footman to retire. The room had emptied of everyone who was not a Vayle. Vayles never washed their dirty linen in public.

She might have been alarmed by these obvious tactics if she hadn't felt mildly resentful. This was, after all, her house. She had provided the excellent dinner her family had just consumed. She was the one who paid her servants' wages, not to mention those of Miss Fairbairn. Yet Daniel had taken charge of her household as if by divine right, and everyone now deferred to him.

The trouble was, old habits died hard, and she supposed the servants were taking their cue from her. This was the first time her family had made the journey to Bath to see her. They'd come down from her brother-in-law's place near Oxford, where they always spent the hunting season, and would be returning to London in the morning for the start of the social season. They'd come out of their way to see her, and she'd wanted to please them. In spite of their faults, she loved them all dearly. That was where she always went wrong. She really must learn to stand up for herself.

This wasn't a problem for her with the friends she had made in Bath. Then again, they had never seen her in the role of dutiful daughter, favorite maiden aunt, or self-effacing spinster. She had taken pains to establish herself as a person in her own right, and she didn't know why it was so difficult to do the same thing with her own family.

Over the rim of her wineglass, she studied the faces of the three people who sat around her polished mahogany dining table. Her mother's elegant eyebrows were raised—always a bad sign; her sister, Harriet, was affecting her usual bored expression; and Daniel was regarding her with a look that was more perplexed than stern.

They were a striking trio, this formidable family of hers, with their dark good looks, refined features, and intelligent green eyes. They were strong-willed, strong-minded characters. It was in their nature to master anyone who was weaker than they. And in her, they'd found the perfect object to work upon.

But that was in the past. She'd had twelve months of glorious freedom, ever since she'd come into her legacy, twelve months as her own mistress, and at the advanced age of seven and twenty, she was just beginning to discover who she really was. So many years to regret, trying to conform to someone else's idea of what she should be! She was determined there would be no more regrets.

It was her brother who broke the long, unnatural silence. "There is something I wish to discuss with you, Abbie," he said.

She tried to head him off. "This isn't the time to have a discussion. We're due at the Gardiners' in the next hour." She smiled to soften her words. "Besides, I can never concentrate when I'm dressed to go to a party. Let's postpone this conversation till later."

"There won't be another time, as you know very well." He smiled whimsically. "Admit it, Abbie. You've gone out of your way to avoid this family conference. Ever since we arrived, you've filled our days and nights with engagements. It we don't talk now, we'll not have the opportunity to do so later."

The very idea of a "family conference" was enough to give her the shudders. Her family liked to think it worked on democratic principles, but this was a fiction. She and her younger brother, George, who were both easygoing and reputed to take after their late father, always came out the losers.

It was her jaunt to Paris, of course, that had brought this on. She'd known better than to give her family advance warning of her intentions. They would have moved heaven and earth to stop her. To give them their due, they wanted what they thought was best for her, and they were no different from others of their class. Single women did not set up their own households and arrange their lives to suit themselves. In short, they thought she should either be married or be devoting her life to them.

That's what she would have done, too, if fate had not taken a hand in things, fate in the shape of her namesake and godmother, Abigail Vayle. Aunt Abigail had needed a nurse in the last year of her life, and the only member of the family who could be spared was, naturally, the only unmarried daughter—namely, herself. When Aunt Abigail died, she left her small house in Bath and her modest fortune to the niece who had nursed her.

Aunt Abigail had left her so much more than that. She'd taught her that she was a worthwhile person in her own right; that it was a waste of time to try to fit herself to someone else's mold. Aunt Abigail had shown her by example that a woman could live richly and fully without a husband. All she had to do was take charge of her own life.

She glanced at the clock on the mantel, then looked at Daniel. "Ten minutes, Daniel, and not one minute more."

"Abbie!" The dowager Viscountess of Clivendon stared at her daughter in open reproach. "I swear I don't know what's come over you. I hardly recognize you as my own daughter. In fact—"

Abbie knew that once her mother got started, there would be a long litany of complaints. She knew them by heart, since her mother wrote to her unfailingly every week in an effort to make her mend her ways. If she didn't take charge of the conversation, they'd be here till doomsday.

"It's Paris, isn't it?" she said, cutting her mother off in midsentence. "That's the reason you're here. Well, as you see, I came to no harm. In fact, I had a wonderful time and I can't wait to go back."

"It's not about Paris," said Daniel, "except, perhaps, indirectly."

Her mother's lips were open, and she blinked slowly. Abbie stifled a smile. She'd never been known to interrupt her mother during one of her tirades. No one did.

Quickly recovering, Lady Clivendon said, "How can

you say this isn't about Paris, Daniel? Mark my words, this is only the beginning. Goodness only knows what she'll get up to next. That a daughter of mine should go off without a by-your-leave, unchaperoned, is more than I can tolerate. Just think what all my friends and acquaintances will say. I don't know what you were thinking of, Abbie."

She'd been caught up in the excitement of the thing. It was an adventure. She'd wanted to test herself, and she'd passed with flying colors. She couldn't tell any of this to her mother without getting a lecture. And she wasn't in the mood for lectures.

"I wasn't unchaperoned," she said. "Miss Fairbairn was with me."

"Miss Fairbairn!" said Lady Clivendon with asperity. "When I insisted you employ a chaperon, Abbie, I meant someone who would be a good example for you. Miss Fairbairn is totally unsuitable. She is blind to your faults and makes no attempt to correct you or guide you."

Which was why, out of twenty applicants for the position, Abbie had settled on Miss Fairbairn. "Mother," she said gently, "Olivia is more of a companion than a chaperon. And when we went to Paris, my own brother was there to protect me, as I wrote you. I would have told you when we broke our journey in London, but you weren't there. You were at Giles's place in Oxford."

"As you knew very well we would be," exclaimed Lady Clivendon wrathfully. "That's why you chose to go to Paris when you did."

This was true, but Abbie saw no reason to argue a point she could not win. She was more interested in Daniel's remark that there was more to this family conference than her unauthorized jaunt to Paris, and she was reviewing in her mind what else she might have done to incur her family's displeasure. Only one thing occurred to her. They'd somehow got wind that she was setting up her own little business, buying and selling rare books.

"I'd hardly call George a proper escort," interjected Harriet at that point. "For one thing he's too young, and for another, our baby brother is a bit of a loose screw. No need to look at me like that, Mama. We all know that George and Abbie take after our father. How else can we explain this harebrained trip to Paris? And where is George now? That's what I'd like to know."

The trip to Paris, in Abbie's opinion, was hardly in the same league as her father's adventures. The great passion in his life had been to find the lost city of Troy. No one could convince him that it did not exist. He'd spent more time in Greece than he had in England. It was only after he died that they discovered he'd practically bankrupted them to finance his expeditions.

Abbie said soothingly, "He met friends in Paris and decided to stay on. I told you that in my letter as well."

"That was weeks ago," said Lady Clivendon. "He should have sent word to us by now, telling us what his plans are. Good grief! It's less than a year since the French were at our throats. I can't sleep well knowing that he's in enemy territory."

"Mama," said Abbie. "Paris is overrun by British visitors, and the French welcome them with open arms. It's quite safe, I promise you."

"Safe!" scoffed her ladyship. "What would you know about it? I've lived in the world a good deal longer than you, my girl, so I think I know what I'm talking about."

This was her mother's invariable reply whenever she found herself losing an argument, as everyone there knew. Abbie turned to Daniel expecting him to share in this private joke with a wink or a smile. He was reclining in his chair, studying her as though she were a strange species of insect he could not classify.

"It was all very proper," she told him. "We attended receptions at the British embassy. We met everyone who was anyone, the cream of society, in fact. And . . . and we went shopping, of course." She did not mention that she'd shopped mainly for rare books to sell to her growing clientele in and around Bath and as far afield as Shropshire.

"Oh, I believe you." He smiled.

The smile pleased her. Daniel was seven years older than she, and she'd always looked up to him. He was the Viscount Clivendon, the head of their family and he took his responsibilities very seriously. She was one of those responsibilities, or so Daniel thought.

Daniel said, "At least one good thing came from your jaunt to Paris. Am I right, Abbie?"

He was looking curiously pleased with himself and that puzzled her. "What?" she asked.

"You were taken up by Hugh Templar."

"I was . . . ?" Her voice trailed away as she pondered where Daniel's thoughts had led him. "Hugh! Taken up by Hugh!" She laughed.

No one laughed with her. They were looking at her solemnly, expectantly, and her own smile gradually faded away. "Oh no," she said, shaking her head. "Hugh and I are friends, nothing more, so you can take that hopeful look off your faces."

"Friends?" Her mother's brows went up another notch. "I've never heard of such a thing. Men and women can never be friends, Abbie."

"That was in your day," replied Abbie emphatically. "Things are different now, Mama."

Harriet let out an exasperated sigh. "Sometimes I find it hard to believe that you are a year older than I. 'Friends' for heaven's sakes! Then do something about it! Flirt with the man! Use your feminine wiles to attach him. If you won't, some other woman will. Think about it, Abbie! This may be your last chance."

The muscles in Abbie's stomach clenched, and she felt her confidence begin to slip. Harriet's words were all too familiar. She'd heard them often enough when she lived at home. She wasn't getting any younger, she was turning into a full-fledged old maid; if she didn't act at once to attach some eligible gentleman, her chances of having her own home and children would be gone forever. Then she might as well be dead.

Steady, she told herself. *Steady*. She might be unmarried, but she still led a full, rich life.

She adopted an amused tone. "Marriage! To Hugh! The thought has never once crossed my mind."

"Well, let it cross your mind now," snapped her mother. "You're not getting any younger, and Hugh Templar has everything to recommend him as an eligible suitor. He is independently wealthy, he comes of good family, he keeps a house in London, and his estate in Oxfordshire is reputed to be peerless."

Abbie's jaw went a little slack. Her mother had done her research well. In the next instant her temper began to rise. She had a picture of Hugh being bombarded with questions from her not-so-subtle family. If they had spoiled her friendship with Hugh, she would never forgive them.

She struggled to keep her tone light. She didn't want to quarrel with her family when she saw them so rarely. She just wanted them to stop interfering in her life. "Poor Hugh," she said. "I would never have asked him to carry my letters to you had I suspected that you would get the wrong idea about us. Hugh has no more thought of marrying me than he has of . . . well, flying to the moon. The trouble with Hugh is he's too nice for his own good. Did you badger him with questions? And he took it all in good part, I suppose. Well, isn't that just like him. But don't let that get your hopes up. As I said, there is nothing between us but friendship."

Daniel shook his head. "That's not how it was, Abbie. We didn't put him on the spot. Why should we? He's way out of your league. It never occurred to us that he would think of offering for you when he could do so much better for himself."

His unflattering remarks stung, but the sting was swallowed up in suspicion. She could believe that Daniel might refrain from putting Hugh on the spot, but not her mother. Where an eligible gentleman was concerned, Mama had all the instincts of a man-eating tiger. The thought brought back humiliating memories that made her cringe inside.

She said incredulously, "You're not saying that Hugh offered for me?"

"No," said Daniel. "He more or less established his credentials, letting us know that he was a man of property, had good bloodlines, that sort of thing."

At these words, a wave of relief flooded through Abbie. If Hugh had offered for her, it could only be because he'd been browbeaten into it. "That explains it then," she said. "Hugh is not very good with small talk. I'm sure he was just trying to make conversation, and you all got the wrong idea."

Harriet rolled her eyes. "Then how do you explain Barbara Munro?" she demanded.

Abbie's brow wrinkled. The name had a familiar ring but she couldn't quite place it. She shook her head.

"Templar's mistress." Harriet did not bother to hide her impatience. "The actress? He pensioned her off before he went to Paris with you. How do you explain that, Abbie?"

Daniel brought his hand down on the flat of the table, making everyone jump. "Try to remember you are a lady, Harriet. What would your husband think if he could hear you now?"

Harriet laughed. "Don't be so stuffy, Daniel. Who do you think told me about Miss Munro? Besides, females are not blind and deaf, you know. We know about mistresses. And Abbie is no schoolgirl. She's lived in the world. She knows the score. And if she doesn't, it's time she did."

Daniel appealed to his mother. "Mother, have you no control over your daughter?"

Her ladyship ignored this moot question. "I want to hear what Abbie has to say."

Abbie's brain was reeling. Hugh had a mistress? And not just any mistress. Barbara Munro was the leading light of Drury Lane Theater. On her way home from Paris, when she stopped off in London, Abbie had seen Miss Munro in performance and had been enthralled. Hugh had accompanied her and he'd been bored. *Philistine,* she'd laughingly called him. *Barbara Munro is divine,* she said, and Hugh had stifled a yawn.

She didn't know where her family was getting its information, but obviously they'd made a mistake. Barbara Munro was an exciting, vibrant woman, and her legion of lovers were equally exciting. Hugh and Barbara Munro? It couldn't be true.

Abbie took a deep breath. "You misconstrued the situation—that's what I have to say. Hugh did not go with me to Paris. I already told you that George was our escort. Hugh arrived later, and the only reason he escorted Miss Fairbairn and me home was because George wanted to stay on."

"What was Templar doing in Paris?" asked Daniel.

"He was . . . ," Abbie had to think before she answered. "Hugh is a diplomat. He spent a good deal of time at the embassy."

"Strange," said Daniel. "I understood Templar had resigned from the foreign office, and that's why he came to reside in Bath."

"Well, he did," said Abbie, trying to remember what Hugh had told her, "but there are loose ends that only he can tie up." Those were Hugh's exact words. "And from time to time, he is invited to Whitehall to consult with the minister on matters of policy."

Harriet made a rude sound. "To consult with his ladybird more like! Abbie, I despair of you. You're so naive about men."

Abbie's eyes flashed with uncharacteristic fire. "A moment ago, you said that I knew the score. Now you're calling me naive. You can't have it both ways, you know, Harriet."

"Not with most people, perhaps. But with you, anything is possible. It was the same with our father. One couldn't help loving him, of course, but . . ."

Lady Clivendon cut in impatiently, "None of that is to the point. What I wish to know is, can Mr. Templar be brought up to scratch with a little encouragement from Abbie?"

"Let me disabuse you of that notion at once," declared Abbie. "Hugh is a confirmed bachelor. He's far more interested in Roman antiquities and his books than he is in females."

"I thought it was too good to be true," said Lady

Clivendon, sighing. "Templar and our Abbie? I just couldn't see it."

Neither could Abbie. In the first place, Hugh was a confirmed bachelor, and in the second place, she valued Hugh's friendship too much to jeopardize it by playing the flirt, a role she'd never had much success with anyway. Beaux, she'd learned from sad experience, came and went. No, she didn't want to do anything that might jeopardize her friendship with Hugh. If she lost him, it would make a hole in her life that no one else could fill.

It was astonishing how much they had in common. They were never at a loss for words. They were both members of the Antiquarians' Society, which met every month in members' homes; they were both avid readers, though the scope of Hugh's education was far superior to hers. Their minds were in tune—but that was as far as it went. They did not share their feelings at a deeper level, nor did she want to. She was no longer the starry-eyed girl who wore her heart on her sleeve. It had taken her a long time, but she'd finally found her niche. She fitted in. She had friends who were comfortable to be with and who were comfortable with her—friends like Hugh.

Comfortable. That was the word that came to mind when she thought of Hugh.

Except for one memorable occasion, she silently amended. Six months ago, when he came to Bath to settle a relative's estate, they'd been introduced at a meeting of the Antiquarians' Society. She'd decided then that Hugh Templar could easily be the reincarnation of a Roman centurion: hard, chiseled features; watchful amber eyes; and a physique that was honed for combat. When he took her hand in his and bowed over it, she'd been overcome by a vague sense of danger, a feeling she recognized as thoroughly feminine in nature.

But she had quickly realized that Hugh Templar wasn't interested in females. He was a real scholar, a former fellow at Oxford University, and a fund of knowledge on all things Roman and Greek. It wasn't a beautiful woman that made Hugh's heart beat faster, but the Roman ruins in and around Bath.

Daniel said, "Well, I'm not going to make up my mind until I talk to Templar in person. Perhaps I should stay for another week. When did you say he was expected back, Abbie?"

Appalled, Abbie sucked in a breath and let it out slowly. "Now you listen to me," she said, looking squarely at each person in turn. "You're not going to palm me off on poor Hugh just because it will relieve your minds to think that someone else is taking care of me. I am not a piece of baggage to be passed from hand to hand." When they began to protest, she held up a hand, silencing them. "I am twenty-seven years old. I am responsible for my own actions. I don't need a man to take care of me."

She scraped back her chair and slowly got to her feet. "Even if Hugh were to offer for me, I wouldn't accept him. I wouldn't accept any man. I am my own mistress. All that would change if I married.

"I am always happy to see any member of my family," she went on, bending the truth a little, "but I won't stand for your meddling. Make up your minds to it here and now—I am not the marrying kind of woman."

Their shocked stares were vastly gratifying, and even more gratifying was the knowledge that she had finally stood up to her formidable family. Aunt Abigail would have been proud of her.

It was the perfect moment to make her exit.

•　　•　　•

I'm not the marrying kind of woman.

Her bold declaration stayed with Abbie all through the Gardiners' delightful party, all through Maria Gardiner's accomplished performance on the pianoforte, lingering into the delectable late supper, persisting on the short carriage drive home, and following her into her own bedchamber, when she finally shut the door on the world and allowed her smile to slip.

As an exit line, it was superlative. How close it came to the truth was open to question. It wasn't that she wasn't the marrying kind of woman so much as she'd outgrown her girlish dreams and yearnings.

And at seven and twenty, she told herself with grim humor, it was no bad thing. There was nothing more pathetic than an aging spinster who refused to face facts. As a young girl, she'd dreamed of being swept into a grand passion; she'd longed to meet her soul mate. Experience and the passage of time had muted her desires. Now she was content to have a few close friends who shared her interests.

She dwelt on that thought as she began to disrobe. She was still thinking about it when she sat at her dressing table to brush out her hair. Her head was aching; her stomach was churning. If this was the result of having her family come for a visit, she'd do well to move to the wilds of Africa and see them only once in ten years.

The thought was unworthy. She really did love her family. Besides, they weren't responsible for her headache and churning stomach, except indirectly. It was the specter of marriage that had led to all this introspection; that's what had opened the doors to memories she didn't want to think about. It was the strain of trying to appear a woman who was having the time of her life. It was the fear that if she let down her guard, she would become an object of pity. That's why she always told people that she would never marry.

And it was the truth, wasn't it?

Then why was she so restless? Why was she questioning the path she had chosen for herself? Only yesterday she'd been happy. Now she didn't know where she was.

Or maybe it was that she didn't know *who* she was.

As if to plumb the enigma of her existence, she studied her reflection in the mirror. A girl with large gray eyes in an oval face, framed with fairish hair, stared back at her. She was pleasant enough to look upon, she supposed, but not in the same class as her sister. Harriet had had men falling all over her since she was a girl in pinafores. It wasn't Harriet's fault that the man she, Abbie, had hoped to marry had taken one look at Harriet and fallen violently in love with her. And had proposed, and was accepted, and was now Abbie's brother-in-law. It wasn't Giles's fault either. She'd read too much into his kisses, he'd told her. What he felt for her was affection. It was Harriet he loved.

Her mother had given her no sympathy. Men did not admire clever females, she'd told Abbie. If she would only stop spouting poetry and flaunting her knowledge of subjects no one was interested in, she would stand a better chance. She should take Harriet as her model. No one would dream of calling Harriet a bluestocking. Her nose wasn't forever in a book. Harriet had put her time to better use. She'd mastered all the feminine arts. She knew how to flirt. She knew when to melt and when to play hard to get.

When her heart mended and she became used to the idea of Giles as her brother-in-law, she'd tried to follow

Mama's advice. But all it achieved was that something inside her, something precious and fragile, had withered away and quietly died.

Aunt Abigail, wise old Aunt Abigail, had brought it back to life. She'd taught her that *bluestocking* and *old maid* were only words. They couldn't hurt her. The important thing was to be true to herself. Yet here she was, all in a flutter, because someone had mentioned marriage in connection with her.

And with Hugh.

She let the thought revolve in her mind. It couldn't be true. It was one of the things they were supposed to have in common, this aversion to the wedded state. They'd even joked about it. Marriage would clip his wings, Hugh had said. He was too set in his ways. He liked living alone, where he could come and go as he pleased. And she'd agreed with him.

If there was a warning in his words, it was unnecessary. She'd stopped thinking of marriage a long time ago. But just in case Hugh had doubts about her, she'd taken extra pains to do or say nothing that could be taken the wrong way. And she wasn't the type to set a man's blood on fire. She was no Harriet, no Barbara Munro.

She frowned when she thought of Hugh with a mistress. She should have anticipated something like this. Even an old fogy like Major Danvers had a mistress. But nothing would persuade her that Hugh had attached someone like Barbara Munro. And as for pensioning her off, the idea was laughable. What man in his right mind would pension off Barbara Munro?

So, Hugh probably had a mistress tucked away somewhere. She could live with that. She wasn't jealous, she told herself. It was just that Hugh was a good friend, and she didn't want anything to spoil that friendship.

Everyone was entitled to keep his own little secrets. Still, it did seem odd that she should be the last to know what Hugh was up to. In fact, when she thought about it, really thought about it, she didn't know much about Hugh at all.

Her eyes lost focus and she gazed into space. When she came to herself, she frowned at her reflection. There was nothing more pathetic than an aging spinster who refused to face facts. On that thought, she picked up her hairbrush and dragged it violently through her hair.

CHAPTER 2

Hugh Templar entered his rented house in Royal Crescent and asked himself, not for the first time, what the devil he was doing in Bath. In summer, Bath was tolerable. In February, it was the dampest, coldest place in the whole of England. But here he was, whistling the chorus of some bawdy ditty he'd picked up around campfires while soldiering in Spain as though he were actually glad to be back.

Abbie was the drawing card, of course, Abbie with her unruly fair hair, her intelligent gray eyes, and a smile that could melt a man at twenty paces. He would see her tonight at the Assembly Rooms, and he wondered which of the dashing ensembles she'd purchased in Paris she would choose to wear. Only Abbie could get away with what would be censured in any other lady in prim and proper Bath, not because she had the confidence to carry it off, but because everyone liked her. Abbie was everyone's friend.

Friend. He grimaced. When he'd first met Abbie, he'd summed her up as a typical spinster, strait-laced, proper and with her mind firmly fixed on bagging the first eligible gentleman who crossed her path. Naturally, he'd tried to keep her at a distance, and by the time he discovered that Abbie wasn't anything like he'd imagined, he'd allowed her to set the boundaries of their odd relationship.

Not that trying to keep her at a distance had worked. Abbie had an inquiring mind and was fascinated by Roman antiquities. When she'd heard about his reputation as an authority on all things Roman, she'd begun her pursuit.

It was the first time, thought Hugh humorously, that a woman had ever pursued him for his brains. Without knowing quite how it happened, he'd found himself elected secretary of the Antiquarians' Society that Abbie's aunt and namesake had founded. Naturally, Abbie was the president. And now Abbie regarded him as something between a well-worn encyclopedia and her favorite Dutch uncle.

The role used to suit him. He'd been disillusioned with England after his years as a soldier in Spain. He was bored with its politics, bored with its class system, and particularly bored with its women. He'd wanted to return to Oxford and take up the things that really mattered to him. He'd wanted to return to a life of scholarship, or go off on some dig for Roman ruins.

That's when he'd met Abbie.

Abbie was a breath of fresh air. He'd soon discovered that she was anything but conventional. She'd set up her own household; she ran her own little business; she didn't have that annoying habit of sizing a man up with her eyes as a potential husband. In fact, Abbie had made it perfectly clear that she wasn't interested in marriage, and that suited him just fine. He'd been married once and he never wanted to repeat the experience.

He couldn't remember when he'd begun to want more

from her than friendship. What he did remember was that he'd become irritated when he realized she was keeping him at a distance, literally. If he got too close or their hands accidentally brushed, she would give him one of her clear-eyed gazes and move away. Which perversely made him want to lay his hands on her boldly and possessively, just to shake her up a bit.

She'd given him one of those clear-eyed gazes once too often. He'd been so annoyed with her that he'd gone off to London to seek consolation. He wasn't used to rejection. When, however, he found himself thinking of Abbie while making love to another woman, he'd known he had a serious problem.

He'd hoped the attraction would pass. But it hadn't passed. And now he was left to wonder how he could make Abbie see him in a different light.

In the white marble entrance hall, his manservant, Soames, took his coat. Soames was tall and thin, in his mid-fifties, with an expression on his face that always made Hugh think of the word *martyr*.

Soames said, "You have a caller, sir, a gentleman. He's waiting in the library."

"His name?" asked Hugh.

Soames sniffed. "He refused to give his name. He insisted on waiting for you."

Curious, thought Hugh, and paused before opening the door to his library. His caution, he told himself, was out of place. This was Bath, the most tranquil, orderly spot on God's earth. Nothing ever happened in Bath. It was time he learned to break these ingrained habits.

He pushed open the door, took one step over the threshold, then either saw or heard something, and in the next instant he lashed out with his balled fist, sending the door flying back on its hinges. He rolled and came up on the balls of his feet. Before the man who was hiding behind the door could recover himself, Hugh launched himself at him and, hooking one leg behind his knee, toppled him to the floor.

"Hugh!" his assailant cried out as Hugh fell on top of him. "Hugh! It's me! Alex! Alex Ballard!"

Hugh's fist froze in midair. "Alex?" he said incredulously. "Bloody hell! I should crack your head open! You and your practical jokes!"

When both men got to their feet, they pounded each other on the back and began to laugh. They stopped abruptly when Hugh's manservant came tearing into the room with a raised poker in his hand.

"It's all right, Soames," said Hugh sheepishly. "Mr. Ballard is a friend. As you see, he's quite harmless. He just likes to play practical jokes on his friends, that's all."

The poker was slowly lowered, but Soames still looked distrustfully at Hugh's friend, then he glanced around the library as if to make sure that nothing had been taken. His eyes came back to Hugh. "I shall be in the pantry, sir, if you need anything."

When the door closed, Ballard let out a chuckle. "I presume the pantry is within shouting distance, just in case I should decide to murder you?"

Hugh grinned. "It's across the hall."

He and Alex had served together in Spain, first as soldiers, then in an elite corps that had been handpicked by Colonel Langley, Wellington's chief of intelligence. They'd worked closely together and had become good friends. When the war ended, Hugh had taken up his old life while Alex had transferred to the foreign office in London.

"What brings you to Bath?" asked Hugh, indicating that his friend should take one of the armchairs close to the fire. "Or is that a leading question?" He poured out two glasses of whiskey and handed one to Alex before taking the chair facing him.

"My mother-in-law lives in Wells, and Mary and the children are there now. Wells is only a short drive from Bath. So here I am."

Mary was Alex's wife. Hugh had met her once at a reception. There were two small boys, as he remembered. He'd learned more about Alex and his family in the short conversation he'd had with Mary Ballard than he'd learned from Alex in the four years they served together in the elite corps.

"How are Mary and the children?" he asked.

"Oh, they are all well. Mary is expecting again. That's why we've made this trip to Wells. You know how it is with women. She wants to be with her mother."

Hugh sipped his whiskey. It seemed a strange time of year to travel the roads, especially for a woman who was pregnant. And this seemed a strange hour to come calling, so late in the day. It was dark outside. Alex would have a long drive ahead of him before he got home.

The blue eyes that were studying Hugh were highly amused. Ballard said, "It's difficult to break old habits, isn't it, Hugh—the suspicion, the constant sifting of a man's words and motives, putting two and two together? So, what have you come up with?"

"You're on an assignment," said Hugh flatly. "This visit to your mother-in-law is a blind to explain your presence in Bath. You think I can help you." His eyes narrowed as he thought things through. He shook his head. "I hope this doesn't mean that Langley has sent you to try and recruit me." When Ballard did not reply, Hugh went on, "I'll save you the trouble of asking. I'm not interested, Alex. I was never more than an amateur. I have another life to lead now. And now we're at peace with France, I intend to enjoy it."

"The chief's talking of retiring, you know."

"Colonel Langley? Retired? I find that hard to believe. He has the energy of a man half his age. Besides, it's the only life he knows."

Ballard laughed. "It's true all the same. He came into some money recently, when his cousin died, and that may have something to do with it. Now he can afford to retire."

"He'll be a hard man to follow. And just in case you think I'd be interested in Langley's job, you can forget that too."

Ballard looked as though he might say more, hesitated then gestured with one hand, encompassing the whole room. "Is this the life you want, your books and Roman artifacts?"

Hugh sat back in his chair and smiled as his friend looked around his library. Fragments of Roman marbles littered every available flat surface. The untidy pile of books on his desk, all opened at noteworthy places, was matched by an equally untidy pile of books on the floor. On top of the high bookshelves were marble busts of various Roman dignitaries. Pinned to the wall between two windows was a large map of Bath with sections circled in black ink.

"That about sums it up."

Ballard rose and wandered over to the map of Bath. "I remember," he said, "that you were once a great admirer of Napoleon."

"That was before he got too big for his boots. And now that he has been stopped, my job is finished." Hugh's curiosity was rising. "What I can't understand is why you're still in the game. You're an amateur like me, Alex. When the war ended, you couldn't wait to get back to your family and that estate of yours in Sussex. You wanted to raise horses. What made you change your mind?"

Ballard turned from scrutinizing the map and shrugged. "We were tying up loose ends, you know how it is, when something came up."

"Then something else came up after that?"

Ballard grinned. "That about sums it up."

"And now?"

Ballard looked at Hugh, measuring him with his eyes. Finally, he said, "In the last month, we've lost four crack agents in Paris. Something big is going on, Hugh. The only thing is, we don't know what or who is behind it."

There was a prolonged silence as Hugh considered Ballard's words. He was very curious. But one question would lead to another, and before he knew it he would be in it up to his neck. That's how he'd been recruited the last time. He had different plans for his life now.

He allowed himself one last question. "Anyone I know?"

"No. They were all French, all Maitland's people. As you can imagine, he's out for blood."

At the mention of Maitland's name, Hugh's head came up. Richard Maitland had been recruited at the same time as Alex and he. They'd been colleagues, but that was the only thing they'd had in common. Maitland was a dour, cantankerous Scot who despised privilege in all its manifestations. He was supposed to be good at his job, but Hugh had regarded his methods as brutal and wanted nothing to do with them. He and Maitland could never work together.

"So Maitland kept his group active after the rest of us got out of it?"

"It was a precautionary measure," replied Ballard mildly. "And it paid off. They were on to something before they were wiped out."

Wiped out. Once, he could have used those words as casually as his friend, but now they made him wince. He'd been away from the game too long. "I'm sorry about Maitland's agents," he said. "What was their assignment?"

Ballard shook his head. "We don't know, and anyway, this is Maitland's operation. I don't have all the facts. Even if I did, you know I can't tell you more without knowing where you stand. I've told you too much already."

Hugh should have known that there was no such thing as one last question, not to a former intelligence agent. "I'm curious, Alex, but not that curious," he said. "If we were at war with the French, my answer might be different. But I have a different life now, and I won't give it up."

"You're a hard man to persuade, Hugh."

"I'm impossible to persuade."

"We always worked well together. There's no one I trust more than you."

"I'm sorry, Alex, but the answer is still no."

For a while, they said nothing as Hugh sipped his drink and Ballard studied the map on the wall. Finally, Ballard said, "I thought Oxford was your home. I thought you liked being close to the university. Weren't you a fellow there at one time?"

"Classics has always been my hobby," said Hugh. He spoke casually, but he was watchful. He wondered what Alex was getting at. "And yes, I was a fellow, but that was before I went off to war. Now I divide my time between Oxfordshire and Bath."

Ballard gestured to the map. "What's that for, Hugh?"

Hugh rose and joined his friend. "It's a map of Bath

and those marks are where we suspect we'll find Roman remains if we're ever allowed to excavate." He fished in his pocket, found his spectacles, and put them on. "Look here," he said, pointing. "We believe that there are Roman baths under the foundations of the present Pump Room, and a Roman temple nearby, possibly under the abbey." He looked at Ballard and grinned. "Am I boring you, Alex?"

"On the contrary, I'm fascinated."

Hugh might have been amused if he weren't so wary of where this was leading.

Ballard said, "Who's we?"

"What?"

"You said that 'we' suspect we'll find Roman remains here. So who is 'we'?"

He wasn't going to mention Abbie's name. "Oh, I meant the Antiquarians' Society here in Bath." He turned from the map and returned to his chair. "We're all very respectable, Alex, all very boring. Not a foreign agent among the lot of us."

Ballard treated his remark as a joke. "Was I asking too many questions? Sorry, bad habit." He took a chair close to Hugh's. "All right, I'll be frank." He grinned. "I have another reason for being here. Mary heard something and asked me to verify it."

"Verify what?"

"That you're engaged to be married to Miss Abigail Vayle."

Hugh stiffened. He was conscious of Ballard's veiled scrutiny, his sensing, his watchful silence. "Engaged to Miss Vayle?" said Hugh. "What gave you that idea?"

"You were with her in Paris in December, weren't you? Bets were being laid at the embassy. It was common knowledge, of course, that you'd terminated your liaison with Miss Munro."

There was a moment of silence, then Hugh said softly, "What the hell is going on, Alex? Why the interest in Miss Vayle? What are you really after? Tell me and I may be able to help you."

Ballard's eyes opened wide. "Hugh, you've got the wrong idea! This is just a friendly conversation. I told you, Mary heard some gossip and—"

He stopped abruptly when Hugh reached across the space that separated them and grabbed him by the lapels. "Listen to yourself! I was wrong about you. You're no longer an amateur. You've become one of them. I thought we were friends, for God's sake."

When Hugh released him, Ballard slowly got up.

"Alex," said Hugh, and pressed his fingers to his temples. "I'm sorry I let my temper get the better of me. I suppose you were only doing your job."

"No, I wasn't," said Ballard stiffly. "If I'd been doing my job, I wouldn't be here." He walked to the door, hesitated, and turned back. "I'm speaking to you as a friend now, Hugh. Remember what I said about Maitland. Remember that you have a poor record with women. And remember to watch your back."

When he heard the front door close, Hugh rose and began to prowl around the room. It didn't take him long to discover that his library had been expertly searched. He'd known where to put his hand on any book he wanted, but now the piles of books on his desk and floor were in the wrong order, while the papers and letters were neatly stacked, too neatly to be his work. What had

Alex been looking for? And what was he, Hugh, suspected of?

His mind began to sift through their conversation. He'd assumed that Alex had come to Bath to try and recruit him, but if Maitland were in charge of things, that didn't seem likely. Then why was Alex here, and why the questions about Abbie and the warning at the end?

Deep in thought, Hugh left the library and made his way upstairs.

CHAPTER 3

Despite the bad weather, polite society flocked to the dress ball in Bath's New Assembly Rooms. Hugh had just come from the card room and was standing inside the entrance to the ballroom, watching the dancing. When he saw Abbie, his lips softened in a smile.

When he first met her, he'd thought she was merely pleasant looking. He couldn't remember when his opinion began to change, but now he considered her one of the loveliest women he knew. Her large gray eyes were her best feature. They could be as cool as ice or they could fill with passion, but that, unfortunately, was the passion for ancient history. If she would only look at him the way she looked at fragments of Roman pottery, he'd be a happy man.

When the dancers parted, giving Hugh a clearer view of Abbie, his smile died. She was wearing one of the daring ensembles she'd purchased in Paris. He stared at the short bodice that revealed an expanse of tender white flesh, then he looked down at the raised hem that gave him a glimpse of trim ankles in white silk stockings.

What the devil had she been getting up to in his absence?

The steps of the dance had brought Abbie within arms' reach of him. He resisted the temptation to grab her away from the young fop she was dancing with, but when her eyes met his, he couldn't hide what he was feeling.

For a fleeting moment, Hugh's jealousy blazed, then sanity returned. This wasn't like him. What was the matter with him?

He was still brooding, he supposed, over Alex's parting shot about his poor record with women and, by implication, that Abbie was up to something behind his back. History wasn't repeating itself, he told himself irritably. Abbie was nothing like his first wife. Then what was behind Alex's pointed warning? And why the reference to Paris? What reason could there be to distrust Abbie?

On that thought, he looked around the rows of spectators, mostly dowagers and chaperones, who were seated at one side of the ballroom, and his eyes came to rest on Abbie's companion. Olivia Fairbairn was tall and stout, in her mid-fifties, with brown hair liberally peppered with gray. He liked her well enough. She was a kind-hearted soul. But he could never converse with her without talking at cross purposes. Miss Fairbairn had the unfortunate habit of hearing only what she wanted to hear. If he were to ask her about Paris, there was no saying where the conversation might end up.

He was on the point of turning away when Major Danvers, the gentleman sitting next to Miss Fairbairn, threw him a pleading look and waved him over. There was no escape now. Stifling a sigh, he sauntered over.

•   •   •

Abbie tried to focus on the question her partner had asked, something about her brother George, but her mind wasn't functioning properly. She was still reeling from the look Hugh had blazed at her. He was angry about something and she thought it was probably because her well-meaning mother had tried to pressure him into marriage. She hoped he didn't think the idea had come from her!

"No," she answered mechanically as the steps of the dance brought her back to her partner. "George is not in Bath. He may have decided to stop off in London, on his way home from Paris, or he might have met some friends and gone off with them."

Mr. Horton or Morton—she hadn't quite caught his name—shook his head, but the steps of the dance separated them and she didn't catch his reply nor did she care. She had far more important things to worry about than George's whereabouts. George came and went as he pleased. He would turn up eventually; he always did. Her most pressing problem was how to salvage her friendship with Hugh.

When the dance ended, she looked around for Hugh. He was in conversation with Olivia and Major Danvers. Pinning a smile on her face, Abbie hurried over. As she drew near them, her steps slowed to a halt. Hugh's face was in profile, and she had the oddest sensation, much like the one she had experienced all those months ago when they were first introduced. A lock of dark hair fell across his broad brow; his features looked as though they were carved out of marble; his coat hugged a pair of powerful masculine shoulders, his arm muscles bunched as he reached for a paper in Major Danvers's hand.

Roman centurion, she thought.

The awesome impression faded when Hugh slipped

on his wire-rimmed spectacles and began to read. Roman centurions were not equipped with spectacles but with great metal shields and swords. Hugh was no warrior. He was a scholarly gentleman who had ruined his eyes by spending too much time with his books. The spectacles were vastly reassuring. He was still the same Hugh, still the best friend a girl ever had.

Be natural, she told herself. *Be natural.*

"Hugh," she said with unnatural brightness, "you're back."

He turned his head slowly, and his tawny eyes gazed at her over the rim of his spectacles. "As you see," he said.

It seemed to Abbie that there was a moment of awkwardness, and she tried to cover it by looking around for somewhere to sit. Every chair and settee was occupied. Hugh solved her dilemma. He rose and held up the paper he'd been reading.

"I shall put this with the rest of the accounts," he said, looking at Major Danvers, then turning to Abbie, "Come along, Abbie. After I've taken care of this, I'll take you to the tearoom for refreshments."

A look passed between Abbie and Olivia. *I told you so,* Olivia was saying. She had tried to convince Abbie that Hugh was too much of an intellectual to understand Abbie's mother's hints.

"What were you and Olivia talking about?" asked Abbie as they left the ballroom.

"The Trojan War."

There was something dry about his tone, and she looked at him quickly. His expression gave nothing away. Deciding she must have been mistaken, she tried again. "What did Major Danvers give you?"

"A bill for candles," he replied. "If we continue to use up candles at this rate, we may have to raise subscriptions."

Hugh was treasurer of the committee that had oversight of the Assembly Rooms, and he took his responsibilities very seriously. Abbie was in the habit of teasing him about it, but on this occasion she felt shy and said nothing.

The office was just off the main entrance. Hugh took a candelabra from one of the hall tables, unlocked the door, and ushered Abbie inside. While he went to the desk and riffled through some papers, she wandered around the room, looking at the pictures on the wall, but she wasn't as casual as she pretended to be. She still sensed an awkwardness between them and wasn't sure whether it originated with herself or with Hugh.

"Hugh," she said, turning suddenly, "I—"

"Who was the young man you were dancing with?"

"What?"

He looked up from the folder of papers he'd been reading. "The young man you were dancing with. I don't think I know him."

"Oh, he's George's friend. Harry Morton or Horton. I can't remember which."

"George?"

"My brother."

"Your brother's friend." The set of Hugh's mouth softened a little. "And you don't know his name?"

"George has many friends, and you know how hopeless I am with names."

"But you never forget a face."

It was a private joke. Hugh was referring to the time Abbie had made a social blunder when she was introduced to one of Bath's leading citizens and claimed she remembered him and his daughter from somewhere. The "somewhere" turned out to be a hotel on the outskirts of Reading when the gentleman had told his wife that he was with his mother in Falmouth. There was no daughter.

"Hugh," she said, "why aren't you wearing your spectacles?"

"I only wear them when the print is small. Why do you ask?"

"No reason. It's just that you look different without them."

Now she knew where the awkwardness between them originated. It was with her. Her damnable family had put ideas in her head. She wasn't seeing Hugh as her best friend but as the romantic figure Harriet had described. She had to rein in her imagination before she spoiled everything.

"What is it, Abbie? Why do you stare at me like that?"

"You haven't told me what you think of my new gown," she said, then she stifled a groan. This wasn't how she'd planned to put their friendship back on the right footing. The question was too personal. She should have asked him about his books or the state of the assembly's finances. Dear Lord, what must he be thinking?

Hugh was thinking that he'd deliberately engineered this private tête-à-tête to question Abbie about Paris, to determine what she'd done to arouse the suspicions of a member of His Majesty's intelligence service. But when he saw the swift rise and fall of her breasts and heard the slight hiatus in her breathing, his thoughts changed direction.

Easy, he told himself, *slowly.* This was Abbie. She wasn't used to thinking of him as a lover. He wanted to tempt her, not terrify her.

As casually as he could manage, he dropped the paper he was holding and slowly crossed to her. "Your new gown?" he said. "I think your gown is . . . ," his eyes moved over her slowly, "charming. Quite rustic, in fact. Is this the rage in Paris, this shepherdess's getup? It suits you, Abbie."

"Shepherdess!" Her confusion was swamped by a tide of indignation. She glanced down at her gown. "It's no such thing! I don't know why I asked for your opinion. You've never shown the slightest interest in ladies' fashions."

"Oh, I don't know." He smiled into her eyes. "I occasionally think of other things besides Roman ruins and the price of candles. I'm not as dull as you think, Abbie."

There flashed into her mind a picture of Barbara Munro, the beautiful actress whom Harriet insisted was once Hugh's mistress. She blinked to dispel the image. Once she would have said that Hugh had never entertained a carnal thought in his life. He was too wrapped up in his intellectual pursuits. Now she didn't know what to think.

His eyes had narrowed on her face, not the clear, guileless eyes she knew so well, but cat's eyes, sharp and watchful, seeing everything.

When he tried to take her hands, she took a quick step back and rushed into speech. "I don't think you're dull. Why, you know more about Roman antiquities than anyone."

"Praise indeed," he said dryly. "Shame the devil, Abbie, and tell the truth. Don't you find me too tame for you?"

"I don't think of you as 'tame.' You're . . . well . . . solid, and dependable."

"I see," he said, and with a whimsical smile, returned to the desk.

"Oh, Hugh!" Abbie went after him, cut to the quick to think that she'd hurt his feelings. "You don't understand."

"What don't I understand?" He propped himself

against the desk, folded his arms across his chest, and regarded her steadily.

"Your friendship means a great deal to me. Hugh, you know how much I admire you and enjoy your company. I wouldn't want anything to spoil what we have."

"What could spoil it?"

She answered with feeling, "My family for a start." When he made no response to this, she foundered a little before going on. "They came to see me last week, and . . . and . . . they've got the wrong idea about us." She laughed lightly to convey just the right degree of amusement. "Oh, I should have foreseen how their minds would work. I should have known better than to ask you to carry letters for me." She touched a hand to his sleeve and quickly withdrew it. "Was it very bad, Hugh? Did they . . . well . . . did they ask you a lot of personal questions?"

"Well, they did, but I found your family quite . . . interesting." He paused. "Oh, I see what it is. They feared I was going to ask you to marry me, and they posted down to Bath to warn you off. Is that it?"

"Feared? It was no such thing! They *hoped* you were going to ask me to marry you, and they came to try and persuade me to bring you up to scratch. They won't accept that I'm not the marrying kind of woman."

"No?"

"No. They think every woman wants to be married. And they don't care who I marry, just as long as—" She covered her mouth with her hand and peeked up at him. "That didn't come out the way . . . that is . . . that's not what I meant."

"Oh, don't apologize. You've always been frank with me, Abbie. That's one of the things I like about you. But this is interesting. Tell me what else you said to your family."

"I told them the truth."

"That I have ice in my veins, and that no warm-blooded female would ever be interested in a dull stick like me?"

When she began to protest, he waved her to silence. "Not all women are like you, Abbie. As a rule, they're not interested in the breadth of my knowledge, the scope of my interests, or my prodigious . . . ah . . . intelligence. They want a man who knows how to charm a woman."

She shot him a quick look, but there was no hint of humor in his eyes. That shouldn't have surprised her. Hugh didn't have much of a sense of humor. She said, "All you lack is practice, Hugh, and that is easily come by."

"Is it? Now there's a thought. Would you mind, Abbie, if I practiced with you? I mean, we are friends, and I know you won't get the wrong idea if I make a fool of myself."

She'd never seen him look so uncertain. Not only did that look stir her softer feelings, but it also made her realize what a fool she'd been. This was Hugh. He hadn't changed. She'd allowed her family to put ideas in her head, and her lurid imagination had done the rest. Poor Hugh. He really was a sweet man.

"Of course I don't mind," she said. "What else are friends for?"

"You won't take offense?"

"How could I take offense when you would only be following my advice?"

"That settles it then."

With that, he tipped up her chin and kissed her.

She froze. This wasn't what she had in mind, but it

was no more than a slight pressure of his lips on hers, then it was over.

"How did I do?" he asked.

She dimpled up at him. "Hugh," she said, "I'm not your grandmother. If you're going to steal a kiss from a lady, do try to put a little feeling into it."

"Why don't you show me?"

"What?"

"Show me."

Boldness could only take her so far, and this was going too far. She searched his face again, looking for signs of humor but his eyes were clear.

It's only a kiss, she told herself fiercely. It didn't mean anything. But what if . . . what if . . .

He took the initiative away from her. He put his hands on her waist and exerted a little pressure to bring her closer. She looked up at him with a question in her eyes.

"You feel good in my arms, Abbie," he said. "Do I feel good to you?"

Now that he'd made her think about it, she couldn't deny that she liked being in his arms. In fact, she liked everything about Hugh—the broad shoulders, the manly features, the thick black hair that looked as though a woman's fingers had just played with it. But she especially liked his mouth. It was full lipped, firmly molded, and made for kissing.

A shiver of feminine awareness rippled through her. Dear Lord, where had that thought come from? This was Hugh, her best friend. She was doing it again, letting her imagination run away with her.

His lips settled on hers, and whatever she'd been about to say was swept away in a flood of sensation. He angled her head back, and the pressure of his mouth increased, opening her lips to him. She felt his hands kneading her waist, the flare of her hips, her back, then his arms wrapped around her, bringing her hard against the full length of his body. He left her mouth to kiss her brows, her cheeks, her throat. She sucked in a breath when he nipped her ear with his sharp teeth, then she moaned when he bent her back and kissed the swell of her breasts.

He kissed her again and again, each kiss more desperate than the last. Abbie had never known such passion. Her skin was hot, her blood was on fire, her whole body shivered in anticipation. She wanted more, more, more.

The kissing ended as suddenly as it had begun. One moment she was in his arms and the next he had set her away from him. Dazed, she stared up at him.

"How was I this time, Abbie?" he asked.

"What?" She steadied herself with one hand on the desk.

"Did I put enough feeling into it? You did say to put a little more feeling into it, didn't you?"

She looked around that small candlelit room as though she'd never seen it before. It was like awakening from a dream. As she gradually came to herself, she touched her fingers to her burning lips, then looked up at Hugh. If he was affected by that shattering kiss, he gave no sign of it.

She stilled the tumult of questions that rushed into her mind. She'd made a fool of herself with Giles. She wasn't going to make a fool of herself this time around.

She cleared the huskiness from her voice, but she could do nothing about her burning cheeks. "Hugh, what can I say?"

His eyes anxiously searched hers. "Was I so bad?"

She blinked slowly. "No. You were . . . very good."

"Oh, I can't take all the credit," he said modestly. "You're quite the accomplished actress, Abbie. But I think I managed my part quite well too."

It was a graceful way out of a tricky situation, and she didn't know why she felt so disappointed. She cleared the worry frown from her brow and gave him what she hoped was a brilliant smile.

"You did very well, Hugh. Very well indeed. In fact, you were quite convincing."

"And so were you." He smiled. "So were you, Abbie."

He kept up a flow of small talk as he ushered her out of the room, but he didn't know what he was blathering about, and he doubted that Abbie knew either. He'd given her something to think about and could tell from her surreptitious glances that his strategy was paying off. It was beginning to register with Miss Abigail Vayle that there was more to old stick-in-the-mud Hugh than his prodigious brain.

"Abbie," he said, "what do you think about asking Major Danvers to be the speaker at our regular meeting of the Antiquarians' Society?"

CHAPTER 4

Abbie was still thinking about Hugh when she climbed the stairs to her bedchamber. She replied mechanically to all Olivia's observations on the ball, but she could hardly wait to be alone with her own thoughts.

Once she was in her chamber and had closed the door, she wandered over to the long cheval mirror with a candle in her hand and studied her reflection. The gown she had chosen to bolster her confidence now made her cringe.

Is this what had brought on Hugh's kiss? Did he imagine that she'd worn this flashy gown to tempt him? Why had she worn it, anyway? And why had he kissed her?

She set the candle on the mantelpiece, wandered over to the bed, and hoisted herself up. Maybe it was just as Hugh said. Maybe all he wanted was a little practice.

She sniffed. She was naive about men, but not as naive as all that. It had to be the gown. Nothing else explained the change in Hugh. If that were the case, he'd got the wrong idea about her.

She picked at the eiderdown with the nail of her index finger. There must be something wrong with her.

She'd never thought of Hugh as the type of man to set a woman's blood on fire, and she wasn't the type of woman to feel passion. But the unthinkable had happened. If she'd got any hotter, she would have burned to a cinder.

Do you like being in my arms, Abbie?

How had she managed to fool herself all this time? What woman in her right mind didn't like tall, handsome men with broad shoulders and a mouth that was made for kissing? Of course he was the kind of man to set a woman's blood on fire! She'd shut her eyes to his potent appeal because she'd lusted after his *brain*. How lowering to discover that she also lusted after his body.

She laughed weakly. Though she would never have suspected it of herself, she was no more immune to a magnificent specimen of masculinity than the next woman.

And that's what Hugh was—a magnificent specimen of masculinity.

Her lips still burned from his kisses. She'd kissed Giles many times and had experienced only a pleasant breathlessness. And she'd loved Giles. In Giles, she'd thought she found a kindred spirit. She'd told him things about herself she'd never told anyone else, that Harriet was her mother's favorite, that her sister was confident and good at everything she put her mind to while she, Abbie, was shy and awkward. And Giles had joked that Harriet's little nose would be out of joint when she saw how he doted on her older sister.

But that was before he met Harriet.

Mama had thought her chances would improve when Harriet was married and no longer there to overshadow her, but Mama had been wrong. Tom, Ambrose, Larry—

she forgot all their names—had taken to their heels when they realized Mama had marriage on her mind. And she hadn't been sorry to see them go. But it was humiliating all the same. She'd made up her mind then that she'd had enough rejection to last her a lifetime. So she'd taken to wearing a lace cap to proclaim to the world that she considered herself well out of the marriage mart.

And the first thing Aunt Abigail did when she arrived in Bath was make her take it off. The lace cap, which everyone knew was the badge of a confirmed spinster, said Aunt Abigail, was a ridiculous custom. When confirmed bachelors took to wearing lace caps, she would too.

Hugh was a confirmed bachelor. But what if he was like her? What if he'd kissed her because . . . because . . .

Enough! her mind screamed. *It was only a kiss, for heaven's sake! So much soul-searching over one little kiss?*

In a flurry of motion, she began to tear off her clothes. Once she was in bed, she pulled the covers up to her chin and composed herself for sleep. Thoughts of Hugh tried to intrude but she ruthlessly suppressed them. She wasn't up to examining all the ins and outs of what had passed between them at the ball. She tried counting sheep, but there was no relief there. Gritting her teeth, Abbie turned on her side and kept Hugh at bay by thinking of her brother. He'd met friends in Paris, George had told her. He would stay on for another week or two, then he would make for—now what exactly had he said?

She was reaching for the words that escaped her when she suddenly plunged into sleep, and straight into Hugh's arms. He was kissing her passionately, making her experience all those thrilling sensations she'd experienced in his office. Her skin was hot, her bones had turned to water. She wanted more, more, more. But Hugh was shocked.

I've never had a carnal thought in my life, he said. *I was only playing a part. After the spectacle you have made of yourself, we can never go back to being friends. You're an old maid, Abbie. An old maid. An old maid.*

All at once, his hands were around her throat and she could hardly breathe. He was going to kill her! She was suffocating! She tried to scream, but no sound came. And as suddenly as she'd plunged into sleep, she awakened to a nightmare.

The pressure on her aching mouth eased a little. "That's better," whispered the man who was kneeling over her. "I'm going to let you go, but one sound out of you, and I'll slit your throat. Do you understand?"

She nodded vigorously. A moment later, the hand was removed from her mouth, but she could feel the sharp point of the knife pricking her throat. There was no candle lit, but impressions were assaulting all her senses. Her assailant was a big man, and his hands were cold. Though he spoke in the cultured accents of an English gentleman, he had calluses on the tips of his fingers. She could tell that he had entered her room by the window because the cold night air ruffled the muslin drapes and the pages of the book she kept on the table by her bed.

Her heart was pounding so hard that she could hear each terrified beat. "I keep my money in the clothes press," she choked out.

"Shut your mouth and listen," he snarled. "I want the book Colette passed to you in Paris. Where is it?"

"Colette?" Her thoughts spun off in every direction. "Who is Colette?"

He slapped her so hard that her teeth jarred into her lip. Tears of pain and terror welled in her eyes.

"Don't make this hard on yourself, Miss Vayle," said

that hateful voice. "I know you have the book. I know you want to sell it to the highest bidder. So here's my offer. Your brother's life for the book Colette gave you."

She was horribly afraid of what he would do to her if she denied knowing Colette again. There was a cold brutality about him that warned her he enjoyed inflicting pain. She swallowed the blood in her mouth as her mind groped frantically to make sense of what was happening.

She didn't know any Colette, but she'd been in Paris with George and Olivia. And she had bought books, a whole trunk of books, for the little business she had set up. But those books were not in Bath. They were locked up at the customs house in Dover.

She felt rather than saw the movement as he raised his hand to strike her again, and she blurted out, "The book isn't here. If you kill me, you'll never find it." Then the full horror of his words cut through her panic. "What have you done to my brother?" she cried out.

His hand instantly covered her mouth, mashing her lips against her teeth. "Keep your voice down!" His lips were so close to her ear that she felt his warm breath fan across her cheek, and her stomach heaved. "I won't hesitate to kill your companion if she comes to investigate. Do you understand?"

She nodded and once again found herself released.

"Your brother is safe, and as soon as you hand over the book, he'll be free to go."

Though she was mortally afraid, her mind was working like quicksilver, adding things up, making connections. One thing stood out clearly. The truth would not save her or George. They would be safe only as long as her assailant thought she had Colette's book to trade.

"A book for your brother's life," he whispered. "Most

people would think that was a bargain. Where is the book, Miss Vayle?"

Where was the book? Tears clogged her throat and squeezed past her lashes as she braced for the blow that would finish her off. "I . . . I don't . . . in a safe place."

"Where?"

Where would she keep a book that was valuable? Not in the customs house. Think! Think! Think!

When his fingers tightened around her throat, she gagged then blurted out, "It's . . . it's in my bank vault in London."

There was an interval of silence. "Where only you can get it?"

Was that good or bad? "Y- yes."

"How very clever."

She knew by his tone of voice that it was a mistake to be clever, and she began to think wildly of how she could save herself. There was a pistol for just such an occasion as this in the top drawer of her bureau, but even if she got to it, she couldn't remember if it was loaded. And if she tried to throw this monster off her, he would slit her throat.

The blackness of terror swam at the edges of her mind and she fought it off by sheer force of will. She squealed when he moved his weight, and he laughed softly.

"Frightened, Miss Vayle?"

"No . . . y- yes. What about my brother? How can I be sure that you have him?"

"What a suspicious mind you have, Miss Vayle. It so happens that I brought a letter from George with me. You'll find it on the dresser. Rest assured he's alive and well, for the moment."

"Please," she said hoarsely. "Please, I'll do anything you say."

"George will be glad to hear it, because if you fail me, he knows we'll do to him what we did to Jerome and Colette when they crossed us."

She swallowed a bubble of panic. She had to ask. "What did you do to them?"

He answered pleasantly, "We skinned Jerome alive, but we were more merciful with Colette. I put a bullet in her brain."

Now she knew she was going to be sick. "I won't cross you. I swear to God. I won't cross you."

"No? I bet that right this minute you're thinking that as soon as you're free, you're going to call in the magistrates and constables to track me down and find your brother."

That's exactly what had been going through her mind! "No," she moaned. "No. I wasn't! I didn't. I promise."

"If you go to the authorities, you'll never see your brother alive again. I'll cut him up and send him to you in little pieces. And if you go to our competitors, I'll make you sorry you were ever born. We'll be watching you, Miss Vayle, and at the first hint of trouble, we'll cut our losses."

She believed him. A wave of despair washed through her. If she didn't have the book he wanted, how could she hope to save her brother? One false step on her part and it would be all over for George. And who were his competitors?

"Don't leave Bath until you hear from me. Do you understand?"

"Who are you?"

"I'm nobody, Miss Vayle. I'm nobody at all. Don't confide in anyone. If you do, I'll find out about it, and you wouldn't like that either." He laughed softly. "And neither would they."

"I—" she said, and got no further. Pain exploded through her head, and she sank back on the pillows as blackness engulfed her.

Nemo was thinking about the girl all the way back to his hotel on George Street. When he entered his bedchamber he locked the door, then took a good, hard look at himself in the looking glass above the washstand. Harry Norton, George's "friend," stared back at him.

He'd finally met the girl who had bested him in Paris, and he wanted to laugh out loud. Miss Abigail Vayle was not what he'd expected. She was no match for him. She was as fearful as a mouse. But that might be a façade. She had certainly fooled him in Dessene's bookshop in the Palais Royal. He'd said something coarse just to get rid of her so that he could deal with Colette. And all the time, this unremarkable English girl was the person Colette had come to meet. Incredible!

Miss Abigail Vayle was, without doubt, quite a surprise. She'd got the book from Colette, and now she was trying to sell it to the highest bidder. Jerome and Colette would be turning in their graves if they knew.

He removed his wig, and then with the precision of an actor, removed all other traces of Harry Norton—the powder and paint, the pale eyebrows and the receding hairline. He'd already removed the wads of tape that had plumped up his cheeks to make him look younger. The tape altered his speech, and he was glad now that he'd used a different voice when he confronted the girl tonight, because he'd decided to keep Harry Norton alive. He was self-effacing and harmless, the kind of young man women trusted. Miss Vayle did not know it yet, but she was fated to meet Harry Norton again.

It annoyed him that he had to waste his energies in tracking down the book. He had far more important things to do. He was an assassin. His real mission was waiting for him in London, and he had still to refine the details of how he would make the kill.

And this kill would be spectacular.

All the same, the book was important. If the authorities learned that Nemo was still alive and in England, it would make his job more difficult. But not too difficult. Jerome had not known who his target was. Even he hadn't known until recently.

He wasn't convinced that the girl had hidden the book in her bank vault. She might be terrified of him, but she wasn't stupid. She must have feared that he would kill her the moment he had the book. It didn't matter. One way or another, she would lead him to the book.

He'd considered delegating the problem of finding the book to his English accomplices, but he was reluctant to do it. They were rank amateurs. They didn't have the nerve to kill anyone in cold blood, least of all a girl. He'd infiltrated their cells months ago, given them a new direction, and had set things up so that they would be there as scapegoats when his real mission was completed. After that, he'd returned to France to bide his time for the right moment to arrive. Then Jerome had intercepted his letter to the Emperor.

First Jerome, then Colette, and now Abigail Vayle. And he never would have known about Miss Vayle if one of *his* spies had not intercepted *her* letter.

Abbie. How English. How boring! It made him think of bland puddings, apple dumplings, and boiled beef. She'd given him quite a start when he asked her to dance at the Assembly Rooms tonight. *He looked familiar,* she'd told him. *She always remembered a face.* He prided himself on his reputation as a master of disguise. No one ever recognized him. That was why the English had given him the nickname Nemo—'Nobody.' He was nameless and faceless, and that's how he liked it.

Had it not been for Miss Vayle, he would have been in London right now. It did not sit well with him that he'd been put to so much trouble by a mere female. She really must be punished for the inconvenience she'd caused him.

He placed his pistol on the table beside his bed, but his weapon of choice, his two-edged blade, remained in the sheath strapped to his arm. He had too many enemies to feel comfortable without it, and though those enemies were for the most part among his own people in France, the habit of sleeping with his knife strapped to his arm had become second nature.

When he blew out the candle and slipped into bed, he folded one arm behind his neck and contemplated when and how he would kill the girl. He would have killed her tonight if she'd given him the book, and that would have been a pity. She'd been terrified of him, but not nearly as terrified as he could make her. He could picture her on her knees, begging for her life and the life of her brother. He knew how to build that terror until she would kill her brother just to please him. The thought made him smile.

There was no doubt about it, he had a weakness for females. Even at the kill, he couldn't help flirting with them. But he preferred women who had some spunk. It made the chase all the more interesting. He suspected that Miss Vayle was going to be a big disappointment. In spite of how she'd outwitted him in Paris, she'd turned out to be a poor, sniveling, spiritless creature. Her heart would give out long before the chase ended.

Colette had been more to his taste. She hadn't been

terrified of him. He'd savored the pleasure of finally breaking her. But at the end, she'd cheated him of his pleasure. She'd leveled an empty pistol at him. She'd forced his hand and that made him angry.

Abigail Vayle was no Colette.

He didn't know how long the game would last. He could spare three days, perhaps four. That would give him plenty of time before he kept his appointment with destiny.

CHAPTER 5

Olivia Fairbairn peered through the lens of the magnifying glass and feasted her eyes on the name of the publisher of the slim volume she was examining. "Colin," she mouthed to herself. There was no doubt in her mind that this was the genuine article. This was one of Marat's tracts that Colin had published during the French Revolution. If her father was alive, he would have paid a tidy sum to add it to his collection. Now Abbie could sell it for a nice little profit, and her own half share would plump up the nest egg she was squirreling away for the proverbial rainy day.

If it hadn't been for Abbie, there would be no nest egg.

She leaned back in her chair and reflected on her changed circumstances. The turning point had come when she applied for the position of companion that Abbie had advertised in the Bath *Chronicle*. Life for an elderly single woman who had once eked out her existence on the fringes of polite society couldn't be better. Courtesy of Abbie, she had acquired a wide circle of friends and acquaintants. She'd seen more of the world in the last six months than she'd seen in the previous half century. But more satisfying by far was the knowledge that it wasn't all one-sided, that she had something to offer Abbie in return. She was the mastermind behind the little business enterprise they had drifted into. In short, she was an authority on rare books.

She had her father to thank for that. His knowledge and love of books had been phenomenal, and he'd passed that love and knowledge on to his only child. His own library, which he built up book by book, had been the envy of the county. It should have all come to her. Unfortunately, her father's knowledge of books was not matched by his knowledge of accounting, and on his death, everything had to be sold to pay off his debts.

She'd fallen on hard times. But all that had changed with Abbie. They were partners, Abbie liked to say. Abbie put up the money and she, Olivia, contributed her knowledge. It was a fair exchange, Abbie said.

There was nothing she would not do for that dear girl.

She gave a start of surprise when the door handle rattled and the door swung slowly open. "Abbie!" she burst out. "Dear Lord! What's happened to you? You're as white as a sheet."

Abbie tried to smile, then winced. She put a finger to her swollen lip. Her jaw was sore as well, but only her lip gave any outward evidence of last night's attack, and even then, the cut was on the inside of her mouth. But she was shaking badly and couldn't hide it. "The silliest thing," she said. "I walked into a door and knocked myself senseless."

Miss Fairbairn jumped to her feet and went to Abbie. "You poor thing," she cried, gathering her in her arms. "I didn't hear anything. When did this happen?"

"Not long after we got home last night." She choked back a teary sob. Olivia's concern after what she'd been through the night before made Abbie want to cry like a baby.

Miss Fairbairn led Abbie to a chair close to the fire and pushed her into it. She glanced at Abbie's warm dressing robe and shook her head. "Have you just come to yourself?"

"No," said Abbie. "I didn't feel like getting dressed. I'm all right. Really."

But she wasn't all right. She was just a hairbreadth away from hysteria. It was a nightmare. She was just an ordinary girl, and things like this didn't happen to ordinary people.

"All the same, I think we should send for the doctor. Concussion can have serious consequences."

"I didn't have a concussion. I wasn't unconscious for more than a few minutes."

Miss Fairbairn's hands fluttered. "You're shaking. Let me get you a shawl."

It was all Abbie could do to sit still while Olivia fussed over her. She wanted to rush around the house and lock all the doors and windows. And even that wouldn't be enough for her. She wanted to arm herself to the teeth so that she would never feel so helpless again. Much good that would do! She'd found the pistol Daniel left for her in the bureau drawer, and she hadn't known how to arm it or use it. When she'd come to herself, she'd locked her bedroom door and window and sat in a chair with a useless pistol clutched in both hands for her only defense. She'd been frightened out of her wits, and too scared to call for a maid or Olivia to come and help her.

As the tears welled up, she sniffed them back.

"Are you sure you're all right?"

Abbie swallowed and nodded. "But I wouldn't mind some tea."

The worry frown disappeared from Miss Fairbairn's brow. "I'll see to it at once."

When Abbie was alone, she found her handkerchief, blew her nose, and curled up in the chair. Last night, she'd fallen asleep worrying about a trivial kiss, and now look at her! She had something real to worry about now. This was a matter of life and death.

All night long, she'd agonized over George, and his note to her. It didn't matter if someone had made a blunder. It didn't matter if she didn't know any Colettes, or anything about a book that was supposed to be passed to her. The important thing was that the horrible monster who had attacked her believed it, and he'd abducted George.

She put her hand in her pocket and withdrew the note that had been left on her dresser. She could hardly read it because she was shaking so hard. Anyway, she'd read it endlessly, and knew the words by heart.

> *Bea, don't do anything foolish. Do exactly as these men say and all going well, you'll see your little brother in Bath again. And this time, I promise to be nice to Miss Fairbairn. Don't worry, I'm well.*

That "Bea" made her bite down hard on her sore lip. Only George had ever called her Bea. It was his child-hood name for her. And the reference to Miss Fairbairn was a private joke. George found Miss Fairbairn a great trial to talk with, because she could never keep to the point of a conversation. But it was said in fun. George was never unkind.

There was no doubt the note was from George.

She carefully folded the note and slipped it into her pocket.

She was going to be sick. Abducted!—and for a book! It didn't make any sense. Abduction was a capital offense. . . . The book they were after must be worth a fortune. But she didn't care what it was worth—they could have it, just as long as they set George free.

She threw off the shawl, jumped to her feet, and began to prowl the room. Would they really kill George over a book? Maybe she should go to the authorities, after all, and let them find George. The authorities had the resources to find George and track down the man who had attacked her as well.

If you go to the authorities, you'll never see your brother alive again. I'll cut him up and send him to you in little pieces. We'll be watching you, Miss Vayle, and at the first hint of trouble, we'll cut our losses.

She hated him! He'd enjoyed terrorizing her. He enjoyed hurting people. No, she didn't dare go to the authorities. Her only hope was to find the book he wanted and hand it over.

The door opened, and a maid with a tray bustled into the room followed by Miss Fairbairn. Olivia's smile faded when she saw Abbie's face.

"Oh, my dear," she cried out, "you don't look at all well. You really should see a doctor."

Once again, she helped Abbie to the chair. Abbie looked at that kindly face and longed to unburden herself of the whole sorry story. She couldn't of course. Olivia was no help in a crisis. She had a nervous disposition and would only become excited and take to her bed. Besides, Olivia couldn't keep secrets.

No . . . until she reached London and could consult with her family, she would have to keep everything to herself.

"Oh, Millie," said Abbie, looking at the maid, "I heard from Mrs. Gordon at the ball last night that there are housebreakers in the area." This wasn't true, but it was the best she could come up with. "From now on, I want all our doors locked and all the windows latched, and if you or any of the other servants see anyone lingering in the street, let me know at once."

Millie's eyes went round with alarm; Miss Fairbairn began to chatter excitedly, asking questions she answered for herself; Abbie let her mind wander.

She was well aware that locking the doors and securing the windows were on a par with barring the stable door after the horse had bolted, but it made her feel safer. And the next thing she was going to do was learn how to use a pistol. There was nothing she would like better than to put a bullet in that villain's brain, just as he'd done to Colette.

What was she saying? Pistols were made to kill people. She'd always hated them. She and George both were good, law-abiding citizens, and this shouldn't be happening to them.

When Olivia's voice trailed away, Abbie gathered her wits. She waited till the tea was poured and Olivia had taken several sips from her cup.

"The books we bought in Paris," she said. "I mean, of course, the ones that are being held at customs. The period of grace is almost up. If I don't claim them soon, they'll be sold at public auction. I was wondering if it was worth our while to pay the duty on them."

"I thought you said that His Majesty could wait till doomsday before you would pay duty on your own property."

Abbie took a sip of tea and winced as her torn lip

smarted. "I said a lot of things in the heat of the moment. I've had a change of heart. Well, it was a great to-do about nothing."

"I don't call nasty, officious men bullying two innocent women a 'to-do about nothing.' You were entirely within your rights."

That's not how Abbie remembered it, not when she was honest with herself. She had been largely to blame for what had happened at customs. It had all started pleasantly enough. She'd answered the customs officers' questions politely and truthfully. No, the books were not for personal use, she'd said. She'd acquired them to sell to her customers at home. The officers had looked impressed, and she couldn't help boasting about how well she and Miss Fairbairn were doing with their fledgling business, or how much profit they would make when they sold the books.

Hugh had been there, too, trying to shush her, but she hadn't listened to him or understood what he was trying to do, not until the officer in charge informed her how much duty she would have to pay. "Articles of commerce," the officer called her books, and after all her boasting she could hardly deny it.

She saw, then, that the officers' politeness and charm had been a blind to entrap her. In her stupidity, she'd exaggerated the value of the books and thus the amount of duty that was owing on them. She'd seen red, of course. On a matter of principle, she'd ranted, she wouldn't pay them a penny, no, not even a farthing. The King could wait till doomsday before she would enrich his coffers by paying an unjust tax. It was getting harder and harder for decent people to make an honest living.

There was more in this vein, and Hugh had hustled her out of the customs house before—as he'd said—they clapped her in irons. His censure had kept her temper hot, and she'd turned on him too. He should have stood up for her, she'd raged. Anyone would think he was afraid of his own shadow.

She always looked back on that episode with mixed emotions. She was sorry, deeply sorry, that she'd let fly at Hugh, but she was astonished and rather proud of the way she'd stood up for herself. The old Abbie would never have shown such gumption. But then the old Abbie wouldn't have opened her mouth, and the question of duty would never have arisen.

None of that mattered now. She had a book to find, and if it wasn't with the lot that were still waiting in Dover for her to pay duty on, she didn't know what she would do. But how was she going to know what book to look for?

She curved the fingers of both hands around her cup and stared at a solitary leaf that floated on the surface of her tea. Aunt Abigail would have told her that the tea leaf was a sign that a tall, dark, and handsome stranger was coming into her life. She didn't want a tall, dark, and handsome stranger. She wanted a tall, fair-haired man she'd known forever. She wanted her brother George.

"What is it, my dear?"

Abbie blinked rapidly before looking at her companion. She tried for a smile, then thought better of it as pain began to spread along her lip and jaw. "I was just thinking," she said, "that we never did get around to cataloging the books we bought in Paris. None of them stands out in my mind. I mean to say, was there anything unusual about any of them that you remember?"

"Well, some of them looked promising, but nothing that would make our fortune or warrant paying the exorbitant duty on them, leastways, I don't think so."

It was the answer Abbie expected, and despair and inertia settled over her like a wet blanket.

Miss Fairbairn sighed. "And to think I had such hopes that it wouldn't come to this."

"Come to what?"

"Paying the exorbitant duty."

"How could we get out of it?"

Miss Fairbairn gave a deprecatory laugh. "I wrote a letter of complaint to the foreign office right afterward, but so far they haven't even acknowledged my letter."

"You never mentioned it to me."

"No. I was hoping to surprise you, you know, if they found in our favor, but as I said, I haven't heard a thing."

"I didn't know that customs is under the jurisdiction of the foreign office."

"I don't think it is. No, I wrote a personal letter to Mr. Lovatt, who works at the British embassy in Paris. His name was on the flyleaf of the book I was reading. I asked our foreign office to pass my letter on to him, and I hoped he would use his influence to help us—if only to get his book back."

"What book?"

"Oh dear, I'm not explaining this very well." Miss Fairbairn's hands were beginning to flutter, a sure sign that she was becoming agitated. "The book that that nasty customs officer snatched from my hand, you know, Homer's *Iliad* in a French translation. I thought I mentioned it at the time. It had notations in the margins, but I couldn't make sense of them."

Abbie vaguely remembered Miss Fairbairn engrossed in a book during their return journey across the English Channel. "I do remember something," she said, "but not the name of the book you were reading." She thought for a moment then went on, "I don't remember purchasing a copy of the *Iliad* when we were in Paris."

"Perhaps it belongs to George. Perhaps Mr. Lovatt is his friend and loaned it to him. At any rate, it's with all the other books we acquired."

Abbie's heart began to pound. "And Mr. Lovatt's name was on the flyleaf?"

"Yes. It was a present from his wife."

Abbie swallowed the question that sprang to her lip. Olivia was looking at her anxiously, and when Olivia was anxious, she invariably lost the thread of what she wanted to say. There was only one way out of the fog and that was to stop pushing her, and let her tell the story in her own words. "I see," was all Abbie said.

Miss Fairbairn's hands stopped fluttering, and she flashed Abbie a grateful look. "But whether the foreign office passed my letter on to him, I have no way of knowing."

"You asked the foreign office to pass your letter on to Mr. Lovatt at the British embassy in Paris?" said Abbie to clarify things in her own mind.

"I thought it was worth a try."

"What did you say in your letter?"

"Only that we had Mr. Lovatt's book, but could not give it back to him until we'd paid the duty, and that wasn't likely. . . ." She stopped. "I can't remember exactly what I said. I just gave him the facts."

"And you kept this all a secret from me?"

"As I said, I wanted to surprise you. Are you upset with me? Have I made matters worse?"

"Of course I'm not upset with you," said Abbie loyally. "What you did showed great ingenuity."

Miss Fairbairn beamed at Abbie. "Well, I wouldn't go

that far, but it did seem to me that we had nothing to lose and a great deal to gain."

For a few moments, Abbie sifted through everything Olivia had told her. Finally she said, "You said that the book was a present from Mr. Lovatt's wife. How did you know?"

Miss Fairbairn screwed up her face as she thought back. "It was inscribed, 'To my dear husband from your own. . . ,' now, what was his wife's name?"

Goosebumps broke out on Abbie's skin. She knew what Miss Fairbairn was going to say before the words were out.

"Her name was Colette," said Miss Fairbairn. "Yes, that's it. Colette. Such a pretty name, don't you think?"

Her injuries had healed. Her boxes were packed. She'd written notes to all her friends, and just as soon as she had left for London, they would be sent out. Miss Fairbairn had been briefed on what might come up in her absence. She'd told her that the reason for this unexpected journey was to visit a married friend in Hampstead who had fallen ill. The pretext had served her well, providing an excuse for her distraction and low spirits. Abbie did not again mention the books that were impounded in customs at Dover.

There was nothing to do now but wait for instructions, and the lack of activity was driving her crazy.

She seated herself on a straight-backed chair beside the fire. If only she could sleep for an hour or two, she would feel better. But she couldn't sleep. A confusion of thoughts hammered inside her head, and she was powerless to stop them. George, Michael Lovatt, Colette, the British embassy, Miss Fairbairn, Hugh, herself, George's abductors—they were all connected to Paris, and she still could not make sense of it.

She wished that there was someone older and wiser she could confide in. She thought of Hugh but discarded the notion. Hugh was a scholar. He dealt in ideas and antiquities. He was more of a diplomat than a man of action, as he'd proved in her quarrel with the customs officers. Hugh had tried to pour oil on troubled waters while she had stood up for her rights. And if she knew Hugh, he would insist that she call in the authorities.

Her brother Daniel was different. No man trifled with Daniel and got away with it. He wasn't hot tempered. He didn't go looking for quarrels or fights, but if they came his way, he didn't turn from them. If Daniel were here, she would feel so much better.

She found her handkerchief and blew her nose just as someone rapped on her door. It was Millie, bearing a small silver salver with a letter on it. It was hand delivered by an urchin only moments before, the maid explained. When Abbie was alone, she tore the letter open and scanned it. It was not written in her brother's hand, but in a beautiful copperplate that George would have scorned to use. She read:

> *Dear Miss Vayle,*
> *We recommend that you set off tomorrow and break your journey at the Castle in Marlborough, the Pelican in Newbury, and the White Hart in Reading, where rooms have been reserved for you. Take only a maid with you, no one else. Once you reach London, place the following advertisement in* The Times *when you have the package and are ready to make the exchange:*
> *"Vicar's daughter wishes to sell her late-father's*

extensive library. Apply by letter to Miss Smith, Rose Cottage, Mayfield, Sussex."

And Abbie, remember we'll be watching you. Now burn this letter and the other. At once.

She felt as though he were standing right behind her. She read the letter through again, crumpled it into a ball, did the same with the note she took from her pocket, and threw them both into the fire.

CHAPTER 6

Abbie used her handkerchief to mop up the vapor on the coach window and looked out. The dismal view of sodden hedgerows in the fading light seemed to mirror her own dismal thoughts. It had been raining intermittently since they left Bath. The temperature was so frigid that she was surprised the rain had not turned to sleet. Nothing had passed them on the road since they changed horses at Devizes. Marlborough was only ten miles away, but at this rate it would be dark before they reached it.

She suppressed a shudder. Now that they were almost at Marlborough, her nerve was beginning to crack. He would be there, waiting for her, the man who'd assaulted her in Bath. He'd told her they would be watching her and she believed him. She felt horribly exposed. He'd had no trouble invading her home, and she didn't think it would be any harder for him to invade her bedroom at the Castle.

It wasn't bravery that made her suddenly decide to defy his instructions, but cowardice. She didn't want him to know where her room was, didn't want to wake up in the middle of the night with his hand over her mouth and his knife at her throat. There was something about him that made her skin crawl, and it wasn't only because he'd attacked her. She'd relived that scene many times in her mind and she sensed . . . evil, depravity, something so corrupt she didn't know how to explain it.

The thought prompted her to move her hand to the small leather portmanteau beside her on the banquette. Daniel's pistol was inside it. She'd taken the trouble to learn how to load it and use it, but that knowledge came from a book. She'd yet to practice what she'd learned. The gun was supposed to make her feel safer, but when she thought of *him*, her precautions didn't seem adequate. Not nearly adequate.

She was afraid to defy his instructions, but she was even more afraid of meeting up with him again. So she'd decided on a compromise. She'd put up at the Castle, but she'd find her own accommodations under an assumed name. It was the book he wanted, and as long as he thought she could get it for him, she was safe, up to a point. He wouldn't kill her, but there were other ways of terrorizing a woman.

She let out a shivery sigh and turned her head to look at her young maid. Nan was sleeping, covered with blankets to keep her warm. The poor girl had embarked on this journey in good faith, but it turned out that she didn't have the stomach for coach travel. The swaying of the chaise nauseated her. They couldn't go on like this. When they reached Marlborough, she'd have to arrange for Nan to return to Bath in the morning, and if possible find someone to take Nan's place.

Her thoughts drifted to the last time she had made this journey, just before Christmas, on the first leg of their jaunt to Paris. The roads had been in no better shape then, but the atmosphere inside the coach had been far different. They'd been jubilant, irrepressible, she and George and Olivia, and they'd carried on like school children playing truant. The least little thing had set them off into gales of laughter.

George. She couldn't believe it had come to this. She half expected to waken and find that she was having a nightmare. But George wasn't the sort of person who turned up in one's nightmares. He was too easygoing, too much fun, too nice.

And these were the very qualities that worried her mother. In fact, her mother's worst nightmares were about George. As the younger son, said Mama, he had to take up a profession. He couldn't always rely on Daniel to give him an allowance. But the professions that Mama thought suitable—the church, the army, the law—bored George to tears. If he had to take up a profession to earn his bread, he said, he'd take up landscape gardening. That was the great love of his life.

There was no doubt about it, Mama had declared. George took after his father, and she trembled in her shoes to think what would become of him. This dire prediction had flowed over George as water over the proverbial duck's back. He never argued. He wasn't rebellious. He simply went his own charming way regardless of what others thought.

He had been the perfect companion to share her adventure in Paris. He wasn't like other young men who were interested only in gaming, drinking, and wenching. He'd come to see the sights, the architecture, the museums, and the magnificent gardens. And when Hugh had arrived on the scene and introduced them to his friends at the embassy, George had enjoyed that too. Then he'd met his own friends and gone off with them. He would write to her, he said. And she had laughed, knowing that George wasn't much of a letter writer.

She covered her face with her hands. How had it come to this? Her brother's life depended on her, and she was no heroine. She wondered if she'd done the right thing by not going to the authorities. Those family conferences that she'd always scorned would have been a great comfort to her now. But she'd set her course, and she would stick to it till together they decided what was best.

If only she had paid more attention to Mr. Horton— Morton—when she'd danced with him at the Assembly Rooms. George's friends, he said, were becoming worried about him. No one knew where he was. She should have listened to him more carefully. She should have taken him seriously. She should have asked him questions about where and when he'd last seen George. Now, she didn't know where Mr. Horton was or how she could find him.

She stayed as she was for several minutes. When Nan began to stir, she dropped her hands and looked out the window. There was nothing to be seen in the thickening dusk but the glisten of raindrops caught in the light of the box lamp.

Abbie was jerked from an uneasy sleep when the chaise came to a swaying, grinding halt. She heard coach doors slamming and men shouting. Horses were neighing and stamping their feet. Her maid moaned and blinked her eyes, but she did not waken.

Abbie let down the window and looked out just as one of her hired postboys came down from his perch.

"Looks like an accident, miss," he said. "I'll go take a look."

She'd thought, hoped, when the coach halted, that they'd reached their destination, but evidently this wasn't the case. Ahead of them, in the faint glow cast by the box lamps on each carriage, she could see a line of stationary vehicles stretching all the way to the bend in the road. There could be no doubt that some unfortunate carriage had come to grief.

When five minutes had passed and her postboy had not returned, she decided to investigate in person. She opened the door, let down the steps, and gingerly climbed down. Beneath her feet, the road was like sheet ice, and she steadied herself with one hand against the front wheel till she found her feet. As she passed her postilion, he half turned in the saddle to look at her.

"What's going on?" she asked. "Have you heard anything?"

"Mail coach," he replied. "It must 'ave taken the bend too fast. They thinks they's real whips, them mail coachmen. That'll learn 'em."

She had just come abreast of the next carriage, when the sudden blast of a tin horn up ahead, followed by the sound of men cheering, shattered the silence. Some minutes passed, then, "All clear!" shouted a coachman before climbing into his box, and the cry was taken up and carried down the line of waiting carriages.

Inch by slow inch, she began to retreat, but she stopped when someone called her name. The young man who came out of the shadows was wearing a many-caped driving coat with a double row of silver buttons down the front. This was the fashion that all young men who aspired to be dandies had taken up. Her brother George had a coat just like it.

"It's Harry Norton," he said, coming up to her. "Don't you remember me? I'm your brother's friend."

He unwound his muffler and pushed back his hat to give her a better look at his face. It was a young face, pretty rather than handsome, fringed by fairish hair and with light blue eyes. He was smiling.

"Mr. . . . Norton," she said, then fervently, "Mr. Norton! Of course! We danced at the Assembly Rooms! You're George's friend! How good it is to see you."

He seemed surprised by the warmth of his reception, but he said easily, "We should be on our way at any moment. Perhaps we'll meet again in Marlborough?"

"Where are you staying?" she asked.

"At the Castle," he replied.

"So am I!"

She was groping for a polite way of asking him to dine with her when he surprised her by taking the initiative. "I don't suppose . . . that is . . . if you have nothing better to do, would you do me the honor of dining with me, Miss Vayle? I understand that the Castle keeps a very fine table."

"Thank you. I should like that very much."

"Then . . ." He looked at his watch and gave her a shy smile. "Shall we say nine o'clock, in the dining hall? That should give us plenty of time."

"Nine o'clock it is," she said, and beamed at him.

The Castle's courtyard was ablaze with the lights from dozens of lanterns and pitch torches attached to its brick walls, and as Abbie alighted from her chaise, she took in the scene with mounting dismay. The yard was choked with vehicles that had been delayed by the mail-coach accident. From snatches of conversation, she deduced that all the inns and posthouses in and around Marlborough were packed to the rafters. It seemed that travelers had decided to stay put rather than chance the highways in these unpredictable weather conditions. She heard the word *snow*, and her heart sank. If it snowed, she could be holed up in Marlborough for days on end.

Her hope of obtaining her own accommodations faded as people who were pushing out of the inn complained vociferously of having been turned away on such a filthy night when there were no beds to be had anywhere. She searched the crush of people for Mr. Norton's face, but there was no sign of him. There was no one to help her but herself.

Squaring her shoulders, she offered Nan her arm. As they crossed the cobblestones, they happened to fall in behind no less a personage than the dowager Duchess of Champrey and her entourage of servants. Her Grace, a stately, horse-faced woman who towered over her footmen, had a formidable voice that soon sent anyone who got in her way scurrying for cover, and this included hapless members of the Castle's staff who were bowing the duchess into the inn's lobby. Though there was a crowd of distinguished guests at the counter, patiently waiting their turn, they parted without protest to allow the duchess to be attended to first.

Abbie kept her maid's arm in a tight grip and stuck to the tail of Her Grace's retinue as though she were part of it. Normally, she wouldn't have had the nerve to jump her place in the queue, but she was desperate. She had a sick maid on her hands; she had a brother to rescue; it was possible that her every move was being watched, and she was terrified of what "they" might do next.

Barely moving her lips, she said to her maid, "Nan, keep your mouth shut, and take your cue from me."

A worried look crossed Nan's face, but she nodded to show that she understood.

The landlord came from behind the counter and led the duchess and her retinue away. Abbie found herself first in line with a crush of people at her back.

"Her Grace's companion and maid," she said on a sudden inspiration.

The harried clerk handed her a key. "In the attics. Her Grace really ought to advise us when she adds servants to her retinue."

Abbie thanked the clerk, then grasped Nan's arm and propelled her to the stairs.

The desk clerk had allotted them two rooms no bigger than closets with an adjoining door.

"Perfect," said Abbie. "We'll be quite comfortable here, Nan."

"We won't be comfortable in prison," said Nan, "and that's where they'll put us for wot we done."

"Nonsense," said Abbie. "Why should they do that?"

" 'Cos the duchess will 'ave to pay our shot."

"I'll tell them it was all a silly mistake, beginning right now, as soon as I find a chambermaid. You worry too much, Nan."

Abbie spent the next little while finding a chambermaid to take care of their needs: their boxes had to be collected from their hired chaise; a fire had to be lit; a tray suitable for an invalid had to be sent up; and hot bricks to warm the beds. At first, the chambermaid, who was as harried as the desk clerk, was uncooperative, but her frown soon changed to smiles when she saw the half-sovereign Abbie proffered as a tip.

When Abbie descended the stairs to keep her appointment with Mr. Norton, she tried to look natural and managed to smile vaguely at an elderly gentleman who passed her on the way up, but she wasn't nearly as composed as she pretended to be. The thought that "he" might be watching her made her tremble all over. If it weren't for Mr. Norton, she wouldn't have left her chamber.

On entering the dining hall, she was dismayed to find that it was thronged with people. She scanned the tables for a glimpse of Mr. Norton. Eventually, she walked part way down one side of the hall, then the other. He was not there.

She retreated to the lobby and concealed herself in one of the curtained window alcoves while she waited for Mr. Norton to appear. There were plenty of people coming and going, but none of them looked suspicious.

She studied the hotel's guests. Two gentlemen had just finished a game of chess, and they pushed back their chairs and began to idle their way toward the stairs. Her eyes moved to a young couple who seemed to be having an argument. The wife dabbed at her eyes with a scrap of lace handkerchief, then stormed out of the inn with her husband hurrying to catch up with her. Two more people who had been turned away to try their luck elsewhere, thought Abbie. A group of noisy young fops entered the coffee shop on a gale of laughter; another almost identical group left it shortly after. Liveried servants in coats of many colors were flitting about like exotic butterflies.

When time had passed, and there was no sign of Mr. Norton, she decided to take a more direct approach. But when she asked at the counter whether Mr. Norton had registered at the hotel, she discovered, to her great disappointment, that he had not. There were no rooms available, the clerk told her. In fact, there were no rooms available at any of the inns in Marlborough. The young gentleman had probably decided to try his luck at the next stop.

She was crossing to the stairs when she heard a familiar voice at her back.

"Abbie! It is you!"

Her jaw went slack, and she turned slowly. "Hugh!" she said. "What on earth are you doing here?"

As soon as Nemo had caught sight of Abbie, he left the two gentlemen who were playing chess and began to mount the stairs. He was no longer Harry Norton. His hair was dark and threaded with gray; his shoulders were slightly stooped. He was dressed like any other guest, and as he passed her on the stairs, she looked directly at him, but gave no sign of recognition. So much for her phenomenal memory for faces, he thought, and allowed himself a small, superior smile. He'd matched wits with the best. This poor woman did not know what she was up against.

The accident to the mail coach had served him well, but if there had been no accident, he would have found another way to meet her and set this up. If she had the book with her, he would find it.

He reckoned he had five or ten minutes to search her room before she returned. It would take her that long to discover that he wasn't in the dining hall. She would wait for him, but not for long. Unchaperoned ladies did not loiter in public places. It just wasn't done.

He'd planned ahead and arranged for the Lavender Room, one floor up, to be assigned to Miss Vayle and her maid. It was at the back of the hotel. After glancing around to make sure no one was watching, he knocked on the door, expecting the maid to answer. He would easily overpower her. But surprisingly there was no response.

The spare key he used to open the door had been given

to him by the desk clerk. He'd simply told the clerk that his key did not fit the lock on his door, and he'd held up the key to prove his point. He was in the Lavender Room, he'd told the clerk, and the keys were exchanged with no questions asked. If he'd been a thief, he could have robbed the hotel guests blind, the security was so lax.

Once inside, he paused. There was no maid, no sound of anyone sleeping or breathing. It didn't worry him unduly. The maid could be in the wash house or the drying room in the nether regions of the hotel. There could be gowns to press, and handkerchiefs to wash out, or shoes to polish. He knew all about being in service, he and his mother both. His mother had been a lady's maid, always at her mistress's beck and call. And he'd been the page.

They'd called him "sweet" and "adorable." And he'd hated them, hated their condescension, hated having to run and fetch for his master's son and daughters, who would be nice to him one minute and turn on him the next. And most of all, he hated his mother for her compliance. The master would only have to wink at her and she would be in his bed. And when the mistress of the house discovered what her husband was up to, they were turned out, only to begin the same sequence of events all over again.

They'd been nobodies, slaves to the rich and privileged.

Nemo. He knew that was what the English called him, and he hated it. It was double-edged, a mark of respect on one hand and a bitter reminder of his origins on the other.

He wasn't a nobody now. He was Napoleon's right-hand man, a full colonel in his Imperial Guard with all the privileges that entailed. *He* was master now. *He* was the one who was nice to his inferiors one minute and turned on them the next.

He felt the quick rise and fall of his chest and took a moment to collect himself. The first thing he noticed was the frigid temperature. The fire had not been lit, and that was unusual. She'd been here for close to an hour. What the hell had she been doing?

The curtains hadn't been pulled, and lights from the courtyard filtered through the window, giving him just enough light to make out shapes and shadows. If he found the book, he would finish her off as soon as she came through the door.

It took him only five minutes to discover that the bitch had bested him yet again. God only knew where she'd hidden her boxes, but they were not here. What was she playing at? What was she up to?

He sat on a chair and took stock of the situation. He could not believe that she was trying to cross him, not when he had her brother. She must be playing it safe, just as he would do if he were in her place. She must have obtained another room under a false name. Now he was sure she had the book with her.

A slow smile spread across his face. She really was a surprising woman. He wouldn't have credited her with so much gumption. He would allow her this small victory. Besides, he had no desire to go chasing all over this labyrinth of a hotel, trying to find her, or linger in the hotel's public rooms, drawing attention to himself, while he searched for her. And the journey was far from over. Tomorrow night, they would be staying at the Pelican. And this time, when Abigail Vayle registered, he would be right there beside her.

This was the one and only sporting chance she would be allowed.

The night wasn't over for him yet. A complication

had arisen. Nothing he couldn't take care of. He looked at his watch. Now that he didn't have to hurry away, all he had to do was wait.

He lit the fire and watched the flames lick around the kindling, then he settled back in his chair.

CHAPTER 7

It was easy to decide to give up agonizing over trivial things when she thought that Hugh was miles away, but now that he was here, sitting beside her in the Castle's gracious wood-paneled dining hall, she realized what a fool she'd been.

Do you like being in my arms, Abbie?

Her mouth was dry just thinking about it.

Hugh didn't seem awkward or ill at ease, but she sensed . . . she didn't know what she sensed. It was probably all in her imagination, but she thought she detected a difference in the way he looked at her, and it made her feel self-conscious in a pleasant way.

He'd told her that he was here because Olivia had given him such a garbled account of her sudden departure from Bath that he'd come after her to make sure everything was all right. But what if there was more to it than that? What if her family was right? What if Hugh wanted to marry her? What if—?

She put a brake on her thoughts. She wasn't going to make the same mistake she'd made with Giles. And anyway, this was the wrong time and the wrong place to think of her own happiness. If she got too close to Hugh, she'd be tempted to tell him everything, and she wasn't willing to risk George's life—or Hugh's—by doing anything rash. All the same, when she first saw Hugh in the hotel lobby, she'd wanted badly to tell him everything. She couldn't, of course. Instead, she'd told him about the accident to the mail coach and the delay in reaching Marlborough. She'd told him about her maid's illness and how poor Nan would have to return to Bath when she was feeling better, when she'd set her heart on seeing the sights of London. She'd told him about her room in the attics, but knowing that Hugh would take a dim view of how she'd obtained it, she hadn't told him about her little deception. When she came to the end of her story, Hugh had asked only one question—when had she last eaten? She couldn't remember. So here they were, in the Castle's dining hall, and she couldn't eat a thing.

In an effort to get a grip on herself, she reached for her glass of Burgundy and took a long swallow. She shouldn't be fantasizing about Hugh wanting to marry her. She should be thinking of "them" and the journey ahead of her. Though she'd surreptitiously glanced around the dining hall from time to time, she could not detect anyone watching her. "They" had probably expected her to eat in her room. Young ladies without the protection of a male escort or a chaperon did not usually eat in a public dining room, not unless they were fast.

Hugh smiled at Abbie. "I think the wine has done you some good."

"Yes, I do feel more relaxed. It's been a horrible journey so far."

"I don't believe," said Hugh, "that you've mentioned this friend before now. Close friend was she?"

"Friend?" said Abbie, blinking slowly.

"The one who prompted this journey of yours."

Enlightenment dawned. "Oh, Sarah! We were very close at one time, but you know how it is. She married. I moved to Bath. But we kept up a correspondence."

Hugh reached for the bottle of Burgundy and topped up their glasses. Not for one moment was he fooled by Abbie's innocent air, and he wondered if she was running away from him because of the kiss they'd shared. The memory of that kiss and Abbie's response to him had kept his body in a constant state of arousal for three days and nights. He couldn't say that no woman had been as hot as Abbie when he kissed her, but those other kisses were bought and paid for. He was very sure that Abbie's passion was genuine. Then why was she still keeping him at arm's length?

There was something else nagging at him. He kept thinking of Ballard's visit and his vague warning about Abbie. If she was dabbling in something dangerous, he wanted to know what it was.

"Abbie," he said quietly, "you would tell me if you were in some sort of trouble, wouldn't you?"

"Trouble?" she said carefully. "What gave you that idea?"

So she wasn't going to confide in him. "It seemed odd that you would leave Bath in such haste. The note you sent me hardly told me anything, and by the time I received it, you'd already left."

This was making Abbie nervous. If she didn't put him off the scent, he would become involved in her problems, and there was no saying what they would do to him. She knew that Hugh had been a soldier at one time, but that was a long time ago. She could never think of him as a man of action—he was a scholar. He'd be no match for them.

She said, "It's Sarah who is in trouble." She was thinking of George, and she had to clear her throat before continuing. "She needs me, Hugh. She was never very strong and now she's taken a turn for the worse. I have to go to her. That's all there is to it."

Before he could ask any more questions, she changed the subject. She looked around the crowded dining room and said lightly, "I never expected the inns to be full, not in February. Where is everyone going?"

"You're forgetting," he said, "that the London season is getting underway. Parents with daughters of marriageable age are taking them to town in hopes of finding them a husband. That's why there are so many carriages on the road."

Abbie groaned. "Of course. That explains it. How could I have forgotten?"

"You had a season in London?"

She nodded. "When I was twenty. Oh, not the kind that costs thousands of pounds, with a presentation at court, a ball to launch me, and a subscription to Almack's Assembly Rooms. That was far above what my family could afford after my father died. But I attended parties and routs, and met people my own age."

Hugh smiled. "Sounds as if you enjoyed yourself."

She'd been a wallflower until Giles came along, but she didn't want to go into that with Hugh.

"Well, I did," she said, "especially when I found myself a beau."

Hugh put down his knife and fork. "Then what happened?"

"Then," she said, "I introduced him to my younger sister, and that was that."

Hugh frowned. "You introduced him to Harriet?" He paused. "We're not talking about her husband, Sir Giles, are we?"

"The same," she said. "Sir Giles Mercer, country

gentleman, with a sizable estate in Oxfordshire—well, you know that—and an income that was not to be sneezed at, especially by my family. Giles was quite a catch—tall, pleasant looking, titled. And he had money."

A smile tugged at Hugh's lips. "You weren't in love with him?"

"What makes you say that?"

The smile vanished. "Well, were you?"

She laughed. "No, I wasn't in love with him, and it's just as well, because, as I said, when I introduced him to my sister, it was love at first sight."

"A love match? I find that hard to believe."

"Oh? Why?"

He wasn't going to fall into the trap of criticizing Abbie's sister, because he knew how defensive Abbie could be about her family. But it was obvious that Harriet was a tyrant. Sir Giles Mercer held one of the most powerful positions outside the Prime Minister's cabinet, yet his own wife treated him as if he were a little boy.

That was the thing about marriage: it changed people. Or maybe it was truer to say that it brought out the worst in them.

He had taken a long time to answer Abbie's question, and she was staring at him curiously. They'd wandered into a subject he had no wish to discuss and he said abruptly, "All I meant was that your sister and brother-in-law seem like any normal couple to me, and most marriages are arranged." He took a sip of wine. "Now," he said, "tell me the truth, Abbie. Why did you leave Bath in such a hurry?"

Her eyes widened and she shook her head. "There's no mystery, Hugh. You know me. I'm not like you. I'm impulsive. Once an idea pops into my head, I'm off and running."

He smiled at this. "Are you implying that I like to plan everything down to the last detail?"

"Hugh, I'm not finding fault with you. I'm just pointing out how different we are."

He said dryly, "My immediate plans did not include taking a hasty trip at this wretched time of year yet, here I am."

"I'm grateful for your concern, but it was quite unnecessary. I know how to look after myself. And as for—how did you put it?—'a hasty trip?' You never do anything hasty. Your coachmen drive at a snail's pace because that's the way you like it."

"I'm only thinking of my horses. And I always send a groom ahead on one of my fastest steeds to reserve a room in my name. So you see, there's no need to travel at breakneck speed."

Her indignation was genuine. "Send a groom ahead! Reserve a room in your name! Hugh, only you could think of such things."

"And I'm glad I did or I'd be sleeping in my coach right now, and we wouldn't be here, eating our dinner in comfort. So what's wrong with that?"

"There's nothing wrong with it," she said in a tone of voice that suggested the opposite. "All I'm saying is that most people aren't as cautious as you. We don't expect inns to be full at this time of year, and they wouldn't have been full if the mail coach hadn't overturned and the weather hadn't changed."

"You don't have to wave your knife under my nose, Abbie. I get your point."

She looked at her knife, blushed, and quickly lowered it. "Sorry," she mumbled.

His eyes narrowed on her bent head. "Abbie," he said, "I've been thinking about your room in the attics."

Her head came up. "I wondered when you would bring that up," she said. "Hugh, just because you'll be sleeping in luxury, and I'll be sleeping in the attics doesn't prove that your way is better than mine. I don't care about spacious bedchambers. In fact, the Castle is too luxurious for my taste, not to mention overpriced."

"Then why didn't you try to find a bed at one of the other inns in Marlborough?"

"How do you know that I didn't?"

There was an interval of silence as he searched her face. "Because I know that you never stay at the Castle if you can help it, so I made the rounds of every inn and tavern before I came here. You weren't registered at any of them. No one remembered you."

She'd stayed at the Castle because "they" had told her to. "I didn't try any of the other inns," she said, "because I thought . . . I thought . . ."

"Yes?"

"I thought it might be fun to give the Castle a try just this once." She laughed. "But my grand scheme came to nothing. No taste of luxury for me, I'm afraid. I still ended up in the attics. It seems to be my fate in life."

Their waiter arrived at that moment and whispered something in Hugh's ear. Hugh looked over his shoulder. Abbie followed the direction of his gaze. A matronly lady in a striking azure blue ensemble with a matching silk turban smiled and raised her hand in greeting. It was a friendly gesture that seemed to include Abbie, and she smiled warmly in return.

Abbie's eyes then shifted to the lady's companion. This young woman—she couldn't have been more than eighteen or nineteen—was a beauty: heart-shaped face framed with tiny dark ringlets, rose petal complexion, and huge shy eyes that were at that moment staring wistfully at Hugh.

Hugh rose. "Good God!" he said. "Little Hetty is all grown up. I wouldn't have recognized her if she hadn't been with her mother. I'll be right back."

Abbie wondered if her own expression was as wistful as the young Beauty's. She hoped not. Age and experience should have taught her something. But she understood Hetty's confusion only too well. Youth, with all its insecurities, could be a horrible burden, and she remembered retreating into her own little world of books and poetry. But she hadn't been a Beauty; she'd been an awkward, lanky girl. In time, Hetty would gain confidence because she would discover that people, and men in particular, were attracted to beauty.

She watched Hugh press a kiss to the young woman's hand, then she tore her eyes away. Now that she was seeing Hugh as a man and not as a friend, she'd become absurdly conscious of everything about him—his looks, his manners, the little gestures that were unique to Hugh, how he swept that dark lock of hair back from his forehead when his mind was elsewhere, and how his smile became crooked when he was unsure of himself.

But what did he see when he looked at her?

She wasn't that awkward, lanky girl of eighteen any more. She'd learned to make the best of herself. Maybe Hugh thought she was beautiful. Maybe he admired her intelligence and her conversation.

And maybe she should remember why she was here.

She picked up her knife and fork, but after one bite of beefsteak, she put them down again. Without Hugh to take her mind off her troubles, she was back to thinking about George. She wondered what he would be eating for dinner tonight, and where they were holding him. It seemed criminal to her that she should be living in the lap of luxury in one of the most expensive hotels in the whole of England, while George was held captive somewhere. Was he warm? Was he cold? Did he have enough to eat? Was he frightened?

A wave of anger swept over her. She wasn't a violent person, but if she could lay her hands on the man who was responsible for all this, she would gladly strangle him.

The waiter arrived to clear their table, and a few moments later, Hugh returned. Abbie rose, and they made for the lobby.

Hugh said, "That was Mrs. Langley and her daughter, Henrietta. You've heard me mention Colonel Langley? He was my commanding officer."

It was all coming back to her. Hugh had talked about Colonel Langley before. He had shared Hugh's interest in Roman antiquities, and though they'd been fighting a war in Spain, they managed to see the Roman ruins. Despite the difference in their ages, they'd become friends.

Mrs. Langley was an army wife, which meant that where Colonel Langley went, she followed. Hugh respected her enormously because although she'd been born to a life of luxury, she'd given it all up to marry the man she loved, and had endured hardships without complaint just to be with her husband.

Abbie said, "You never mentioned that the Langleys had a daughter."

"No? Well, Hetty was a child when I knew her. She was all arms and legs when they sent her home to relatives in England to finish her education. It almost broke their hearts to part with her. They'd given up hope of having children when Hetty came along. And you can imagine how they spoiled her."

"She's grown into a lovely young woman."

"And all set to make her come-out," replied Hugh.

"Are they going to London, then?"

"For the season. Colonel Langley is there now. He works at the foreign office. Mrs. Langley is staying with relatives in Marlborough while their house in Chelsea is being done up for Henrietta's come-out ball."

"I'll bet her father is screaming blue murder at the cost of everything."

"How do you know?"

"Men always do."

Abbie didn't hear Hugh's response. She was scanning the faces of the people they passed in the lobby and on their way up the stairs, but her fears were groundless. Nobody spared her a second glance. When they came to the narrow staircase that led to the attics, Abbie halted, and offered Hugh her hand.

"This is good-bye, then, Hugh. I won't see you in the morning because I shall be leaving early. It was very kind of you to come after me, and I mean that sincerely. Give my love to Olivia, and tell all my friends I shall write to them soon."

He took the hand she offered and stared down at it. "Abbie," he said softly, "don't you trust me?"

"You know I do."

"Then tell me what's troubling you. Tell me why you're running away. Whatever it is, I'll protect you. I won't let anything hurt you. You know that, don't you?"

Her heart expanded then seemed to contract. She looked at him, at the lock of dark hair that fell across his brow, at the amber eyes that were studying her intently, at that firmly molded mouth, and a yearning uncurled in the pit of her stomach and spread out in waves. She was worn out with worry about George and Hugh seemed like a rock that nothing could shatter. She wanted that strength for herself.

Their eyes met and held, hers wide and fragile, his heavy-lidded. She was dimly aware of other things: lights flickering in wall sconces, a door slamming along the corridor, the muted sound of voices, the beat of her own heart, the rise and fall of his chest.

She couldn't seem to focus on any one thing. Her head was buzzing. Her responses were slow. Why was he looking at her like that? "I think I've had too much wine," she said.

His hand tightened around hers. "Abbie, tell me!"

She had to fight to hold back the words. But she wasn't made of stone. She couldn't resist the appeal in his eyes or the strength he was offering. "Hold me, Hugh," she whispered. "Just hold me."

A door opened and someone stepped into the corridor. "We must talk," said Hugh, "but not here. Come with me. We'll talk in my chamber."

She felt bereft when he stepped away from her, but it was only for a moment. He took her elbow in a loose clasp and led her along the narrow carpeted hall. When they came to his room, he unlocked the door, took one of the candles from the hall table and ushered her inside. Abbie took a few steps toward the fire that burned low in the grate while Hugh lit several candles around the room. And in those few moments, she began to realize she'd made a terrible mistake. Hugh wanted to question her, and that was the one thing she could not allow.

He stood in front of her, his eyes searching her face.

His hands grasped her shoulders. "Now tell me everything," he said quietly.

She kept her eyes steady on his. "There's nothing to tell. Honestly, Hugh."

"Abbie—"

With some vague idea of throwing him off balance then making her escape, she stopped his words with a kiss. But when his mouth sank into hers, she was the one who lost her balance.

The flavor of wine was on his tongue and she parted her lips to absorb his taste. Pleasure began a slow beat deep in her body. Her skin was hot; her bones were turning to water. It was heady; it was intoxicating. It was too much; it wasn't nearly enough.

Hugh gave her what she wanted, needed. His mouth was ravenous on hers; his arms were wrapped around her like bonds of steel. When she was held like this, she felt that nothing could hurt her ever again.

When he suddenly broke the kiss, she murmured a protest. He gave her a shake to get her attention. "Abbie, you haven't told me anything yet."

"I don't want to talk."

Hugh resisted when she tried to draw his head down. "I won't—"

"Kiss me, Hugh."

"If we don't talk now, we'll talk later."

"Later," she said. "We'll talk later. Now, kiss me."

He kissed her swiftly. "Are you sure, Abbie? Are you sure this is what you want?"

The question seemed irrelevant. She had never been more sure of anything in her life. One night was all she asked. Tomorrow seemed a long way off.

"I'm sure."

He laughed softly and pulled her to the bed. His hands cupped her face and he brushed his lips lightly over hers.

"Easy," he said when she tried to deepen the kiss. There was a smile in his voice. "This is one sphere where I won't let you hurry me."

He shrugged out of his coat, then his waistcoat, his eyes on Abbie all the while. "You've turned my life upside down. You know that, don't you?"

Awareness was coming back to her, and she shook her head.

"Why do you think I stayed on in Bath?" He reached out and brushed his thumb along her cheek.

His touch made her tremble. "Because . . ." She cleared the huskiness from her throat. "The Roman ruins?"

"Hardly. You were what kept me there, Abbie."

She was afraid to believe what her heart was telling her, but every cell in her body was humming in anticipation of his next words. "What are you trying to say, Hugh?"

He undid the buttons on his shirt, dragged it over his head then tossed it on a chair. *Roman Centurion,* she thought as he came to stand over her.

He knelt on the bed and tipped up her chin. "Isn't it obvious? One night isn't enough for me. I want us to be together. There are so many places I want to show you— Italy, Greece, France." His voice thickened and turned husky. "I've wanted you for a long, long time and now it seems that you want me too." He flashed her a crooked smile. "Undress for me, Abbie?"

Though her fingers trembled as she began on the buttons of her bodice, she obeyed him all the same. It didn't seem possible that this magnificent male animal could want to spend the rest of his life with someone like her. In the past, he'd made it perfectly clear that he wasn't the marrying kind of man, just as she'd made it perfectly clear that she wasn't . . .

Then she knew, she *knew* that marriage was the farthest thing from his mind.

She blurted out the words. "Are you asking me to be your *mistress?*"

For a fraction of a second he seemed puzzled, but he quickly recovered himself. "I wouldn't put it like that. A mistress is a man's . . . plaything. I want us to be equals. I want us to be lovers as well as friends." He gave her a searching look. "Isn't that what you want too?"

Abbie felt as though someone had just punched her in the stomach. Tears of pain welled in her eyes, and all her pent up longing and softer feelings were swallowed up in a flood of humiliation.

"Abbie."

When he reached for her, she slapped him hard on the shoulder and slid from the bed.

Hugh raked a hand through his hair. "Abbie, what's got into you? What did I say?"

She was so furious, the words tumbled from her lips in a torrent. "You said you brought me here to talk. Well, Mr. Templar, I have only one thing to say to you." She paused to draw in a breath. "You are an out-and-out"—she discarded the word *cad* as too tepid—"an out-and-out bastard."

Hugh rose from the bed, his look of bewilderment quickly changing to one of annoyance. "I don't understand. You said you were ready for this. I'm offering you more than one night of pleasure. So why does that make me a villain?"

She was at the cheval mirror, arranging her gown. She hadn't the patience to argue the logic of the situation with him. All she knew was that she felt horribly, horribly cheapened.

Having tidied herself, she turned and confronted him. "If you don't know why that makes you a villain, I can't explain it." And that was the truth.

He put his hands on his hips and his eyes narrowed on her face. "Marriage is your price. Is that it?"

Her chin lifted. "For a clever man, you can be incredibly stupid." And that was the truth as well.

She slipped by him, quickly opened the door, and sailed out.

"Abbie," he roared. "You come back here and give me a straight answer."

He would have gone after her if he had not been half-naked. He reached for his shirt and pulled it over his head, but when he dashed into the corridor, there was no sign of Abbie.

CHAPTER 8

Outside the Castle, it was as black as pitch; snow was in the air and nothing was stirring. Inside, a few night lamps were burning, and Abbie could hear faint rumblings coming from the nether regions of the great house. In another hour or two, the inn would burst into life as early bird travelers descended the stairs calling for their carriages before they sat down to a hearty breakfast in the dining hall.

Just thinking about food made Abbie realize how hungry she was. She'd hardly eaten a thing at dinner, and it would be hours before they stopped to water the horses, hours before she could ease her own hunger pangs. It couldn't be helped. After last night, the last thing she wanted was to come face-to-face with Hugh Templar. The very idea of seeing him again made her cringe inside. She was ashamed of the way she'd behaved, ashamed of giving him the wrong impression. *Undress for me*, he'd said, and like a trollop, she'd obeyed. But she'd been swept up in the emotion of the moment. Her actions had sprung from her heart. His were premeditated. He'd admitted that long before she'd entered his room, he'd known he wanted her. And his base offer had cheapened something precious that she would have given him without counting the cost.

She hadn't been thinking of marriage. But Hugh had, as he'd proved when he'd asked her if marriage was her price. The man had the soul of a bookkeeper.

She wanted to hit him. She wanted to smack that crooked smile clear off his face. She wanted to tear that dark hair out by the roots so that an unsuspecting female would never again be seduced by the lock of hair he was forever brushing from his broad brow. But most of all, she never wanted to see him again. That's why she was creeping down the stairs at this ungodly hour to make her escape.

Everything was set. After she made her decision last night, she'd sent a message to her postboys through one of the maids, letting them know that she wanted to be on the road before five o'clock. Her box and portmanteau had been sent down. All that she had to do before slipping away was make arrangements for her maid with the clerk on duty.

And pay her bill.

Then, when she'd left Marlborough, she'd head for London—no stopping in Newbury or Reading and she didn't care what "they" made of it. She'd been terrorized to the breaking point, first by "them," then by Hugh Templar, and she couldn't take any more. She wanted her family; she wanted to see their dear faces. Just to know that she wasn't alone in her worry for her brother would make all the difference in the world. Then, together, they would find a way to save George.

On a teary sniff, she began to cross the vestibule to the front desk. She caught a movement from the corner of her eye and turned slightly. A gentleman was sitting at a small table in the same window embrasure she'd occupied the night before.

"Hugh?" she said faintly, hoping desperately that she was wrong.

Hugh threw aside the newspaper he'd been reading, got to his feet, and crossed to her.

"What are you doing here?" she asked rudely.

His reply was no more civil than hers. "I promised Olivia that I would escort you to London, and I mean to keep my word. She was worried about you, Abbie."

"I absolve you of your promise."

"The promise wasn't made to you but to Olivia." He paused. "I've just finished breakfast. Why don't you sit yourself down, and I'll order something for you too? That's what I like about the Castle. You can order anything you like at any time of the day or night."

His conciliatory words did not soften her. "Now you listen to me, Hugh Templar. I do not want your escort, do you understand? In fact, I never want to see your face again."

With all the dignity of a queen, she made to step by him, but he caught her wrist and brought her to a standstill. In a low, driven tone, he said, "Will you stop behaving as though I were a seducer of young innocents? We're both adults, for God's sake. Last night, I made a mistake, an error in judgment. You corrected it. So come down off your high horse and stop acting like an outraged—" He stopped.

Two flags of color bloomed in her cheeks. "Oh, don't stop there," she said through clenched teeth. "Like an outraged *what*, you lecher?"

He spoke through clenched teeth as well. "Like an outraged old maid."

She sucked in a breath and let it out slowly and audibly.

"Abbie, I'm sorry. That remark was uncalled for. But if you—"

She rushed into speech. "I'd rather be an outraged old maid than a . . . an unscrupulous libertine. You disgust me, Hugh Templar, and that is no exaggeration."

He lowered his head till they were practically nose to nose. "I didn't disgust you last night. You were on fire for me."

She tugged to free her wrist, without success. Her voice rose a notch. "Last night I had too much wine to drink."

"Liar!"

She gave him a shove that rocked him back on his heels. Finding herself free, she picked up her skirts and marched to the counter. The spotty-faced clerk appeared to be busy, but he was wearing a snide smile that Abbie was sorely tempted to wipe from his face.

"I have a bill to pay," she said.

The desk clerk's smile widened. "Mr. Templar paid your bill, Miss Vayle."

"Oh, he did, did he?" Her gray eyes sparkled with anger.

Hugh was right at her elbow. "Yes, I took care of everything, Abbie. I knew you'd want to get off to an early start, so I settled our accounts before I sat down to breakfast. You can settle with me later."

The glitter in his eyes warned her not to make a scene in front of the desk clerk. As though she needed a lesson in manners from a libertine! In as natural a voice as she could manage, she said, "I have a maid who has to be cared for."

"I've already made those arrangements, Abbie. Rest assured, she'll have the best of attention until she's fit to travel."

Abbie smirked. Obviously, since there was no record of her in the attics, Hugh had paid for the room "they" had reserved for her. She hoped it had cost him a fortune, because she had no intention of ever repaying a penny of that debt.

"Fine," she said, "then I'll be on my way."

The clerk came from behind the counter and unlocked the back door for her. Hugh was right beside her. When the clerk had locked the door on the inside, she said tightly, "If you attempt to enter my chaise, I shall have my postboys throw you out."

Hugh ignored the threat and went to speak to the ostler on duty. When he returned, he said, "We're not traveling in your hired chaise."

"What does that mean?" she asked sharply.

"It means," said Hugh, "that I took the liberty of telling your postboys that you'd be making the rest of the journey in the comfort of my carriage."

"You did what?" she cried.

"I told them that we wouldn't need their services, and that when your maid is fit to travel, they're to return her to Bath. Oh, and your boxes have been transferred to my coach as well."

She bristled. "I'm not going to make the journey to London in that, that . . . hearse you call a carriage! A snail could outrun us! And I'm in a hurry."

"A hearse? Oh no, Abbie. My carriage was built by Robinson and Cook of Mount Street. It's made for speed and stability. I'll get you to London in good time, weather permitting."

"Your carriage," she said scathingly, "was built in the last century. It must be at least twenty years old. It may have been all the rage then, but it's past it."

He scratched his chin. "I suppose it is rather shabby,

but it's still got many good years left. Trust me, Abbie. They don't make carriages like they used to."

Her voice rose a notch. "A carriage is only as good as the man who drives it, and your coachman knows only one speed—slow, slower, and stop."

"That's three speeds, Abbie, and Harper can be a daredevil when the occasion arises, but with the roads in the state they are now, and with snow threatening, it wouldn't make any difference if Isaac Walton were to take the reins. He was a mail coach driver, by the way, and could pick a fly off his leader's eyelid with a flick of his whip. Quite an achievement, that."

"I don't care who Isaac—" She broke off in mid-sentence. This was all beside the point, and she didn't know why she'd allowed herself to become involved in such a useless argument.

She breathed slowly and deeply. He was doing this on purpose, keeping her arguing here till his coach was brought round so that she wouldn't have time to think of how she could escape him. But she couldn't escape him, not as long as he had her boxes. And if she caused a scene, she would only draw attention to herself, and even now, they might be watching her.

The decision was taken out of her hands. Hugh's coach, with its team of matched bays and lamps glowing, came rattling over the cobblestones toward them.

Her voice betrayed her fury. "If your idea is to seduce me once you have me alone in that carriage, you can think again."

"God have mercy!" He sounded thoroughly bored. "Can't you understand that I'm only fulfilling my promise to Olivia? You can't go traveling around England without an escort. That's asking for trouble."

She pressed her lips together as the coach came to a stop.

"Good mornin' to you, Miss Vayle."

The greeting came from Tom, Hugh's assistant coachman. Abbie liked this young man. He was always smiling, always cheery. She wasn't going to take her temper out on Tom. "Good morning, Tom. And good morning to you, too, Mr. Harper."

Harper was Hugh's head coachman. He merely grunted a reply, but that came as no surprise. He was taciturn to the point of rudeness, and Abbie had never understood why Hugh did not get rid of him.

When Hugh handed her into the coach, everything was just as she expected. Hugh really was meticulous about details. There were hot bricks for her feet and a sheepskin blanket to keep her warm, and, in case they got bored, there were newspapers to read. But none of this mollified her.

The first thing she did when she was settled was pick up a newspaper and retreat behind it. There wasn't enough light to read by, but she didn't let that deter her. If he said anything, she would hit him.

"Abbie?"

"What?"

"If you're hungry—"

"I am *not* hungry."

"Fine."

He yawned, adjusted his broad shoulders in a corner of the banquette, and closed his eyes. Within minutes he was snoring.

She rustled her newspaper, but it made no difference. He continued to snore. After a while, she lowered the paper. Since she couldn't read and couldn't vent her anger on her companion, she tried to sleep too, but her head was buzzing with thoughts. As time passed and her temper cooled, inevitably she thought of George.

She could picture him as if were sitting beside her on the banquette. His hair was much lighter than hers, a true blond, in fact. They had the same gray eyes, the same mouth and smile, but George smiled far more often than she did. He'd been born with a sunny disposition. Everyone who came into the nursery remarked on what a happy child he'd been. And he'd grown up into a fine young man.

He was only twenty. His whole life was in front of him, and though he hadn't made much of a mark on the world yet, that would come. He wasn't ambitious; he might never excel in law or politics or the army, but there were other ways of excelling. George was one of those people who knew how to enjoy life one day at a time, and that was a rare gift.

This shouldn't have happened to someone like George.

Isn't that what everyone said when someone they loved was hurt? Colette and Jerome would have had loved ones who would have wept over them too, just as she was weeping inside for her brother.

Where is the book Colette passed to you?

She still had no recollection of Colette, much less a book the girl was supposed to have passed to her. But she was certain that all the books she had acquired in Paris were at the customs house in Dover. She just prayed God she had the right one.

She'd begun to think more about Colette and Jerome since she'd embarked on this terrifying journey, and she'd racked her brains to try to figure out how they fitted into the picture. If they were not booksellers like herself, she didn't know what they were.

Yet, it didn't seem likely that Colette was a bookseller, not if she'd been married to Michael Lovatt of the British embassy. Again, her memory failed her. She'd attended the odd reception at the embassy, but she had no recollection of meeting a couple by that name. Then, she had no memory for names.

She quietly folded her paper and looked at Hugh. He was still sleeping, still snoring. He might know something, but she was reluctant to ask him. He seemed to know that she was in some kind of trouble, and that seemed odd. He'd also told her that Olivia was worried about her, and that seemed odd as well. When she left Bath, Olivia had been in her element because she'd been left in charge of things. As she said, she'd never been left in charge of a cabbage patch much less a thriving book business.

So why was Hugh here? Why was he hounding her? Why wouldn't he leave her alone?

She pressed her fingers to her throbbing temples. Her anxiety for George was making her suspicious for no good reason. Hugh was here because . . . because—she pursed her lips—because he was a libertine and he thought she was an easy mark.

She let out a long sigh. There was no getting round it: if she wanted to find out about Michael Lovatt, she'd have to talk to Hugh. But she would have to do it casually, without rousing his suspicions, or she'd never get rid of him.

Colette. The girl seemed to haunt her. If Colette had passed a book to her, she must have done it in secret. But why would Colette have chosen her, Abigail Vayle? And what did Colette want from her?

She pressed her face to the cold window as the thought turned in her mind.

• • •

Abbie was sound asleep with her head resting in the crook of his shoulder, and his arm was loosely encircling her waist. He'd tried budging her a time or two, but all that did was make her nestle closer. He had no doubt that when she finally woke up, she would accuse him of taking advantage of the situation, and it wouldn't do a bit of good to point out that she had crowded him into his corner of the coach. No. He was the villain of the piece, and that was that.

Libertine. That was a baseless accusation, as she knew very well. He'd had his share of women, but he wasn't a skirt chaser. And since taking up residence in Bath, he'd become as celibate as a monk. She must know that, because he'd never even looked at another woman. As for being unscrupulous—now that really stung. He hadn't tried to seduce her. He hadn't misled her. She had misled him. From the very beginning, she'd made it clear that she wasn't the marrying kind of woman. And he'd certainly made it clear that he wasn't the marrying kind of man.

He had good reason to avoid the trap of marriage. His wife had been a nice, conventional girl when he'd met her, and she'd cost him his peace-of-mind, his reputation, and his self-respect. He'd married Estelle soon after he arrived in Portugal. She was pretty and sweet, with eyes the color of cornflowers. And he was abysmally ignorant about women. He was an academic, having just given up his fellowship in Oxford to fight for king and country.

It was odd how things had turned out. The last thing he'd ever expected was that he would become a soldier, and he never would have if Bonaparte had been content to be ruler of France. Like many academics, he'd admired Napoleon, but that admiration had turned to ashes when his hero had tried to make himself master of Europe. It was idealism that made him decide he had to do his part to put a stop to it. And that's when he met Estelle.

She was visiting her brother Jerry, who was one of Wellington's aides, and he, Hugh, had fallen hard for her. Two months after the marriage, he discovered he'd married a shrew.

If Jerry had lived, things might have turned out differently. But Jerry was killed while on patrol and Estelle had no one to turn to. He'd done his best, but most of the time, he was on assignment, and when he did come home, it was hell on earth.

It was the scenes that got to him, and the constant quarrels that always ended in bouts of weeping. He was a failure as a husband, Estelle never tired of pointing out. Estelle wanted a man who would dote on her, and he was too involved in his job.

She'd found consolation in the arms of someone else, someone who showered her with attention and knew all the pretty words that women liked to hear. It all came to light when Estelle's lover, a Spanish diplomat, was unmasked as a traitor. Estelle, it turned out, had been his willing accomplice, passing information she'd gleaned from her husband's private correspondence.

Hugh clenched his hand as the memory of that awful scene in Colonel Langley's office came back to him: Estelle, screaming at him that it was all his fault, that if he'd been any kind of husband, she would never have strayed.

A failure as a husband was one thing, but he'd also failed as an agent, and that was unforgivable. There was no doubt that innocent people had died because of his carelessness. He'd wanted to resign there and then, but Colonel Langley wouldn't hear of it. Everyone made mistakes, he'd said, and if a man couldn't trust his own wife, who could he trust?

Estelle had been incarcerated in a convent in Ireland on the clear understanding that if she ever left it, she would be facing a charge of treason. She didn't care. Her lover had been executed and her reason for living had been taken away. When she died not long after, they said it was from a broken heart.

He wasn't to blame, said Langley. Estelle had brought it on herself. But that's not how Hugh felt about it. He never should have married her. He wasn't husband material. He didn't know how to make a woman happy. He became preoccupied, involved in whatever job he'd taken on.

After that, he'd steered clear of women who had marriage on their minds. Women had a place in his life, but it wasn't an important place. And if he'd used them, they'd certainly used him. He was openhanded, he was easy to please, but at the first mention of marriage, he immediately severed the relationship.

The coach lurched, dislodging Abbie from her comfortable position. Her lashes fluttered, and she involuntarily stretched her cramped muscles, but she did not waken. Now that he could see her more clearly, he studied her at leisure.

She looked so helpless and trusting, curled into him like a sleeping kitten. But she didn't look relaxed. Her brow was furrowed, and every once in a while, he could hear her breath catch.

He was still angry and confused about last night. He didn't see why she had taken offense. She'd offered herself to him. He wanted more. He thought she'd be pleased.

The truth was, he didn't understand women at all.

He couldn't deny that Abbie appealed to him more than any woman he'd ever known, but the thought of marriage appalled him. Not even for her sake would he go through that again. Now that he knew where she stood, he'd make damn sure he kept his distance.

Only he couldn't keep his distance. Not until he'd got to the bottom of this.

Abbie snuggled closer. Hugh sighed and adjusted his position to make her more comfortable.

They stopped at the Black Boar near Hungerford to water the horses and get a bite to eat. The inn's dining room was everything Abbie had hoped for. It was small by the Castle's standards, but that suited her just fine. A cheery coal fire burned at each end of the room, making it seem warm and cozy. Her coat was folded over a chair, with her bonnet on top, and on the floor by her feet were her muff and reticule. It was really pleasant, and she was sorry that soon they would be on the road again.

The cuisine appealed to her as much as the cozy interior. It was unashamedly English—beefsteak and Yorkshire pudding, or beefsteak and kidney pudding, or plain beefsteak, followed by rhubarb jam pudding or apple tart. She ordered a little of everything, not because she wanted to eat it all, but because when she was chewing, she could ignore Hugh. She loathed him; she really loathed him. She should have listened to her mother. Mama always said that the quiet ones were the ones to watch, and how right she was!

Hugh wasn't the least bit embarrassed by their odd situation. He chatted as though they were the best of friends, ignoring her long silences. He'd mentioned making a short detour to a place nearby called Endicote, to visit Mrs. Deane, his late tutor's widow, but Abbie had scotched that idea. If they left the main road, George's abductors, supposing they were watching her, might get the wrong idea, and that was the last thing she wanted.

She occasionally glanced around the crowded dining room, and her eyes kept returning to a swarthy gentleman seated all by himself at a small window table. He'd entered the inn shortly after she and Hugh had arrived. He looked familiar. Like Hugh, he was picking at the food on his plate. She wouldn't have noticed him except for the fact that although he was seated at a window table, he rarely looked outside. When he wasn't reading the newspaper he'd brought with him, he looked casually around the dining room.

Hugh looked out the window. "It's snowing, Abbie," he said. "And I don't like the look of it. Why don't you finish your tea while I settle our bill. Then I'd like to speak to some of the drivers who've come from the east, just to satisfy myself that it's safe to go on. I'll meet you back at our coach, all right?"

She glanced anxiously out the window. Hugh was right. It was snowing, but that didn't mean they couldn't go on. They *had* to go on. Sighing, she topped up her cup and sipped slowly.

Shortly after Hugh left, the gentleman at the window table rose abruptly. As he buttoned his coat, she studied him covertly. He was in his early twenties, of medium height, stocky, with dark hair and complexion. He was wearing a brown coat, but he hadn't been wearing a brown coat when she saw him last. Green, she remembered, and she'd seen him very recently. Maybe she'd met him at the Castle.

She hadn't met anyone at the Castle, and the only people she remembered were Mrs. Langley and her daughter and the guests she'd studied in the hotel lobby when she was waiting for Mr. Norton.

Then it came to her. He'd been one of the gentlemen who had played chess. He and his friend had finished their game almost as soon as she'd taken a seat in the window embrasure.

When he moved past her and left the dining room, she reached for her own coat, then she wandered over to the window. The man in the brown coat was striding across the courtyard, hailing someone who was in conversation with an ostler. The man turned just as the stranger reached him.

Hugh!

Then why hadn't the man in the brown coat spoken to Hugh in the dining room when he had the chance?

Her heart began to pound. Turning on her heel, she returned to the table, picked up her bonnet and reached for her muff. She was halfway to the door before she remembered her reticule. Turning quickly, she ran back and snatched it from the floor.

When she came out on the porch, she halted. Hugh and the man in the brown coat had vanished.

CHAPTER 9

She hesitated on the front porch and looked around the courtyard. There was no sign of Hugh, yet she knew he had to be here somewhere. Only a few minutes had elapsed since she watched him conversing with the man in the brown coat. But there was no sign of the stranger either.

Taking a deep breath, she took her time and studied the courtyard in detail. The stable wings were attached to the main building and with the high brick wall at the far end formed a square. The entrance ran under an arch in the inn itself, and opposite the entrance was the exit, a gateway in the brick wall that gave onto a lane. There were several carriages in the yard, close to the buildings, but only Hugh's vehicle was ready to roll. The others were horseless, either waiting for ostlers to harness a fresh team, or they were in the process of having their horses un-hitched and led away. She saw stableboys with shovels and brooms clearing the snow from the cobblestones, and a few hardy gentlemen who were walking about to stretch their legs. But there was no Hugh and no swarthy gentleman in a brown coat.

When she saw Harper, Hugh's coachman, her panic ebbed a little. He was stamping up and down the cobblestones, trying to keep warm. She picked up her skirts and dashed across the courtyard just as a carriage came rumbling through the archway and ground to a stop. It was so blustery that she held up her muff to protect her face. Harper had seen her coming and had the door open and was ready to hand her in. She put one foot on the step and looked into the coach. Hugh was not there.

"Where is Mr. Templar?" she asked.

He glanced around the courtyard. "I saw him here a moment ago."

"So did I. He was speaking to a gentleman in a brown coat. Did you notice him too?"

"No, I didn't," replied Harper. "Maybe they went for a walk."

Her panic returned. "Went for a walk?" she said despairingly. "In this kind of weather? Mr. Templar wouldn't do that, not willingly."

As if to add weight to her words, a blast of cold air came tearing through the entrance tunnel, driving snow in a torrent of icy pellets. Abbie held on to her bonnet, Harper held on to the door, and Tom held on to the reins as his team stamped, tossed their heads, and jostled forward only to be brought back as they felt the pressure of their bits.

When the gust had spent itself, Harper said, "I'll take a look around."

"I'll come with you," Abbie said quickly.

"No. you wait here."

"But—"

"No buts. Get inside the carriage. At once."

Abbie was shocked into silence. Harper wasn't exactly

one of those servants who was always touching his forelock, but he'd never spoken to her, or anyone in her hearing, in this rough fashion. She peered into that hard, grim face, and it came to her that Harper was almost as worried as she was.

She nodded and entered the carriage. Harper didn't leave at once. He said something to Tom, and when he passed her window Abbie saw him thrust a pistol into the waistband of his trousers. Her own pistol was in her portmanteau and stowed with the rest of her baggage where she could not get at it. She had no idea what she would do if she had it, but she was no longer thinking rationally.

She looked around the coach and reached for the pocket in the corner of the banquette. Most private coaches were equipped with pistols in case of an attack by highwaymen, and most pistols were useless because their owners forgot to check them to ensure that they were primed and ready. Hugh wasn't like most owners. He was meticulous about details.

The pistol was much larger and heavier than she'd anticipated, and she almost dropped it. Clutching it tightly, she frantically searched her mind for the instructions she'd read on the use of firearms. *She could do it. It wasn't that difficult.* The hardest thing was to keep the pistol steady when she leveled it.

Before her nerve gave way, she thrust the pistol into her muff and reached for the door handle. When she stepped onto the cobblestones and scanned the courtyard, Harper was nowhere to be seen. First Hugh, then the man in the brown coat, and now Harper. Her panic took a gargantuan leap.

"Tom!" she cried out.

He didn't hear her. His eyes were trained on the exit

into the lane. A young man, a dandy, was entering the courtyard from the lane, and he was furious.

"Snowdrift," he yelled at the ostler who came forward to assist him. "My gig is stuck in a bloody snowdrift in the lane. Aren't you people supposed to keep the lane clear? And bring two shovels, man. There's a carriage behind me that's stuck as well."

Abbie's brain raced ahead of her, making connections, seizing on images that flashed into her mind. If there was a carriage behind the curricle, it must be on the other side of the gateway. It must have been waiting there while Hugh talked to the man in the brown coat. And the only reason it hadn't taken off was that the back lane had become impassable. She began to run.

She shot into the lane like a runner crossing a finishing line. She saw horses pawing the snow and beyond them three men and a chaise. Two of those men were trying to heave one of the chaise's wheels clear of the snow whole the third was giving directions. The third man was the swarthy man in the brown coat.

Her sudden appearance startled the horses, and they reared up and lashed out with their hooves. The three men looked up, then the swarthy man cursed and started forward. She glanced around for someone to help her. The driver of the curricle had wandered into the lane and was eyeing her curiously.

"Please, help me," she cried out, but when she dragged the pistol from her muff, his jaw gaped and he backed away with his hands in the air. Then he turned and ran into the courtyard.

"What do you think you're doing, Miss Vayle?"

Her head whipped up. The swarthy gentleman was shaking his head. And he knew her name. That proved it. He must be one of them.

Her voice was shaking as badly as her hands as she tried to level the pistol. "You're going to back away from that carriage, or I'm going to shoot you."

His two companions put their hands in the air.

The swarthy man said, "She won't pull the trigger."

"No, but I will." Harper's voice came from high above them. Abbie chanced a quick glance up. He was on the iron gallery that ran the length of the stable block, and his pistol was pointed at the man in the brown coat.

"Harper," she cried. "Thank God you're here! I think Mr. Templar is inside the chaise."

"Then let's find out. You there, back off, away from the carriage, if you please. Now!" he bellowed when they hesitated.

The three men cleared the coach and retreated with their hands in the air. "Do you know how to use that thing?" asked Harper, looking skeptically at Abbie's pistol.

"I know how to use it," she said.

"Then pull back the hammer," he said dryly. "Gently, now, gently."

She'd forgotten about the hammer. She gently pulled it back.

"Now cover them."

Keeping close to the wall and with her pistol pointed at the man who seemed to be in charge, she followed them along the lane until they'd cleared the chaise. "That's far enough," bawled Harper.

Harper shoved his pistol into his waistband, swung over the rail of the gallery onto the wall, then lightly dropped down. Abbie heard the coach door open, and Harper entered the coach. It seemed to take forever before he came out. She allowed herself one quick glance. Hugh was slung over Harper's shoulder.

"How is he?" she asked.

"He'll live." When she sucked in a harsh breath, Harper said quickly, "No, no. He'll be fine. Really. God, he weighs a ton!"

Abbie thought she was going to laugh, but the sound came out a sob. Hugh was safe. Now she could think about other things. She didn't want the authorities to take these men into custody, not as long as they held the power of life and death over her brother. And she had to act quickly. At any moment she expected the curricle driver to return with a band of armed men.

She edged toward the back of the chaise to conceal her movements from Harper. Keeping her voice low and her eyes fixed on the man in the brown coat, she said, "Now get out of here and don't come near me until I reach London."

"Miss Vayle?" It was Harper's voice, and he sounded suspicious.

She raised her pistol and fired into the air. Several things happened at once. Hugh's assailants took off down the lane. The horses reared up in their traces and tried to bolt. Harper flung himself clear. And a bullet plowed into the snow right at Abbie's feet.

Abbie yelped and dove for the cover of the wall beside Harper. The horses, maddened with fright, plunged and reared, dislodging the wheel that was stuck, and made a dash for it, only to become stuck in another snow drift a few yards farther on. They were now blocking the exit from the courtyard into the lane.

"Where did that shot come from?" Abbie quavered.

"There's a man on the gallery."

A voice from the gallery called out, "They're over there, behind the wall. In the lane, man, in the lane."

Abbie looked at Harper in stark horror. There was no way out, no way for Hugh's coach to get through the gateway and into the back lane, not when the chaise was blocking the exit. "We're trapped."

"Then," said Harper, "we'll just have to leave the way we came in."

"We'll never do it. There isn't enough room to swing a cat in the courtyard, let alone maneuver a carriage. That's why there's a separate exit."

Harper's reply was to put two fingers to his mouth and emit a shrill whistle. She heard wheels rattling over cobblestones in the courtyard, then the voice of the man on the gallery again.

"You, down there! What do you think you're doing?"

"Who me?" Tom's voice.

"Yes you!"

"I'm not doing anything, guv'nor. It's them bleeding 'orses of mine. Now why don't you lower that pistol before I blasts your 'ead off with my brown Bess? That's better. Thank you, sir." Then he yelled, "Ready, Mr. 'arper!"

"Now!" said Harper, giving Abbie a shove toward the gap in the wall. Then hoisting Hugh more securely on his shoulder, he went after her.

Hugh's carriage was hard by the exit now. Abbie squeezed past the chaise that was stuck in the snow, went through the gap into the courtyard, then she opened the carriage door. She clambered in, then turned to give Harper a hand with Hugh. When Hugh was settled on the floor, Harper said, "Stay on the floor. And brace yourself!"

She looked worriedly down at Hugh. He'd been badly battered about the face and blood trickled from his nose. But there were no serious wounds that she could detect, no patches of blood on his clothes. Tears welled in her eyes and spilled over. She heard Harper's voice. "Clear the way or my friend here will blast you away."

"Don't be stupid, man!" The voice of authority. "You can't escape."

She jumped when the blast came, but it wasn't the blast of a pistol or a blunderbuss. It was the blast of a tin horn.

Hugh moved restlessly. "Maitland?" he murmured. "Maitland? What's he doing here?"

The coach suddenly lurched forward, then tipped backward as the horses reared up. Abbie was thrown back against the banquette. She heard the scrape of metal on stone as the coach hit the wall, and in the next instant she was thrown to the floor as the horses jolted forward.

"What the devil—?" gasped Hugh.

"It's all right," she soothed. "It's all right."

But it wasn't all right. Harper, she was convinced, had taken leave of his senses. Brace yourself, he'd said, and that's what she did. She flung herself full length on the floor and clasped Hugh tightly, trying to cushion him against her softness. Out in the courtyard, it sounded like an insane asylum—men shouting, women screaming, a dog barking.

"Hold your fire!" The man on the gallery. "They're not going anywhere. Hold your fire. There are too many innocent people here to take chances."

Harper's voice. "Clear the way! Clear the way or I'll run you down."

Abbie shivered in apprehension. Hugh had told her that Harper could be a daredevil when the occasion arose, and she had scoffed at the idea. She wasn't scoffing now.

They struck something with an impact that jarred her teeth, then they struck something else. Screams. Shouts. She sensed the horses check and falter, but either Harper or Tom cracked the whip, for they sprang forward as though they were on the open road.

She clambered to her knees and braced herself with

one hand on either banquette, then winced as her ears were assaulted by the piercing blast of the tin horn. She looked out the window. "Oh no!" she breathed. "Oh no!"

Harper was going to drive them straight through the entrance into the High Street. That's why he had made Tom give a blast on the horn, to warn other vehicles to keep out of his way.

The horn gave another piercing blast, and she braced herself for a collision. When they entered the tunnel under the archway, it was as if someone had suddenly put out the light. Though she could not see, she could still feel and hear. They were going too fast, rattling over the cobblestones, making straight for the houses on the other side of the road. "Oh, dear Lord!" The words were wrung from her as she heard two more blasts in quick succession, one from Tom's horn and a fainter blast from an approaching vehicle.

They shot out of the tunnel like a ball from a cannon. Abbie saw a coach bearing down on them and she gasped. Before she could scream out in terror, the coach tilted as it turned the corner and she fell in a heap on top of Hugh. The carriage righted itself with a resounding thud, and Hugh made a movement to push her away.

His eyelashes fluttered open. "Abbie," he said faintly.

She had pulled back to her hands and knees. "Yes, Hugh?"

"My head aches."

She probed his skull with her fingers. There was a bump as big as a cricket ball on the back of his head, and her fingers came away sticky. "You've taken a nasty knock," she said.

He made a feeble attempt to get up, then sank back. "Abbie, there's a bottle of whiskey under the seat."

She pulled herself up and looked out the small peep

window at the back of the carriage. The snow was falling so heavily that it was impossible to tell if they were being followed. Harper evidently wasn't taking any chances. He had not slackened their pace. "Slow, slower, and stop" Harper had certainly fooled her.

She found the whiskey and held Hugh's head as she dribbled some of it into his mouth, but most of it went down the front of his shirt. "Just a little," she said. "It's not the best thing for you if you have a concussion."

She considered helping him onto the banquette and decided against it. If Harper made another sharp turn, Hugh could topple to the floor. She reached for the sheepskin blanket and was surprised to discover that it was wrapped around hot bricks. Hugh must have seen to the bricks before going off with the man who attacked him. She sniffed.

She wrapped him with the sheepskin blanket and tucked the hot bricks at his back and feet. It was too cold to strip off her coat and use it as a pillow, so she used her muff instead.

"Don't fall asleep," she said. "You may have a concussion, and it's the worst thing you can do."

"Abbie?"

"Yes, Hugh?"

"Who were those men?"

"I don't know."

"I was careless. I should have expected . . . but next time . . . next time . . ." Silence, then, "Where are we going?"

"Hungerford, I presume."

"Is that wise?"

"Don't worry about it, Hugh. Harper knows what he's doing."

"Says who?"

"Says me."

Hugh smiled at this. "That doesn't sound like you."

"Maybe not, but I've seen Harper in action now, and I've changed my mind about him. No, don't go to sleep."

"I won't."

He looked so vulnerable, with pain etched in his pale face, so vulnerable and mortal. If anything happened to him, she knew she would never forgive herself. This was all her fault. She'd let a silly quarrel cloud her judgment. She should never have allowed Hugh to accompany her, never have allowed him to share a carriage with her. She'd been warned of what they would do if she didn't travel alone, but she'd been so caught up in her grievances against Hugh that she hadn't been thinking straight.

Well, she was thinking straight now. She'd been taught a lesson. These people meant business, and the first chance she got, she would hire her own chaise and do what she was supposed to do.

"Abbie?"

"Yes, Hugh?" She fished in her pocket, found her handkerchief, and blew her nose.

"Is it raining in here?"

She gave a teary laugh. "No," she said.

"Then you're crying. Why?"

Because everything was in such a muddle. "Because I misjudged your coachman," she said.

The coach was slowing down. Abbie looked out the window and saw that they'd come to a crossroads. One way led to Hungerford the other to Endicote. The coach made the turn onto the Endicote road.

"Looks like we're going to Endicote," she said. "So you'll see Mrs. Deane after all."

"We'd never make Hungerford in this weather," he replied.

She sighed. "No. I suppose not."

She wouldn't get the book George's abductors wanted in three of four days now. In silent misery, she looked out the window and watched the snow fall.

Nemo was fit to be tied. He was dressed as an English country gentleman and he'd watched the whole thing from under the gallery. He could not believe how stupid his accomplices were. They'd ruined everything. He'd ordered them to maim Templar and put him out of action for a long time to come. When they saw that Templar was getting away, they should have used their initiative and killed him on the spot. They must have known that he, Nemo, couldn't do anything. He was in full view of two of the men who had trained their guns on Templar's coach. But his men had panicked when British agents had suddenly appeared. And now Templar and the woman had vanished into the snowstorm, taking the book with them.

He'd been told that Templar was harmless, that he wouldn't know anything because he was no longer in the service. But when Templar had unexpectedly turned up with Miss Vayle that morning and they'd left the Castle in Templar's coach, he hadn't known what to make of it. His first instinct had been to kill Templar when he caught up to him. Now he wished he'd paid attention to his instincts.

And his instincts were telling him right now to cut his losses and make for London as long as the roads were passable. He was far more important than the book, and now that British agents had arrived on the scene, it was time to take himself out of the game. Like it or not, he would have to leave his accomplices in charge of finding the girl's trail.

The ostler led his horse out of the stable and Nemo mounted up. They'd already exchanged a few words on the coach that had run amok.

The ostler shook his head. "You'll never get far on them there roads, guv'nor."

"I'm not going far." Nemo's glance shifted to two men he knew were British agents. They were mounting up as well. "Only to Newbury," he added absently.

"You'll be lucky to make it that far."

Nemo focused his attention on the ostler. "What did you say?"

"You'll be lucky to make it that far, guv'nor, sir."

Nemo threw back his head and laughed. "But I am lucky."

And it was true. If he hadn't been lucky, Napoleon would never have favored him. The Emperor was super-stitious that way. When he chose his generals and closest aides, he didn't ask about their years of service or what schools and universities they'd attended. He wanted to know only one thing: Were they lucky?

As he rode out of the courtyard and turned his mount's head toward Newbury, Nemo felt his spirits rise. He'd had near misses, but his luck had always held.

No one could beat him. He was unstoppable.

CHAPTER 10

Endicote was only three miles from the main highway, but the road was treacherous and their pace slackened. The village was no more than a church, a smithy, and a cluster of thatched cottages, and there wasn't a person in sight. A mile farther on, they turned into the drive of a modest two-story stone house. There were no lights in the windows and no smoking chimneys.

"It looks deserted," said Abbie.

Hugh was sitting on the banquette with the sheepskin blanket draped around his shoulders. "Mrs. Deane must have gone to her sister's in Newbury," he said, looking out the coach window. "She said she might. The house is for sale, so I suppose she got tired of waiting for a buyer."

When the coach came to a stop and Abbie tried to open the door, it was stuck. Harper finally got it open and she quickly jumped down. She marveled at the condition of the coach. There were several dents and the paint was badly scraped, but nothing more serious than that.

Hugh stepped down gingerly and halted. "No," he told Harper, "you're not going to sling me over your shoulder. I'll walk on my own two feet, thank you very much."

He took one step, staggered, and sank to his knees.

"I slipped on the ice," he said irritably, when Abbie and Harper each grabbed an arm to prevent him from falling on his face, then he sucked in a breath when they tried to raise him. "Not that arm, Abbie. My shoulder aches like the dickens. But I'm perfectly capable of walking unaided."

"Aye," retorted Harper, "and I'm the king of England. Tom, get our rig out of sight, and be quick about it. We're not in the clear yet."

Abbie looked nervously over her shoulder, but the snow was falling so thick and fast that she could not see much beyond the stone pillars at the entrance to the drive.

Harper hoisted Hugh to his feet, then drew his good arm tightly around his neck. "Now perhaps Your Honor will tell us how we're supposed to break in to that there house," he said.

"This is the country." Hugh gritted his teeth as he and Harper slowly ascended the front steps. "No one locks their doors in the country."

Hugh was right, and within moments they were inside.

"Where is the kitchen?" asked Abbie.

"Through that door," answered Hugh.

Harper said, "He should be in his bed."

"Not," replied Abbie, "until I've had a chance to look at him."

The house was cold and damp, and Abbie guessed that its mistress had been absent for several days. She went ahead of the others and passed through a small dining room, but there was not much to see in the fading light. The kitchen was reached through a flagstone corridor. Abbie used the flint box on the mantel to light the candles. There was a fire set in the grate, requiring only a flame to light it. She opened the damper and set her candle to the papers and tinder beneath the coal. When the papers caught and flared, she turned to survey the room.

There were two stone sinks and a pump in front of one of the windows. A plain wooden worktable sat in the center of the room, and hanging from pegs on all the walls was an array of pots and pans. Everything was as clean and tidy as a doctor's surgery.

"I can manage!" This was from Hugh as Harper carefully lowered him into one of the shabby stuffed armchairs that flanked the grate.

"Now," said Harper, "tell us what happened back at the inn."

"I was talking to one of the ostlers," Hugh said, "when I was approached by a gentleman, a stranger, who invited me to go for a walk." He paused for a moment. "I couldn't refuse because he had shoved a pistol in my ribs. We went through the exit into the lane. I saw another man, and behind him a carriage and coachmen. I resisted and they beat me with their pistols. That's all I remember until you pulled me from the carriage."

"What did they want?"

"I haven't a clue. They didn't ask me for money or my valuables, so they weren't thieves. Now it's your turn. What happened next? I have only the vaguest recollection after you pulled me from the carriage until we were on the open road."

"What happened next," said Harper, "is all hell broke

loose. We got rid of one lot of scoundrels only to come under fire from another lot."

Hugh said, "I wondered about that. I thought I heard—"

"Two lots of scoundrels!" exclaimed Abbie suddenly, and both men turned their heads to look at her. She shrugged helplessly. "That's not how it seemed to me. I thought they were all part of the same gang."

"Not likely," said Harper. "Why do you think those villains ran away? Not because you fired a shot. Your pistol was spent. They could have rushed you. No. They ran away because they saw the man on the gallery. Why *did* you fire that shot, Miss Vayle?"

"One of them made a move toward me," she said weakly, "and I panicked."

Hugh said, "I would have panicked too. You did very well, Abbie. Go on, Harper. What happened next?"

Harper looked at Hugh, caught something in his expression, then went on, "Well, as I was saying, they wasn't waiting for no explanations, so I decided to leave the party. So here we are." He looked at Hugh again. "We'll talk later," he said, "after you're rested. I'll take a look outside, just in case them blighters followed us."

Abbie said, "Surely they can't have followed us in that storm."

Hugh looked out the window. The snow was driving against the glass in a wild dervish. "Abbie's right. We were lucky to get through ourselves, and they wouldn't be expecting us to leave the main road."

Another look passed between Hugh and Harper, then Harper said, "I'll go help Tom with the horses, then. I'll talk to you later."

"You do that," said Hugh. "There's a stable at the back of the house. You'll find everything you need there."

When Harper left, Hugh relaxed into his chair. Abbie slowly removed her coat and hung it on a hook on the back of the door. Her brain was still reeling. Two lots of villains! It made perfect sense when she thought about it. She was remembering something the man who had attacked her in Bath had said, something about not trying to sell the book to his competitors. So now she had two lots of villains after her, two lots of villains to terrorize her. Far from frightening her, the thought infuriated her. They all seemed to think she was as easily cowed as a timid little rabbit.

Hugh watched her as she picked up the black kettle on the stone hearth and went to fill it from the pump. He was well aware that there was a lot more to what had happened at the Black Boar than appeared on the surface. This wasn't a random attack, and he suspected that it had far more to do with Abbie than with him.

She used two hands to carry the kettle back to the hearth, then she stooped down to hang it on its hook before swinging it over the open fire. Hugh gazed appreciatively at the rounded curve of her bottom. That was one of the things he liked about Abbie. She had generous curves.

"Now let's see what the damage is," she said.

Hugh didn't usually like people fussing over him, but this was different. He liked Abbie's hands on him, liked the way her cool fingers felt his pulse then his brow to test for fever. Her skirts were brushing his trousers, and if he leaned forward, he could plant a kiss right between her breasts.

"So far so good," she said, "now open your eyes wide."

Hugh obediently opened his eyes and stared up at Abbie.

"Well, that's a relief," she said. "Your pupils are not dilated."

"Mmm," said Hugh, inhaling the scent of her, part flowery and part something that was uniquely Abbie. He liked everything about her, from . . .

He suddenly realized where his thoughts were taking him and he was appalled. Marriage was definitely not in his stars, and that was the only way he could have Abbie.

Well, maybe he could have her if he was the unscrupulous libertine she'd called him. He had only to touch her and she melted for him. He could seduce her easily if he went about it the right way. Then she'd feel guilty, and he'd feel like hell, and in spite of what Abbie thought, he wasn't dishonorable. So, he'd feel obliged to marry her.

Better to burn than be caught in that trap again.

"Ouch," he said irritably. "That hurt."

"Mmm," said Abbie. "Well, now we know. You don't have a concussion, and you don't have a fever. You haven't broken any bones, or you wouldn't have managed to walk in here. It's your shoulder I'm worried about. These injuries to joints can be serious if they're not treated properly."

"Oh?" he said. "And how did you come to be such an authority?"

"George was forever—"

He waited, then prompted, "Your brother George?"

"Yes." She paused then went on, "When we were children, George was forever falling out of trees or from walls, and I would help Nurse look after him. So you see, I came to know all about concussions and how to set broken bones very early in life."

She'd moved behind him to examine the gash on his head. He couldn't see her face, but he'd heard the odd huskiness in her voice. *George?* He thought. What scrape had George got himself into?

"What is that young cub up to now?" he asked casually.

"Who?" Her fingers stilled.

"George. Isn't that who we were talking about?"

When she stood in front of him again, her expression was blank. "Oh, you know George," she said. "He comes and goes as he pleases." Then on the next breath, "There must be a medicine chest here somewhere. I'll need a plaster for that nasty cut on your head, and something to put on your cuts and abrasions. Do you know where Mrs. Deane keeps these things?"

"In the pantry," he said. "That door there."

"You seem to know the house very well."

"Dr. Deane was my tutor. I lived with him for a number of years."

"I see."

She took a candle from the mantel and went through the door he'd indicated.

Hugh watched her go with a puzzled frown. She'd adroitly changed the subject, but what was there about George that made her nervous? Could George be mixed up in this insane misadventure? What had these two innocents got themselves in to? And maybe not so innocent if British intelligence was involved. That thought was still revolving in his mind when Abbie returned. She put down the tray she was carrying and set to work with all the competence of a surgeon. When she was ready, she came to stand over him with a cloth wrung out in hot water in one hand, and a small black bottle in the other. He sniffed the bottle. "Extract of Yarrow and

Betony to clean my wounds. One of Mrs. Deane's home-made remedies. I remember it well, and yes, I know this is going to hurt."

She began by cleaning the dried blood from the abrasions on his face. "You said you lived in this house for a number of years?"

Hugh nodded. "I came here not long after my mother remarried, when I was six. And I lived here until I went away to school, when I was twelve. But I always came back here for holidays."

"Six! Isn't that very young? I mean, I know that boys sometimes go to live with their tutors, but not at that tender age."

"My mother and stepfather were involved in their own lives. They thought this would be the best solution all round."

"Best for whom?" she demanded indignantly.

He answered her with a smile. "Now don't let your imagination lead you astray. Once I got used to the Deanes, I was happy here. And when my mother died, well, it didn't seem such a catastrophe. This was my real home."

"I see." She said softly, "What were you like as a boy, Hugh?"

"I loved books. I was interested in history. I liked nothing better than to go out with Dr. Deane on scavenging expeditions, looking for fragments of pottery. Did you know that there are Roman ruins in this area, and stone circles similar to Stonehenge? So you see, I was in my element."

Their eyes met. She smiled. He smiled. The silence that followed was pleasant, companionable. But as the silence lengthened, it changed subtly. Hugh's chest began to rise and fall. Abbie's breathing became audible. Smiles faded.

They spoke at the same moment.

"Abbie, about last night."

"I'll need strips of linen to bind your shoulder. Don't move. This will only take a moment."

She left him in a rustle of skirts.

After Abbie had bound Hugh's shoulder, she went upstairs to prepare a room for him. The fire was already set and flared to life when she put a flame to it. She found freshly laundered bedclothes in the linen cupboard in the hall, and made up the bed in five minutes flat. There was an empty water carafe on the table by the bed, and though she felt that she should go downstairs and fill it from the pump as well as heat bricks in the oven to take the chill off the sheets, she didn't want to face Hugh right now.

They were becoming too cozy. She'd almost blurted out that in spite of his atrocious family, he'd turned out a fine, upstanding man. Then they'd get around to talking about last night, and she just wasn't up to it.

It was all a colossal misunderstanding. That's the approach she would take if the subject ever came up. And all things considered, maybe it was the truth.

She plumped herself down in front of the grate and used the tongs to add small lumps of coal to the crackling kindling, thinking all the while of Hugh as a boy in this very room.

Hugh had referred to his tutor many times, and always warmly, but she'd never understood that he'd actually lived with Dr. Deane, year in and year out. It wasn't unusual for boys to take up residence with their tutors, but not for years at a time, and only when there were no relatives to take them in.

She was appalled at the idea that Hugh had been abandoned. Despite his apparent indifference, she couldn't believe that he'd come through it unscathed. No child could. This was a nice comfortable house. Mrs. Deane was obviously an excellent housekeeper. But it wasn't the same as being raised in a loving family.

Not that her family was perfect, far from it. They bickered; they quarreled. Sometimes they liked each other. Often they did not. But, when one member was hurt or in trouble, they all rallied round. That was one thing that could be said of Vayles: they might dislike each other, but they never abandoned each other.

It was an unfortunate thought, for her mind immediately pictured George, in deep despair in some darkly lit, moldy cell, convinced that his family had abandoned him. She got to her feet and hugged herself with her arms. "No!" she said aloud. "No!" George would remember all the family rules they'd always lived by. *Vayles never forget to say please and thank you. Vayles never wash their dirty linen in public. Vayles stick together.*

The list was endless. And maybe they'd derided these sayings as they'd grown older, but the words had stuck in their minds all the same. They were practically the tenets of their faith—the Vayle dogma. No matter what, George would know that his family would never abandon him. They would move heaven and earth to get him home safe.

She swung away from the fire and went to look out the window. Snow. She used to love snow. Now she wanted to torch it. This could only happen to her. She was marooned in the middle of nowhere, going nowhere, with two lots of villains after her, and George's fate hanging in the balance. A fine rescuer she'd turned out to be! She didn't even know how to load a pistol and fire it. Harper had had to remind her to pull back the hammer. And the force of the shot had practically broken her wrist.

Even worse, she'd actually believed that Hugh's attackers ran away because she'd fired a shot over their heads. How stupid could she get? She'd left herself defenseless. They could have rushed her and overpowered her. If it hadn't been for the man on the gallery, it would have been a catastrophe.

She thought for a long time about the men who had attacked Hugh. The man who had accosted her in her own bed wasn't one of them. She let the thought turn in her mind and wondered how she could be so sure.

She didn't know. Instinct or intuition. Hugh's attackers were too fearful, almost as afraid as she was herself. The man in the brown coat was obviously the leader, and he didn't fit the bill at all. He wasn't big enough. He wasn't bold. And he didn't make her skin crawl. They'd all run away and she just couldn't see the man who had accosted her running away from anything.

The man on the gallery didn't fit her impressions of her assailant either. It was something in his voice. She didn't know what. Not his accent. She'd recognized a trace of a brogue, Irish or Scottish, but it was more than that. The voice on the gallery belonged to a baritone. The voice that she'd awakened to on that harrowing night was much lighter. And much more terrifying.

It didn't help. Nothing helped. She didn't know how she could hope to save George against such a man.

Just thinking about how pathetic she was made her temper boil—she, Abigail Vayle, who didn't have a temper! Maybe, if she asked him nicely, Harper would teach her how to use a gun.

On that thought, she went in search of Harper.

Three hours later, having emerged from a dreamless sleep, Hugh had the conversation with Harper he'd promised himself. He was propped up in bed, with hot bricks to keep his feet warm and a cup of contraband whiskey to do the same for his insides. The whiskey was contraband because Abbie had expressly forbidden wine or strong spirits on account of possible effects on any inflammation that may have set in. She'd made a pot of tea instead. They'd drunk the tea and were now working their way through the last of the whiskey Harper had found in the coach.

Hugh said, "Abbie didn't look too happy when she brought me my tea. What's got into her?"

Harper made a face. "She's as mad as a hornet 'cause she couldn't hit the target I set up for her when she asked me to show her how to use a pistol."

"I didn't hear anything."

"Didn't you? Well, you was out like a light and we was some ways from the house."

"Why does she want to learn how to use a pistol?"

Harper shrugged. "She said that she felt like a clown

when I had to tell her to pull back the hammer when she was covering those bastards who attacked you."

Hugh thought about this for a moment and his lips began to twitch. "What was the target?"

"A broken-down barn door."

"And she couldn't hit it?" Hugh asked incredulously.

"I suppose she could if she was standing three feet in front of it. She won't give up, though. She says we're to practice again tomorrow. What she lacks in skill she makes up for in sheer determination. She's a regular trooper."

Since his coachman didn't have a high opinion of women, this tribute made Hugh stare. Harper, in his time, had contracted four irregular "marriages," without benefit of clergy, and his sad experiences had turned him into a confirmed misogynist. Harper had been Hugh's sergeant in Spain, the man who, as Harper would have it, had "saved his arse" on more occasions than he cared to remember.

Hugh had discovered that there was no shame in this. Most greenhorn officers who saw active service were either made or unmade by their sergeants. He'd been lucky to have Harper, and Harper never let him forget it.

They might have gone their separate ways except for something that happened after Hugh was recruited to British intelligence. During a battle, with all the officers dying around him, Harper had been promoted to lieutenant on the spot. But Harper's friends were enlisted men and he didn't want to be an officer. So he'd taken matters into his own hands. When the battle was over, he'd started a brawl and was hauled off to the block house. All he'd wanted was to be demoted. What he'd got was a court-martial. Hugh heard about it, had intervened, and had Harper transferred to British intelligence where, much to Hugh's surprise, he'd proved invaluable. They'd made a good team.

But that was during the war. In peace time, Harper had no skills that were in demand. He was wasted as a coachman, but it was the only employment Hugh could find for him. Harper was a born soldier, but the army wouldn't have him back at any price.

Harper said, "Now would you mind telling me why you gave me all them strange looks when we first got here? I wasn't sure what to make of them."

"I didn't want Maitland's name to come up. Miss Vayle doesn't know about the time I spent with British intelligence and that's the way I'd like to keep it."

Somehow, he didn't think Abbie would appreciate knowing that he had once been a spy. Besides, that part of his life was over, and he was going to make damn sure that it stayed that way.

"You said that Miss Vayle sounded the alarm?"

Harper nodded. "She'd seen you speaking to a stranger in a brown coat, and when she couldn't find you, she came to me."

"Were you as alarmed as she?"

"Well, I was and I wasn't. After all, you'd only been gone a few minutes. But when I saw how worried *she* was, that worried me too."

Hugh frowned. "It strikes me that she was expecting trouble, which is why she jumped to the conclusion that something had happened to me. But then she risked her life to save me."

Harper nodded. "She saved your arse. There ain't no doubt about that."

Hugh smiled. "She did, didn't she?"

There was a long, unbroken silence. Hugh held out

his cup. Harper lifted the china teapot with flowers on it and poured out a generous measure of whiskey, then he did the same to his own cup. Both men sipped their drinks as they reviewed the events at the Black Boar.

Finally, Hugh said, "Tell me about Maitland again."

Harper looked at Hugh with a question in his eyes and a half smile hovering at the corner of his mouth.

"What?" demanded Hugh, frowning.

"I never could understand," said Harper, almost drawling the words, "why you and Maitland was always at each other's throats. You was on the same side. You was both good agents, or so I heard the colonel say. But you never could work together without falling out."

"You'll have to ask Maitland that." When Harper's bushy eyebrows rose, Hugh said, "Look, it happens sometimes. Two people just take a dislike to one another." And when those brows climbed another notch, Hugh gave a reluctant laugh. "We were recruited at the same time," he said. "Maitland always felt he was at a disadvantage. He didn't go to the right schools; he didn't have the right background. I believe his father was a country solicitor. He was out to prove himself and didn't care what methods he used. And he didn't like me because he thought I was born with a silver spoon in my mouth, and that the colonel favored me. That's how it started, and as time went on, it only got worse."

"Mmm," said Harper, looking only half convinced.

"So tell me again," said Hugh. "What happened with Maitland?"

"At first, when I saw him on the gallery, I thought that he and his merry band of men had come to rescue us. But they pointed their pistols straight at us, and would have used them, too, if there hadn't been innocent people standing around."

"But why would Maitland turn on us? It doesn't make sense."

"Maybe it's Miss Vayle he's after. But that don't make no sense neither."

Hugh reflected on this then said, "The men who tried to abduct me—they weren't working for Maitland?"

"It was Maitland and his crew that scared them off. Well, think about it. Miss Vayle had emptied her pistol so those thugs could easily have overpowered her."

"A woman wouldn't think about that," said Hugh, "especially a frightened woman." He paused as he tried to visualize exactly what had happened. "But you're right. They wouldn't have run off after Abbie discharged her pistol. So, there must be two units working against each other. British intelligence and—?" He looked a question at Harper.

But Harper could only shake his head.

Hugh sank back against the pillows and closed his eyes. There were so many loose threads, and he didn't know how to knit them together—Abbie, her brother, Maitland, and the thugs who had beat him up with their pistols.

There was only one way to get at the truth, and that was through Abbie. But if she refused to confide in him, he didn't know how to make her talk. When they reached London, he could go straight to Colonel Langley. The colonel would know what his men were up to.

Unless Maitland was working alone.

It wouldn't be the first time. He was a secretive bastard, and guarded his territory jealously. He wasn't a good agent, in Hugh's opinion. He didn't share information with his colleagues, and that was dangerous. He liked nothing better than to show them up as incompetent while taking all the credit himself.

Hugh opened his eyes. "Maitland can tell me what I want to know. And I bet he knows more than Abbie."

Harper choked on a swallow of whiskey. When he had cleared his throat, he said, "I hopes that doesn't mean what I thinks it means. You're surely not going back to the Black Boar?"

"He'll get the surprise of his life when I turn up."

Harper shook his head. "Just like that? You're going to walk into the lion's den?"

Hugh snorted. "Credit me with some sense. I'm going back there to give Maitland a taste of his own medicine. I'll do whatever I have to do to get the truth out of Maitland."

"If I was you, I'd start with Miss Vayle. She knows more than she's telling."

Hugh straightened and winced at the pain that pierced his shoulder. Gritting his teeth, he said, "I intend to. But I can't believe that Abbie would involve herself in anything criminal. Maybe she does know more than she's telling, but her motives are pure. I'm sure of it. She's an innocent pawn. But Maitland—he'd use his own mother to advance his career."

Harper stared into space. "She reminds me of wife number three," he said.

Hugh stifled a groan. Every woman reminded Harper of one or another of his "wives," and he had a fund of horror stories on each one. Hugh wasn't in the mood to hear them right now. "Don't your wives have names?" he asked testily.

Harper ignored the bad temper. "She looked as innocent as an angel, but looks can be deceiving. One night, she bashed me with the kettle, just because I had one too many, then she run off with all my money."

"Maybe you deserved it!"

"Oh, I didn't care about the money. But she run off with my mate as well, the one she was always telling me was a bad influence. He was a good mate, none better, and I never found anyone to replace him."

"Harper," said Hugh, pressing a hand to his brow, "this isn't helping."

Harper grinned. "No? Well, maybe this will help." He pointed to the window. "That there snow is coming down like pigeon shit in one of them Spanish plazas. Now, it's true that Maitland won't be going anywhere, but neither will we, see? We're stuck here until the snow melts or we digs ourselves out. And if that wasn't enough, there's you to think about. In your condition, you couldn't fight your way out of your bathwater, so how can you hope to take on Maitland?"

"I'm not going to take him on in hand-to-hand combat. I intend to take him by surprise, if necessary with a pistol to his head. And as for getting out of here, I know this area like the back of my hand. I've walked out of here in snowstorms before."

"And I suppose you'll want me to go along with you?"

Hugh grinned. "I couldn't do it on my own," he said.

"In that case," said Harper, "we'll leave it till tomorrow night."

"But that could be too late."

"I means it. I'm not having no invalid on my hands to worry about."

When the door suddenly opened and Abbie entered with a laden tray, both men jumped like guilty schoolboys.

"How's the patient?" she asked pleasantly.

"Feeling much better, thanks to you," Hugh replied, eyeing her pleasant expression with some mistrust.

As she drew closer, she sniffed the air. "What's that I smell?" she asked.

Hugh and Harper exchanged a quick look. "It's—it's the salve you put on my cuts," said Hugh.

"It smells like whiskey."

Harper rose abruptly. "Well, I best be getting along. I has to look after—"

"The horses," supplied Abbie. "Yes, I know."

Harper left with a sheepish grin. Hugh's grin was calculated to melt a heart of stone. "Did Harper give you the box of provisions from the coach?" he asked.

"You mean the basket with steak pies, and cold chicken and ham and French champagne? Yes, I was surprised, though I suppose I shouldn't have been. You *do* like to plan for every possibility, don't you, Hugh? Too bad that this time it's not going to do you any good."

"Why not?"

"Because you're an invalid, Hugh, and invalids must be very careful about what they eat. *And drink.*" She whisked off the silver cover from the server on the tray. "There's plenty more where that came from," she said cheerfully, "so don't stint yourself."

Hugh looked down at a bowl of watery mush. "What," he asked ominously, "is that?"

"Gruel," she replied, drawing out the word. "Fortunately, I found oatmeal and butter in the larder, so I was able to make a full pot." She touched a small glass of slimy black liquid. "And that's your purgative. It's always important to purge a patient who has an inflammation. So be sure to drink it to the last drop."

Hugh was rendered speechless.

"Shall I hold the glass for you?"

His eyes glinted. "If you do, it will be the last thing you do."

She smiled unpleasantly. "I'll be back later to collect the dishes." She walked to the door.

"Abbie!" he roared. "You've had your joke! Now get me my dinner!"

"Joke? Who said anything about a joke?" Arms akimbo, she glared at him. "I warned you that in your weakened condition you weren't allowed to touch strong spirits, and you went behind my back and got Harper involved in your underhanded scheme. Well, now you'll pay the consequences," and she flounced from the room.

Not long after, she relented, as Hugh knew she would. It was Harper who brought the dinner tray. "What, no champagne?" asked Hugh.

"Miss Vayle," said Harper, "plucked the glass off the tray before I could get out the door. She said I should tell you that you're to make do with tea until she says differently."

"Tea?" said Hugh hopefully, eyeing the china teapot on the tray.

Harper shook his head. "It's more than my life's worth."

Hugh sighed, and reached for a chicken drumstick.

Her wrists ached, her arms ached, her back ached, not from all her housework, but from Harper's pistol practice. The book she'd read had not told her how much physical effort was required to shoot a pistol. She thought all one had to do was pick it up, aim, and shoot. No one had told her that when she pulled the trigger, she would feel the report of the shot all the way from her shoulder right down to the tips of her fingers. She couldn't even hit the door at fifteen paces. How was she ever going to learn to protect herself?

The weight of the water in her bucket made her groan as she raised it and emptied it into the sink. She could scarcely believe how puny she was. She was young, healthy, and strong, yet after an hour's pistol practice she felt as weak as an old woman.

And she'd wheedled a promise out of Harper to put her through the same torture tomorrow? She must be crazy.

She wasn't crazy, she was scared. Those thugs had abducted her brother. They'd got to Hugh as well. She just couldn't see them holding to their bargain once she handed over the book. They'd killed Colette and Jerome. What was to stop them from killing George and her as well?

She would stop them if she could only learn how to shoot a gun.

It wasn't all bad. Maybe she couldn't hit a door at fifteen paces, but she'd learned a few things. She knew how to load a pistol now, quickly and efficiently. She'd learned not to waste her shot because one shot was all she was going to get. She knew not to get too close to an opponent because it would be easy for him to disarm her. That's why Harper had insisted that she try to hit the door at fifteen paces. And she'd learned that each pistol was different—some threw to the left and some threw to the right. All that meant was that few pistols ever hit what they were pointed at.

Then what was the use of trying? she asked herself angrily. She didn't know why guns had been invented if they couldn't shoot straight.

Or maybe it wasn't the gun; maybe it was her. After all, Harper hadn't had any trouble hitting the target.

She replaced the bucket beneath the sink, picked up a damp rag, and spread it out to dry on the draining board rack. She jumped when the kitchen door opened, then relaxed when Hugh entered. He was wearing a dark blue dressing robe, and his injured arm was bound tightly to his chest. If he tried anything, she wouldn't need a gun to protect herself. One slap on that weak shoulder would send him to his knees, and she was just in the mood to take him on.

He said, "I've been waiting for you to come upstairs so that we could discuss what happened at the Black Boar."

She made a vague gesture with one hand. "I've just finished cleaning up in here. Besides, I'm sure Harper has told you everything already."

"I don't think so. Sit down, Abbie."

She blinked at his tone of voice and took the chair he indicated, because it gave her something to do while she marshaled her thoughts. This wasn't the kind of threat she'd been expecting.

Hugh edged one hip onto the tabletop and eyed her blank expression. "Those men at the inn . . . You know who they are, don't you, Abbie?"

"I've never seen them before in my life!"

His eyes narrowed fractionally. "Let's not mince words. You're in some kind of trouble, you and your brother both."

Though her heart leaped, she kept her voice and gaze steady. "And I think you must have come down with a fever. You're raving, Hugh."

"Will you stop lying? Don't you know how serious

this is? Harper recognized the man on the gallery. He's attached to British intelligence."

She looked at him without comprehension, then her jaw went slack. "British intelligence? You mean . . . he's a *spy*?"

Hugh paused before answering. There was no doubt in his mind that her shock was genuine. "That's exactly what I mean."

She jumped to her feet. "Now I *know* you're raving. We're not at war with anybody. Harper must have been mistaken. And anyway, what have spies to do with me?"

"All right. So you didn't know about British intelligence. But you're not being completely honest with me. I want to help you, don't you see? So please, no more lies between us."

Her pulse was pounding so loudly she could hear it thrumming in her ears. She looked up at him with unseeing eyes. Her mind was paralyzed and she was afraid to make connections—Paris, the British embassy, George, spies.

Hugh saw that dazed look and cursed himself under his breath. He slipped from the table and took the one step that separated them. With his good hand, he cupped her neck, anchoring her to him. "It's all right," he soothed. "It's not that serious. I have connections. I'll take care of everything, Abbie. I would never let anything happen to you."

When she stared at him with the same unseeing expression, he tilted her chin up and pressed his lips to hers in a chaste kiss. "Let me take care of you, Abbie," he murmured. "I promise, I'll take good care of you."

He kissed her again and this time his mouth was open, warm, wet. His hand moved from her neck and cupped her breast. When she accepted that intimate touch, a powerful shudder wracked his body. He dipped his head and kissed her chin, her throat, her breasts, then his mouth closed over one taut nipple through the fabric of her gown.

With a choked sob, she leaped back.

Hugh combed his fingers through his hair. "I'm sorry. It just happened. I wanted to comfort you."

"*Comfort* me? By telling me a pack of lies? You wanted to frighten me so you could take me off guard."

"Now who's raving? I came in here with only one thought in my mind: I want to protect you."

Abbie struggled to find her balance. As she gained control of her senses, she took another step back.

It wasn't his kisses that had shocked her, as he seemed to think, but the sudden suspicion that he would use any means to get the truth out of her. But that didn't make sense. Hugh wouldn't use those underhanded methods. He wasn't the enemy, but an innocent bystander. If it hadn't been for her, he wouldn't be involved at all.

All her instincts told her to trust him, and that's where the danger lay. This was a lethal game they were playing, and she didn't want Hugh involved at all.

She had to find a way to take him out of the game.

Her voice was cool and controlled. "You want to protect me? If this is a renewal of your insulting offer, you can go to Hades. I value my self-respect."

"I never meant to insult you. In fact—" He broke off, paused, then went on, "That's beside the point. When I came in here, I wanted to talk to you, that's all. Then, well . . . things got out of hand." He grinned crookedly. "I can't resist you, Abbie, and that's the truth."

He meant what he said. She could see it in his eyes: desire tempered by ruefulness. It would be so easy to give him back the same words. Then he'd enfold her in his arms and make love to her, and. . . .

And then she'd never get rid of him.

She said lightly, "What a pretty compliment, Hugh. Truly, I'm flattered. But it comes too late. You see, I realize that I could never be happy with a man like you."

Temper heated his eyes, then cooled to ice. "A man like me? Would you mind explaining that remark?"

"I've lost interest, Hugh. That's all I meant."

"You have an odd way of showing it."

"As I said, you took me off guard. I'm not saying this to make you feel guilty. I'm telling you so that you'll take my no as final. I can't deny that when I'm in your arms, I forget . . . well, everything but being in your arms. But I could never be happy with what you offer. So I'm asking you to give me a chance to find what I really want."

"Which is?"

"There must be some nice man out there who isn't too fussy; someone who would be content with a solid, affectionate relationship based on mutual respect; someone who wants children as much as I do. That's what I want, Hugh."

It was the truth and it was all lies. But she'd done what she'd set out to do. She could see that he believed her. Behind the fury, she detected the hurt pride. One day, if everything turned out well, she would beg his forgiveness. One day, when this was all over.

At the door, she turned back as though a thought had just occurred to her. "When we get to Newbury, I shall hire my own chaise. We have nothing more to say to each other, so there's no point in traveling together."

Hugh's face was grim when she closed the door. *Babies,* he was thinking. Abbie wanted *babies?* Babies were the one thing he never thought about.

Some nice man. . . . If he found that man, he would kill him.

CHAPTER 12

Richard Maitland drained his coffee cup and glanced around the dining room, hoping to catch the eye of a waiter so that he could settle his bill and return to his room. He usually liked to linger over his after-dinner coffee, but because the Black Boar had more guests than it could accommodate, he'd had a long, long wait in the taproom. When he was finally called into the dining room, he learned that dinner was not served after ten o'clock, and all that was available were cold meats and sandwiches. To add insult to injury, he'd had to share his table with a talkative bore of a man, and his patience was wearing thin.

There were, however, no waiters in that besieged dining room willing to look anyone in the eye, and Maitland resigned himself to another five minutes, ten at the most, of utter boredom. Not that boredom was anything new. Since they'd lost Templar and the woman in the storm, they'd been marooned here for over twenty-four hours, sitting on their hands. Meantime, he'd sent two of his men to check the road to Newbury. As soon as conditions improved, they would be out of here, even if they had to take off in the middle of the night.

The gentleman sitting opposite him, who'd introduced himself as Mr. John Compton, was eyeing him speculatively. "You're Scottish!" he declared, as though he'd just trumped his opponent in a game of whist.

"How did you guess?" asked Maitland indifferently. He already knew what the answer would be. Five years of striving to erase his own accent so that he would fit in with his uppity English colleagues had proved only moderately successful.

"It was when you said the word 'waiter,' " responded Compton. "You rolled the *r*. Otherwise, I would have taken you for one of us."

Maitland bared his teeth in a stiff-lipped smile. "Praise indeed," he murmured laconically.

Arrogant English bastard! he thought. Did he think that all the Scots had red hair and freckles? Or maybe he expected to see heather growing out of his ears?

Compton went on innocently, "It's one of my hobbies, you know, trying to place a man by his accent. I had pegged you as an Oxford man until that *r* betrayed you. Or perhaps you did go to Oxford?"

"No," said Maitland, and began to drum his fingers on the tablecloth.

"Then it must be Cambridge!"

God, did the English never give up? They could not be satisfied until they had put everyone in pigeonholes. And if you didn't fit into the right pigeonhole, God help you. There were only a handful of schools the members of the uppercrust would dream of sending their sons to, only two universities that amounted to anything in their estimation. Education was the furthest thing from their minds. What they wanted was that exclusive accent and polish that set them apart from the herd.

Though he despised their arrogance, the unhappy truth was that in his profession, a man's background and accent could make or break him. He couldn't afford to be different, so he'd done everything in his power to fit in with his colleagues. He'd had one asset to start with: he looked like a typical Englishman, or what they thought was a typical Englishman—fair hair, regular features, average height and build. He'd learned to wear the right clothes; he copied his colleagues' manners, their habits, and their modes of expression. What he could not copy was their easygoing attitude to things, and that betrayed him far more than his accent.

He was ambitious—a sin in his colleagues' eyes. The intelligence service was his profession. He had to excel. He had no family fortune to fall back on if and when he left the service. His father was a solicitor in Aberdeen, highly respected in his own sphere, but not a wealthy man. His son had to stand on his own two feet.

And he had talent. In fact, he was Langley's best agent, as he'd proved time and time again. But all that had earned him was a slap on the wrist.

"Richard, you're too intense," Langley once told him. "This isn't a competition. We're all friends here. You're not working on your own. You must learn to cooperate with your colleagues."

So here he was, at four and thirty, a misfit Scot, stuck in a rut, going nowhere because he took his job too seriously while his English colleagues acted as though they were involved in nothing more serious than a game of cricket.

He was exaggerating, of course, but not by much. Langley was a case in point. Now that the war with

France was over, he was thinking of retiring so that he could enjoy life more—whatever that meant. Actually, it would be better if the colonel did retire. He wasn't as vigilant as he used to be, and delegated a greater share of the work to his subordinates. That's why he'd put him, Richard Maitland, in charge of this investigation.

"There's probably nothing to it," Langley had told him, "but we've got to check it out. Tread carefully here, Richard. I understand that Miss Vayle is a close friend of Hugh Templar."

Nothing to it. That's what they'd all thought, except him. That's what made people careless, and when people in his business got careless, they paid for it with their lives.

Hugh Templar had a lot to answer for. Had it not been for him, he would have captured the woman, and even now could be questioning her.

The bore was speaking again. "You're a military man, too, are you not?" He nodded sagely. "I can always spot a military man."

Maitland let out a long sigh, placed both hands on the flat of the table, and leaned toward the older man. "Two can play at this game, you know."

"I beg your pardon?"

"Mr. Compton," said Maitland pleasantly, "does your wife know that you are traveling with a young woman half your age?"

Compton went white around the mouth. "I—I don't know what you're talking about," he said.

"I thought not." At last he'd caught the eye of a waiter. He waved him over, then turned back to his companion. "The young woman near the door who keeps looking our way? Serving girl, is she? No, on second thoughts, I'd say from her dress that she's a cut above that. Maybe your wife's maid? You know, you're not fooling anyone by sitting at separate tables."

All the color drained out of Compton's face. "Who are you?" he asked hoarsely.

There was no humor in Maitland's smile. He spoke in a theatrical whisper. "If I told you my name, Mr. Compton, I'd have to kill you."

He paid his bill, smiled pleasantly at Compton, tipped his hat to Compton's pretty young traveling companion, then sauntered outside.

Nothing much was happening in the courtyard. A few stableboys were having a snowball fight. It had stopped snowing. Now if only they could get underway, they might catch up with Templar and the woman when they were least expecting it.

He looked at his watch. It would soon be midnight. Middler and Leigh should have returned by now, unless they'd lost their way. He wouldn't put it past them. They were still wet behind the ears and didn't know their elbows from their arses. He didn't know what the service was coming to.

He stood for some time lost in thought, then returned to the inn and made his way upstairs to his room. When he inserted the key in the lock and turned it, he realized the door was unlocked. He set down his candle, reached in his pocket for his pistol, then burst into the room.

Hugh Templar looked up from the table he was stooped over. One arm was in a sling, and in his free hand he held a bottle of brandy. "Ah, Maitland," he said. "What kept you?" He raised the brandy bottle. "I was looking for whiskey, but this seems to be all you've got. I've just poured myself a drink. Shall I pour one for you?"

Maitland kept his pistol trained on Hugh and shut the door with his foot. His eyes flicked around the room, but there was no one else there and no place for anyone to hide. Reaching back with one hand, he locked the door and pocketed the key.

"Where's Harper?" he asked.

"You forgot to look under the bed," said Hugh.

Maitland ignored the taunt. "I'm not in the mood for games. Put that bottle down, Templar, then sit down, and don't make any sudden move or it could be your last."

Hugh put the bottle on the table, picked up his glass, and carefully sank into a chair. "Careful with that pistol. I'm not armed, so there's no need to point it at me. As for Harper, he's been delayed. I left him tying up two of your men in the coal cellar. When he gets here, he's going to keep watch outside the door. But once you and I have our little tête-à-tête, he can join us if you like, and we can all reminisce about old times."

Maitland took the few steps to bring him to a tall mahogany dresser. He propped his shoulder against it, then cradled his pistol in the crook of one arm. "Where is the woman?" he asked.

"In a safe place. She was sleeping when I left her."

Maitland smiled. "You do know how to pick them, don't you, Templar?"

Hugh was silent for a moment. When he spoke, he said simply, "I want to talk to Langley."

"And tell him what? You'll never talk your way out of this one."

Hugh took a healthy swallow of brandy. "Where is Langley?"

"In London, hanging out with all his old cronies now that he's practically retired."

Hugh snorted. "So that's why you're in charge."

Maitland leveled his pistol. "I could put a bullet in your brain right now, and claim it was self-defense."

"Not you, Dickie boy," replied Hugh. "You would never do anything to put a blot on your record. That's the difference between us. I don't give a damn, and you've got your eye fixed on . . . what exactly is your eye fixed on? Langley's job?"

"So you admit that you killed Alex Ballard?"

Hugh frowned. "What in hell's name are you talking about?"

"Ballard. He's dead. Don't pretend you didn't know, because it won't wash."

Maitland went on speaking, but Hugh didn't hear him. His mind seemed to crack wide open, then slowly come together again. "What do you mean, he's dead?" he suddenly burst out, cutting Maitland off in midsentence. "I spoke to Alex a few nights ago. His wife is about to have a baby. He'd taken her down to Wells to be with her mother. He can't be dead."

"You sound very convincing, I'll give you that."

"Listen to me! I don't know what's happening. Why do you think I'm here? Not for the pleasure of your company. Talk to me, Maitland. Tell me what this is about. Maybe I can help you. Maybe the two of us can work together."

Maitland stood unmoving, like a man who had come to a fork in the road and didn't know which way to go. Finally, he put his pistol in his pocket, moved to the table where he poured himself a glass of brandy, then sat down on the chair facing Hugh's.

He said, "We found Ballard's body yesterday morning in the Castle Inn, when we went looking for Miss Vayle. He was on the floor of her bedchamber. His skull was crushed. There was a brass candlestick on the floor beside the body."

Hugh stared at the other man without seeing him. He was seeing Alex Ballard's face, hearing Ballard's voice. *Remember you have a poor record with women. Remember to watch your back.*

"Where is Miss Vayle?" asked Maitland softly.

The fog in Hugh's brain cleared. "You can't believe that she had anything to do with this!"

"I do believe it. In fact, I'm sure of it. And until a moment ago, I thought you were protecting her. Maybe I've misjudged you."

Hugh said angrily, "It's Miss Vayle you've misjudged. Somebody, somewhere, has his facts mixed up. Who put you on to her?"

"She did." Maitland took a long gulp of brandy, then another, and said, "We didn't approach her. She approached us."

"Abbie did?" Hugh sounded incredulous.

"Several weeks ago, she sent a letter to Mr. Michael Lovatt of the British embassy in Paris, care of Whitehall. The letter sat on some insignificant clerk's desk until he finally got around to sending it on. The Paris people know of Michael Lovatt and sent Lovatt's letter back to London, but addressed to me. So you see, there was a delay in getting the letter, a delay in getting started."

" 'Michael Lovatt' is one of your aliases?"

"It's a code name my Paris agents used whenever they wanted to communicate with me—but that was before I was recalled to London."

Hugh sat on the edge of his chair, carefully sifting every word as Maitland reviewed the sequence of events. His cell in Paris, Maitland said, had been wiped out, but no one knew why. They were on to something, but he didn't have a clue what it was. No one at the foreign office took his agents' deaths seriously, assuming that old scores were being paid off now that the war was over. Only Alex Ballard had shown any sympathy. But there was nothing to go on . . . not until Abigail Vayle wrote that letter to Michael Lovatt, offering a trade.

"I can't remember exactly what was in her letter," Maitland said. "She was too clever to come right out and demand money."

"Then what did she offer to trade?"

"She said she would return Michael Lovatt's copy of the *Iliad* if he would help her out of her difficulties. She knew the book was priceless because it was a gift from his wife, Colette."

"Colette was one of your agents?"

"Yes. And that's how she passed on messages—with a book. The day she died, she had an appointment with an embassy official in a bookshop in the rue de Rivoli, but she never turned up. Whatever those agents died for . . . it's in that book. You can bet on it."

When Hugh shook his head, Maitland said roughly, "Good God, man, Colette was murdered the day before you and Miss Vayle left Paris!"

"That doesn't prove anything!"

Maitland laughed mirthlessly and shook his head. "What will it take to convince you?"

"A hell of a lot more than that!" Hugh considered for a moment or two, then said, "Tell me about Ballard's murder."

"I don't know what happened. I didn't know he was down here until I went looking for Miss Vayle and found his body in her room. I thought I was in charge of this case. They were my agents who were eliminated, for God's sake! I should have known Langley would send someone to make sure that I didn't step on anyone's toes." Another unpleasant smile. "Do you know what Langley's parting words to me were?" He mimicked the words. " 'Tread carefully, Richard. Miss Vayle is a close friend of Hugh Templar. This may be a colossal misunderstanding.' A misunderstanding!" he said violently, and as more emotion crept into his voice, his accent became less cultured, betraying his origins. "We've become soft! Well, Langley won't be soft when he hears that one of his blue-eyed boys has been murdered."

"It's ridiculous to think that Miss Vayle murdered him! Even if she tried to, Ballard was a trained agent—he would have easily overpowered her."

"Obviously she had an accomplice. A man with the strength to inflict the blow to Ballard's skull."

"Or it happened after she left."

"In that case the body would have been warm, and it was stone cold."

Hugh drained his glass and set it aside. His thoughts were running off in every direction. He knew Abbie was in some kind of trouble; he knew she was nervous about something. But he also knew she was innocent.

Maitland abruptly stood up. After topping up his own glass, he offered the bottle to Hugh, but Hugh shook his head.

"We were only a few hours behind you." Maitland took his seat again. "I mean, after we left Bath. I thought I would catch up with Miss Vayle on the road. I didn't expect you to be with her." He leaned forward in his chair and his eyes locked on Hugh's. "Where is she, Templar? Give me five minutes alone with her, and she'll tell me everything."

Hugh's eyes narrowed to slits. "How is that going to help you find the book? If she's guilty, and you threaten her, she'll get rid of it."

"It's gone beyond that now. She murdered Ballard."

"I know her!" Hugh bit out. "She couldn't murder anyone."

Maitland made a slashing motion with one hand. "You're thinking with your balls! Try thinking with your brain. It's in your interest to cooperate with me. You're not in the clear yet."

"You're out of your mind."

"Am I? Fact: You and Miss Vayle were both in Paris when two of my agents were murdered. Fact: You and Miss Vayle are traveling together and Ballard's body is discovered in her room. Fact: In the courtyard of this very inn, when I asked you to give yourselves up, you defied me and tried to run down my men."

"Fact—" retorted Hugh, almost snarling the word— "I'd just been attacked by footpads. Why do you think my arm is in a sling? When you ordered us to surrender and trained your guns on us, we didn't know what to think. Fact: I'm here now, aren't I? Would I have come back to confront you if I had something to hide?"

"Footpads? You expect me to believe that?"

"They were right under your shagging nose. Are you blind as well as irrational? Look," said Hugh, "supposing Miss Vayle has this book, why would she murder Ballard? Wouldn't she hand it over to him? Isn't that what she wanted to do? Isn't that why she wrote that letter?"

"We were too slow off the mark. I think she's sold it to our enemies or is trying to sell it. She said in her letter that she would." Maitland's words were slurred.

There was a moment of silence, then Hugh said slowly,

"Listen to me, Maitland. This *has* been a colossal misunderstanding. Miss Vayle buys and sells books. It's a sort of hobby with her. Maitland!" He raised his voice. "*Maitland!* Don't go to sleep on me now! Not yet!"

Cursing violently, Hugh rose and crossed to the other man. Maitland's eyes were closed, and his head lolled against the back of his chair. Hugh removed the empty glass from his inert fingers and set it on the table, then he poured what was left of the brandy into the slop pail beside the wash basin. Having done that, he felt in Maitland's pocket and removed the key.

Harper was waiting for him on the other side of the door. "Well?" he said.

"How much of that narcotic did you put in the brandy bottle?" demanded Hugh irritably.

"I told you you'd have ten minutes at the most if he drank a glass."

They heard a step in the corridor. "Let's get the hell out of here," said Hugh.

They left the inn by the front doors, with no attempt at concealment except to pull up the collars of their cloaks, and pull down their hat brims, but that was more to protect their faces from the night air. Their destination was a smaller inn, the Swan, at the other end of the High Street, where they'd left their horses. As they trudged along, Hugh filled Harper in on his conversation with Maitland.

When Hugh was finished, Harper said only, "So what are you going to do about Miss Vayle?"

"What I'm going to do," said Hugh savagely, "is get her away from here. I don't trust Maitland. He's crazed because he lost four agents. He doesn't care who pays for it, as long as someone pays. He's already tried Abbie in his mind and found her guilty. I'm going to get this sorted out, then I'm going to take Miss Vayle straight to the colonel in London. He'll give her a fair hearing."

"Mmm," said Harper.

Hugh gave him a sharp look. "What?" he demanded.

"I always thought Maitland had a good head on his shoulders. I mean, I knows he's not easy to get along with, but he's a good agent."

"Oh? Don't stop there."

"If you're going to take that attitude," said Harper stiffly, "I'll keep my mouth shut."

"Fine," retorted Hugh.

They made the rest of the journey in thin-lipped silence. When they arrived at the Swan, they went to the stable and led out their horses.

They left the main road almost at once and took the track to the river Kennet. It was slow going because trees hemmed them in and the darkness was almost absolute. When they came to the river, the trees and the darkness thinned out. They turned onto the bridle path but still kept their horses to a slow walk. When the bridle path widened, Harper came abreast of Hugh.

"How's the shoulder?" he asked.

"It's perfectly—" Hugh's horse jogged sideways, and he stifled a groan. "It's bloody awful, if you must know."

Both men chuckled. After a while, Hugh said, "You think Maitland is such a good agent, but can't you see that in this case he's blinded by anger? He's lost four agents. He suspects Abbie of murdering Ballard, and he's out for her blood."

"What I thinks," said Harper carefully, "is that you're both good agents, but in this case, you're both at fault. Maitland is blinded by anger, and you are blinded by your fondness for Miss Vayle. He wants to punish her, you wants to protect her. You're both overlooking the most important thing. If you takes your blinkers off, I'm sure you'll see it."

"The book," said Hugh. "No, I hadn't forgotten about it."

The bridle path narrowed again and Harper fell back. Hugh drew his cloak more snugly about him and leaned into the breeze that lifted off the river.

Four agents had died to pass on a message, five counting Ballard. Clearly the book was crucial. And both sides seemed to think that Abbie had it.

He'd mentioned the attack on him to Maitland. When Maitland had time to think about it, he would realize the other side did not have the book either, and try even harder to capture Abbie.

It all seemed so farfetched. He knew Abbie as well as he knew himself, and he would trust her with his life. But that was Hugh Templar, thinking as a man. When he thought as an agent, he wasn't so confident.

CHAPTER 13

They expected the house to be dark except for the porch lantern, but there was a light in one of the upstairs bedrooms.

"Ain't that Miss Vayle's chamber?" asked Harper.

"I hope not."

They'd left the house long after Abbie had gone to bed. He'd checked on her before they went out, and she'd been sound asleep. He'd expected to return before she was awake, and she would never have to know that they'd left the house.

Tom was watching for them and met them with a pistol in each hand. He peered into the gloom. "Is that you, Mr. Templar, sir?"

Harper snapped, "You're supposed to say, 'Who goes there?' What if we was the enemy?"

"What is it, Tom?" asked Hugh quietly. "What's happened?"

"She woke up, sir," replied Tom, "and when she found that you was gone . . ." he swallowed, "there was no reasoning with 'er. She wanted to go after you. But I 'ad my orders. Only, she wouldn't listen."

"Get to the point, Tom."

"I . . . I 'ad to restrain 'er. She didn't take it kindly, sir. I . . . I 'ope I did the right thing. She said she'd set the magistrates on me, and that I'd be transported to the colonies for what I done."

"You had to restrain her?" asked Hugh sharply. "What does that mean?"

"I was only doing what you said, Mr. Templar, you knows, to keep 'er safe."

"And?"

Tom straightened and spoke as though he were addressing his commanding officer. "So when she tried to leave, I locked 'er in 'er room. She carried on something awful. I could 'ear the dishes breaking and 'er cursing me, so I tried to speak to 'er through the door. She was in a right temper, so I just left 'er to it."

"Bloody hell!"

Harper said, "I told you she reminded me of wife number three. Come on, Tom. Our work ain't done yet. Let's get these horses rubbed down and stabled. Mr. Templar will see to Miss Vayle, 'cos if anyone is going to be transported to the colonies, it's 'im. You was only doing your duty. . . ." and going on in this vein, he walked the horses to the back of the house with Tom following along.

Hugh entered the house and made straight for Abbie's room. When he crossed the threshold, he stopped. Fragments of glass and china littered the floor. One of the bed drapes was hanging by a thread. Abbie was sitting in the middle of the bed, in her nightgown, head bowed and her hair spilling over her face in a wild, unruly cascade.

"Abbie," he said softly.

At the sound of his voice, her head jerked up. Her eyes were red rimmed and her cheeks were streaked with dried tears. The sight of her, the change in her, slammed into Hugh like a physical blow.

For the last twenty-four hours, she'd treated him with an aloof dignity that had kept him firmly in his place. He hadn't tried to smash through the wall she erected because he'd been deeply shaken by what had happened between them in the kitchen last night. He hadn't exaggerated when he said he couldn't resist her. She'd looked at him in that appealing way of hers and he was lost. He hadn't lied either when he told her he only wanted to comfort her. At least, that's how it had started out. Then he'd lost control.

She'd said some harsh things to him, and maybe he'd deserved them. But as he absorbed the naked pain in that tear-bright gaze, it came to him that Abbie had lied. She hadn't lost interest. She cared too much.

The instant he realized that, his world seemed to tilt on its axis, and when it righted itself, everything was different. The first thing that occurred to him was that life without Abbie was unthinkable, and hard on that thought came the realization that he would do anything to keep her. He wanted to protect her; he wanted to make her happy. He wanted to give her everything she'd ever dreamed about. As long as he had breath in his body, no one and nothing would ever hurt her again.

He quickly crossed to her. Her eyes were fastened on his face as if she could not believe he was real.

"It's all right, Abbie," he soothed. "I'm here. Nothing happened. Did you think I had abandoned you? You know I would never do that."

She made a soft mewling sound and tentatively reached out and cupped his cheek with one hand.

"Yes. It's me," he said. "You're not dreaming. I'm real."

Fresh tears flooded her eyes.

"Abbie," he murmured, and he took the hand that cupped his cheek and pressed a passionate kiss to it.

That's when she slapped him. Then, with fists flying, she flung herself on him. He had the presence of mind to grab her wrists, but he still felt the blows that rained on his chest.

"Vile . . . rodent . . . worm!" she panted. "Cur . . . louse . . . maggot!" She sucked in several long breaths. "You . . . you . . . tricked me."

She said more, much more, and each word was punctuated with a wild punch. Hugh felt helpless. He didn't know what to do to comfort her. Falling back on instinct, he wrapped her tightly in his arms and began to rock. "It's all right," he said. "I'm here. Did you waken, love, and think I had deserted you? You should know me better. It's all right. Don't take on so. I'm here."

As he repeated the soothing words, he ran his hands over her arms, her back, her shoulders, pressing her into the shelter of his body. Gradually, her struggles diminished till she lay limp in his arms.

After a long time, she lifted her head and looked up at him. "Why did you do it, Hugh? Why did you go back there? They almost killed you last time. Wasn't that enough for you?"

He found his handkerchief and dried her cheeks, then he made her blow her nose. Smiling into her eyes, he said, "You worried for nothing, Abbie."

This provoked an infuriated outburst. Hugh gathered that she had no time for heroes and she didn't want him to be one, and that living dangerously was for lunatics and the feebleminded, not for ordinary people like themselves. Finally, she said, "I just want you to be safe. I just want you to be safe."

He smoothed back her tangle of hair and pressed kisses to her eyes, her cheeks, her brow. "And I am safe. Harper and I went to the Black Boar and asked a few questions. We didn't expect trouble, and we didn't get any."

He half expected her to ask him questions about what he'd found out, but she showed no curiosity. She kept staring at him unblinkingly as though she were afraid he would vanish if she closed her eyes.

After a while he said, "Feeling better?"

She nodded.

"Then let's get you into bed."

He pulled back the bedcovers and settled her in the bed. If his shoulder hurt, he didn't feel it. He was totally focused on Abbie.

When he tried to move away, her fingers curled into his coat, holding him fast. "No," she whispered. "Stay with me."

He spoke to her as he might speak to a hurt child. "I won't leave, not for long, but there are things I have to do. You're cold, and the fire is almost out. I'm going to add some lumps of coal, then I'm going downstairs to get the brandy bottle. If you don't need it, I do. This will only take a few minutes."

She nodded, but he had to pry her fingers loose. "Now stay under the covers," he said. "We've got to keep you warm."

He pulled the covers up to her chin, kissed her chastely on the brow, and stepped back. "Will you be all right?"

"Yes," she said.

After adding coal to the fire, he took one of the candles and went downstairs. He found Mrs. Deane's medicinal bottle of brandy in its usual place in the larder. When he returned to Abbie's room, the fire was beginning to catch. He poured out a small measure of brandy, then carefully picked his way over broken glass and china to reach the bed. Holding her head up, he set the glass to her mouth and forced her to swallow. She was strangely passive, and that worried him. When the glass was empty, he set it aside and eased her down on the pillows.

As he picked up the broken glass and crockery, her eyes followed him as a compass follows a magnet. He thought about going to his own room to wash and change, but he decided against it. She was afraid to close her eyes in case he was gone when she opened them again. The knowledge was both sweet and chastening. It showed how much she cared for him, as well as how unthinking his own actions had been. If she had left him without a word, he would have done more than break a few ornaments.

He spent the next few minutes concentrating on menial tasks—adding coal to the fire, trimming the candlewicks, and generally tidying the room. It was only when he pulled a stuffed armchair close to the bed, however, and sipped at the brandy he'd promised himself, that she seemed to settle. Her eyelids gradually began to droop. Finally, her eyelashes fluttered and her eyes closed.

Sleep was the farthest thing from his mind. He was brooding. A short time ago, on the bridle path, he had decided to set aside his feelings as a man and act like an intelligence agent. It was easier said than done. He should have questioned her when she was at her most vulnerable. Instead, he'd been shattered to see the state she was in.

It didn't matter. They would have that heart-to-heart

talk in the morning, and this time he would insist on answers. The murder of a British agent had taken them into a different realm altogether.

He thought about Alex Ballard for a long time, speculating, adding things up. Something Ballard said came back to him, something he'd forgotten in his concern for Abbie. *There's no one I trust more than you.*

Maybe it meant nothing; maybe Alex spoke without thinking, hoping to persuade him to come back into the service. But Hugh couldn't shake himself of the feeling that if he'd agreed to help Ballard, he would still be alive.

He brooded on that thought for a long time.

When Abbie stirred, dislodging the covers, he rose and gently tucked them around her again. She smiled in her sleep, and he wondered what kind of smile she would wear after she'd spent the night in his bed.

It wouldn't be a bed in some sordid hotel where they gave false names and crept in and out through the back door. He knew now that such an arrangement would destroy Abbie by small degrees.

Marriage. He tested the word gingerly and wondered why he'd thought it was something to dread. When he thought about it, there were many advantages to marriage. For a start, he'd have peace of mind knowing he had some say in Abbie's affairs. He'd know what she was getting up to. She couldn't defy him and tell him to mind his own business. And when he took her to bed, Abbie need not feel guilty and he wouldn't feel like an unscrupulous libertine.

He leaned over and caressed her lips with the pad of his thumb. Her lips opened. She was like sleeping beauty, waiting to be awakened by his kiss. And this time she would accept him. After all that had happened tonight, she was vulnerable. He could have whatever he wanted from her.

He raked a shaking hand through his hair and damned himself for the lecher Abbie had called him. He shouldn't be mooning over her like this. He had plans to make, things to do. Maitland was no slouch. As soon as the weather changed, he would come after them.

He rose and began to prowl. When Abbie did not waken, he stopped prowling, and his movements became deliberate. He found her box and portmanteau in front of the window, under her neatly folded clothes. The box was locked. Her reticule was on a table nearby. He opened it, riffled through handkerchiefs, odd receipts, a bottle of perfume, and found what he was looking for— an embroidered pochette. Inside were a few coins and two keys.

He felt no shame for what he was doing. A British agent had been murdered, and that was a serious matter. The best way to protect Abbie was to get at the truth. If she had confided in him, this wouldn't have been necessary.

The first key he tried opened the box. His experience as an agent had become second nature to him, and he went through her things methodically without disturbing anything. He found a leather purse and counted out fifty sovereigns—more than enough for her needs if she were staying with friends. He set the wallet aside and slid his hands under a pile of lacy undergarments. He stilled when his hands closed around a book, then he let out a pent-up breath when he opened it and read the title. It wasn't the book Maitland was after. He leafed through it and a book-marker, a folded piece of paper, fluttered to the floor. He picked it up and smoothed it out. It was a receipt from His Majesty's customs at Dover, a receipt for a box of books.

Frowning, Hugh sat back on his heels. He'd forgotten about the episode in the customs house when Abbie had refused to pay duty on the books she'd bought in Paris. He began to bring that memory into focus: Abbie, as mad as a hornet when the customs officers confiscated her books. She'd been taken by surprise. In fact, she was shocked. She'd begged, she'd cajoled. The officers would not budge, and neither would she.

There was no doubt in Hugh's mind that Abbie's outrage had been genuine. She hadn't planned to have the books impounded. She'd even turned her wrath on him.

The memory made him smile.

But this was no smiling matter. Abbie was in trouble up to her neck. The receipt might be just what it appeared to be, a book marker, or it might be something else entirely.

He folded the receipt and held it in the palm of his hand as though weighing its worth.

After a long time, he sighed, put everything back the way he had found it, then went through her portmanteau. There was little in it besides a shawl, a few pairs of gloves, and a muff. Inside the muff was a loaded pistol, but he couldn't find extra balls or powder to arm the piece once it was spent. He shook his head. Harper was right. Abbie was a novice with guns. She didn't think ahead. Her portmanteau would be stored with the baggage when she was traveling, where she could not get to it. So even the pistol was useless. He would have to point out to her that one did not carry a pistol for show. It was too dangerous.

He returned to his chair, and for a long, long time, sat there, slumped inelegantly as he went over everything he'd learned tonight. Sighing, he shook his head. He did not have much choice. The book was crucial. He had to get Abbie to hand it over or tell him where she was hiding it, even if it meant frightening the truth out of her.

Better that he should question her than Maitland.

CHAPTER 14

Abbie rolled to her side and slowly opened her eyes. The pale light of dawn filtered through the gauze curtains at the window and glazed the empty chair that was pulled close to her bed, the chair Hugh had occupied last night. The fire was reduced to embers and the candles had gone out. From downstairs came the comforting sounds of the house stirring—doors opening and closing, the murmur of voices, faint laughter.

A sigh shuddered out of her, then another, but her eyes were dry. She'd done all her crying yesterday when she awakened to find Hugh gone. Until then, she'd been in command of herself; she'd found reserves of strength to go on when everything that could possibly go wrong had gone wrong. She hadn't lost hope. She'd told herself that as long as she had the book, nothing could happen to George.

She hadn't counted on anything happening to Hugh, not again. It had never occurred to her that he would return to the inn to try to discover who their assailants were. They'd beaten him with their pistols. Next time, they might kill him! All this had gone through her head, and before Tom stopped speaking she'd turned into a spitting, snarling wild cat.

Then, as suddenly as the madness had come upon her, it subsided, and she'd plunged into black despair. She'd tried to pray, but she couldn't find the words. All she could think about was Hugh, how she'd failed him, how she was responsible for putting him in danger. If it had not been for her, he'd be safe in his own house in Bath.

When he walked into her room and said her name, she'd felt like a murderess whose death sentence had been commuted. She'd wanted to touch him, hold him, just to make sure he was all right. The next minute, her mind must have snapped, because she'd wanted to kill him. She hated him for all the torments he'd put her through. But when her anger was spent, she knew it wasn't true. She could never hate Hugh.

She was on the point of rising and had just pushed back the covers when there was a knock at the door. At her command, the door opened and Hugh entered.

"Good. You're awake," he said.

He crossed to the bed, tipped up her chin, and kissed her with a proficiency that made her head swim. Her fingers clenched and unclenched around his arms. Her skin began to heat, and her blood pumped wildly through her veins.

Her head was still swimming when he broke the kiss. He took her hands in his and said seriously, "We're leaving in a few minutes, Abbie, on horseback, so I want you to get dressed in something suitable and come downstairs."

The gravity of his expression brought her abruptly to her senses. "How can we leave? What about the roads?"

"The snow is melting. And it's started to rain. In another hour or two, the roads will be passable."

"Passable?" she repeated dully, as her mind grappled with her growing alarm. "Then why don't we take the carriage?"

He shook his head. "It's too risky, too easily recognized. We want to slip away quietly. We'll ride out on horseback, go around Hungerford, and come out at Newbury where we'll hire a chaise to get us to London."

"But why all the secrecy? What's wrong, Hugh?"

He looked down at their clasped hands and caressed the back of her fingers with his thumbs, then he looked up at her. "I couldn't tell you the truth last night," he said, "because you were distraught." He paused. "The authorities are looking for us. They say that we murdered a man, that they found his body in your room at the Castle."

She stuttered, then got out, "Murdered someone? In my room? But that's impossible! Who—who was he?"

"Alex Ballard. He and I worked together for a time at the foreign office. Do you remember him, Abbie?"

She nodded numbly. "I met him in Paris, at the embassy. You introduced us. He talked about his wife and children. He was a nice man."

Hugh waited, and when she was silent, he went on, "He turned up in Bath recently and came to see me."

"But they can't think *we* had anything to do with his murder!"

"I'm afraid they do. What's worse is that I know the man who is in charge of the investigation, and I don't trust him. It's Richard Maitland, and he'd do anything to discredit me. He seems to think that you stole a book that belongs to him, that Ballard was murdered trying to get it back, and that I knew about it and am trying to protect you."

Her mind was numb with fear, and the anguished words tumbled out before she had time to consider them. "It wasn't supposed to be like this. It seemed so simple. I would get the book, and George . . ."

When she looked up at him with huge, frightened eyes, he grasped her by the shoulders. "So that's the real reason for this journey—the book!"

She gazed at him mutely, but the answer was in her eyes.

"And what about George?" he went on relentlessly. "Finish what you were saying. You would get the book, and George . . ."

When he administered a rough shake, she cried out, "George would be safe!"

He straightened and frowned down at her. "George is behind all this?"

"No!"

"Then who is?"

"I don't know."

"Where is George?"

"I don't know."

"He's gone into hiding, is that it? And he's letting you help him out of a scrape?"

"It's not like that," she said miserably.

"Then what is it like? Tell me!"

She felt as though she were standing on the edge of a precipice. One false step and she would go over. Everything was happening too fast. She wanted time to think, time to consider how much she should tell Hugh. But time was something he wasn't going to give her. She'd never seen him look so stern.

She moistened her lips. "All I know is that I have to get the book."

"Tell me about Colette. How did you meet her? What happened there, Abbie?"

"I don't know! I don't know anyone by that name!"

"I'll wager George does. Did he tell you what to write to Michael Lovatt?"

"No!" she cried out.

"What's in the book?"

"I don't know."

"Where is it? Where did George hide it?"

She raised her head. He'd got the wrong idea about George. For a second, a fraction of a second, the words trembled on her lips, and in that moment of indecision, she took a step back from the brink. "In the vault of my bank in Pall Mall."

He frowned. "If it's in your bank vault, then you must have put it there. When did you do that, Abbie?"

She'd almost blundered, but she recovered herself well. "The last time I was in London. You remember, on my way home from Paris, I stayed on in town for a while?"

"George gave you the book in Paris?"

Hugh would know that all the books she'd acquired in Paris had been impounded by customs because he'd been there. "No. He sent it to me at Vayle House and asked me to keep it safe for him. Oh Hugh, I wasn't supposed to tell anyone."

At those words, he exhaled a long, telling breath, cupped her face in both hands, and smiled into her eyes. "Don't look so guilt stricken," he said. "You did right to tell me. And don't worry about betraying George's confidence. You've saved his neck and ours as well. Silly young cub. I suppose he got mixed up in this in Paris and got in over his head. Well, we can sort that out later. The important thing now is to get hold of that book and get it to the right people."

"Who are these people? What are you talking about?"

"British intelligence. I know some of these people from my work at the foreign office. Their chief is . . . well . . . a personal friend. Colonel Langley. He's a good man. He'll listen to us."

She cried out, "How will that help us when a man has been murdered?"

"The men who attacked me were probably the ones who murdered Ballard. They want that book and they want it badly. That's another reason we have to leave here as quickly as possible."

He kissed her swiftly. "Now get dressed and come downstairs. We'll go through this in more detail when we've put some miles between us and our pursuers."

At the door, he turned back. "Just one last question, Abbie. Once you had the book, what were you going to do with it?"

She looked directly into his eyes. The time for indecision and second thoughts was over. She'd burned her bridges. She had to brazen it out. "I was going to send it back to myself at Bath," she said. "That's where George would pick it up."

His eyes flared. "It was a good plan. Then what?"

He had the tenacity of a bulldog. It was one of the traits she'd always admired in him, this refusal to let things go until he'd plumbed their depths. That's how they'd come to suspect there was a Roman temple beneath the abbey in Bath. In this context, it was unnerving.

"He said it would save his life," she said. "And that's all he would tell me."

His voice gentled. "Nothing will happen to George. Abbie, trust me. George is out of it. It's us they want now. And I'd die before I'd let anything happen to you. Now, get dressed," and he left her.

She stared at the closed door in abject misery as Hugh's words sank into her. With a soft cry of despair, she slid from the bed and, after opening her box, began to hunt through it for something suitable to wear.

She'd made a pact with herself. When this was over, she would never lie to Hugh again. And she would do everything in her power to bring these villains to justice.

After it was over. When George was safe.

She could visualize how it would be. She would go to Hugh and confess everything. She would explain how she'd felt, and that she'd had no choice, and she could not take chances with her brother's life. These were desperate men. There was nothing they wouldn't do. When she explained all this to Hugh, she was sure he would understand.

The reality was, she was not sure of anything. She'd toyed with the idea of asking for Hugh's help, but she couldn't bring herself to do it. He kept telling her how important it was to get the book to the right people. But the right people, in Hugh's view, were members of British intelligence.

If she gave the book to them, she might as well sign George's death warrant. She couldn't do it. She simply could not do it. Did that make her a traitor?

It was so unfair. She was as patriotic as the next person. No one should have to make these choices. If England had been at war, it would have been different. . . .

It wouldn't have been different. She would still choose George first.

"Abbie, what is it? What are you thinking?"

At the sound of Hugh's voice, she came out of her reverie. There hadn't been much opportunity to talk when they were on horseback, but now that they were in a closed chaise, he'd gone over her story again and again. She'd tried to keep it simple and vague, but he'd pressed her on things she had to know. And with each lie she told, the web of deceit became more and more tangled.

"Abbie?" he prompted.

"It all seems so fantastic," she said, "like a bad dream."

His hand closed around hers. "It won't be for long. We'll reach the outskirts of London tonight. And tomorrow, when we get the book and give it to Langley, the nightmare will end, and we'll be out of it. It will be up to others to track down those murdering swine and punish them. Just one more day, Abbie."

He tipped up her chin with one long finger and gave her a searching look. "Abbie," he said, "don't be so hard on yourself for telling me the truth. You did the right thing, not only for George's sake, but for ours as well. I already suspected that you and George were in some kind of trouble. I was waiting for you to confide in me. So no more secrets, Abbie. Promise you won't lie to me again."

She swallowed the lump in her throat. "I promise."

"Try to get some sleep. This has been a grueling day. I'm proud of you, Abbie. Even Harper said you were a regular trooper, and coming from him, that is as extravagant a compliment as you'll ever hear."

She smiled, then she rested her head in the crook of his shoulder and obediently closed her eyes. But she couldn't sleep for thinking. The nightmare wasn't over yet. Tonight they would reach the outskirts of London, and tomorrow Hugh would discover that she'd told him a pack of lies.

He had everything planned down to the last detail, or so he thought. She would only get in the way, he'd said, so she would remain behind with Tom while he and Harper went to the bank. When he had the book he would give it to Colonel Langley, but only in exchange for amnesty for her and George. If they could prove their innocence—and Hugh was sure that they could—well and good. But in any event, he would insist on amnesty for them before he handed over the book.

Tomorrow, when Hugh got to the bank, he would learn the truth. And when he came back for her, he wouldn't find her. She planned to be well on her way to Dover.

Hugh smoothed back loose strands of hair from Abbie's brow. Her lashes were like smudges against the parchment of her skin. She was exhausted, worn out by the punishing pace he'd set. They'd covered the distance to London in record time, but only because they'd stopped for nothing but a change of horses and provisions to eat on the way. They'd been traveling since dawn and they weren't done yet. Night had fallen a long time ago, but he was determined to push on until they reached the outskirts of London. No one could trace them there.

He'd had no choice but to go at this grueling pace. Not only was he determined to get to Langley before

Maitland could prejudice the colonel's mind, but he would not risk being caught by the other side, not now that he knew what he was up against.

The men who'd murdered Alex were scum, fanatics, and traitors besides. He'd dealt with their kind before. Nothing stopped them but a bullet or a hangman's noose.

When Abbie moaned in her sleep he reached down, slid one arm under her legs and lifted them to lie across his lap. She nestled against him, murmured something incoherent, but she did not waken.

He was proud of her in more ways than one. She'd made the journey without a word of complaint. But more important by far, she'd finally told him the truth.

As for George, when he caught up with that scapegrace, he'd kick his backside to kingdom come. Undoubtably, there was a woman in it somewhere.

He wondered what Abbie made of it all. She'd asked a few questions about his work at the foreign office, and how he knew all these intelligence people, and he had said something vague about meeting them at university or during the course of his work.

He hadn't wanted to tell her the truth. For one thing, all agents were sworn to secrecy, even when they left the service. But there was more to it than that. Hugh Templar, the agent, wasn't the man he was now. He'd been a warrior. He'd seen things, done things, that only another agent could condone. As soon as he'd left the service, he'd slammed and locked the door on that episode of his life. He didn't want Abbie opening that door because he didn't want her to change towards him. She respected him, and that's the way he wanted to keep it.

There must be some nice man out there. . .

Maybe he didn't fit the description. Maybe his past was murky, and maybe it didn't matter. He could take good care to make sure that Abbie never found out. And when this was over, he would gladly sink into the obscurity of his books and scholarship.

He pillowed his head on the banquette and let his thoughts drift.

CHAPTER 15

They stopped for what was left of the night at a hostelry in Chiswick, well off the main road. Another hour or two would have taken them to their own doors, but Hugh was convinced that Maitland would not be far behind, and would expect them to make for home. Maitland might think twice about arresting him, but he would have no such reservations about Abbie, and Hugh's object was to keep Abbie out of it until he had a chance to speak to his former chief.

The landlord had obviously risen from his bed to answer the pounding of the door knocker and spoke to them rudely until Hugh slapped several gold sovereigns into his palm. Before long, Hugh and Abbie, now posing as Mr. and Mrs. White, were shown into a small but comfortable room, while Harper and Tom went off to the stable block.

The first thing Hugh did was light the fire. "We could have posed as brother and sister," he said. "Then we would have been given separate rooms."

"No," said Abbie. It was she who had told the landlord

they were husband and wife. "I don't want to be alone, not tonight."

Hugh straightened and turned to watch her. She was wandering around the room, looking at everything but, he suspected, seeing nothing. When she let out a sigh and sat on the edge of the bed, he crossed to her.

"It's George, isn't it?" he said. "That's what's put that look on your face."

"What look?"

The look of a trapped animal waiting for the hunter to catch up to it. "Anxious, worried," he said. "But George will have his amnesty, I promise you."

"I wasn't thinking about amnesty for George."

"Then what were you thinking?"

She was thinking that she couldn't save George by herself, that she wasn't brave enough or clever enough. She was thinking that the urge to confess was like a constant shadow on her heart. She looked at Hugh and wanted to lay all her burdens on his broad shoulders.

"I was thinking about tomorrow," she said. "It could be dangerous."

He sank down on his haunches and took her hands. "I'll be on my guard at all times. Nothing will go wrong."

"Those men are dangerous. They've already killed a man."

He got up and sat beside her on the bed. "They don't know where we are. They don't know where we're going. And once Langley has the book, they're finished. They won't care about us. All they'll care about is saving their own skins."

"What will happen to them if they're caught?"

"They're traitors, Abbie. They'll hang."

"What about me? Am I a traitor too?"

"Put that thought right out of your mind. You thought

you were helping your brother. You didn't know then that British intelligence was involved. You're in the clear."

The urge to confess quietly died.

When she nodded, he stood up. "I'm going to check on Harper and Tom," he said, "and have a look around. I'll get our saddlebags at the same time. Will you be all right?"

She made an effort to show some life. "Don't worry about me, Hugh. I'll be fine. I'll just sit in front of the fire and warm myself until you return."

"This will only take a few minutes."

"Really, Hugh, I'm fine."

He wasn't convinced. She was very pale, and she would hardly look him in the eye. When she stifled a yawn behind her hand, he felt reassured. Maybe all she needed was a good night's rest.

"Lock the door behind me," he said, "and don't open it to anyone but me."

She walked him to the door and locked it behind him. When she heard his steps recede along the corridor, she put her fists to her mouth to stifle a long pent-up breath. She took a few halting steps into the room and was caught by her own reflection in a long cheval mirror. The woman who stared back at her was barely recognizable. Her coat and frock were mired with mud. Her expression, her whole appearance, was one of hopelessness. This woman didn't look as though she could stand up to her own shadow. How could she hope to stand up to these vicious, desperate men?

She would stand up to them the same way she had stood up to them when Hugh was attacked, or she would die in the attempt.

The thought terrified her, but fear wasn't the only emotion she experienced. She was mourning the loss of all that might have been. Whether she lived or died, whether she succeeded or failed, she would lose Hugh's friendship. He would despise her. He would know that she was unprincipled, that she was prepared to betray her own country. The names she had called him paled into insignificance beside the names he would call her. And it wouldn't matter if, once she got the book, her family decided that their best course was to go to the authorities. Hugh would know she had tricked him.

She took the chair by the fire and stared at the flames that licked around a log. Her dreams had burned to ashes a long time ago. It was more than time that she accepted it. She would never marry; she would never have children. She would never know a lover's embrace.

Lover. She tested the word carefully. She'd always thought she understood the difference between right and wrong, but now she realized she didn't know anything at all.

She covered her face with her hands. What was the good of being good when it felt so bad?

When she opened the door, Hugh strode into the room and threw the saddlebags onto the bed. They'd left their boxes at Mrs. Deane's place because he'd wanted to travel light. All they had with them was a change of clothes and a few articles of toilette.

"Did you pack a nightgown, Abbie?"

"I don't remember."

He opened one of the saddlebags and removed a white lawn shirt. "You can sleep in one of my shirts if you forgot," he said.

"Thank you, Hugh, but I'd rather go to bed as I am."

He stopped rummaging in his saddlebag when he noticed the chair by the bed. The garments she'd worn that day were neatly folded over the backrest; her white lacy underthings were on the cushioned seat. A pair of embroidered silk stockings trailed from her underthings to the floor. He looked at those stockings and his mouth went dry. Imprints of her calves and thighs were clearly evident.

Slowly, very slowly, he turned to face her.

She'd taken the gold taffeta counterpane from the bed and wrapped herself in it, leaving her shoulders and arms bare. Her hair was loose and streamed around her shoulders in a fiery torrent. Flickering candlelight played over her skin, drizzling it with honey. Her appeal was staggering. Her intent was patently clear. But giving the lie to her bold attempt at seduction was the alluring smile that wobbled at the edges, and the fragility in her eyes.

"I thought—" he cleared his throat, "I thought I'd bed down in front of the fire, if you'll spare me a blanket and one of your pillows."

Her chin lifted, and she took a tentative step toward him, then another. "I want you to sleep with me, Hugh," she said simply.

A wave of heat roared through him, and beads of sweat broke out on his brow. He had to struggle to find his next breath. "Abbie," he shook his head, "this isn't what you want. What about your self-respect? What about that nice man out there who wants the same things you do?"

He was trying to be noble, trying to spare her. She had no idea how it would be if he took her right now. She was at a low ebb; she was frightened and in need of reassurance. She wanted comforting.

And he wanted to take her on a wild ride to oblivion. He was wound up like a coiled spring. He was always like this on the eve of a mission. In spite of his assurances to Abbie, he was well aware of the danger involved, and the threat of danger aroused long forgotten instincts in a man. It stripped him of the veneer of civilization and reduced him to little more than a barbarian. Every soldier who had fought in a battle knew this. If he were to take her now, his body would demand a fast and furious release. Abbie deserved a slow, careful initiation with all the finesse at his command.

And she would have it, when the conditions were right.

She held on to the edges of the taffeta counterpane as she took another rustling step toward him. Her voice cracked. "What nice man out there? There isn't one. If there were, don't you think I would have found him by now? And what's the good of self-respect when the future is so uncertain? All I want is this one night, Hugh. If I had that, I think I'd be more reconciled to my lot in life and stop pining for the impossible."

He wanted to tell her that she wasn't pining for the impossible. He wanted to tell her that she'd found that nice man out there who wanted the same things she did. He ached to hold her, reassure her, convince her that she was more of a woman than he had ever known. He could do none of those things. Even now, his control was slipping away. If he didn't get out of here, he would fall on her like a rutting bull.

She drew in a big gulp of air and swallowed it. She hadn't expected Hugh to be so skittish, but that's how he appeared. He looked as though he'd rather be anywhere than in this small room, alone, with her.

At any other time, her pride would have rushed in to save her from making a fool of herself. But this was too important to be swayed by pride. This night would be all she would ever have of him. She refused to let him turn her away unless he could convince her he really meant it.

She began to edge forward, but carefully, so as not to make him more nervous than he appeared. "Don't go all moral on me now, Hugh. Isn't this what you wanted? You kissed me. You touched me. You changed things between us."

He saw that he was mangling the shirt he'd offered her in lieu of her nightgown, and he tossed it aside with a grimace of self-derision. Wonderful. Now he'd given her the impression that he was rejecting her. He didn't want to hurt her, but he didn't want to disgust her either.

The irony in the reversal of their roles would have made him laugh if he hadn't been grinding his teeth together. The taffeta wrap was slipping, and his imagination had just taken a wild plunge into hell and damnation. He hardly knew what he was saying. "I've changed my mind. This isn't for you. You're not a camp follower. You're a respectable, gently bred girl."

She stopped edging forward as the hurt started in her heart and spread out in waves. She spoke in a painful whisper. "You've changed your mind? You don't want me anymore?"

He took a sideways step, giving him a clear path to the door. "Go to bed, Abbie. I'm going to find Harper. There are still some things we have to go over before we leave tomorrow."

"But you've just talked to Harper."

"Well, I want to talk to him again."

She took a sideways step as well, blocking his exit.

"Don't you understand anything?" he said fiercely. "This is the wrong time and place. And I haven't had a woman in an age. This is not a good idea, Abbie."

This was something new, this reference to past lovers.

She wasn't surprised; she simply wasn't interested. All she could think about was the present moment. She wanted something for herself, something to warm her in the cold black nights that lay ahead.

"I'm not afraid of you, Hugh," she said.

"Well you damn well ought to be," he roared.

She was only an arm's length from him when her courage began to ebb. She'd thought it would be simple. She'd offer herself and he'd take her. But all he'd done was try to put her off. He stood there, as loverlike as a pillar of stone, while she was all trembles and shivers inside.

Then she saw the pulse beating at his throat, and the muscle that tensed in his cheek. But more than anything, it was his eyes that betrayed him, dark as midnight and helpless with wanting her.

"Hugh," she softly cajoled, "this is what I want. Don't be noble, not for my sake. Just this one night, please?"

He closed his eyes against her powerful appeal, then he heard the rustle of taffeta, and the air in his lungs froze. When he opened his eyes, she was standing before him as naked as the day she was born. The taffeta counterpane was pooled at her feet.

He tried to keep his eyes on her face, but he couldn't help looking: rose-crested breasts, beautifully molded curves and valleys, and the flower of her femininity veiled in a golden shadow.

Through clenched teeth, he got out, "I wish you hadn't done that."

When he caught hold of her, he meant only to push her aside and storm from the room. But the feel of her warm, satiny skin savaged his noble intentions. He could no longer think with his brain; he was thinking with his body, and that appalled him.

Abbie had twined her arms around his neck, and her soft womanly contours were pressed against his hard length, enticing him, tempting, driving him wild to have her. Then she pleaded with him in that throaty, husky voice of hers, and his control snapped. With a groan of surrender, he crushed her mouth beneath his. One step took him to the bed. Without severing the kiss, he lowered her to the mattress and rolled with her.

He was starving for her taste and touch. The ache inside him was so fierce, his whole body trembled. He couldn't resist fisting his fingers in her glorious hair and holding her steady as he plundered her mouth the way he'd dreamed of, his tongue thrusting in a wild intimate dance with hers. But there were other treasures he wanted to plunder. He was fascinated with the tips of her breasts, and how each rosy nipple puckered and darkened when he laved it with his tongue and lips. The slope of her shoulders, the swell of her hips, every feminine hill and valley lured him on.

She'd never known that passion on this scale existed. Everything that had seemed so difficult was natural. She reveled in the intimacy he demanded, reveled in the pleasure that he could bring to her with the brush of his hands and lips. But it wasn't enough. She wanted to feel his bare skin against her bare skin. She wanted to touch him the way he touched her. She wanted him to take off all his clothes. She reached for the buttons on his coat.

The only candle in the room flared, sputtered, and went out. The fire still burned, and though it took the edge off the darkness, the room was dappled in long, flickering shadows. When Hugh rose from the bed, Abbie could just make out his silhouette.

Her senses had never been so acute. She heard the soft

rustle of each garment as he gradually disrobed; she heard the thud of his boots as he dropped them on the floor; she knew when he was naked; the heat from his body seemed to pass into hers; he smelled like a dark wind-swept night on the lonely moors.

Then he was on her, bearing her back against the pillows. She felt the smile on his lips when he kissed her. She knew he was different, but it was so subtle, she couldn't puzzle it out. Then she stopped trying to puzzle it out as her fingertips took the impression of his sleek, hard flesh and coiled muscles. She rubbed herself against him and smiled when she heard his sharp intake of breath.

She had no conception of the control he exercised for her sake. She was lost in each new sensation as his tongue, lips, and hands bathed her in pleasure. Passion and love seemed to flow together. Her mind, soul, and senses were filled with him. *Hugh,* she thought. *Hugh.*

He didn't try to hurry her, and if he had, she wouldn't have allowed it. She was making memories to take with her for the rest of her life. She wanted to know every inch of him intimately. But it wasn't all taking on her part. She wanted to give as much as he gave her.

Remember me, she said silently as she stroked his shoulders, his ribs, his flanks. This was the truth. This was reality. This was the Abbie she wanted him to remember. Nothing else mattered, if only he would remember that she'd loved him. And with her shy, intimate touches, she drove him to the brink.

He knelt between her legs and positioned himself to take her. "Forgive me, Abbie," he whispered hoarsely, knowing he was about to give pain when what he wanted was to bring pleasure.

With the first thrust, a cry of pain tore from her throat. He gritted his teeth and held perfectly still, giving her body time to adjust to his. When he finally lifted his head, he saw that her eyes were filmed with tears.

"Abbie," he began, and froze when she moved sinuously beneath him.

Eyes locked and held, then glazed over as he began to move in slow, easy lunges. At his hoarsely muttered command, she wrapped her arms and legs around him and followed the rhythm he set.

She couldn't stop moaning, couldn't stop writhing. Something was terribly wrong. She was going to shatter; she knew she was going to shatter. She wanted him to stop.

Hugh locked his body to hers. He spoke soothingly, calming her fears. It was all right. This was how it was supposed to be. He wasn't going to hurt her. She had to trust him, trust him, trust him. . . .

When he changed the tempo of his rhythm, sensation raged to a sudden, white hot fever. She couldn't breathe. She couldn't think. She could only feel. He rained hard, fast kisses on every exposed inch of skin. A rainbow exploded behind her eyes, and she went hurtling into infinity.

Hugh watched her face as the pleasure took her, and a fierce possessiveness surged through him. She was his, and he would never give her up. Then rational thought dissolved as he surrendered himself to the driving beat of his own body.

They lay for a long time afterward, entwined in each other's arms. When he could move again, Hugh rolled to his side and looked down at Abbie. Her eyes were closed. He frowned when his fingers touched her cheek and came away wet.

"Tears?" he said. "What's wrong, Abbie?"

Her eyelashes fluttered and she said something low

and inaudible, but she did not waken. Hugh wrapped her in his arms and drew the bedclothes up to cover them both.

He brooded on those tears for a long time. She'd given herself to him freely and generously without counting the cost. Now, when it was too late, she was counting the cost.

He tried shaking her awake. When her lashes lifted, he said, "We have a lot of talking to do, Abbie. Do you understand? This isn't the end of it. This is only the beginning."

"I understand." She sighed and curled into him.

She hadn't heard a word he said. He smoothed back her hair and kissed her brow. Maybe it was better this way. This wasn't the way he wanted to ask her to marry him. This time, she was going to have everything just as she'd always dreamed.

He kissed her on the lips. "I may even go down on my bended knee," he whispered humorously. "But don't expect me to beg. That would be asking too much."

She seemed to rally. "I love you, Hugh," she whispered.

No one had ever said those words to him. He didn't know what those words meant, but on Abbie's lips, they were the sweetest sound he'd ever heard.

He had no words to give her back. All he knew was that she came first with him.

He adjusted his body to hers and nestled her head in the crook of his shoulder.

CHAPTER 16

Hugh rose as the first rays of dawn began to chase the darkness away. He dressed himself, lit a candle, and looked down at Abbie. He'd always wondered how she would look after they'd made love and now he had his answer. Her lips were turned up in a smile. *Sleeping Beauty.*

He couldn't resist. He bent over her and awakened her with a kiss.

She came awake instantly and hauled herself up. "What happened? What's wrong?"

"Nothing," Hugh soothed. "Everything is fine. I wanted to talk to you . . ." he couldn't resist another kiss, "since we didn't do much talking last night."

Her alarm subsided. "Is it time to go?"

"Not for you. Tom will stay here to protect you while Harper and I go to your bank for the book. I'll need a note, signed by you, giving me permission to act as your agent."

"My bank?"

"Isn't that where you told me you'd hidden the book?"

"I . . . yes, of course."

It was all coming back to her. She must remain in

hiding, Hugh had said, until he got the book and traded it for amnesty for her and George. She couldn't hide with relatives or friends or at his house because that's where the authorities would look first. She would be safer here. And once the bargain was made with Langley, she would be immune from prosecution. Then he would come for her.

And she wouldn't be here.

"Langley will want to question you," Hugh said, "but I'll be with you, and you'll have nothing to fear."

His gentle tone and the tender look in his eyes were more than she could bear. "I'll get you the key to my trunk," she said quickly.

The last few minutes were taken up with mundane affairs: writing the note that Hugh asked for; his instructions on what she should do in his absence. Then Harper was there, and there were no more precious moments to share.

When Hugh took her in his arms and kissed her, she clung to him. "Don't look so sad," he said. "I know what I'm doing. Just be patient."

"Hugh!" she called frantically as he opened the door.

"What is it, Abbie?"

Her heart was in her eyes. She shrugged helplessly. "I love you."

A slow, slow smile softened his lips. "When I come for you we'll talk, when this business is over, I mean, and we can think about ourselves. All right?"

She nodded.

"And remember what I told you. Don't go anywhere without Tom."

She locked the door behind him as she'd been told, then sat on the edge of the bed, staring into space. Everything had worked out for the best, she told herself. She could deal with Tom more easily than she could deal with Hugh and Harper.

Don't think about the future. Take it one step at a time.

It was a long time before she came to herself and a long time after that before she had worked out how she was going to get away from Tom and make for Dover to get the book.

Hugh stared dully at the items he'd spread out on a table in the bank's strong room, the items he'd removed from Abbie's trunk. There were letters and legal documents, concert programs and sketches of various places she'd visited, and other odds and ends, but there were no books, not one. He'd examined the trunk inch by inch, unwilling to accept that he'd been duped, but there were no secret compartments. This was all there was.

Harper looked at Hugh's face and shifted uncomfortably from one foot to the other. He knew his employer well enough to recognize the seething resentment beneath the blank facade. Harper was well aware that things looked black for Miss Vayle, but he wasn't ready to accept the evidence against her. In spite of his deeply ingrained prejudice against females, he'd come to respect this young woman. She was plucky. They'd made a good team these last few days. She was one of them and deserved a chance to explain herself.

There was more to it than that, though, for Mr. Templar. He didn't see Miss Vayle as a good little soldier. He saw her as a woman, his woman, and that always twisted a man's brain in knots.

Weighing each word carefully, Harper said, "It's possible that her brother lied to her and that he's hid the book someplace else. Maybe Miss Vayle misunderstood. Maybe the book is in another trunk, in another bank."

"She didn't misunderstand," said Hugh. He suddenly moved, sending papers and sketches fluttering to the floor with a vicious swipe of his hand, then he turned his back on Harper and stared blindly through the bars of the small basement window.

After a long silence, Harper said, "But it don't make no sense. She knows we'll find her out. What does she hope to gain?"

"Money," said Hugh bitterly. "How should I know? Who can tell how a woman's mind works?"

"You think she'll sell the book to our enemies?" demanded Harper incredulously.

"Not for herself, but for her brother. George has no fortune of his own. It could be he's doing this for the money, and somehow he's drawn Abbie into his deadly game. I don't know. I just don't know."

"But she must know that she won't get away with it, that we'll catch up to them both sooner or later."

"Maybe she thinks that once she gets rid of the book, there won't be any evidence against her."

"That don't sound like Miss Vayle."

Hugh's voice was like ice. "I hardly think you're an expert on women, Harper, and Miss Vayle least of all. Now get the horses. I'll be with you in a few minutes. And be careful. It's possible this is a trap."

"A trap? That Miss Vayle has arranged?"

"It's possible."

Harper shot Hugh a look that would have soured cream, but his only comment was short, sharp, and unintelligible. He rapped on the door, and when the clerk came to open it, he left with one quick, troubled glance at Hugh.

When Hugh heard the clerk turn the key, locking him in, he forced himself to take a long steadying breath. He had to fight the urge to do something violent—kick in the door, throw Abbie's trunk against the wall and smash it to smithereens. He stood there, a muscle working furiously in his jaw, as he battled the loss of control. Finally, he got hold of himself and he picked up the papers that were strewn on the floor. When everything was back in the trunk, he shut the lid gently and used the key Abbie had given him to lock it.

I love you, she'd said when he left her that morning. *I love you.*

He was ashamed now of his own feelings. He'd been exalted and humbled at the same time. As he and Harper had ridden into town, he'd relived every moment of the seduction scene Abbie had engineered, and he'd been filled with determination to prove himself worthy of such an extraordinary woman. She had asked nothing for herself. She'd given herself freely and generously. She was a woman in a million.

God help him, he'd even woven fancies of the deeply satisfying life they would have together when they were married. She would share his life as few women shared their husbands' lives because she was interested in the same things as he. They would go on digs for Roman ruins, and when they had children, they would instill a love of history in them too. And at night, when he and Abbie tumbled into bed, they'd share the sweetest passion he had ever known.

He must have been out of his mind. She'd lied through her teeth. Even her sweet surrender was a lie. And now that he'd found her out, he couldn't believe how blind he'd been—falling for that seduction that was so out of character for Abbie, believing her touching words at the end. She'd wanted him to trust her so that he would become careless and she would be free to get the book by herself.

Careless wasn't the word for it. He'd *stupidly* handed her the perfect opportunity to slip away. She wouldn't be waiting for him to return empty-handed from her bank vault, because she'd know that the game was over.

Tom would be no match for her and maybe it was just as well, because he knew now where she had hidden the book, and the rules of the game had just changed.

One part of his mind flinched from thinking the worst of Abbie, but he'd been through this before with his first wife. He'd convinced himself that Abbie was different, when he, of all people, should have known better. But the sense of betrayal he felt with Abbie was far greater than anything he'd felt with Estelle.

From the very first, the evidence against Abbie had been damning, and he had chosen to ignore it. Alex Ballard had tried to warn him, and Alex was dead. Maybe Abbie hadn't struck the blow that killed Alex, but her accomplices had, and that made her an accessory. He'd come damn near to losing his own life as well, and still he'd continued to believe her lies. She'd lied about the friend in Hampstead, lied about her brother, lied about the men who had attacked him. And the final lie, the most bitter of all, the grand seduction and the passion they'd shared.

He should hand her over to Langley and walk away without looking back. But treason was a capital offense and he wasn't prepared to go that far. That didn't mean she was going to get off scot-free. Miss Abigail Vayle would be taught a lesson she would never forget.

Harper was waiting with the horses right outside the

bank's front door. He took one look at Hugh's expression and said quietly, "What do we do now?"

When they were mounted, Hugh said, "First we see Langley and make a bargain with him."

"But you don't have the book."

"No, but I know where to find it."

"How do you know?"

"At Endicote, I searched her belongings and came across a receipt for books she had purchased in Paris, books that are at this moment, impounded by English customs. I thought at the time that that receipt struck an odd note, but I got caught up in her lies and forgot about it."

"I see." When Hugh didn't elaborate, Harper said in a puzzled tone, "And after we see Langley, what then?"

"Then," said Hugh, "we go down to Dover and wait for Miss Vayle to come and collect the book."

"What if she don't come?"

"She'll come," said Hugh harshly, then he wheeled his horse in the direction of Whitehall and moved off.

Harper gave one short expletive under his breath and went after him.

Colonel Langley's office was at the Horse Guards, only a five-minute ride from Pall Mall. Harper stayed in the street to look after the horses while Hugh went up to see Langley.

The colonel was standing at the window looking down on the parade grounds when Hugh walked in. He turned, a slow smile spreading across his face when he saw Hugh.

"I was sure," he said, "that the stories I've heard about you must be grossly exaggerated. How are you, Hugh?" and he came from behind his desk to clasp Hugh's hand.

Hugh saw immediately that Langley already had a visitor. Richard Maitland, looking as if he'd ridden all night to get there, was slumped in an armchair in front of the fire.

Ignoring Maitland, he grasped Langley's hand. James Langley did not look like a chief intelligence officer, but like the proverbial, absent-minded professor. He was in his mid-sixties, tall, with stooped shoulders and a limp that came, not from battle, but from a nasty fall he'd taken while digging for Roman ruins on his property and had fallen through the roof of an old, underground icehouse that he'd forgotten existed. The colonel, like Hugh, forgot everything when he was searching for ancient relics.

"Colonel," said Hugh, "I'm happy to see that the rumors of your retirement are grossly exaggerated as well."

Maitland was on his feet and he and Hugh nodded coldly to each other.

"The rumors are not exaggerated, Hugh," said Langley. "The war is over. I'm not getting any younger. It's time I was put out to pasture."

He moved to a tray of decanters on a table between two long windows, poured out a glass of whiskey and handed it to Hugh.

Hugh sat in the chair the colonel indicated. "Pasture, sir? That doesn't sound like you." Hugh was deliberately engaging in the kind of aimless conversation that he knew would annoy Maitland, whose mind was always firmly fixed on the business at hand.

Langley sat at his desk. "You're right, of course. I may be an old war-horse, but there's plenty of life in me yet. However, Mrs. Langley thinks it's time I spent more time with her and our daughter."

Hugh mentioned that he had met Mrs. Langley and Henrietta in Marlborough. Langley responded by joking about the expense of introducing a daughter to society.

Maitland couldn't take it anymore. At the first pause in the conversation, he said, "Colonel, sir, may I remind you that this man is a fugitive from the law? Shouldn't we—"

"Yes, yes, Richard! I was coming to that." Langley's face lost none of its good humor. "You see how it is, Hugh," he said. "I can't resign until this wretched business is cleared up."

In a sudden transformation that was characteristic of Langley, his good humor died, and his eyes became cold and determined. "So give me one good reason," he said, "why I should not have you hauled off to Newgate as a traitor."

"Because," said Hugh, "I have the book you want, and I'm willing to strike a bargain with you."

Langley sat back in his chair. "You have the book?"

Hugh met Langley's eyes unflinchingly. "I know where it's hidden."

Maitland was standing now. His tone was scathing. "What did I tell you, sir? He's in it up to his neck."

Langley studied Hugh for a moment, then said gently, "Sit down, Richard, and let's listen to what Hugh has to say."

Hugh went over everything that had happened during the last several days. He told them about Ballard's visit, and how Alex had tried to recruit him; he told them that Abbie had become involved to help her brother. But he did not tell them everything. In fact, he deliberately gave the impression that Abbie and George were a couple of innocents who had not weighed the consequences of their actions, and were now in over their heads.

"She's on her way to get the book now," he said finally. "Once she has it, she'll pass it on to her brother. If we move quickly, we can intercept her."

In the silence that followed, Langley searched Hugh's face. "And you want amnesty for this girl?"

"No, I want amnesty for the girl and her brother. As I told you, they are innocents who have got in over their heads. They are no threat to national security, or they won't be once I give you the book. So make up your mind. Do you want the book or don't you?"

Langley's eyebrows rose slowly. "What if I were to call your bluff, Hugh? Would you really allow the book to fall into the hands of our enemies?"

"I'd have to think about that," said Hugh, "and time is wearing on."

The glacier gradually melted. "So that's the way of it." Then, without taking his eyes off Hugh, "Richard, what do you advise me to do?"

There was a silence, then reluctantly, "I want that book."

Langley smiled. "Then it's settled. You have your bargain, Hugh, and not because of your empty threats. And when we have the girl and the book—what then?"

"I leave that up to you, sir. I know you'll have to question her, and I'm not asking you to make it easy for her."

Langley's eyelids drooped. "I see," he said.

Of course Langley saw. And so did Maitland. A blind man could have seen that the woman had duped him, was continuing to dupe him or there would be no need to intercept her when she went to get the book. If she had confessed everything to him, he would have been the one to get the book.

Langley gathered some papers on his desk. "I have an appointment with the minister before he keeps his appointment with the Prime Minister, so I must excuse myself. Richard, bring the girl and the book back here. But don't wait for me. Short of torture—and that's a joke Hugh, as you know very well—I want you to give her the scare of her life."

When Langley rose, so did Hugh and Maitland.

"Sir, what's in this book?" Hugh asked. "Why is it so important?"

Langley shook his head. "Until today, I would have said the book was unimportant. But events have proved me wrong."

"But if it was unimportant, why did you send Ballard down to Bath?"

"I didn't send him. He was taking his wife to be with her mother. That's what he told me. Of course, he lied. He had to know about the book. What other reason could there be for him to turn up dead in Miss Vayle's room? My theory is that he got hold of Miss Vayle's letter before it reached Richard's desk."

"Wouldn't he have mentioned it to you, sir?"

"Not necessarily. I think Alex was onto something but was keeping quiet about it until he had gathered all his facts."

Maitland said, "It's possible that Ballard was up to no good. Maybe he and Miss Vayle were in this together and had a falling out."

Hugh gave a snort of derision. "Are you implying that Alex was a traitor?"

Langley retorted, "Of course not! But he shouldn't have been working alone. That's not how I trained him."

When Langley left them, his shoulders seemed more stooped than usual. Hugh knew that there would be hell to pay with the minister and wished he could take part of the blame on himself. But that's not how it worked. A commander was always held responsible for his subordinates' mistakes.

When they were alone, Maitland said, "I don't know about you, but I'd rather be caned than see our chief like that."

"We both made a mess of things, didn't we?"

"You don't have to worry about it. You're no longer in the service."

"No," said Hugh bleakly. "What do you think is in the book, Maitland?"

Maitland's eyes bored into Hugh's. "I think the book will tell us who murdered my agents in Paris, and if your Miss Vayle had any part in it, amnesty or not, I warn you, I'll find a way to make her pay for her crimes."

Hugh's voice was lethally soft. "Do you want the book or don't you?"

A tight-lipped silence, then, "I want the book."

"Then we'll do this my way. Agreed?"

After a moment, Maitland nodded.

They descended the stairs in silence.

It was late afternoon when Abbie's hired chaise entered the outskirts of Dover. To the east, on the summit of the highest cliff, the castle soared above the huddle of small dwellings that clung to the hillsides. This dark and forbidding fortress was, Hugh had told her, the first line of defense not only for Kent but for the whole of England.

That was months ago, when Hugh had still been her best friend. She'd been in a temper, having just come from customs after being told of the exorbitant duty she had to pay on her books. Hugh had distracted her by taking her inside the castle to see a relic of the original Roman fortress that had once looked out over the English Channel. They'd been happy then.

She tried to shake off her despair by reminding herself that for once on this ill-fated journey, things had gone right for her. With Hugh and Harper out of the way, it had been easy to deal with Tom. She'd pretended to come down with a raging toothache and had sent Tom to fetch a doctor. Then she'd slipped away.

They would know by now that she'd lied about everything. What must they think of her?

It didn't matter what they thought. The only thing that mattered was saving her brother.

How simple it had all seemed when she'd set off from Bath. She would get the book and trade it for George. Now, everything was a nightmare. She'd been delayed by the storm, and time was running out. She was on the run from the law. They thought she had murdered a man; they believed she was a traitor. They would be looking everywhere for her, at Vayle House in London, at the homes of all her friends.

She focused on the one thing that gave her any control over the situation: the book. The book was the key to everything, the key to saving George.

In contrast to the last time, Abbie was quiet and subdued when she entered the customs house. One of the postboys went with her, to help carry her box of books to the chaise when she'd paid the duty on them. The packet from Calais had just docked, and Abbie felt inconspicuous among the many people opening their bags for the customs officers to examine. She said as little as possible, and after watching most of her horde of precious sovereigns disappear into the customs officer's strongbox, was free to collect her books.

The postboy carried her battered box to a table that the officer indicated. Abbie undid the leather straps and opened it. Homer's *Iliad*, a slim dark green leather volume, was right on top, almost the first book she saw. Her hand closed around it as though she were touching the Holy Grail. Tears welled up, and she was afraid to let out a breath in case she started bawling like a baby. Until that moment, she had not admitted to herself how terrified she'd been that the book would not be there.

When she could breathe again and her fingers had stopped trembling, she opened the book. On the flyleaf, just as Olivia had described, was the inscription to Mr. Michael Lovatt from his wife, Colette. She stared at that inscription for a long time before going on. At first glance, she would have said that it was a schoolboy's book. There were notations penciled in the margins, but as she studied those notations, she could make no sense of them, though she was quite fluent in French. A code, she thought, and her pulse, which was already racing, began to throb unpleasantly.

This wasn't the time or place to examine the book in detail. But without a shadow of doubt, she was convinced that this was the book everyone wanted, the book that would save George's life. With one comprehensive glance around, to make sure that she was unobserved, she slipped the book into her reticule, then she made a show of going through the rest of the books in the box. That done, she shut the box, fastened the straps, and told the postboy she was ready to go.

Outside, it was raining, and Abbie, head down, hurried across the cobblestones to the waiting chaise. She had only a yard or two to go when her steps faltered. The man who was standing beside her chaise was not the postboy. It was Hugh's coachman, Harper.

He shook his head and said sorrowfully, "Oh, Miss Vayle, why did you do it?"

Like an animal at bay, she whirled to face the danger she sensed was behind her. Hugh was there, and a man she did not recognize. She stared at Hugh in mute astonishment.

He held out his hand. His voice was oddly unlike his own, without inflection. "Give me the book, Abbie. I know it's in your reticule. I saw you put it there."

In a purely reflexive action, she brought the reticule up and hugged it to her body. Her eyes never wavered from Hugh's face, but whatever she was searching for was not there. She took a step back, then another. She found her voice. "You're not in Chiswick."

He replied dryly, "Apparently not."

"But how did you know, how *could* you—? You followed me."

"No, I didn't follow you. You should have remembered that I always pay attention to details. Now give me the book."

Harper said, "Give him the book, Miss Vayle."

She jerked when Harper's hands cupped her shoulders, but she was too numb, too shocked to fight him off.

Hugh's fingers closed around her reticule. For a moment, he hesitated, taken off guard by a rush of doubt. This was Abbie. She could never betray anyone.

But she'd lied through her teeth to him.

Hugh wrenched the reticule from her hands and found the book inside. "Is this the book you want, Maitland?" he asked.

Abbie flinched when Hugh tossed the book to his companion. But it was the name that made her brain begin to thaw. Richard Maitland. This was the man Hugh said was his enemy, the man who was hunting them down.

"This is the book," said Maitland, and pocketed it.

Abbie reached for Hugh, but her hand fell away when he stepped back. His coldness frightened her. She cried out, "Hugh, if only you would let me explain!"

"You can explain everything to Mr. Maitland," he replied in the same frighteningly flat voice. "He'll listen to you. I'm afraid I've had my fill of lies." He began to pull on his gloves. "A word of advice, Abbie. Lies won't save you now. Your only chance is to tell everything you know."

His frosty glance swept over her, plunging her into a boiling sea of emotions—guilt, despair, anguish, fear. "Please," she said, her voice breaking, "please, Hugh. Help me."

He ignored her eloquent appeal. Looking over her shoulder to Harper, he said, "We're finished here. Let's go."

When Harper released her, she sagged against the side of the chaise. It was raining harder now, but she wasn't aware that she was becoming soaked to the skin any more than she was aware of the curious glances of pedestrians who were scurrying for cover, or that red-coated soldiers had converged on the scene, or that Maitland was speaking to her, or that a carriage with barred windows had emerged from a side street. Her eyes were fixed on the two figures who were striking out along the side of the customs house. Harper looked back once, but Hugh did not waver from his purposeful stride.

When they turned the corner and were lost to view, she looked stupidly at her wrists. The man called Maitland had manacled them.

CHAPTER 17

T hey've decoded the message."

Maitland wordlessly accepted the sheet of paper Langley passed across his desk. He scanned the first few sentences and quickly looked up. "Nemo is now operating in England? But that's impossible."

"Why is it impossible?"

"Because he's dead. I saw his corpse with my own eyes. I was there when Napoleon's personal staff identified the body."

"Where and when was this?"

"It was in my report."

"Refresh my memory."

"In a cellar of the Château Fontainbleau, right after Napoleon was exiled. Nemo killed himself rather than fall into the hands of his enemies. Well, you know he was hated as much by his own people as he was by us."

"Oh yes, I remember him well."

He was more legend than man, thought Langley, this agent who, British intelligence suspected, had indiscriminately murdered his way to the top of his profession in

France. He was Napoleon's master spy. An assassin. Everyone feared him, but no one knew anything about him. No one knew his real name. No one knew his nationality. What was known was that he was fluent in many languages and was a master of disguise.

"It could be," said Langley, "that Napoleon's household staff lied."

Maitland thought about this, shook his head, and read the rest of the decoded message. It didn't tell them nearly enough, but it did give them a list of names. Nemo had evidently infiltrated a group of dissidents in England to plan something big.

Langley said, "Miss Vayle's name isn't there, nor her brother's. And . . ." He leaned across his desk to emphasize his point. ". . . neither is Alex Ballard's. So your theory that Alex was working hand-in-glove with Miss Vayle doesn't hold water."

"They could have been recruited later, after the message was written."

"I can't believe Alex would betray his country. No. I'm betting that he was onto something."

Maitland threw the paper onto Langley's desk. "It doesn't mention anything about Nemo's mission. He's an assassin—who is he after? I mean, he's Napoleon's man, and Napoleon is cut off on Elba. And there's no one of any interest in England right now. All the bigwigs like Wellington are at the Congress in Vienna."

"We'll know more when we start tracking down the names in that book."

Maitland sat quietly as he watched his chief pick up a pencil and begin to drum rhythmically on the flat of his desk. Langley was deep in thought, and this was not the time to interrupt him. They had a saying in the service about the colonel, a parody on one of his own father's favorite quotes: the brains of the chief grind slow but they grind exceedingly small.

The minutes passed. Finally Langley tossed his pencil aside and looked at Maitland. "This is a hell of a way to end my career: one crack agent murdered in a quiet English backwater—and we have no idea what Alex was doing there—and now Nemo turns up on my doorstep. He's a vicious operator, and I was always thankful I never had to deal with him in Spain."

Maitland said carefully, "He's not invincible, sir."

"No. You're damn right he's not! He's ruthless and clever, but he has his weakness like anyone else. His weakness, Richard, is women."

"He's a womanizer?"

"Just the opposite. He hates women. He abuses them. And I had that from Bell-Smythe who ran our operation in Russia. He reported that Nemo likes to terrorize women; he likes to have them plead for their lives. Sometimes he tortures them and sometimes he spares them, depending on the mood he's in. Charming character."

"I bet Miss Vayle doesn't know that or she would never have become involved in this business."

"I want her followed at all times."

"I haven't finished questioning her yet, sir."

"You've already had twenty-four hours," Langley said. "I'll give you until dawn tomorrow, and that's all the time I'm giving you."

Maitland knew when it was useless to argue with the colonel. "Yes, sir." He rose slowly and hesitated.

"What is it now, Richard?"

"I was thinking about Hugh Templar."

"What about Hugh?"

"I was wondering if it was wise to speak so freely

about our work in front of him. I mean, he did resign. He's no longer one of us."

Colonel Langley seemed puzzled. "You can count on Hugh's discretion."

"Yes, but can we count on Hugh?"

Langley frowned. "What are you talking about, Richard?"

Maitland cleared his throat. "Don't you think it's odd that he happened to show up in all the places where our agents were being eliminated? And he knows the Vayle woman and her brother. That's quite a coincidence, sir."

The silence was unnerving. When Langley spoke, though he did not raise his voice, Maitland winced. "Major Maitland," he said, "let me remind you that I trained Templar myself. I know him; I watched him develop into one of the finest agents who ever served under my command. He's the best there is. And if we can persuade him to help, we'll have a much better chance of catching Nemo. Do I make myself clear?"

"Yes, sir."

"And, you're forgetting that if it weren't for Major Templar, we would still be looking for that book."

When the door closed, Langley let out a long sigh. The minister had suggested that Richard Maitland might be just the right man for his job once he retired, and he'd agreed with him. Now, he was beginning to wonder if he'd made a mistake.

She was sitting at the other end of the table, her head cushioned on her arms as she slept. Her hair was a mass of tangles; her breathing was soft and regular, except for the occasional start of breath that made her shoulders lift.

Richard Maitland drummed his fingers on the scarred

tabletop and wondered why this woman was proving so hard to wear down. He'd thought he could break her in a matter of hours. She was, he'd reasoned, a gently bred girl and used to a soft life. If she dropped a handkerchief, a maid or a footman would hasten to pick it up. God forbid that women of her class should lift a hand to help themselves.

So he'd deliberately arranged things to be as unpleasant for her as possible. She'd been conveyed to London like a felon in an armed coach and incarcerated in a cell for the condemned in Newgate Prison. She was wearing the same grubby clothes she'd worn in Dover. The straw mattress on the bed and the threadbare blanket she'd thrown around her shoulders smelled distressingly of the unwashed bodies of former inmates of this rank cell.

He'd threatened, he'd cajoled, he'd offered to set her free if she would only cooperate. He couldn't shake her from her story. Her brother wasn't involved. Hugh Templar wasn't involved. She'd been acting alone, and she'd done nothing wrong.

He'd tried a different tack. He'd told her about Jerome and Colette, how they were in love and soon to be married. He'd told her how Colette had been shot to death in the vicinity of the Palais Royal when a member of the embassy staff waited for her, not far away, in a bookshop in the rue de Rivoli. Colette must have been desperate. She'd written Michael Lovatt's name and address inside the book as well as her own name. She must have known she was going to die and had wanted to make sure the book reached the right people.

Miss Vayle insisted that no one had given her a book.

She moved in her sleep, and the blanket slipped from her shoulders. She was pathetic. Templar had handed her over to British intelligence, yet she refused to believe it, or if she did believe it, it made no difference. She continued to protect him. In her position, he would have damned Templar to hell and back. Right or wrong, her loyalty to her friends was unshakable. Pathetic, he thought again. At the same time, she'd won his grudging respect.

He looked down at the leather folder in his hands. She might not believe him, but once she read the file, she wouldn't be so loyal to Templar. She was in love with him. That had become patently clear as he'd questioned her. But the man she was in love with bore no resemblance to the man he knew. She seemed to think he was a bumbling academic who had been inadvertently caught up in a nightmarish misadventure. If he could get her to read this file, she would discover that Templar was no bumbling academic. He was an experienced operator with nerves of steel.

And whatever Langley said, he was convinced that Hugh Templar knew more than he was telling. Alex Ballard had visited him in Bath. What had Ballard told Templar?

He had to know what he was up against, and the only way to do that was to turn the girl against Templar. He knew he was breaking every rule in the book, but this was too important to let rules stand in his way.

He wakened her by deliberately jerking the table.

She gave a start and came to herself slowly as the dream began to fade. The Palais Royal, Dessene the bookseller, and a French girl who had tipped over her basket of books—it wasn't a dream, it was real, and it was all coming back to her. This was the only bookshop she had visited on the day Colette was killed. It was too great a coincidence to dismiss. She remembered a pretty young girl with a tremulous smile and a plea in her eyes. Their hands had met on the handle of her basket. The girl's hand had trembled, as hers was trembling now. She was cold.

As awareness returned, she looked up and saw Maitland staring at her. "You're back," she said faintly.

"I told you I'd prove that Templar isn't the man you think he is, and I keep my word." He edged the folder to the center of the table.

Gradually, a change came over her. She straightened, rubbed her wrists where the manacles had pinched them, and stared at the folder with dull, wary eyes. "What is it?" she asked.

Maitland got up. "It's Templar's file. His record as a British agent."

He gave her credit for the way she gathered her poise. She looked at the folder, looked up at him, and her brows rose. "You keep files on agents? That seems like a dangerous practice. What if they were to fall into the wrong hands?"

A slow smile curved his lips. "This file is inactive. And our files are better protected than the Bank of England. Only two people have access to them, myself and my chief."

She glanced at the folder. "How can I be sure that what's in that folder isn't a pack of lies?"

"There's nothing in there that discredits Major Templar. He was, at one time, one of the best agents in the service."

She shook her head. "I don't believe you."

He edged the folder toward her. "Read that file and you'll change your mind. Or are you afraid to face the truth?"

"I've told you the truth, but you won't believe me. Hugh is innocent. He didn't do anything wrong. Where is he? What have you done with him?"

He laughed unpleasantly. "What do the rich do when they come up to town? They go to parties and balls, or gamble the night away in their exclusive gentlemen's clubs. That's where he'll be."

"That's a lie," she cried out. "Hugh wouldn't abandon me."

He placed his hands on the table and leaned toward her. "He has abandoned you, Miss Vayle. Who do you think told us where to find you? He came to us; we didn't go to him. My God, you saw him with your own eyes. What will it take to convince you?"

Her poise began to show signs of cracking. She said stubbornly, "It wasn't like that. Hugh wouldn't abandon me. He wouldn't."

"Oh, wouldn't he? He abandoned his own wife, so why not you? What makes you so special?"

There was a long, eerie silence broken only by a muffled wail from the women's quadrangle two floors below. When the sound died away, he said softly, "So you didn't know about Estelle?" When she remained silent, he went on, "He abandoned her too. Shortly after they were married, he sent her back to Ireland where she died of a broken heart."

No response, but he could see that she was shaken. "Read the file, Miss Vayle," he said. "Then we'll talk."

Long after he left, she remained as she was, her eyes fastened on the leather folder, her arms hugging her sides. She knew her brain was sluggish from lack of sleep and all the questioning she'd been subjected to, and she feared a trap. She'd thought that all she had to worry about was George, but Hugh had come under suspicion too.

Hugh, she thought despairingly, *Hugh.*

More than once, she'd hovered on the brink of telling her interrogators everything. In fact, when she was first brought here, she'd tried to. If her brother was involved, she'd told Maitland, it was against his will. But Maitland had laughed in her face. "That's what they all say when they're captured," he'd replied. And after that, the conviction had grown that they didn't care what happened to George. Whether he was guilty or innocent was all the same to them. They were desperate to catch the men who were after the book, and wouldn't lift a hand to save anyone who got in their way.

But there was more to it than that. She was beginning to have doubts about her own brother. What if Maitland was right? What if George was part of a conspiracy? If that were true, it could only be because he hadn't known what he was getting into. George had no interest in politics.

She pressed her fingers to her temples in a vain attempt to blot out the doubts Maitland had raised in her mind, not only about George, but about Hugh as well. Maitland was very clever. She supposed she'd had her doubts about Hugh ever since he caught up to her in Dover. And she was haunted by the look on his face when he'd handed her over to Maitland. It was the face of a man she did not know—menacing, frightening in its coldness. She'd blotted out that memory on the drive to London, but Maitland's words had brought it back to her.

So, you didn't know about Estelle? He abandoned her, too.

Her gaze slid to the folder. With a little sob of resignation, she reached for the folder, dragged it toward herself, and slowly opened it.

The first page contained no surprises. It was a short biography of Hugh's early life. The next part dealt with his career as a soldier. Almost as soon as he had arrived in Portugal, he'd been recruited as an observing officer. Abbie knew about such men. They were spies in uniform, honorable men who risked their lives by riding into enemy territory to gather information on the deployment of enemy troops. But Hugh hadn't remained an observing officer for long. His facility with languages had made him a candidate for more dangerous assignments. He'd shed his identity, shed his uniform, and had become a spy behind French lines, working under a string of Spanish and French aliases.

Maitland had not lied. Hugh's career was spectacular. The victories he chalked up had won him many commendations from his superiors. Wellington had mentioned him in dispatches several times, but always under the code name of El Centurion. No one was more fearless or successful in pursuing his objectives than El Centurion. Certainly, the secretary who had recorded Hugh's career was very impressed. Major Templar was a hero.

The entry of Hugh's marriage was terse and to the point. Major Templar, she read, had married Miss Estelle Saunders on December 9, 1812, in Lisbon. There was another entry on the next page. Mrs. Hugh Templar, formerly Miss Estelle Saunders, had died of a fever in Lismore, Ireland, the following year, while her husband was on active duty in Spain.

Abbie read that short entry several times, but couldn't see anything scandalous about it. Nothing to explain why Hugh had never mentioned his marriage—not to her, not to all their friends.

She noticed other names interspersed throughout the file. Desdemona, Mercedes, Catalina—all vaguely described as "collaborators." It didn't take her long to work out that these were the names of Hugh's mistresses. It seemed that spies were not entitled to a private life. In the interest of security, their mistresses must be investigated as well. Her eyes dwelled on the last entry in the file. In Paris, on April 30, 1814, the major had resigned his commission and returned to England accompanied by the actress Miss Barbara Munro.

Abbie sat back in her chair and stared at the candle in the center of the table. Maitland had left the candle so that she could read Hugh's file. Inmates weren't supposed to be left alone with candles in case they set fire to themselves. She had no need of a candle. She was already on fire.

She glared down at the folder in her hands as though Hugh's face were stamped upon it. Without a shadow of a doubt, she knew that everything in the file was true. Her instincts, her intuition, her powers of reasoning, at long last, were perfectly in tune.

El Centurion, the centurion. The first time she'd seen him, the picture of a Roman centurion had flashed into her mind. But Hugh had dispelled that impression by showing her a different Hugh, the quiet, unassuming scholar who was interested in the same things as she.

But why had he wanted to be her lover? That's what she couldn't understand, unless he'd found it amusing to make her, a confirmed spinster, his next trophy. Daniel had warned her about such men. They'd done everything, seen everything, and life had become one long bore. They were always looking for the next challenge, the next novelty.

He'd deliberately misled her, pretending to be one kind of man when he was really another. At one time she'd even thought he was too tame for her. And he'd mocked her unmercifully, pretending to be a dull clod who was only interested in ancient civilizations. How he must have laughed at her. If she'd known what he was really like, she would have kept far away from him.

Instead, she'd seduced him.

She moaned. She had totally humiliated herself. She was beyond lying to herself now. He hadn't wanted her. That sleazy, immoral, unscrupulous libertine who had left a trail of mistresses all the way from Lisbon to Paris had not wanted her. It was *she* who had forced herself on *him*. And now that she'd seen the list of women he'd bedded, she understood his reluctance only too well. Desdemona, Mercedes, Catalina—there wasn't a plain Abbie among the lot of them. She was obviously not in their class. He'd even told her he'd changed his mind, and he'd meant it.

He'd been married and never mentioned it. Barbara Munro had been his mistress, and while she was raving about the beautiful actress and her performance at Drury Lane, Hugh had pretended to be bored. The cad had actually yawned behind his hand several times! How could she have been so naive? So trusting? So stupidly, stupidly gullible? So stupid?

When she felt the sting of scalding tears, she angrily dashed them away. She wasn't going to mope over a man who had deceived her, a man who wouldn't lift a finger to help her. It was all there in his file. He was the hero and she was the enemy. She and George would only be two more names to add to his illustrious war record. Maybe Wellington would commend him for that, too.

Every moment of their acquaintance was now examined in minute detail; every kindness on his part became suspect. She went over the last few days, sifting every conversation, every incident, to determine why he'd come after her. Not from the goodness of his heart, as he'd led her to believe, because she knew now that Hugh Templar didn't have a heart. A man with a heart wouldn't have abandoned her to this chamber of horrors, no matter what she'd done.

If their positions were reversed, she'd be moving heaven and earth to get him out of this place. She wouldn't care whether he was innocent or guilty. She would go to her brother-in-law and beg him to help; she would ask him to speak to the prime minister if need be. She would appeal to the king. She would do anything to get Hugh off. She would . . .

The emotions she'd held in check suddenly swallowed her, and a great gasping cry tore from her throat. Without knowing what she was doing, she stumbled to her feet, groped her way to the bed and flung herself down on the mattress. Many minutes passed before there were no more tears to shed.

With emotions spent, she turned on her side and scrubbed her face with the hem of her gown. By slow degrees, she forced herself to think calmly. There was more to consider here than her broken heart. She had to think of George.

She fell asleep on the comforting thought that she would offer Maitland Hugh Templar's head if he would only help her save her brother.

CHAPTER 18

The first rays of dawn were filtering through the bars of the double grated window when she awoke. She knew at once where she was and what had awakened her. Heart pounding, she hauled herself up and stared at the door as it swung open on its rusty hinges. One of the female wardens, a sour-faced woman with a candle in her hand, entered. Behind her was a gentleman.

He took a few steps into the cell and said uncertainly, "Abbie?"

She expected Maitland and stared at him without recognition until he approached the bed.

"Abbie! Good God! What have they done to you?"

"Giles," she said faintly, "have they arrested you too?"

"No," he said, "I've come to take you home."

Her brother-in-law wasn't particularly handsome, he wasn't particularly tall or fashionable, but he was one of the nicest men she knew, and the look of concern on his face—in marked contrast to the looks she had received in the last little while—shattered what was left of her control. With a little cry, she flung herself from the bed and catapulted herself into his arms.

"It's all right, Abbie," he soothed. "It's all right. I'm here now. You're safe. I won't leave without you. It's all right. We'll have you home in no time."

He tried to hold her at arm's length, but she wouldn't allow it. She buried her nose in his broad, comfortable chest and clung to him with the tenacity of a monkey. He patted her awkwardly and made the same soothing sounds he might have made to his own infant daughters, Lizzie and Vicki, when they were hurt.

At length, when she went limp in his arms, he said, "I'll have someone's head for this."

Those fierce words, coming from her mild-mannered brother-in-law, startled a laugh out of her, but it verged on the hysterical and she quickly cut it off. Blinking back tears, she took a step back and looked up at him.

His brown wavy hair was receding at the temples, making him look older than his years. His brows were pulled in a frown, and his eyes were deeply troubled.

This was the man she had once loved, or thought she had—the man who had chosen her sister over her. Giles was a good husband and father. He was a good man. If he were her husband, she would cherish him.

"Harriet," she said with feeling, "doesn't know how lucky she is."

"What?" He frowned, puzzled.

She passed a hand over her eyes. "I'm babbling, Giles. Put it down to nerves. Is it true? Am I really free to go?"

"Yes, it's true."

"But how can that be? They caught me red-handed. They know I'm guilty."

"All I know," said Giles, "is that you and George have been given amnesty."

"But how? Why?" Hugh had mentioned amnesty, but that was before he'd become her enemy, and after what had happened, she knew he wouldn't lift a hand to save her.

Aware of the warden nearby, Giles said, "We'll talk later in private."

He began to bark out orders. From the warden he wanted water and soap and towels for Miss Vayle, and a comb for her hair. And if his orders weren't carried out at once, he threatened to bring a regiment of militia to Newgate and have them all arrested for wrongful confinement.

Abbie didn't care about cleaning herself up. She just wanted to go home. But Giles insisted. Harriet was waiting in the carriage right outside the prison, he said, and he knew she wouldn't want her sister to see her with a grimy face and her hair like a bird's nest. And they weren't going home straight away. They had to make a small detour first. She wouldn't want strangers to see her like this either.

"A detour?" she repeated, alarm suddenly coursing through her.

"We'll talk in the carriage," he said. "Now hurry. I'll be waiting for you right outside that door."

When she was ready, she looked around for the green folder, but it was gone. It didn't matter. Every word was indelibly branded in her brain.

She was even more alarmed when she came out of her cell to find two red-coated soldiers waiting to escort her. She began to tremble. Giles saw it and threw his cloak over her shoulders.

"This place is like an icehouse. This should keep you warm," he said.

It all seemed too easy, and she half expected that someone would try to stop them before they could get away. But the turnkeys unlocked every door when one of the soldiers showed his pass.

Outside, she breathed deeply of the cool morning air, unpolluted by the misery of Newgate. She'd been incarcerated for forty-eight hours. It felt like an eternity.

Giles put an arm around her shoulders and urged her toward the carriage. When she looked into Harriet's worried face, tears rose in her throat, cutting off words, but Harriet's greeting was the perfect antidote to self-pity.

"If you'd stayed with your family instead of going to live in Bath, none of this would have happened. Do you realize we've been up all night trying to find out where they'd taken you? Do you know what we've suffered these last few hours?"

"Harriet!" chided Giles, then stopped when his wife suddenly burst into tears and flung herself into Abbie's arms.

"I'm going to kill that man!" sobbed Harriet.

"Who, dear?" asked Abbie.

The carriage was moving off, and she couldn't help looking out the window, at the grim redbricked building that had almost no windows. She still didn't feel safe, and she wondered if she would ever feel safe again.

"Hugh Templar!" retorted Harriet.

"Oh, no," said Abbie. "I'm reserving that pleasure for myself. But how do you know about Hugh?"

"He was the one who told us that you'd been held for questioning," sobbed Harriet.

"Oh, he did, did he?" said Abbie bitterly. "When did you see him? What did he say?"

Giles did most of the talking. He stuck to the facts, but it was Harriet's nasty asides that fleshed out the picture that formed in Abbie's mind. Harriet and Giles had attended the opera that evening, and during one of the intermissions, when they were strolling in the corridor, they'd come face-to-face with Hugh.

"And that showy actress was hanging on his sleeve," hissed Harriet. "Barbara Munro!"

Harriet was so incensed at this perceived betrayal of her sister, that she'd shaken off her husband's restraining hand and planted herself directly in their path. "I asked after you, of course," said Harriet, "and was dumbfounded when he said that he had escorted you to London."

Giles said reasonably, "Naturally, we were alarmed because you had not turned up at the house. I think that shocked Templar too."

"No, it didn't," said Harriet nastily. "He shrugged his shoulders and moved past us. I wouldn't have known him, he was so changed."

"But he did come back," Giles pointed out. "He told us that he was confident you would turn up soon, but if not, I should apply to Colonel Langley at the Horse Guards. He'd held you for questioning on a matter of national security."

"Then he just walked away," declared Harriet, "as though he had not blown our world apart."

"He's good at doing that," said Abbie.

There followed hours of trying to track down this elusive Colonel Langley. He wasn't in his office, and he wasn't at his club where, they'd been told, he was living while his house in Chelsea was being refurbished. Giles wanted Harriet to go home, but she flatly refused.

"How could I face our mother and Daniel with the news that you were missing too? We've all been so worried about George."

"What have you heard of George?" asked Abbie.

"He arrived home from Paris when we were visiting you in Bath. There was a note waiting for us when we reached London. He was going off to visit some famous landscape gardener. He would write to us, he said. But that was weeks ago. Daniel and Giles have approached all his friends, but no one knows where he is. And now this!"

"There's a lot more to it than you know," said Abbie.

Giles cut her off. "We don't have time to go into all this right now. We're almost there. To cut a long story short, I eventually tracked down Colonel Langley's aide, Mr. Richard Maitland. He's waiting for us now, Abbie. This won't take long, then you'll be free to go."

"Maitland!" Abbie shuddered in reaction. "He's worse than the Spanish Inquisition. Giles, I can't face him again. I can't!"

"You have no choice."

"I don't like it," said Harriet. "Either Abbie's under arrest or she's not, and if she's not, no one can force her to do what she doesn't want to do."

"It's not a case of force," said Giles. "It's a case of clearing up a few minor details."

"I still don't like it," said Harriet. "What does he want with her?"

"Let's wait and see, shall we?"

Abbie didn't like it either. She didn't like the look of the rundown area they were driving through. She didn't like the omissions in her brother-in-law's replies to her sister's questions. Her instincts were telling her to run for her life, but Giles had grasped her elbow, as though he was well aware of what her instincts were telling her.

When the coach came to a stop, Harriet started to get up.

"You're not invited," said Giles.

Harriet's mouth dropped open. Quickly recovering herself, she said, "I don't care whether I'm invited or not. I'm not letting Abbie out of my sight."

"Sit down," said Giles in an awful voice.

Harriet sat. "Wait," she cried when he opened the door. "What is it now?"

She peeled out of her sable-lined coat. "Abbie is not going in there looking like a street hawker. Abbie, take off Giles's cloak and put this on. At least it will keep you warm."

Harriet had never allowed anyone to borrow her clothes, not even when she was a girl, because she was always so particular about her things. That she was doing it now gave Abbie an eerie sensation of approaching doom.

She should have run while she still had the chance. Now her legs had turned to jelly.

"Good girl," said Giles, looking at his wife, then he stepped down from the coach and helped Abbie alight.

A few steps from the carriage, he turned to face her. "Abbie," he said, bringing her eyes to him, "we don't have much time, so listen carefully. You must prepare yourself for something of an ordeal. Early this morning, soldiers surrounded this house and tried to arrest the occupants. When the men inside resisted, the soldiers stormed the house and everyone inside was killed." He paused. "Are you with me, Abbie?"

She was ahead of him. "George?" she got out on a shaken whisper.

"I don't know," he said gravely. "I don't know. But it's not only George they're interested in. Maitland thinks you may be able to identify some of the others. I'll be right with you, so you'll have nothing to fear. Do you understand?"

She nodded and thought how odd it was that she could think at all.

"Good. Then let's get it over with."

The house, unlike the others in the area, was detached and stood back from the road on its own little garden. Its front door was off its hinges, and glass from broken windows littered the paths and barren flowerbeds. A line of soldiers was keeping back small clusters of people who had congregated outside the iron railings. Richard Maitland met them on the front steps.

"This way," he said quietly.

Giles slipped an arm around Abbie's shoulders, as though he were afraid she would faint. She wanted to tell him that she wasn't going to faint. She knew she had to go through with this; she had to find out if George was among the dead.

The bodies were laid out on the floor in the front room, with a blanket covering each one. There were four of them in all. She saw blood on the walls and dark stains on the carpet, but no blood on the blankets that covered the bodies.

She noticed other things: a pair of worn boots flung into a corner; a man's jacket draped over a chair. Two men in dark coats were going through the drawers of a desk, and soldiers were coming and going on the stairs, laughing and chatting to one another, as though nothing out of the ordinary had happened here.

It was obscene. It was sickening. She couldn't go through with it. She wasn't strong enough.

Giles's arm tightened around her shoulders, and his eyes searched her face. "I wouldn't ask you to do this," he said, "but it's a condition of your release. Do you understand, Abbie?"

She looked into his kind brown eyes and blinked back tears. If anyone had to be with her, she was glad it was Giles. He was as steady as a rock, and she trusted him.

She thought of Hugh, of how she had trusted him once, and pain twisted inside her.

"Abbie, what is it?"

"It's all right, Giles," she said. "I'm stronger than you think."

He didn't look convinced, but he nodded all the same, then turning to Maitland, he said, "Who are these men?" and he indicated the inert shapes beneath the blankets.

Maitland answered, "Suspected traitors. The name of one was in the book Miss Vayle gave us. He's a student at the university. We don't know about the others yet. All we know is that they resisted arrest."

"Then let's get this over with."

At a nod from Maitland, a soldier rolled back the first blanket to reveal the face of a young man with red hair. He looked as though he were sleeping. It was horrible, but he wasn't George, and Abbie wondered if it was blasphemy to feel such joy.

"Do you recognize this man?" asked Maitland.

"No," she whispered.

He was looking at her intently. "No, I swear it," she cried.

Each time a blanket was raised to reveal the face of the man it covered, her heart would lurch, then subside when she saw it was not George. Apart from the redhaired boy, she recognized them all. They were the men who had attacked Hugh at the Black Boar. But they did not all look as though they were sleeping. The last man looked hideous in death. It was the man in the brown coat.

"For God's sake!" Giles burst out. "Is this really necessary?"

Maitland spoke in the same controlled tone. "Miss Vayle, do you recognize this man as well?"

"Yes. He seemed to be the leader. I told you, these are the men who attacked Mr. Templar at the Black Boar."

Suddenly, it was too much for her. She tore out of

Giles's clasp and stumbled from the room, through the hall and onto the front steps. Her stomach began to heave, and as though it mattered she quickly removed her sister's coat and handed it to Giles as he caught up with her. "Harriet is so particular," she got out, then she began to retch. When the spasms were over, she collapsed against the wall.

After some minutes had passed, Giles said, "Shall I carry you to the carriage?"

She waved vaguely at the room she'd just exited. "They all look so young. Their whole lives were in front of them. Why, Giles? Why?"

"I don't know, Abbie."

She straightened when Maitland appeared behind Giles, then she turned her head when someone called her name.

Hugh Templar was striding up the path to the house. He was immaculately turned out in evening clothes, and looked as though he were on his way home from a ball. It was quite possible. Most people went to balls or private parties after they'd taken in the opera.

As he leaped up the steps and stood towering over her, she detected the faint smell of a woman's perfume on his clothes. Maitland had told her the truth. While she was incarcerated in Newgate, Hugh had been enjoying himself; while the lives of the young men in this house had been snuffed out, he had been amusing himself with a woman.

Their eyes collided, hers wild and dilating, his flaring with shock as he noted the sickly pallor of her skin and her disheveled appearance. She looked like a homeless waif of the streets.

"My God, Abbie, what happened to you?" When she

was silent, he looked beyond her to Maitland and Giles. "What is she doing here?" he demanded.

Maitland said, "The same as you. She came to identify the bodies."

The murderous rage in Hugh's eyes dimmed when he looked down at Abbie. "I didn't know you were being held in Newgate," he said. "That was no part of our bargain. I've been trying to find you all night."

She cowered away from the hand he held out to her. "This was not supposed to happen," he said. "I made a bargain with Colonel Langley: amnesty for you and your brother if I gave him the book. Tell her, Maitland."

Maitland smiled as though he were enjoying every moment of this encounter. "That's perfectly true, Miss Vayle," he said. "We were to let you go after we questioned you. And we've held to our part of the bargain. You should be grateful to Mr. Templar for all he's done for you."

Hugh's eyes never left Abbie's. "There are no charges pending against you or your brother. Do you understand, Abbie? I did that much for you. Go home and forget about all this."

As though she could forget all the grief and misery she'd endured because of this man. She thought of the room she'd just left, and of the lifeless young men who were huddled beneath dirty blankets, and all the time she'd feared one of them would be George.

Before she knew what she was going to do, she lashed out at him, and the impact of her open palm sent his head jerking back. A fierce pleasure surged through her as she saw the imprint of her hand on that handsome face.

Drawing on the fragile reserves of her strength, she turned to her brother-in-law. "Giles, please take me home."

Hugh watched her until she had passed through the line of soldiers at the gate. When he spoke to Maitland, he sounded shaken. "Is her brother among the dead?"

"No."

Hugh let out a breath. "Thank God for that."

"But she identified three of the bodies. They're the men who attacked you at the Black Boar."

"I could have done that. There was no need to involve Miss Vayle."

Maitland shook his head. "I wanted to see her reaction. She was very shaken. Now you're much harder to read, Templar."

"I'll make it easy for you," said Hugh.

With the speed of a striking cobra, he smashed his fist into Maitland's jaw, sending him reeling against a glass door. When the glass shattered and Maitland fell heavily to the floor, soldiers inside the house came running with their pistols drawn.

"Hold your fire!" roared Maitland. He wiped the blood from his mouth and grinned up at Hugh. "I'm going to stuff that silver spoon right down your throat and make you choke on it," he said.

"And I," snarled Hugh, "am going to teach you the manners your mother should have taught you. Where is Colonel Langley?"

"He left a while ago, so there's no one to stop us. It's just you and me."

"That's what I wanted to hear."

Maitland rose cautiously. "Let's make ourselves comfortable first, shall we?" he said.

This was the signal for both men to remove their coats.

"No holds barred?" asked Maitland pleasantly.

"No holds barred," agreed Hugh.

Before he had finished saying the words, Maitland's booted foot connected with Hugh's flank. But Hugh was no novice to unarmed combat. When he fell to the ground, he brought Maitland down with him, and the soldiers watching the fight roared their approval. Then they began to make bets.

Abbie had one foot on the carriage step when she heard that roar. "What is it? What's going on?" she asked anxiously, and she looked back at the house.

"Something that's been brewing for a long time, I think," said Giles. "I only wish I could stay and watch it." When he saw the alarm in Abbie's eyes, he spoke soothingly, though not quite truthfully. "The soldiers will put a stop to it before it gets out of hand. Now let's get you home and into some decent clothes. Then we'll talk."

"Home," said Abbie. "I want that more than anything."

One of the soldiers watching the fight edged his way to the back of the crush. Nemo was congratulating himself on a job well done. There had been a moment of alarm when the girl noticed him on the stairs and looked at him for a long time. But she hadn't recognized him in his red uniform. She was in shock and didn't know what she was seeing.

He'd lost the book to British intelligence and that infuriated him. He wasn't used to failure. It wasn't his fault, but the fault of his incompetent subordinates who'd let the girl get away from them. If he'd been there, it would never have come to this.

But he'd had other things to do in London, more important things. He was an assassin. He'd had to set things up so that he could make the kill and disappear without a trace. The loss of the book was a serious setback. His enemies knew he was in England now. They would take extra precautions to guard likely targets, and that would make his job more difficult, but not too difficult. He was too daring and too clever for them. He was standing among them, in the uniform of a British soldier, and he might as well have been invisible.

When the soldiers had stormed the house, he was already inside, waiting for them to appear. Then he'd efficiently shot his accomplices one by one. Now that they could be recognized, their usefulness was over. Their days were numbered anyway. British intelligence would have relentlessly hunted them down, and he could no longer afford to associate with them.

He had another cell waiting in the wings, virgin, untried. The irony was that these young Englishmen were as committed to Napoleon as he was. They were idealists, either students or professional men, who really believed that if Napoleon were master of England, he would put an end to the class system and make all men equal. They didn't think of themselves as traitors but at patriots.

He, on the other hand, was a realist, so he'd used their idealism for his own ends. Napoleon would return like Phoenix rising from the ashes, and these young hotheads would have a hand in it. And not one of them would live to tell the tale.

Ballard had come close to telling the tale and that infuriated him, too. He should have been warned about Ballard long before he turned up in Bath. He'd originally meant to kill him on neutral ground, but after the trick Abbie—he no longer thought of her as Miss Vayle— played on him, he'd appreciated the irony of killing Ballard in the room registered in her name. He wondered what British intelligence would make of it. And he'd been very sure Ballard would come looking for Miss Vayle. They'd both been after the book.

They said that cats had nine lives, but that little mouse had more than her share of good luck. There was no need to go after her now. Her usefulness had ended as well. But it irked him that she, and only she, could boast of how she'd bested Nemo. He really couldn't allow that to happen.

He had her brother. It gave him pleasure to imagine all the tortures she would be suffering on his behalf. She would know that now that she no longer had the book to trade, George's usefulness was over. Every waking hour, she would remember that he'd promised to send her brother to her in pieces if she crossed him. He was in no hurry. Let her wait; let her suffer. Besides, he had other plans for the boy now.

No one was watching him. Everyone was intent on the fight. So many soldiers milling around, and not one of them doing his job.

With a contemptuous yawn, Nemo broke away from the crowd and sauntered to the back of the house. He went to the privy, and when he came out, he was dressed in the rough clothes of a common laborer.

CHAPTER 19

It was late in the morning when Hugh's carriage pulled up outside his house in Berkeley Square. Harper walked him to the front door.

"You done Major Maitland a grave disservice, Mr. Templar, sir," said Harper. "If his superiors gets to hear of it, he could be court-martialed for striking you."

"Nonsense!" said Hugh irritably. He hated when Harper put on his "governess's" voice and tried to make him feel guilty when he had nothing to feel guilty about.

Well, maybe he did have something to feel guilty about where Abbie was concerned. In spite of Maitland's threats, he hadn't expected him to go so far, but after he spoke to Harriet and Sir Giles at the opera last night, he'd begun to worry. As soon as the opera was over, he'd dropped a tight-lipped Barbara at her front door and had gone looking for Abbie. He'd missed her at Newgate by only a few minutes.

Newgate. He felt his rage begin to boil all over again. He'd wanted to teach her a lesson, but he hadn't wanted it to go that far. He'd left the prison with only one thought in mind: He was going to find Maitland and tear him limb from limb. But Maitland found him first.

There had been a soldier waiting for him outside the prison. "You're a hard man to track down, sir," he said, and handed him a note from Maitland. If *"his lordship" could spare the time from his amusements,* he'd read, *there are several corpses in a house in Chapel Street he might want to view.*

And beneath Maitland's signature: *Don't bother to dress up. We're all friends here.*

Bastard!

The last thing he had expected was to find Abbie there. He didn't think he would ever forget how she looked when he'd found her with her brother-in-law. Her eyes were wide and haunted, and all the life seemed to have drained out of her.

No, he had no regrets about Maitland. He'd got what he deserved. His one regret was that he hadn't killed the bastard.

"They drummed *me* out of the army for striking another soldier," said Harper pointedly.

Maybe, thought Hugh, he had got what he deserved as well. He felt as though a regiment of infantry had just marched over him. Breathing hurt. He knew by the pain in his jaw that he wouldn't be eating much besides baby food for the next few days. All things considered, Maitland had given as good as he'd got.

Bastard!

Harper was watching him. "Look," said Hugh, "if anyone asks, we were demonstrating the art of hand-to-hand combat to a group of soldiers. We were giving them a few pointers, that's all. I'm not going to make a complaint, so nothing will happen to Maitland."

Harper scratched his chin. "You hurt him pretty bad, sir."

Though it cost him something, Hugh grinned. "Yes, I did, didn't I?"

"But no more than he hurt you." This time, Harper was the one who grinned. "You fought each other to a knockout draw, both of you, so all bets was off. I've never known that happen before."

"Harper," said Hugh patiently, "use the bloody door knocker and let's get out of this freezing cold while I can still walk."

The porter who opened the door to them was as welcoming as a gravestone. All his servants were like this, except for Harper and Tom, and Hugh accepted it philosophically. He was reserved by nature, and his servants respected that reserve.

Step by slow step he made for his library where he knew a fire would be lit. When Harper left him to see to the carriage, Hugh felt oddly let down. A fine state of affairs, he thought, easing himself into a chair, when a man's only real friend was his coachman. He had many acquaintances, but no one who knew him intimately. He supposed he wasn't an easy man to get to know.

Abbie had come as close to knowing him as anyone. If only he'd kept her at arm's length, as he did everyone else, he wouldn't be reeling from all the unfamiliar emotions that churned inside him right now.

In short, he felt like hell, and if this was what happened when he let someone get too close to him, he would never let it happen again.

Because he was chilled to the bone, he asked the footman who was standing by to bring him a large whiskey. Harper would have said something caustic about the road to ruin, but this servant—he forgot his name—was as talkative as a doorpost.

As he sipped from his glass, morosely reflecting on his uncaring servants, he was gripped by an ache so profound it seemed like a physical pain. Abbie's image filled his mind. They were in the kitchen at Endicote, and she'd got the fire going before turning her attention to him. He remembered vividly the gentle touch of her fingers as she felt for broken bones. Her fragrance. Her softness. Her warmth.

He'd do better to remember the wallop she'd given him earlier that night. At least that slap was something he could trust. She'd meant it. Everything else that had passed between them was an illusion. She'd wanted to disarm him, and she'd succeeded.

So, she'd suffered the indignity of Newgate. He was damn sorry for it, bitterly sorry. But treason was a capital offense. She'd got off lightly in more ways than she knew. He could still feel the residue of the shock that had frozen him when, after their fight, Maitland had taken him to view the bodies and had murmured, "We think they were Nemo's accomplices."

If Abbie and her brother were mixed up with Nemo, they were lucky they had lived this long.

She would return to Bath, and he would take up his life in London as though they'd never met. The years seemed to stretch out endlessly in front of him, years of cold houses, cold servants, and cold, calculating women who sold their favors for money.

At least they were honest. He'd take a Barbara Munro over a dishonest, repressed old maid any day.

His lips twisted in a bitter smile. A repressed old maid? Who was he trying to fool? In bed, she was as passionate and wanton as a man could hope for in his woman. She'd wrapped her long legs around him and taken him on a wild ride to rapture. He'd been counting the hours until she could do it again.

I love you.

The fire sputtered and quietly died.

He stared moodily at those smoking black coals, then suddenly reaching for his empty glass, he hurled it into the grate.

In Vayle House, just off the Strand, Abbie and her family had congregated in the upstairs parlor. Because this room was small and easily heated in winter, and because it had a fine view of the river Thames, it was the favorite meeting room in the house.

Abbie had undergone a transformation since she arrived home. She'd bathed and washed her hair and was wearing one of her sister's gowns, an olive-green worsted that buttoned from throat to hemline. She was seated on a cushioned stool in front of a blazing fire, drying her hair, and once in a while she would absently run her fingers through it to fluff it out.

With few omissions, she'd told her family the whole story from beginning to end, answering questions as they arose. At first, they were incredulous. They were inclined to believe that she was suffering from dementia. But they couldn't dismiss the fact that George was missing or that she'd been imprisoned in Newgate, or that she'd had to view the bodies of young men who had died in a house in Chapel Street.

When there was a lull in the conversation, Abbie looked around the parlor as if to convince herself that it wasn't a dream. She was home. She was safe. The people she loved best in the world surrounded her. If only George were here, it would be perfect.

The difference between Hugh Templar and the members of her family couldn't have been more striking or more painful. There was nothing she could do to turn the people in this room against her. They'd had their differences in the past; they didn't always get along; but when a Vayle was in trouble, they all rallied around.

They were so fiercely biased in her favor that when she told them how Hugh had betrayed her to the authorities, their outrage had been ferocious. Daniel had vowed to challenge Hugh to a duel; Harriet swore she would find a way to make him suffer; their mother promised that after she had finished blackening his character, no hostess in London would invite him to her house; and Giles had murmured that hanging was too good for him.

It didn't help when Abbie told them there were no charges pending against her or George because Hugh had made a bargain with Maitland. They saw at once that if Hugh had really wanted to protect her, he could have given the book to Maitland without bringing her into it. Obviously he'd wanted Abbie to suffer, wanted her sent to Newgate.

Abbie couldn't bring herself to tell them the rest, that she'd been fool enough to go to bed with Hugh. Daniel might take it into his head to try and force Hugh to marry her, and she'd been humiliated enough as it was.

She would drown in tears of self-pity if she didn't get a grip on herself.

Let it go, she told herself fiercely. There were more important things to think about than Hugh Templar. He could hurt her only if she allowed him to, and she wouldn't let that happen because she was a Vayle, and Vayles had their pride.

They were all quiet now as they tried to come to grips with the incredible story she'd told them. She could have wept at the change in them. This wasn't how they'd looked the last time they had a family conference. They'd been sitting at her dining room table in her house in Bath, and she'd felt intimidated, as she usually did, by the force of their personalities. Now they looked as helpless as children. She would have given anything to have things back the way they were, before this nightmare burst upon them.

"I wonder," said Daniel, breaking the long silence, "if you did the right thing, Abbie. Maybe you should have told this Maitland fellow the whole story. These people have the resources. If anyone can find George, they can."

"I did try to tell Maitland." she said. "I told him that George was involved against his will. But Maitland only laughed and said that's what everyone says when they're caught. Then later," she shook her head, "I began to think maybe Maitland was right, that George was a conspirator too. I was terrified that if they found him, they would shoot him on sight."

"Abbie!" cried her mother, deeply shocked. "How could you think such a thing of your own brother?"

"Newgate will do that to you," said Abbie, and was sorry she had said so much when she saw the look of grief that convulsed her mother's face.

Giles quickly interposed, "What do you think now, Abbie?"

"George is innocent. There's no doubt in my mind. He would never have involved me in such an ugly business if he'd had any choice. No, I'm the one who got *him* involved because of that—that book." She looked directly at Daniel. "But George means nothing to Maitland—it doesn't matter to Maitland whether George was abducted or if he's a conspirator. I saw what happened to those young men this morning when the soldiers tried to arrest them, and if I can help it, it won't happen to George. I don't trust Maitland and his crew any more than I trust George's abductors."

Daniel's face was ashen. "You see what this means? When George's abductors find out that Abbie no longer has the book—that the authorities have it . . ." He looked at his mother, and broke off.

"What?" asked Lady Clivendon. Her voice rose in her alarm. "Daniel, finish what you were going to say." As she worked it out for herself, her face crumpled. "They'll have no reason to keep George alive. That's it, isn't it?"

When Lady Clivendon burst into tears, Harriet sent her brother a withering look and went to comfort her mother.

Giles said, "Let's stay calm. Let's not allow our imaginations to run away with us. And let's not look for trouble before it finds us. As far as we know, George is alive. If we accept that, then we can do something to find him. But if we lose hope, we'll be of no use to anyone, least of all George."

Lady Clivendon dried her tears, and Harriet threw her husband a grateful look. Abbie felt grateful to Giles as well. Her hope of saving George had been almost extinguished when Hugh gave the book to Maitland. Now her hopes began to revive.

Lady Clivendon spoke in a quavering voice. "Then what's to be done, Giles? Where do we begin to look?"

Giles smiled at Abbie. "Oh, I think Abbie should answer that. She's had more time to think about it than we have. And, if I'm not mistaken, I believe she has a plan."

She was nervous, because everyone was looking at her, and in the old days, her opinions hadn't counted for much. "It's not much of a plan," she said, "but I think it might work with a bit of luck." She breathed deeply, then went on, "What if I were to do exactly what George's abductors told me to do? What if I were to place the advertisement in *The Times*?"

"But you don't have the book," said Harriet.

"They might not know that. And I would think they'd want to make sure before they do anything drastic. I'll demand to see George before I hand over the book. Then we'll have to figure out what to do from there."

"In spite of your misgivings, Abbie," said Daniel, "I still think our best bet is to go to the authorities."

"What could they do that they're not doing now? I mean, they're already looking for George, and the men who abducted him. What have we got to lose?"

Giles said, "She has a point."

There was an interval of silence, then Daniel said, "And if no one answers the advertisement, what then?"

Then she really would give up hope. "It's possible that George has managed to get away from his abductors. Maybe he's in hiding. Maybe he thinks the house is being watched and he's afraid to show his face. I don't know. I just don't know. But I do know that we can't sit around here waiting for the world to end. We've got to do something. And I say we make it as easy as possible for George to find us."

Harriet said uncertainly, "But Abbie, we've already looked everywhere for George, and we haven't found him."

"Let Abbie finish," said her ladyship. "Go on, Abbie. How do we make it easy for George to find us?"

"We do what we usually do when we're in London. We go out and about. We go to the theater, the opera, to balls and parties. George knows this. If he's afraid to come to the house, he'll look for us there."

Everyone saw they had little to lose by going along with Abbie's plan. They saw something else in Abbie. The shattering experience she'd come through, far from breaking her, had made her stronger.

Daniel blew out a stream of smoke, then went to the window and opened it. "Mother hates the smell of tobacco," he said.

Giles drew on his cheroot and exhaled with slow pleasure. "You're lucky," he said. "Harriet won't let me smoke in the house."

Daniel smiled. "I know. I see you sometimes when I look out the window. Rain or shine, after dinner, there goes poor Giles in the garden enjoying a solitary cigar."

"That's the trouble with living next door to your relatives," said Giles reflectively. "You can't have any secrets."

"Then why did you buy the house next door?"

"Harriet wanted to be close to her mother. And it's a convenient location for Whitehall and the shops. Harriet loves to shop."

Daniel shook his head. "Though she is my own sister, sometimes I wonder why you put up with her."

Giles said, "Oh, she suits me in other ways."

This was said with a big smile on his face, and Daniel, to cover his embarrassment, pretended that his cigar had gone out, and used a taper to light it again.

"I have to say this, Giles. I'm surprised that you went along with Abbie's desire not to call in the authorities. They have the resources, and they know what they're doing. We're the blind leading the blind."

"By 'the authorities,' you mean magistrates and constables?"

"Of course."

"But they're not the ones who would be investigating this case. This is no ordinary crime. We're dealing with national security, and there's a special branch of investigators that handles that."

"How do you know?"

Giles stretched out his legs in front of the fire. "I work for the Prime Minister. Anything worth knowing always stops at the Prime Minister's desk."

Daniel turned his head and stared at his brother-in-law with an oddly arrested expression. "I had not realized you were so well connected at Whitehall."

"Oh, I'm not. But an aide gets to hear things. You know how it is."

"No, I don't think I do know."

"I keep my eyes and ears open. That's all I meant. Now, where was I? Oh, yes. These special investigators play by their own rules, and it's a dirty game, as Abbie discovered. I think she's right. They won't care what happens to George. They're after bigger fry."

Daniel said bleakly, "Are you saying there's no hope for George, that we might as well give up?"

Giles's voice softened. "No," he said, "we won't give up. Abbie has the right idea. At the very least, she's going to keep everyone busy and keep family morale up. And I have a few ideas of my own."

"Like what, for instance?"

Giles hesitated, then said, "How serious were you when you said you would challenge Templar to a duel?"

"I was never more serious in my life."

"I wouldn't if I were you," said Giles. "In the first place, Abbie would never forgive you."

Daniel protested, "She expects it! She would applaud!"

"Are you sure of that?"

"She said so! We both heard her."

"Yes, she said it today. But what would she say tomorrow, or next week, or next month? Take it from one who knows, Abbie would never forgive you."

Daniel took a moment to digest this, then said cautiously, "You said 'in the first place.' What's the other reason to stop me from giving that snake what he deserves?"

"Only this," said Giles. "I'm counting on Templar to help us find George."

CHAPTER 20

They quickly put Abbie's plan into action. Within hours of arriving home, she had visited *The Times* offices and placed her advertisement. The next order of business was to acquire suitable clothes, for most of her garments remained in Bath or had been lost on the trip to London. Again, Harriet surprised her, offering to let her pick out whatever she needed from her closets. While the ladies trooped over to Harriet's house to go through her wardrobe, the gentlemen followed their normal routine. Giles went to his office in Downing Street, and Daniel went off to his club in St. James's.

They met again at dinner and compared notes. Giles was the only one with any real information. There was a rumor circulating around Whitehall, he said, that some notorious French spy had arrived in England. The special branch people were looking for him and his accomplices. Meanwhile, as a precaution, extra security measures had been taken to protect the royal family and the Prime Minister.

"So you see," he said to Abbie, "how lucky you were

that Templar interceded for you. If he hadn't, the charges against you would be very serious."

This observation was met by stony silence.

Taking this as encouragement, Giles went on, "I'm wondering whether we shouldn't ask Templar to help us. Considering what you learned about his background, Abbie, it sounds like he'd be the perfect person to help us find George."

This suggestion acted on all present as though a firecracker had been tossed among them. Everyone spoke at once. Hugh Templar was beneath contempt. What he had done to Abbie was unconscionable. The man was not to be trusted. Someone should put a bullet in his brain, or run him through with a sword. No Vayle would ever speak to him again.

Abbie had the last word, and her paper-white cheeks and the haunted look in her eyes added to the weight of what she had to say. "Did he do us a good turn, Giles? How can you be sure? Isn't it possible that they let me go so that I could lead them to George? I wouldn't be surprised if they're watching the house right now. I wouldn't be surprised if I'm followed wherever I go. Time will tell. And I assure you, I didn't take any chances this morning when I went to *The Times* offices, and I won't be taking any chances in the future."

She looked around the table, and her eyes filled with tears. "I'm not prepared to trust Hugh Templar. In fact, the only people I'm willing to trust are the people in this room, the people I love and who love me."

Her words affected each person powerfully, but before they were overcome with emotion, she brought them up short. "Keep in mind that we've embarked on something dangerous. I'm not thinking only of Maitland and his people. I cannot forget that I was assaulted in my own house." She breathed deeply to steady herself as the memory of that night came back to her. "These are desperate men. They won't hesitate to kill anyone who gets in their way. Harriet, you and the children can't stay here. It's not safe. I would feel much easier in my mind, if you and Mama and the girls were to go to your place in Oxfordshire until this is over."

This provoked another emotional outburst. Harriet didn't mind sending away her daughters, who could go to Giles's mother in Henley. But her own place was at her sister's side, and nothing would change her mind. Her ladyship expressed the same passionate opinion. Vayles stuck together.

The ladies dabbed their eyes with their napkins; Daniel and Giles refilled their glasses of brandy. Then they began to map out their strategy.

In the week that followed, Abbie and her family were to be seen everywhere. During the day they went shopping or riding or driving in Hyde Park; they made calls on friends and acquaintances. At night, when Giles was free to join them, they went to the theater or to the pleasure gardens at Vauxhall; they went to musicales and parties. There had never been a London season where Vayles were so visible.

And where they went, so did their shadow.

"One of Maitland's crew," said Giles, surreptitiously looking down on the street from one of the upstairs bedrooms of Vayle House.

Abbie twitched the curtain and looked down on the man who was strolling past the house.

"I think it's horrible," said Harriet.

"No," said Giles. "It means they think George is still alive."

Inevitably, they ran into Hugh. The first time Abbie came face-to-face with him was in Bond Street, when she and Harriet were shopping. He was with Barbara Munro and had just exited from an exclusive millinery shop, followed by a footman laden with hatboxes. When he saw Abbie, his jaw dropped.

Recovering himself, he left Miss Munro's side and approached Abbie. Without a pretense of civility, he said, "What the devil are you doing in London? I thought you would have the sense to go home to Bath."

Abbie's only response was to give him "the cut direct." She linked her arm through Harriet's and, as though he were invisible, embarked on an animated discussion of the weather.

She heard Hugh come after her, but Daniel was watching for them from the carriage. He quickly alighted and blocked Hugh's path.

"So that's the way of it," said Hugh quietly, taking in Daniel's belligerent stance, then turned and went back to Miss Munro.

After that, whenever their paths crossed, which happened too frequently for Abbie's comfort, they might have been icebergs passing in the night. She discovered, however, that though she could avoid looking at Hugh, she could not always avoid hearing about him, as on the night they attended Mrs. Montague's musicale.

It was during the intermission, when Daniel and Giles had wandered off to the billiard room for a smoke, that she heard the first titillating piece of gossip. She and her mother and sister were replenishing their punch glasses at the refreshments table, when they were joined by Lady Greer. Hugh was somewhere in the crush, and though Abbie hadn't seen him for over an hour, her un-erring instinct told her he was at one of the windows that overlooked Hyde Park.

Lady Greer was one of her mother's cronies, and Abbie scarcely heard a word until Hugh's name was men-tioned. No one was sure, confided Lady Greer, whether his affair with Barbara Munro was blowing hot or cold. But she had heard from her modiste, who was also Miss Munro's modiste, that the actress was spending money like water, and Hugh Templar was footing the bill. On the other hand—she glanced over Abbie's shoulder to the window that overlooked the park—what was he doing here, at a boring musicale, where only virtuous ladies were to be found? And why was he spending all his nights at White's, gaming his fortune away, when Miss Munro had a snug little house on the edge of Mayfair?

The ironclad smile that Abbie had been wearing all evening remained intact. She was determined that noth-ing concerning Hugh Templar would ever shake her composure again. She'd walled him off in the deepest, darkest recesses of her mind, and that's where he would remain.

Her sister was not so controlled. When Lady Greer moved away, it was obvious that Harriet was seething. "And to think," she exclaimed, "that we all had such hopes that Abbie could bring him up to scratch. I was never more deceived in a man's character in my life. Thank God, Abbie, that you were not in love with him."

Lady Clivendon glanced in Hugh's direction. "There was always something about him I did not like. He's a cold man. Our Abbie could never be happy with a cold man."

Abbie heartily agreed with them and quickly steered the conversation into less turbulent waters. She was fighting a losing battle, because there were others who took up where her mother and sister left off. By the time she arrived home, she'd heard enough about Hugh Templar to last her a lifetime.

One thing had been made patently clear to her: the Hugh Templar who had resided in Bath was not the Hugh Templar who was known in London. He was a dangerous charmer; he was a shameless flirt; every young woman's heart beat just a little faster when he walked into a room. And if it was true that his affair with Barbara Munro was over, he'd have all the bold hussies as well as matrons with marriageable daughters throwing out lures to him.

Not all women are like you, Abbie. As a rule, they're not interested in the breadth of my knowledge, the scope of my interests, or my prodigious . . . ah . . . intelligence. They want a man who knows how to charm a woman.

And she'd thought that Hugh Templar did not possess a sense of humor. Well, the laugh was on her.

As one day slipped into the next and there was no reply to her advertisement, and not one word or sign from George, Abbie's hopes began to falter. She awoke each morning feeling dead inside. What kept her going was sheer force of will. Everyone's hopes were pinned on the strategy she had mapped out. So she dragged herself out of bed, saw to her toilette, and after consulting her calendar, dressed for whatever event she had marked down for the day. Then she pinned her ironclad smile to her face and sallied forth.

She was close to the breaking point, and that point came when she was riding in Hyde Park with Harriet. She suddenly drew rein and looked around her as though she were lost. She noted that the trees were in bud, and beneath them, the first crocuses and hyacinths were just coming out. It was late in the afternoon, and the promise of spring had drawn many people out of doors. She saw riders and pedestrians and carriages of every description.

"What are we doing here?" she asked.

Harriet had stopped a few yards farther on. She turned her mount and trotted back. "What is it, Abbie? What's wrong?"

Abbie repeated her question.

Harriet said, "Don't you remember, dear? Mama is making her afternoon calls, Giles is at the office, and Daniel has gone to Tattersalls, you know, in case George shows up there."

"What on earth made him think that George would show up at Tattersalls?"

"Because that's where gentlemen gather, you know, to buy and sell horses."

"But we don't need any horses."

A look of alarm crossed Harriet's face. "Are you all right, Abbie?"

Abbie looked around the park as in a daze. When she turned back to Harriet, tears were streaming down her face. "Why did you listen to me?" she cried out. "This is a harebrained scheme. George will never show up, and do you know why?"

"Don't say it, Abbie!" cried Harriet. "Don't you dare say it!"

"Dear God, I shouldn't have to say it. More than a week has passed. A week! You were mad to listen to me. Didn't you realize I was just clutching at straws? George is never coming back."

With that, she dug in her heels and sent her horse plunging across the turf. They bolted through a strand of plane trees at the edge of the drive, straight into the path of an oncoming curricle. Abbie's mount reared up, almost unseating her. The driver of the curricle swerved to the right, avoiding her by inches, and the curricle came to a grinding halt. With a roar of rage, the driver jumped down and started to berate her.

Abbie stared at him with blank, hollow eyes, then she sent her horse flying across the turf.

Hugh witnessed the accident. He was coming from the other direction, driving his curricle, and Barbara Munro was sitting beside him. She recognized the girl on the horse and gave Hugh a sideways glance.

He reined in his team of chestnuts and stared after Abbie till she was lost to view.

The lighting became her. In fact, everything in Barbara's house became her and had been chosen as a backdrop to show off her dramatic, dark beauty. The walls, the carpets, the upholstery, were in varying shades of gold. Her ermine-trimmed pelisse and matching muff, for which he'd paid a pretty penny, were in wintry white, and a startling contrast to the furnishings. He almost missed the maid who was kneeling in front of the grate adding coal to the fire. Her uniform matched the backdrop, and she seemed to fade into it.

It was like watching a performance on stage, thought Hugh. Barbara couldn't help herself. As the maid murmured a greeting, her mistress deliberately stole the scene by gracefully removing her pelisse as she glided across the room. The gown beneath the pelisse was a midnight blue velvet, again, a contrast to the backdrop.

It was all very amusing. And very tiresome.

"Mary, dispose of these. I'll ring if I need anything."

Her voice matched the velvet of her gown, and she

knew just how to use it to play on the emotions of her audience. And that's what he was, he supposed—an audience of one.

When they were alone, he moved to the sideboard, opened a door, and removed a decanter of whiskey and a crystal glass. Having poured himself a drink, he seated himself on one of the gold chairs. At least the chair was comfortable.

"We have to talk," he said.

She laughed lightly, crossed to him, and boxed him in by placing one hand on each arm of the chair. "Let's talk later," she murmured.

She took his mouth with a skill and thoroughness that left him shaken. She was trying to seduce him. It couldn't work, not only because he didn't want to be seduced, but because he was remembering another seduction, one that owed nothing to skill or art.

When she raised her head, she was smiling, but her eyes were cold. "All right," she said, "we'll talk first."

She disposed herself gracefully on the chair facing his. He had to give credit where credit was due. Barbara never did anything without grace. He was counting on that grace to get them both out of an awkward situation that was entirely of his making.

After taking a fortifying swallow from his glass, he said, "Barbara, this isn't going to work. It's not you, it's me. I should have told you that there's another woman involved. I think you must have guessed. I'm suggesting that we cut our losses and part as friends."

The losses, he wryly reflected, were all on his side. The amount of money she'd spent on clothes this last week could have kept Abbie in style for a year. All he'd got out of it were a few glasses of whiskey and the pleasure of squiring Barbara around town. But that wasn't Barbara's fault. Every time he kissed her or touched her, he'd sensed Abbie right there beside him, looking over his shoulder.

It played hell with a man's love life.

Barbara must have known something was wrong. He'd dropped her off at her house every evening before taking off on a scouting expedition to find Abbie. She wasn't hard to find. He knew whose parties the Vayles were likely to attend, and though sometimes he had to attend several, in the end he'd always found her.

It amazed him that he went to so much trouble. He didn't know what in Hades he was playing at. Here he was, seeking her out, and she looked through him as if he were a plate-glass window. He must be out of his mind.

Suddenly conscious that Barbara was waiting for him to reply to something she'd said, he coughed into his hand, then said, "Beg pardon?"

"Are we talking about the girl in the park?"

His eyelids drooped. "I saw many ladies in the park when we were out driving."

"Yes, but only one Abigail Vayle."

He set his glass to his lips and took another healthy swallow.

When it was evident that he wasn't going to respond, she said, "I realize that a man of your rank must eventually marry, but Hugh, you could do much better for yourself."

"Could I?" he murmured.

Encouraged, she went on. "Her family has been trying to launch her for years, without success. She's an eccentric, a confirmed old maid. She has no style; she doesn't know how to dress. She'd be an embarrassment to a man in your position."

His expression remained pleasant. "There's more to Miss Vayle than you realize. She has many fine qualities I admire."

"Like what, for instance?"

She was genuinely amused, and that annoyed him. "Would you believe," he said, "her intelligence? Her curiosity? The scope of her interests? Her knowledge of books?" *Her warmth, her softness, her boundless passion for life, her passion.*

When he smiled to himself, her dark brows winged upward. "That won't hold you, Hugh. Not for long."

"And you know me so well?"

She rose in one fluid movement and crossed to the sideboard. After pouring herself a drink, she returned to the hearth and knelt at this feet. Her appeal really was staggering. Large, expressive blue eyes fringed by long dark lashes gazed invitingly into his. She was offering herself to him, and he might have been tempted if he could have convinced himself that there was some genuine feeling behind the offer.

After studying her for several moments, he said, "How do you see me, Barbara? I mean, what kind of man am I, in your opinion?"

A slow smile curved her generous mouth. The velvet in her voice turned to silk. "Dangerous. Easily provoked to violence or passion. A ruthless warrior. An insatiable lover. The kind of man a woman dreams of in her deepest, darkest fantasies."

He was repelled, but not surprised. She wasn't the first woman who had wanted to share his bed because she believed he was barely civilized. "And you think I'm that kind of man?"

"I know it."

"What if I were to tell you that I'm not like that at all,

that I prefer books to people, that I'm never happier than when I'm digging around in the dirt, looking for broken pottery and old coins?"

"I'd say you were lying. Is that how Miss Vayle sees you? If she knew what you were really like, she'd be overcome with terror."

They'd bandied about Abbie's name too much for his comfort. He chuckled, and said easily, "The man you describe fills me with terror as well. I have something for you."

He reached in his pocket and produced a black velvet box. She took it from him, opened it, and stared down at the diamond bracelet inside. It was a parting gift, and they both knew it.

She looked at him curiously. "Is this really necessary? So marry Miss Vayle. Your marriage need not affect our arrangement."

"And you wouldn't mind?"

"Why should I? It's the way of our world."

His answering smile was touched with cynicism. "So it is. But it's not the way of Miss Vayle's world. My dear, she would kill me. Anyway, this conversation is pointless. I'm not marrying Miss Vayle."

"I see."

She rose and went to stand at the window, with her back to him. In a voice he'd never heard before, she said, "If you are so besotted with the chit, why did you take up with me again?"

"Besotted?" He looked at her with a pained expression, as though she'd just said a four-lettered Anglo-Saxon word. "I don't know where you got that idea. The truth is, I'd like to wring her neck."

She had turned to face him, and because he felt he had treated her badly and owed her an explanation, he elaborated. "We had a difference of opinion, a serious difference of opinion on a matter of principle. She was in the wrong. There's no doubt about that."

"So you decided to—how did you put it?—cut your losses?"

"That's it exactly."

It was only when he was making for home in his curricle that it occurred to him that he didn't give a damn anymore who was in the wrong.

Abbie stormed into the house and stopped in the hallway to pick up the post. She quickly riffled through the letters, but there was nothing addressed to her, and nothing that looked interesting or out of the ordinary. She flung the letters down on the hall table and went tearing up the stairs.

She heard Harriet calling her name as she pushed into her chamber, but she was beside herself and could hardly breathe, much less answer anyone. As she crossed the threshold, she began to tear off her clothes. *Harriet's clothes*, she mechanically corrected herself. She was all dolled up in her sister's finery. What was the point? *What was the point?*

A few moments later, Harriet burst into her room. She looked as wild as Abbie. Her hair was undone, her bonnet listed perilously to one side of her head, and her eyes were red with crying. "Abbie, what's wrong?" she cried. "What's wrong with you?"

Abbie pointed to the riding habit she'd just pulled over her head and flung on the bed. Through great wrenching gasps, she got out, "I . . . hate . . . puce."

"Puce? You mean the color?"

Abbie nodded.

"But you chose it yourself. And the color suits you."

Abbie stamped her foot.

Harriet put out both hands in a placating gesture. "Don't move. Just stay as you are. I'm going to get you a large glass of brandy. All right?"

When she rushed from the room, Abbie sank into a chair and covered her face with her hands. She couldn't breathe. She was going to suffocate. Why couldn't she breathe?

Then Harriet was there, pushing away her hands, forcing brandy past her lips. Abbie gagged, then swallowed.

"More," said Harriet, and tipped up the glass.

The brandy burned her throat. She didn't like it. But it worked. When she pushed Harriet's hand away, she could breathe again.

Harriet thrust the glass at Abbie. "Drink the rest of it," she said. "You're shivering. I'll get your dressing gown."

Abbie sipped on the brandy as Harriet went to the wardrobe. The dressing gown was puce too, and though she knew she was being absurdly childish, she cried even harder.

When Abbie was wrapped up in the dressing gown, Harriet pulled up a chair and prompted her to drink down the brandy every time she tried to lay the glass aside. Gradually, Abbie stopped shivering; her breathing became regular; her tears dried; and the madness that had possessed her faded, leaving her spent and without hope.

After a long silence, Harriet looked anxiously into Abbie's eyes. "You didn't mean what you said back there at the park, did you, Abbie?"

Abbie stared at the glass in her hand. She said miserably, "Harriet, we've got to face facts. There's been no reply to my advertisement. No one has tried to approach us, and we've given them every opportunity. A week has gone by, more than a week." She looked up at Harriet, and the words of finality, of hopelessness, died unsaid. But her silence spoke for her.

Harriet shook her head. "You heard what Giles said. We shouldn't go looking for trouble. And nothing has changed, has it? We're all being watched by Maitland's people, and that's a good sign. And if George were dead, surely his body would have turned up by now?"

A look of horror crossed her face, as though by voicing that last thought she had made George's death more real. "No," she moaned, "I won't believe it. He can't be dead. It will kill our mother." She dug her nails into her arms as if she wanted to hurt herself. "And I'll never have the chance to tell George how sorry I am."

"Sorry?" said Abbie. "Sorry for what?"

"For all the unkind things I ever said to him." Harriet bent her head in shame and began to rock. "I was always making fun of him, even when we were children. And later, when he became interested in painting and . . . and landscape gardening, I made fun of that too." Tears splashed onto her hands. "But I didn't mean it, Abbie. I just wanted him to find a profession that would make him secure."

Abbie set down her glass and went to kneel by her sister's chair. She put her arms around Harriet's shoulders and rocked with her. "I'm sure he understood that, Harriet. I know I did."

Harriet went on as though she had not heard. "Don't you remember how it was when Papa died? Mama was always in tears, and Daniel was preoccupied. We couldn't spend a penny because we were so deep in debt. I used to lie awake at night worrying about it."

Abbie remembered having to do without, but it had

never affected her to this degree. She was ashamed now that she had been blind to her sister's pain. "You should have told me," she said.

"Haven't you ever wondered why I like shopping so much? It's to make up for all the things we had to do without." Harriet looked up and managed a tired smile. "It's taken something like this to make me see how foolish I've been. Money isn't everything. We should enjoy each other, don't you think? I don't care if George turns out to be a gardener, or a painter, or even a dancing master. I don't want to lecture him, or tell him how to live his life. Giles says that's one of my failings, always thinking I know what's best for everyone. Well, I've learned my lesson. I just want to see his face and know that he's all right."

"I think he *is* all right."

"What?"

"You said something just now that jogged my memory." Abbie straightened and rubbed her brow as she searched for the memory.

"What did I say?" asked Harriet, finally losing patience.

"You said that if George were dead, his body would have been found by now, and you were right." Abbie's voice became more animated. "That awful man who assaulted me in my bed? He said that if I crossed him he would . . . well, he would punish me by . . . by hurting George. He'd want me to know, don't you see?"

"No, I don't see."

"It's hard to explain. He—" Abbie shook her head as she groped for words. "No one ever crosses him and gets away with it, and he thinks I crossed him in Paris when Colette passed me the book." She paused, then said in a surprised tone. "He *hates* me and wants to hurt me. No, 'hate' isn't the right word. He despises me. He wants me to know how powerful he is. The point is, if he'd done anything to George, he'd want me to know."

Harriet caught Abbie's hands and held on to them. "Abbie, I don't like the sound of him. What can we do against someone like that?"

"We'll talk about it tonight, when we're together as a family."

"Giles thinks we should ask Hugh Templar to help us. I don't like him any more than you do, but for George's sake, I'd be willing to bury our differences."

A shutter came down on Abbie's face. Just to hear Hugh's name mentioned was like pouring acid in an open wound. She'd been hurt before, but those other times she'd managed to put a face on things. She couldn't put a face on this, couldn't make light of it, couldn't fall back on bravado. The only way she could cope was not to think of Hugh at all. And there wasn't one hour in the day when she did not think of him.

Both women turned to face the door when they heard their names being called. "It sounds like Daniel," said Harriet. She went to the door and opened it. "We're up here, Daniel."

There was the rush of feet pounding up the stairs, then Daniel burst into the room. He was breathless and flushed, and waved an envelope under their noses. "Abbie, you were right," he said. "No, George wasn't at Tattersalls. But this note is from him. It's in answer to the advertisement."

She took the envelope out of his hand. "But how did you get hold of it?" Her heart was pounding.

"At Tattersalls, I put down my catalogue to examine a bay gelding, and when I picked it up again, that envelope was tucked inside. There's no doubt the letter is from George. He's alive. Read it and see for yourself."

With trembling fingers, she opened the envelope. Inside was a folded sheet of vellum. She smoothed it out and began to read.

Bea,

   I knew you wouldn't let me down. I'll be waiting for you at the second intermission in Box 10 at the King's Theater on Wednesday night. The Clandestine Marriage. Isn't that one of your favorite plays? Don't forget to bring the book.

George

CHAPTER 21

"Not the puce, Harriet. I don't think I could bear to wear it."

Harriet draped the puce silk evening gown over the back of a chair and glanced at Abbie. "I wasn't thinking of the puce for you, but for myself. But you know, Abbie, it occurs to me that if I'm going to pass myself off as you and you're going to pass yourself off as me, you should dress in colors I like and vice versa, if you see what I mean."

"I do see what you mean, Harriet, and I agree, but not the puce. It depresses me. Now, what else do you have for me to try on?"

They were in Harriet's house, in her bedchamber, selecting the gowns they would wear to the King's Theater tomorrow night. It was Harriet's idea that they should impersonate each other. That way, she said, if Maitland's people were watching, they'd be looking at her while Abbie slipped away to Box 10. Their mother had contributed the blond and black wigs that would complete their costumes, wigs, she'd said with a faraway look in her eyes, that she'd worn as a young woman when she first met their father and they fell in love. Those were the days, according to the dowager, when men were men and ladies knew how to be women.

Harriet said, "Giles thought you might like the silver tissue. It's memorable, so when people see it, they'll know it's my gown and they'll think you're me. At least from a distance."

The gown she held up for Abbie's inspection was a pale gray gauze, shot through with silver threads. Scattered on the bodice and around the hem were silver satin appliquéd leaves.

Abbie stared at the gown and looked up at her sister. "I can't accept the gown," she said.

"Why can't you?"

"It's too . . . beautiful, too costly. I would never have a moment's peace all night, wondering if I was going to tear the hem or spill something on it."

"I don't care about that."

"Hah! You say that now, but what will you say when you see the tear on the hem?"

Harriet's brows rushed together. "A fine opinion you have of me! I don't know why I bother. Can't you see that I've changed? What must I do to convince you?"

Abbie retreated a little. "You've been wonderful, Harriet. I couldn't ask for a better sister. And really, I wouldn't blame you for being cross if I ruined your dress. Anyone would be. It's a beautiful dress. But you must have something less . . . well . . . irreplaceable for me to wear?"

A reluctant smile tugged at Harriet's lips.

"What?" asked Abbie.

"It's not irreplaceable."

"Not?"

"No. Giles has promised that if anything happens to it, he'll have my modiste make up an exact copy, and he doesn't care how much it costs. So you see, you can wear it with a clear conscience."

Abbie ground her teeth together, reached for a cushion, and threw it at Harriet. Then both girls began to laugh. As quickly as the laughter had sprung up, it died away.

"How can we laugh at a time like this?" asked Harriet.

"I don't know. Maybe it's because we have hope now, and we didn't have much to hope for before."

"It's going to be all right, isn't it, Abbie?"

"I . . . Of course it's going to be all right."

"Yes, but so many things can go wrong."

Abbie was well aware of it. George's message implied that he would be waiting for her in the box at the theater, but she couldn't believe that it would be that easy. His abductors would want to verify that the book she would hand over was the genuine article. Giles had scoured the bookshops and found a French translation of the *Illiad* that he'd doctored to make as near to the original as Abbie remembered. He'd even invented a code to make notations in the margins. The most she could hope for was that the exchange would be made before his abductors realized they'd been duped.

She struggled to produce a smile and finally managed it. "It's the book they want, and when I hand it over, I'm sure they'll let George go. Besides, what can they do in a crowded theater? They'd be fools to try anything, and these people are no fools."

"That may be, but it sounds too easy for my liking."

Abbie avoided a discussion that could only add to her panic by changing the subject. "Do you know how lucky you are to have Giles for a husband? Not many men I know spoil their wives as he spoils you." She was fingering the delicate silver tissue gown that Harriet had spread out on the bed. "And he's such a wonderful father, so patient with Lizzie and Vicki. No wonder the girls adore him. I sometimes regret," she went on, "that I did not snap him up while I had the chance."

Harriet blinked. "You do? I thought—" she cleared her throat, "I thought that was water under the bridge, Abbie. I thought you had forgiven me for taking Giles away from you."

"Well, I had," said Abbie, "but that was before I knew how rich he was."

There was a long, uneasy silence, then Harriet giggled. "You're teasing me!"

"Of course I'm teasing you, ninny. But I am envious of you, and if I could find someone as nice as Giles, I'd snap him up in a minute."

"You're not really envious, Abbie, are you?"

Abbie looked up from the satin leaf she had been idly tracing. "Why should that surprise you?"

"No reason." Harriet shrugged. "It just seems so strange to hear you say those words. I thought you were happy. I thought you had everything you wanted."

"What I have," said Abbie dryly, "hardly compares to a wonderful husband who dotes on me and two beautiful and charming infant daughters. I'd have to be an idiot not to envy you."

Harriet edged onto the bed. "We never did get around to talking about—" she coughed delicately, "Giles and me. I couldn't help falling in love with him, you know. He made me feel . . . I don't know . . . good about myself, I suppose."

"Oh, he did, did he?" Abbie's voice was now as dry as a desert.

Harriet nodded. "Giles taught me that though I could never be as clever as you, I wasn't as stupid as I thought I was."

Abbie said slowly, "Harriet, you were never stupid."

"That's easy for you to say. You got all the brains in the family!"

"And you got all the beauty! Men were always falling all over you, even before you were out of the schoolroom."

"Yes, and what a curse that can be! It wasn't me they wanted! They didn't care if I was stupid. In fact, they preferred me that way. I was just an ornament to them. But not to Giles."

A picture formed in Abbie's mind. She was remembering Giles after that first dinner at Vayle House, telling her that Harriet wasn't anything like he'd expected. She wasn't the least bit conceited, said Giles. In fact, she was just the opposite. And she'd wondered if they were speaking about the same Harriet. "I always thought—"

"What?"

She looked at Harriet. "That you beauties had an easy time of it."

"And I always thought that you clever girls had an easy time of it. I'd open my mouth and say something stupid and everyone would laugh. I would have given anything to be more like you."

"And I would have given anything to be more like you."

There was a moment of silence as both girls smiled. Then a thought occurred to Abbie and her brows rushed together. "You don't have to say all this, you know. I got over Giles a long time ago."

Harriet beamed. "That's what I wanted to know. But I wasn't lying just now. I really did envy you when we were girls. Well, you must have noticed how I'm bringing up my own daughters. I want them to be educated like you, Abbie. No one is going to laugh at my Lizzie or Vicki when they open their mouths."

"What on earth," said Abbie emphatically, "has brought this on?"

Harriet sighed. "George, I suppose. It could have been you, or Giles, or Daniel. I don't know how to explain it, except to say that it's shaken me. I've done more soul-searching in the last week than I've done in my entire life. If you promise not to laugh, I would tell you—" she looked suspiciously at Abbie.

"Tell me what?" asked Abbie.

"You'll only laugh."

"I promise I won't."

Harriet hesitated, then blurted out, "That I love you."

Abbie flattened her lips, but a moment later she began to laugh.

"You're just like Daniel!" exclaimed Harriet wrathfully.

"What? Did you tell him that you love him too?"

"I hate you, I really hate you."

"It's nerves," Abbie cried out as a pillow came flying. "Sheer nerves! Honestly, Harriet, I love you too."

They were brought up short by a knock on the door. Harriet answered it. The elderly footman who entered shocked them both when he politely droned that Mr. Hugh Templar was waiting downstairs and wished to speak to Miss Vayle.

Abbie's eyes flew to Harriet's. "How did he know I was in your house?"

Harriet shrugged. "I suppose one of the servants told him."

"You may tell him, Brewster," said Abbie, looking at the footman, "that Miss Vayle is not at home."

Brewster said apologetically, "It won't do no good, miss. Mr. Templar said that if you refused to see him, he would search the house until he found you."

Color was high on Abbie's cheeks, and there was a militant light in her eyes. "In that case," she said, "you may tell Mr. Templar I shall be down in a few minutes."

When the footman bowed himself out of the room, Abbie went to the mirror and ran a comb through her hair. Harriet said, "I wonder what he wants. You don't think—"

"What?"

"Maybe he knows something about George or the men who abducted him. Giles said that when he was riding in Whitehall this morning, he saw Templar coming from the Horse Guards. He's still on the best of terms with his commanding officer, Colonel Something-or-Other."

"Langley?"

"Yes, that's it."

Abbie looked at Harriet with a startled expression. "Then I'd better find out."

"I'll come with you."

"No. He may not speak freely in front of you, but don't be too far away in case I need you."

She walked into the front parlor believing that she had a tight grip on her emotions, but when he turned at her entrance, all the anguish of betrayed love invaded every part of her as easily as fog penetrates a fortress. She could feel it in her fingers, in her belly, in her throat, behind her eyes.

Gritting her teeth, she fought against the pain. She'd

told herself time out of mind that she didn't know this man, that the man she had fallen in love with was a figment of her imagination. She'd relived every moment of the indignities she suffered after he handed her over to Maitland. Her dreams were invaded by the sightless faces of the young men who had died in the house in Chapel Street. The stench of Newgate could never be washed from her skin. Any sane woman would want to drive a dagger through his black heart. All she wanted was to curl up and die.

Had it not been for George, she would have turned on her heel and run from the room. The last words she spoke to Hugh Templar outside the customs house in Dover had been a plea for help. She'd begged him, with tears running down her face, and he had walked away without looking back once. She'd promised herself she would never willingly speak to him again. Only her anxiety for her brother could make her go through with this.

She did not invite him to sit, but for George's sake, she tried to maintain a neutral expression. "What is it you wish to say to me?" she asked.

He spoke easily and without embarrassment, as though nothing had happened between them. "I saw Colonel Langley this morning, and some interesting facts came to light."

Her heart lurched, and she clutched the back of the chair for support. "What facts?"

He studied her for a moment. "Why didn't you tell me that you didn't write that letter to Michael Lovatt?"

This wasn't what she expected to hear, and she said blankly, "What letter?"

"You know what letter! The one Miss Fairbairn wrote in her usual vague way, then signed with *your* name."

"Oh, that letter." He had no news of George. She didn't know whether to be relieved or let down. "Olivia always signs my name to our business letters. Does it matter?"

"Of course it matters. It was because of that letter that British intelligence was convinced that you were trying to sell the book to the highest bidder."

"I wasn't."

"No," he said softly. "I realize that now."

She didn't want his approval; she didn't want anything from this man. "Is that all you came to tell me?"

"No. Your maid has exonerated you as well. She told a very interesting story of how you came to have rooms in the attics of the Castle Inn. It was so farfetched that Langley didn't believe it until I told him it was just like you to pass yourself off as a duchess's servant."

"How does that exonerate me?"

"Ballard's body was found in a room on the second floor, but the odd thing is, the room was reserved in your name. But you didn't reserve a room, did you, Abbie? You never do."

Her head was buzzing with a confusion of thoughts, and she absently touched a finger to her brow. She had to tread carefully here. "A room was reserved for me? By whom?"

"We don't know. Could it have been George?"

"Not to my knowledge. And anyway, I don't see what difference that makes either."

The difference was that he felt as though a millstone had been removed from around his neck. He'd entered Langley's office that morning feeling disgusted with himself. He'd known he was going to try to get Abbie back, and he despised himself for it. She had lied to him; played upon his emotions; tricked him. And it didn't make any difference. He still wanted her back.

He tried to convince himself that things would be different between them. She'd had too much freedom; she was too independent, too used to having her own way. He'd take her to his estate in Oxfordshire, well out of harm's way, and keep her so busy looking after their children and digging in Roman excavations with him that she wouldn't have time to get into trouble.

Then Langley had introduced him to an agent called Harris, who had just returned from Bath after checking out Abbie's story. Langley had also shown him the letter that Abbie supposedly wrote. He'd recognized Miss Fairbairn's writing at once and her convoluted style, and after reading it, he'd known, he'd *known* that he'd misjudged Abbie. All Miss Fairbairn had wanted was to bribe the fictitious Mr. Lovatt into getting back the books impounded by customs.

And that innocent letter had set off a train of events that resulted in Ballard's death and the uncovering of a plot involving a notorious French spy and his English accomplices.

There were still many questions, but as the meeting with Langley went on, he'd begun to feel almost carefree. What it all added up to was what he'd originally thought: that George and Abbie had become involved in something over their heads, and they hadn't known how to get out of it.

"What this means," he said, "is that I was wrong to doubt you, and I see that now. If only you hadn't kept secrets from me. . . ."

When he took a step toward her, she recoiled, and he halted. "Abbie," he said, "you don't need to hide anything from me anymore. You and George both have amnesty— you're both safe. And the book is no longer an issue."

Her gray eyes were wide and unfaltering in her pale

face, and he was suddenly conscious of just how fragile she was. He noticed other things. Her lips were colorless and there were dark smudges under her eyes. He hadn't expected smiles, but he'd expected something more than this. She was as lifeless as a china doll.

This was his doing, he thought bitterly, and he would have given anything to erase the last two weeks. He would make it up to her, he promised himself, just as soon as this business with Nemo was cleared up. He'd take her to his estate in Oxfordshire and get the bloom back in her cheeks and the sparkle back in her eyes. They'd talk, as they'd never talked before. They'd make a new beginning, just as soon as this business with Nemo was settled.

He took another cautious step toward her. "Listen to me, Abbie. We still haven't caught the mastermind behind all this. If there's any danger to you or George, it will come from him. All I want to do is to protect you both, but George must first tell me all he knows. Where is he, Abbie? Where is George?"

His expression was so sincere, so like the old Hugh's. If she hadn't known him better, she might have been tempted to take a chance on him. But she would never trust him again.

"I don't know where he is."

"You told me you would hand over the book to him in Bath, but Langley's people haven't been able to pick up his trail."

Her breath quickened. "Even if I knew where George was, I wouldn't tell you. Haven't you done enough to me? Do you know that the house is being watched even as we speak? Do you know I'm followed wherever I go? How can anyone live like that?"

He spoke calmly and slowly. "Yes, I know, and it's for your own protection."

"Then," she flashed, her bitterness spilling over in spite of herself, "why aren't they protecting me from you?"

"Look," he said, "I admit I made a mistake. But I had no idea Maitland would take you to Newgate or that you would be so stubborn in your resistance. I thought you would be home in a few hours. But if you had told me the truth from the beginning, none of this would have happened."

"The truth," she flared, her voice shaking. "You're a fine one to talk about the truth—*El Centurion*."

In the long silence that followed, she could hear the clock on the mantel ticking, and the rumble of a carriage as it passed over the cobblestones outside the front door.

"You had that from Maitland, I suppose?"

"He gave me your file to read."

"What file?"

"The one with your name on it."

He raised a skeptical eyebrow. "He was lying to you, Abbie. There are no files on agents. It would be too dangerous if they fell into the wrong hands."

"Really?" she scoffed. "Well, someone kept a file on you. It was extremely edifying, Major Templar. You should have told me you were a hero."

He folded his arms across his chest and studied her with narrowed eyes. "I'm not ashamed of my war record," he said.

She was doing exactly what she'd told herself she wouldn't do. She was practically begging him to justify his actions when she knew there was no justification for what he'd done, not after they'd become lovers. And that was the crux of the matter, not his war record, not his duplicity, pretending to be one kind of man when he was really another, but that he'd taken her as casually as he'd taken all those other women she'd read about in his file. She'd given him the gift of her love and he'd cast it aside like so much dross.

She was losing the struggle to hold back her tears. Horrified, she turned to run, but he stepped in front of her, blocking her path to the door.

"No," he said, "I won't let you run away from me. You brought this up, Abbie. If there is someone keeping a record on me, I want to know what's in it. So what else did you read?"

She clenched her hands together as she struggled to hold back the words. She didn't want to embark on this. It was too humiliating. The words came anyway. "Desdemona? Mercedes? Catalina? Does that jog your memory?"

He blinked slowly. "Who?"

"Don't pretend you don't know. It's all in your file. You left a string of women behind you from Lisbon to Paris. Desdemona? Mercedes? Catalina? To name a few."

He looked at her as though she'd taken leave of her senses, then, as enlightenment dawned, his shoulders began to shake. When he saw the pain flash in her eyes, he stopped laughing and let out a long sigh. "Those were the code names of my contacts. Desdemona was a priest, and Mercedes and Catalina were, if I remember correctly, the leaders of bands of Spanish guerrillas. The messages we exchanged were in the form of love letters, but that was only to fool our enemies. You've misunderstood, Abbie."

Her smile was laced with acid. "And I suppose Barbara Munro is your sister?"

"Ah, no. That was not well done of me. I made a mistake there, which I've since corrected. Nothing happened, Abbie. I couldn't . . . well, I wouldn't . . . She's not you, you see."

She felt herself weakening, and that horrified her. "And what about Estelle? Is that another code name for one of your Spanish contacts?"

He regarded her through narrowed eyes. "Maitland has been thorough, hasn't he? No. I would have told you about Estelle before much longer."

"She was your wife?"

"Yes."

She didn't feel anything, she told herself; she wouldn't allow herself to feel anything. She said coldly, "Is it true what Maitland told me—that you sent her home to Ireland to die of a broken heart?"

He was very still, very watchful. "What do you think, Abbie?"

"I think," she said, "that it would be just like you."

"You little hypocrite!" His voice was low and intense. "Are you trying to make me feel guilty? Well, it won't work. Yes, I sent my wife home to Ireland. One day I may tell you about her, but not now.

"And if I did break my wife's heart, and if I did take up with Barbara Munro or leave a string of women behind me in Spain, what difference would it make to us? Not the slightest difference. And you know why as well as I do."

When he made a movement toward her, her nerve broke. With a squeal of fright, she dodged past him and made for the door. He caught her by the waist and spun her to face him. She found herself imprisoned in the circle of one arm while he used his free hand to force her chin up. She braced for his kiss but it did not come.

Long moments passed, Abbie not daring to provoke him, so threatening did he seem as he loomed above her. Then the violence in his eyes died away.

"You little spitfire!" he said on a shaken laugh, and kissed her.

She slammed her fists into his ribs, and his response was to tighten his arms till she could scarcely breathe. She strained, she struggled, she squirmed, and the kiss went on and on. And because she couldn't breathe, so she told herself, she stopped struggling and clung to him.

When he raised his mouth from hers, she let out a teary breath. He spoke against her lips. "I've missed you. I've missed this. Haven't you missed me, even a little?"

"No," she said not very convincingly.

Another shaken laugh, then he took her lips again.

He had to touch her, had to feel every small bone in her spine, the hollow of her waist, the curve of her hip, just to reassure himself that she was all right. But she wasn't all right. She seemed helpless and lost, and not like the Abbie he knew. He wanted to give her his strength; he wanted to wrap himself around her like a shield so that nothing could hurt her ever again.

He shifted slightly and drew her closer. Her arms crept around his neck; her body softened against his. "It's all right," he murmured. "It's all right."

Huge gray eyes shadowed with needs that had nothing to do with passion or a pleasuring of the senses stared up at him. He felt his body clench in response. "It's all right," he said again, "I'm here."

His hands slid along her shoulders, and his fingers

tangled in her hair. He kissed her eyes closed, then his lips moved to her brows, her cheeks, the long sweep of her throat. She was trembling, but so was he. It was only a kiss . . . and it was more than a kiss.

She was lost in him, lost in the comforting protection of the arms that held her, in the granite-hard pressure of his chest. When he held her like this, she felt as though nothing could stop her. She wasn't going to fail. She could do anything. Just as long as Hugh was there.

They slipped into passion as easily as day slips into night. She breathed out an inarticulate sound, and he took it in to his own mouth. Their lips became fevered. As his body hardened, hers became more pliant. His hand found her breast, and she shifted to give him freer access to her body. Pure sensation blocked out rational thought. Their kisses became greedy.

When he pulled back he had to struggle to even his breathing. "Not here," he said, "where we can be disturbed. We can go to my house—no, that's no good either. Let's go to a hotel."

She touched her fingers to her burning lips and stared at him in a daze. But as his words registered, she took a quick step back. "Now why should we do that?"

His dark eyes were suddenly watchful. "To make love. To make up our quarrel."

She crossed her arms over her breasts and hugged herself as though to keep warm. "I don't think so."

"Then what?" He stopped. "You were paying me back in my own coin?" His eyes searched her face. "No. Some women could, Abbie, but not you. You're not made in that mold."

Is that how he saw her, as a doormat? It didn't matter. He'd handed her a perfect excuse to explain her temporary insanity and keep him at arm's length. "Don't be too sure of that, Hugh. You were an excellent teacher and I'm a quick study. And we Vayles never forget a wrong."

She left him with her head held high and pride stiffening her spine. It would have been a magnificent exit, thought Hugh, if he had not caught the glint of tears in her eyes.

CHAPTER 22

Abbie tested the weight of the pistol in her hand. It came from Daniel's collection and was supposed to be a suitable firing piece for a lady. It was much smaller and lighter than the pistol she'd practiced with at Endicote, but it was still too large to fit into an evening pochette or be carried in the folds of a diaphanous gown. Her mother had solved the problem by producing a white swansdown muff with its own matching scarf.

She couldn't look at a pistol now without thinking of Harper. Strange as it seemed, she actually missed the old buzzard. Not that he was old. He couldn't have been more than forty. He was just battered and worn around the edges. But he had a soft center. *He'd* looked back after Hugh handed her over to Maitland. *Harper*, whom she'd once disliked intensely, who was supposed to be a misogynist. And the man she loved, or thought she loved, had sent her to hell.

If she had to swallow any more lumps in her throat, she would gag. Frowning in concentration, she tried to recall all that Harper had told her about the use of firearms. She would only have one shot, so she should hold back until she could make it count. She mustn't get too close to an opponent because, inexperienced as she was, it would be all too easy to disarm her. She must keep her eyes on the target and break the nasty habit she'd got into of turning her head away just before she pulled the trigger.

She could almost hear Harper's exasperated sigh when she'd explained that she turned her head away because she didn't like the smell of gunpowder or the deafening report of the shot.

Her faint smile faded completely as she set the pistol on her dressing table. This was hopeless. It wouldn't matter if she *were* an expert shot. She could never fire at anyone, not even the monster who had murdered Colette, the man who had attacked her in her own bed. She simply did not possess the killer instinct.

Nemo. That was his code name, and he possessed the instincts of a jungle cat. Giles had found out more about him, and they knew they were up against a professional. According to Giles, Whitehall had been thrown into a panic by the report that Nemo was in England. They'd never had to deal with anyone of his caliber before.

For her to be taking on Nemo was so ludicrous that she would have laughed if she were not so scared. Who did she think she was? Is this how David felt when he went out to meet Goliath? But David was brave. She would rather run than fight. Why had Colette chosen her, of all people? Why?

Hopeless, she thought again, and her shoulders drooped.

When she looked up, she saw that her mother had entered her room and was watching her with dull, troubled eyes, and that gave her a pang. The poise that Abbie had always taken for granted in her mother had been savaged.

Her mother would start to say something, stop in mid-sentence, then walk out of the room. She suffered more than any of them, and her children had become fiercely protective of her. They shielded her as much as possible from their own doubts and uncertainties.

Abbie made a small movement with her hand. "The pistol is only a precaution, Mama. I promise I'll be careful."

Lady Clivendon said, "I can't help worrying, Abbie. I've always worried more about you than the others. You and George, well, you always needed looking after." Her hand went to her hair in a vague, distracted gesture; her eyes filmed with tears. "How could it have come to this, with everything depending on you?"

"Would it make you feel better if everything depended on Harriet and Daniel?"

Lady Clivendon bit her lip. "No. I don't know. I love all my children. I just wish—"

"What?"

"I'd been a better mother to you all."

This was one of the hardest things to bear, this constant soul-searching. Everyone felt guilty; they all felt they'd failed George in some way, and now they were trying to make up for it with each other.

It had certainly brought them closer together as a family, but Abbie would have given anything to return to the old days when they could be careless of each other's feelings, quarreling and bickering without hesitation.

She put her arms around her mother. "I don't remember being deprived as a child," she said.

Her ladyship said, "Deprived of love is what I meant. Your father always said I didn't know how to show my feelings, and he was right."

"You did know how to show your feelings," said Abbie. "Maybe not in words but in actions. No, listen,

Mama. When we were children and Papa would send us wonderful presents from faraway places, well, that wasn't Papa, was it? That was you."

Her mother's mouth gaped. "You knew about the presents? But how could you have known?"

"Because when Papa came home, he had trouble remembering what gifts he'd sent, and you were right there beside him to prompt his memory. It wasn't hard for us to figure out."

Not hard at all when some of the presents they received were silks from China and ivories from Africa—places their father had never visited. To Mama's way of thinking, "foreign" was anywhere that was not England.

"You all knew?"

"All of us. And we thought it was sweet."

"I wanted you to remember that you had a father, and that he loved you. And he did love you. It was just that he was away so much and he was—"

"Busy," supplied Abbie when her mother faltered. "But you were never too busy for us, Mama. Sometimes we children wished that you were."

Her mother did not smile. "Your father was a good man."

"I know."

"I still miss him."

"I know that too."

"Well, well." Her ladyship dabbed at her eyes with a lace handkerchief. "I don't know what I'm trying to say, except that I'm proud of you. I want you to know that, Abbie."

The tickle in Abbie's throat threatened to become one of those awful lumps, and she said lightly, "And I love you, too, Mama."

"Yes, *that's* what I wanted to say. Well, well, stand back and let's have a look at you."

Abbie obediently took a step back, and her mother made a critical inspection, studying the raven black wig laced with Harriet's diamonds, the sooty eyebrows and lashes that she herself had darkened with blacking, and the ravishing gown that had cost Giles a small fortune. "If I were not your mother," she said, "I would not recognize you. Until this moment, I did not realize how much you and Harriet look like each other."

She looked steadily into Abbie's eyes. "Abbie, you will be careful?"

"Of course, I will. We're not fools. I'm not going into that box with the book in my hands. I'll talk to these people, that's all. Then after that, Daniel and Giles will make the exchange." Her mother didn't look convinced, and Abbie went on, "Mama, the theater will be crowded. They won't do anything in a crowded theater. And remember, it's the book they want, not me or George."

"George," whispered her ladyship, and she turned away as her face began to crumple. "No, I'm not going to cry. He's alive. Daniel is sure the letter is genuine. But I can't help wondering . . . imagining . . . ," She straightened as if gathering herself to face an onslaught. "At least I don't feel so useless now." She gave Abbie a weary smile. "That's the worst part, the waiting. But that's over."

Abbie felt anguish blooming inside her. She had been imagining things, too, things no one dared put into words. Had they hurt George? Was he frightened? Was he cold? Was he hungry? Did he think every moment would be his last? Did he think his family had forgotten him? And where was he? Where, in God's name, was he?

She forced her fears to recede. For her mother's sake,

she had to appear calm and in control of the situation. "It's time," she said quietly.

She picked up the pistol and was about to thrust it into her muff when she remembered something else Harper had told her. She could almost hear his voice roaring in her ear.

"Just who do you thinks you is? A bleeding officer? Get that glove off your hand! You're supposed to feel as though the pistol is a part of you. Think of it as a lover, you knows, bare skin to bare skin." And he had winked at her.

What a rogue he was! But a nice rogue. Hopeless though it might be, she couldn't disobey Harper. She peeled the glove from her right hand, stuck it in her pochette, then picked up the gun and thrust it into her muff.

They were crossing to the door when Harriet entered. She was dressed very demurely in a puce gown. Her eyebrows had been lightened and her blond wig was threaded with ribbon.

She unfurled her fan, peeked over its rim, and dipped a curtsy. "Miss Abigail Vayle," she said, "at your service. Well, will I do?"

"Oh my," said her ladyship, looking from one daughter to the other. "I think you'll both do very well."

Daniel and Giles were waiting for them at the foot of the stairs. They, too, were amazed at the transformation in Abbie and Harriet.

"Do you have the book, Daniel?" asked Abbie.

He patted his coat pocket. "Right here."

Everyone looked grim. "We're supposed to be having a good time," said Giles. "Let's act like it."

They left the house laughing and talking and did not stop until their carriage had turned the corner into the Strand. Giles was looking out the window.

"We're being followed," he said.

It was what they expected to hear. Maitland's people were vigilant. They never let up.

Harriet leaned across the width of the carriage. "Don't worry, Abbie," she said softly. "I'll draw them off. I won't let you down."

Abbie smiled and nodded, but the nerves in her stomach began to twist themselves into knots.

Those nerves got tighter and tighter as the evening wore on. The first act was a comic opera, and the audience in the pit was so unruly that the performance had to be halted until order was restored. This wasn't unusual, but Abbie was so wound up that any delay only added to her agony.

When the first intermission came, they kept the door to their box locked to deter unwanted visitors. The minutes dragged by endlessly. They spoke very little. Everything had been said. Daniel kept looking at his watch; Giles's hand strayed frequently to the waistband of his trousers where he'd concealed his pistol, and Abbie's fingers flexed and unflexed around the butt of the firing piece inside her muff. It seemed so unreal, so preposterous. They were just ordinary people. How could it have come to this?

They breathed out a collective sigh when Colman's *Clandestine Marriage* got underway. Abbie had seen it with George at Covent Garden and considered it a masterly production. Tonight, the actors might as well have been reciting the Bible backward for all she heard. She was numb with fear, thinking of all the things that could go wrong.

She jumped when Giles put his hand on her shoulder. "It's time," he whispered.

"So soon?"

He nodded, and with an encouraging wink, slipped out the door.

He wasn't going far. His job was to look around before the second intermission. When he came back, they'd put their own little play into motion.

Not long after the curtain came down, he returned. "Just as we thought," he said. "Maitland's man is out there."

"Which one is it this time?" asked Daniel.

"Cassius."

"Ah. The one with the lean and hungry look. What is he doing?"

"Strolling around. There's plenty of people out there already."

"This is it, then." Daniel stood up. "Come on, Harriet, Mother. Let's see if we can draw off this Cassius fellow. Abbie—"

"I know," she said. "Don't take any foolish risks. Believe me, I won't."

They all looked at each other, nodding and passing silent messages with their eyes, as though they could read minds. Then Daniel ushered Harriet and his mother out and shut the door firmly behind him.

"Give them five minutes," said Giles.

She nodded. They'd rehearsed each step so often, she had it down pat. Box 10 was in the upper circle, one floor above. They were in the dress circle, in the box Daniel had rented for the season. While Daniel and her mother and sister went one way to draw off Maitland's watchdog, she and Giles would slip out and go in the opposite direction, toward the stairs. When they were out of sight, Harriet and her mother would stroll back to their own box and lock themselves inside. On the assumption that Maitland's man would keep "Abbie" under surveillance at all times, Daniel would be free to take the other staircase and meet them in the vicinity of Box 10.

She had thirty seconds to convince whoever was inside that box to deal with Daniel. She had to be the one to enter the box, Daniel had pointed out gravely, to reassure George's abductors that they were following orders. But if it was too much to ask—

It wasn't too much to ask, she'd protested. He and Giles would be right outside. Nothing would happen to her, not when Daniel had the book. And until he saw George's face, he would not hand it over.

And that's as far as they'd thought things through.

"Ready, Abbie?" asked Giles.

She would never be ready for this. "Quite ready."

Giles opened the door and gave a quick look to the left. "Our little ploy has worked," he said, and stood aside to let Abbie pass. "Don't look toward Harriet," he warned.

She stepped into the hallway ahead of Giles. The place was crowded with patrons, and the babble of their voices and laughter echoed from the high ceiling and was thrown back against the walls. The babble inside her own head was no less deafening.

She felt Giles's hand on her elbow, urging her forward, but she took only a few steps and halted.

"What's the matter, Abbie?"

She'd caught sight of a Guard in a blue tunic. She shook her head. "I don't know. It doesn't feel right. I wonder—" She blinked up at him "I wonder if it was wise to let Harriet impersonate me. Giles, look at her. Is she all right? What do you see?"

Shock registered in his eyes, then he swiftly turned

and looked beyond her. "No, Abbie, you're wrong. Everything—"

"What?"

"Cassius. What the devil is he doing? He's leaving."

She threw caution to the winds and turned around. After a moment she found him. Maitland's man was walking toward the far staircase with a blue-coated Guard's officer at his elbow.

A Guard in a blue tunic. Now why did that alarm her? Something hovered at the edge of her mind, but she could not bring it into focus. Her heart was racing so fast, she could feel her pulse pounding in her throat.

Her eyes darted around the corridor, taking lightning impressions. There were two other Guards in blue coats, not together, but converging casually on Harriet. Daniel hadn't seen them yet. He was looking her way, and the expression on his face demanded to know why she and Giles were hovering around instead of making for Box 10. He said something to Harriet, then started toward her.

"Go to Harriet," she told Giles. "Tell her to remove the wig. And whatever you do, don't let those Guards take her away."

"What?"

"Do it *now*!"

All the color faded from Giles's face, and he immediately thrust himself into the crush of people, elbowing them aside as he made for his wife. Fear rooted Abbie to the spot. Guards in blue uniforms. Colette. The Palais Royal. The memory was there just out of reach. What was it? What *was* it?

"I believe we have an appointment, Miss Vayle?"

She thought she screamed, then realized she couldn't have because no one was looking at her. With skin prickling and the fine hairs on her neck rising like a cat's fur, she slowly turned to face the man who had addressed her.

He was looking along the corridor, toward Harriet, then he dropped his gaze to her. His teeth gleamed white in his tanned face as he smiled. "You're late, Miss Vayle."

He was handsome, very handsome. If Hugh was El Centurion, this man was the Charioteer. Nemo. She'd come face-to-face with Nemo.

Where was Daniel? Where was Giles?

Don't cower! she warned herself. She knew intuitively it was the worst thing she could do.

"You know my name," she said for something to say, "but I don't know yours."

Again, the white teeth flashed. "There's no point in introducing myself, Miss Vayle. We won't meet again. No, don't look alarmed. All I meant was, I'll be leaving England in a matter of days."

His words chilled her. If he was leaving in a matter of days, that meant his business in England would be over. Why was he telling her this?

She flinched when he took her elbow and began to escort her toward the stairs. It was her right elbow, and that meant that the pistol concealed in her muff was pointing away from him. It was just as Harper said. She'd got too close to her opponent, and he had disarmed her.

In the same pleasant, conversational tone, he said, "I presume that was your sister back there?"

"Yes."

"Did you really think I would fall for that trick?"

"Where is my brother?"

"He's waiting for you in Box 10."

She was silent as they began to ascend the stairs. She

felt defenseless with his hand on her elbow, controlling her movements. He knew about the gun. She was sure he knew about the gun. He was playing with her as a cat plays with a mouse.

Something else was wrong. He hadn't asked about the book. He wasn't interested in the book. Then why was he here? What did he want with her?

As they reached the top of the staircase, he looked over his shoulder and his hand tightened on her elbow. She felt him tense, and her own arm moved faster than her brain. She lashed out with her muff and struck him in the chest just as he lunged for her. A knife fell out of his hand, and as he staggered back, she hit him again.

A woman screamed. Some gentlemen made ribald catcalls. They thought this was a lovers' tiff. Abbie took off along the corridor. She was terrified, but she couldn't give up now. She pushed people out of her way, uncaring of their angry protests. When she came to the box she wanted, Box 10, she looked back the way she'd come. There were too many people crowding the corridor for her to determine whether he was closing in on her or not.

Where was Daniel? Where was Giles?

Taking a deep breath, she pushed into the box. There was no one there. She was numb with grief and shock. They'd never had any intention of trading George for the book. They must have known it was worthless all along. Then what was the point of bringing her here?

As the answer came to her, she frantically groped for the key in the lock. There was no key. She was trapped. What did this mean for George? What would it do to their mother? How could she ever forgive herself for persuading her family to do things her way?

Blind rage drove out fear. She stepped back from the

door, slightly to one side where she could not be easily seen. After throwing off her muff, she raised her pistol with both hands and leveled it. Her thumb pulled back the hammer, and her index finger curled gently around the trigger. *Harper, oh Harper, what do I do now?*

She did not have long to wait. The edge of the door swung inward inch by inch. *Hold your fire! Hold your fire!*

Her nerve broke, and just as she pulled the trigger someone called her name. "Hugh!" she screamed.

He was standing in the corridor, unharmed, when she stumbled out of the box. Her ears were ringing from the report of the shot, and she breathed in the acrid smell of gunpowder. The people nearby took one look at her and began to scream as they ran for cover.

Hugh's voice was awful. "Would you mind telling me what the hell is going on?"

Her hand was sticky. Frowning, she looked down and saw that Harriet's priceless gown was smeared with blood. Tears filled her eyes. The gown was ruined, just as she'd known it would be.

Pain, across the back of her hand. Where had that come from? Someone was trying to take the pistol away from her, but she fought him off. A mist swam before her eyes. As her knees buckled, strong arms closed around her.

"Abbie, what is it?"

Hugh's voice. She tried to open her eyes but couldn't. "Don't let him get away."

"Who?"

"The Charioteer."

"Who is the Charioteer?"

He was the man who had murdered Colette, the same man who had assaulted her in Bath. He hated women.

She didn't know why she knew this, but she was convinced of it. This whole charade tonight had been for her benefit. And he would try again.

Then where did that leave George?

She tried to fight the mist so that she could explain all this to Hugh, but it sucked her into a sea of darkness.

Nemo was descending the stairs when he heard the shot. He hoped she'd killed the bastard. Templar wasn't supposed to be here. He was supposed to be attending some tedious meeting on Greek and Roman coins. In fact, he was to be the speaker. That's why he'd chosen this particular night to take care of the girl. Obviously, his information had been false.

It was one more proof that he was dealing with incompetents. From now on, he would rely on no one but himself.

To appear as natural as possible, he paused to do what everyone else was doing. He looked up the stairs to where the sound of the shot had issued. People were puzzled, but no one was alarmed. Someone mentioned a young buck's prank with a firecracker. He had a good idea of what had happened. He'd watched her enter the box. Now I have her, he'd thought, but he'd drawn back when he saw Templar approach from the other direction. That's when he'd decided to make himself scarce.

There was no sign of his "Guards" in the dress circle. Their task had been to cause a distraction so that he could get to the girl. He'd known she wasn't stupid. He'd expected her to take some precautions to protect herself, but he'd thought he would take her by surprise and deal with her almost as soon as she left her own box. So many people crowding around. So much panic. It would have been over in seconds, before anyone was the wiser. He'd been on the point of sauntering over, when he saw the woman remove her wig. And he was stunned.

Then he'd spotted his quarry right in front of him, and she'd dropped into his hands like a ripe plum. That's when he should have slipped the knife between her ribs. But he'd been so confident that she was no match for him that he'd taken chances he would not normally take. He'd wanted her to look into his eyes before he knifed her. He'd wanted her to know who he was, see the terror in her eyes. He'd wanted her to understand that the chase was over and he was making the kill.

People were beginning to drift back to their boxes. After casually glancing around, he opened the door to his own box. It was only six doors along from the girl's box and would have served him well if everything had gone as planned.

"Did you hear the firecracker, Uncle?" he said, then he entered and locked the door. There was no one else in the box.

He'd picked up his knife in the confusion and had slipped it into the sheath strapped to his arm. He checked it now to see that it was secure. Under one of the chairs was a damp towel. He used it to remove the thin layer of greasepaint that made his face look tanned. In his coat pocket he found his gray wig. When he was ready, he put on his hat, threw his cloak over his shoulders, and picked up his cane.

Bitch! He'd been too complacent, too sure of himself. That pale, colorless, stupid English bitch thought she could outwit him. She'd tried to cross him. Next time he would make no mistakes. This wasn't a mater of expediency now, it was a matter of pride. Grown men trembled when they heard his name. He would not be bested by a mere girl. In two days, his mission would be over and he would be returning to France. There was plenty of time to take care of the girl first.

He needed no mirror to know how he looked. But looks weren't everything. He had mastered facial expressions and gestures so that he could pass for any age. Now he looked like a sober middle-aged merchant banker.

He unlocked the door and opened it a crack. As though speaking to someone in the box, he said, "I'll see you back at the house then."

He didn't overdo it but managed to convey his advancing years by slowing his movements and, literally, watching his steps.

They were coming down the stairs, and he paused to let them pass. Templar was still very much alive, unfortunately, and carried the girl in his arms. They did not spare him a glance. The mother was weeping into her son's shoulder. The sister, a brunette again, and her husband were white faced and grim. He'd watched them all come and go this last week and felt that he was beginning to know them intimately.

Now they would think that the younger brother was dead. He would be soon enough. It was too bad the girl would never know for sure. Maybe he'd tell her before he slit her throat.

The Vayles and Templar soon outdistanced him. Outside the theater, he lifted his cane and a hackney pulled up. He took it to Covent Garden and, after paying off the driver, entered the theater. A few minutes later, he exited by a side door. He'd shed the wig but kept the cane. His movements were no longer slow, and he didn't watch his steps. He looked about thirtyish, and no footpad in his right mind would want to tackle him.

It took him ten minutes to walk to the little house he

had rented in his first week in England. This was the only time he would use it. No one knew where to find him now, not even his closest associates. But he knew where to find them.

He would change his clothes, then have something to eat at one of the many coffeehouses in the Strand.

Then he'd go and deal with the girl.

CHAPTER 23

Hugh was pacing. Giles was sitting close to the fire, nursing a large brandy. They were in the upstairs parlor in Vayle House.

"It's only a scratch," said Giles in answer to Hugh's question. "She didn't lose much blood. I think it was nerves that made her faint."

"Who attacked her?"

"We don't know."

"What did he want?"

"I can't say."

"Why did she go to Box 10?"

"Look, she'll be here in a minute. You'll have to ask her."

Hugh slammed his open palm against the flat of a small side table, making Giles jump. "Why have I been left here to kick my heels? Why won't anyone tell me what's going on?"

Giles answered him mildly, placatingly. "Be patient. You'll know everything soon enough."

"If it's only a scratch, what's keeping her?"

"I don't know. I honestly don't know."

Hugh looked closely at Giles and decided that he shouldn't be taking his frustration out on him. He was slumped in his chair and looked as though he'd aged ten years in the last half hour. He pulled up a straight-backed chair and seated himself. "All right, I'll wait," he said quietly. "But I'm not going to be put off now. You invited me into this when you sent me that cryptic note."

He'd been attending a meeting of the Dilettante Society in the Thatched Tavern when the Vayle footman finally tracked him down. His mood had ranged from gloomy to downright irritable, and he could hardly concentrate on what he was saying about ancient trade routes and Greek coinage. At the back of his mind hovered the ever present problem of Abbie. She'd made it clear that she wanted nothing to do with him, and he couldn't force himself on a woman who didn't want him.

Then Giles's note arrived, saying that he was worried about Abbie, and that if Hugh could attend the performance at the King's Theater that evening, he'd appreciate it.

He'd been out of the Thatched Tavern like a shot, with no explanation to his friends, most of whom he'd known at Oxford, except to say that something urgent had come up. And it was urgent. It had taken the footman two hours to discover where the Dilettante Society held its meetings, and a lot could have happened in two hours.

He'd arrived at the King's Theater during one of the intermissions. He knew Daniel's box was in the dress circle, and he headed straight for it. What kept going through his mind was that George was up to his old tricks and Abbie was helping him again. Apparently she still didn't understand that this wasn't a game for amateurs.

But just beneath the anger was stark, raw fear.

When he'd rounded the corner into the dress circle, he came to an abrupt halt. He saw Giles and Harriet and the dowager, Lady Clivendon, but there was no Abbie. They all looked shaken. Giles beckoned him over.

"Daniel is looking for her in the crush," he said. "I hope I'm wrong, but I think she may have gone by herself to Box 10. It's in the upper circle. I'm going to take Harriet and her mother back to our own box, then I'm going up there."

He hadn't waited to hear more. And when he arrived at Box 10 and tried to enter it, he'd practically had his head blown off.

He looked at Giles. "Why didn't you send for me sooner?"

Giles let out a weary sigh. "I don't know. I wanted to. It makes no difference now. It's too late to save George."

The door opened at that moment, and Lady Clivendon, Daniel, and Harriet filed into the room. Hugh and Giles rose at their entrance.

When no one else entered, Hugh said, "Abbie?"

Harriet answered him. "She's resting." Something in his expression prompted her to add, "She's all right. Truly."

Her words mollified him, but only fractionally. He looked at Daniel. "I'm not leaving here," he said, "until I know exactly what's going on."

"Please," said Lady Clivendon, "take a chair, Mr. Templar. We don't want you to leave. We want to ask your advice. You see, we don't know what to do."

When everyone was seated, she said starkly, "George has been abducted, and someone tried to kill Abbie tonight."

•   •   •   •   •

She knew it was a dream, but try as she might, she couldn't wake from it. She was in the bookshop in the Palais Royal, and she was all that stood between Nemo and Colette. Nemo was in the blue uniform of a French Lifeguard, but that didn't fool her. He was Nemo; he was the Charioteer; he was the man who had assaulted her in her own bed, the man who had abducted George. She had a pistol in her hand. All she had to do was pull the trigger and Colette and George would be safe. But she couldn't do it. Her finger was paralyzed. He was reaching for her, reaching for her . . . Why couldn't she pull the trigger?

She sat bolt upright in bed, fighting for every breath.

"It's all right," a voice soothed. "It's me. Harriet. I didn't mean to frighten you."

"It's George, isn't it?" Abbie cried out.

"No, this isn't about George." Harriet spoke in the same soothing tone. "You're to leave at once with Hugh Templar, and I'm here to help you dress."

As awareness came back to her, Abbie wiped the sweat and tears from her face with the edge of the sheet. "What are you talking about, Harriet? I'm not going anywhere with Hugh Templar."

"Oh, yes you are!" Hugh came striding into the room. "You had a lucky escape tonight, but you may not be so lucky next time. You're coming with me. You're going into hiding until we catch this thug. Now show me your hand."

He didn't wait for her to comply with his order but reached for her right hand and studied the red line and puckered skin.

"It's only a scratch," Abbie said.

"Yes," said Hugh somberly. "But it could have been so much worse."

Her panic had faded but she was still overwrought,

and because she was tempted to disgrace herself by throwing herself into his arms, she spoke sharply. "What are you doing here? How did you get in? If Daniel—"

Hugh made a vicious motion with one hand, silencing her. "Now you listen to me. I'm here with your family's approval. You're leaving with me if I have to bind and gag you, and that's flat. I know everything, Abbie. Your family told me about George and about your close shave with Nemo tonight. *Nemo!* My God, he's a cold-blooded assassin. He'll try to get to you again. You can count on it. And this is the first place he'll look. Even now, he may be watching the house." He looked at Harriet. "Pack a small bag for her—with only the essentials, do you understand?"

Harriet nodded wordlessly.

When Abbie began to protest, he reached for the blankets and dragged them back. His eyes were like flint. "Either Harriet dresses you or I do."

"I'll dress her," said Harriet, coming to life. "Abbie, I'm ashamed of you. Mr. Templar is going to help us find George. This is too important to let your differences stand in the way. Anyway, it's what Mama wants, and we all agreed to do whatever he says." Then, in a shaken plea, "Abbie . . . please?"

Abbie spoke through her teeth. "I'd do anything for my brother."

"Good," said Hugh. "Now get dressed! And quickly!" And turning on his heel, he left the room.

When the door closed, Abbie angrily swung her legs over the edge of the bed and stood up. Harriet had already laid out the clothes she was to wear.

"When I went to bed," said Abbie, "I thought we'd decided to call in the authorities. You said you'd waken me when they got here."

Harriet slipped a lawn chemise over Abbie's head. "It was Mama," she said. "She trusts Mr. Templar, don't ask me why. And how could we go against Mama?"

Abbie sank onto the edge of the bed as the familiar despair and inertia washed over her. It wasn't true to say that Vayles never gave up. She had given up. Why couldn't her mother see that there was no point in going on with this? No point in getting dressed, no point in going with Hugh, no point—

Harriet had turned to see what Abbie was doing. Aghast, she cried out, "Why are you just sitting there? Put on your stockings. Didn't you hear Mr. Templar? You're to hurry!"

Abbie snatched up a stocking and began to pull it on.

Hugh planned their exit as if they were escaping from Newgate prison. The carriage was ordered round, and Giles and Harriet went off as though they were leaving for another engagement. They were, in fact, going to Hugh's house with a message for Harper. When the carriage pulled away from the front doors, Lady Clivendon turned to Hugh.

"Now tell me the truth, Mr. Templar," she said. "Do you think George is still alive?"

He didn't know. He just didn't know. It didn't seem likely, but he hadn't had time to reflect on all that he learned tonight. When he looked into the anguished eyes of Lady Clivendon, however, and sensed Daniel's and Abbie's stillness, he couldn't bring himself to destroy the little hope that was left to them.

He said, "When an agent goes missing, we never give up on him until we have proof that he has been killed. That hasn't happened here, so I'm working on the assumption that George is still alive. I won't give up on your son, Lady Clivendon, I promise you."

Tears filled her ladyship's eyes. "Thank you," she whispered.

Hugh's quiet assurance to her mother had moved Abbie to tears as well. Not only that, but his graciousness made her feel small. She didn't know what his motives were in helping her family. Maybe all he wanted was the glory of being the one to stop Nemo. And maybe he wanted to make amends for all that she'd suffered after he handed her over to Maitland. Whatever his motives, he was going to track down Nemo and, God willing, rescue her brother. She should be kissing the ground he walked on.

She couldn't go that far, not nearly that far. But at least she could be civil to him and properly grateful.

Her mother clasped her in her arms. "You will be careful, Abbie?"

"Don't worry, Mama. Mr. Templar knows what he's doing. I've read his file, remember? He's . . . well . . . a gladiator. If anyone can beat Nemo, he can."

Her ladyship nodded. "And now," she said, "I'd best go along and do my part to help you get safely away."

As she began to ascend the stairs, Hugh spoke to Daniel. "Daniel, do something for me. Ask Giles to get me a list of all the engagements of the royal family for the next few days. No, make that the royal family *and* the Prime Minister and his cabinet."

Daniel said, "Nemo is going to complete his mission in the next few days, isn't he?"

"Yes."

"That's what he meant when he told Abbie he'd be leaving England and they wouldn't meet again."

"Yes."

"But why did he give himself away like that?"

When Hugh hesitated, Abbie answered, "Because he was going to kill me. Because he thought I'd be in no position to tell anyone."

They fell silent as the strains of Mozart floated down to them from the upstairs formal drawing room. Abbie felt a bubble of hysteria rise in her throat and quickly swallowed it. Her mother was playing the piano to a captive audience of maids and footmen on the understanding that when she came to the end of each piece they would applaud.

Everything had returned to normal at Vayle House, or so they hoped anyone watching would think.

"Now!" said Hugh, and they turned and made for the kitchen door at the back of the house.

The grounds sloped down to the river, to the jetty where a small rowing boat was tied up. Hugh wouldn't tell Daniel where they were going. His coachman would be their go-between, he said. All messages were to be left at his club, and Harper would pick them up every day. And if anyone were to ask about Abbie, they were to say she'd gone home to Bath. Meantime, the Vayles were to keep up appearances as though nothing had happened.

"Don't you think you're being overcautious?" asked Daniel. "Shouldn't we at least tell your special branch people what's going on?"

"If we do," replied Hugh, "they will want to question Abbie. They may decide to use her as bait to catch Nemo. It's what I would do. They'll promise, of course, that they'll keep her safe, but there's no guarantee of that. I don't want Maitland and his men looking for Abbie. Do you understand?"

There was a silence, then Daniel chuckled. "Oh yes," he said, "I understand perfectly now."

"Good," said Hugh curtly. "It's about time someone did."

Abbie did not hear any of this. She was looking back at the lights of Vayle House, listening to the faint strains of Mozart that wafted over the lawns. Her mother was playing to a roomful of servants. She, herself, had to creep away like a thief in the night from her own house because someone was trying to kill her. Her brother had been abducted. Her world had tilted on its axis, and she didn't know how it could ever be put right.

They went downstream, past Somerset House, making for Blackfriars Bridge. They weren't alone on the river. The Thames was never idle. Lights winked from boats and watermen called to each other as they passed.

"Are we being followed?" she asked at one point, the only words that had passed between them since they entered the boat.

"I doubt it, but even if we are, I don't think anyone can catch up to us now."

Hugh spoke with far more confidence than he was feeling. Nemo had become a legend in his own time, and Hugh only hoped that the stories that had circulated about him were exaggerated. Nemo wasn't only ruthless, he was pitiless. He remembered something else. Nemo had a thing about women.

That's what really disturbed him. The attack on Abbie tonight had been carefully engineered. It had nothing to do with trading the book for George. She and only she had been Nemo's target. He'd become obsessed with her, and the thought chilled Hugh's blood by several degrees.

Gladiator, she'd called him, and that stung. But that's exactly what it might come down to. Two gladiators fighting to the death in a Roman circus. There would be no mercy shown, no quarter asked or given.

Hugh docked the boat at the Blackfriars Stairs. There was a tavern close by, and they heard the sounds of riotous singing as they approached it. But this wasn't their destination either. There was a stand of hackneys at the top of the road. Hugh hailed one, and as Abbie wearily settled herself on the banquette, he gave the directions to a hotel in Gloucester Street.

They were returning the way they had come, all the way back, past Vayle House, to the edge of Mayfair.

CHAPTER 24

Hugh had no trouble renting a suite of rooms on the top floor. It was the beginning of March, and visitors to London were still scarce. Their servants, he told the landlord, would be coming later with their baggage, after they'd taken care of a repair to their carriage. He registered Abbie and himself as Mr. and Mrs. Sterne, then took the key from the landlord and said they'd show themselves up.

They had to walk up three flights of stairs to reach their suite of rooms.

"I'm sorry about the stairs," said Hugh, "but this way if someone tries to find us, they'll have to climb these stairs as well, and they'll be easy to spot."

He unlocked the door and followed Abbie into the suite. There was a small parlor, one fair-sized bedchamber, and two smaller rooms that were not much bigger than closets. He lit the candles in the parlor first, and while Abbie used a taper to light the fire in the grate, he looked over each room more carefully. There was another exit from one of the closet bedchambers, an exit that led to the back staircase. He'd particularly asked for a suite of rooms with a back exit, because he had no desire to be pinned down in a position with no means of falling back.

He locked the back door and wedged a chair under the doorknob. When he turned, Abbie was watching him from the corridor.

"You really do know what you're doing, don't you, Hugh?" she asked softly.

His jaw set. "Yes."

"You think Nemo will come looking for me?"

"He'll try. He's a cold-blooded killer. Don't underestimate him, Abbie."

"Did you come across him in Spain?"

"No. He and I are like Wellington and Napoleon. We've never had to fight each other. Somehow, our paths never crossed."

"You sound as though you're sorry."

"What if I am?"

There was something about his expression, something about his voice—a taunt? a challenge?—that made her hesitate to respond.

"It was just an idle observation," she said, and quickly turned away.

He followed her into the parlor. She removed her outer things, then kneeling in front of the grate, used the poker to lift the kindling so that the draft made the flames flare up. But all the time she was burningly aware of him standing just inside the door, watching her. Her heart picked up speed and her breath became audible. When she could stand it no longer, she put down the poker, rose, and slowly turned to face him.

"What's the matter, Abbie?" he said. "Am I too much of a man for you? Have I too much red blood in my veins?"

She shook her head and managed a neutral, "No."

"Maitland told me how you saw me. 'A bumbling academic,' I believe his words were. Good old Hugh, the Brain. Is that what you want? Shall I put my spectacles on? Will that make you feel safe?"

He was angry, and she didn't know what she'd done or said to provoke him. "Hugh—" She stopped, unsure of what she wanted to say, then started over. "I liked the man I knew in Bath, if that's what you mean. What's wrong with that?"

His face went so taut that his bones stood out starkly. A shiver of feminine alarm chilled her skin. This was the man who had handed her over to the authorities in Dover.

He approached her with the slow, stealthy stride of a jungle cat. Trembles began deep in her belly and spread out, but she held her ground. He halted only an arm's length away. She lifted her chin.

His voice was low and intense; his dark eyes were alive with fury. "What about the man with you now? How do you feel about him?"

"It . . . it isn't the same," she said weakly.

"How am I different?"

"You can ask that, after what's happened between us?"

The bitterness in his voice lashed out at her. "I'm good enough to save your brother, good enough to stand up to Nemo. But I'm not good enough to be in the same room with you. Just look at you! You're trembling in your shoes. You think I'm barely civilized. You think I'll attack you, ravage you."

"How can you say that?" she cried out. "I'm grateful to you—" She flinched when he reached out and grasped her arms.

"I don't want your gratitude! I want you to see me as I

really am. I'm a man, Abbie, with all a man's strengths and weaknesses."

"I know that," she said quietly, hoping her reasonable tone would placate him.

It didn't placate him. Her cool-eyed stare made his anger burn hotter. "You think you're the only one who has feelings? You think you're the only one who felt betrayed? You seduced me! You told me you loved me! Then you betrayed me!"

"You're wrong! It wasn't like that."

"You would have done anything to save George. Admit it, Abbie."

"He's my brother," she cried out.

He snarled the words. "And I'm only a gladiator."

"Yes," she hissed.

She regretted her outburst almost at once. She didn't mean it. It had been a horrible night and she was still shaken from her encounter with Nemo. And she was grateful to Hugh for his offer of help, more than grateful. He deserved better than this from her.

"Hugh—"

"Then what have I got to lose?"

One jerk brought her against the hard length of his body. His arms clamped around her, then his lips claimed hers in a brutal, suffocating kiss that was far more punitive than loverlike. Her words of apology were forced back into her mouth. Her lips burned; breathing became difficult. He was using his body like a vise to subdue her.

This was Hugh. Why was he punishing her like this?

She thought she could offer him a passive resistance, but she was wrong. His hands slipped lower, holding her steady as he ground his body into hers. The intimate contact made her gasp, not in shock, not in anger, but in sheer animal arousal.

Hugh recognized the sound for what it was. He should stop, he told himself, now that he'd made his point. He should let it go, let *her* go. But the wound she'd inflicted was still too raw. He was going to prove to her that in spite of who and what he was, she still wanted him.

She didn't put up much of a struggle when he lowered her to the floor. She wasn't betrayed by her own passion, but by his. It awed her, thrilled her, humbled her. It made her feel more of a woman than she'd ever felt in her life. They'd made love before, but not like this. This was primitive and darkly sensual. And she wallowed in it.

He absorbed the change in her through his senses. His mind had ceased to function a long time ago. Her desperation made him frantic to get at her. He wrenched her bodice open, spilling tiny pearl buttons over the carpeted floor. She wasn't wearing stays and her chemise was quickly dealt with. Her breasts spilled into his hands. When he put his mouth on one sensitive crest and feasted on it, her back arched off the floor to give him more.

That one act of surrender ripped his control to shreds. He tore off his jacket and shirt and tossed them aside. Her fingers nimbly undid the rest of her buttons, and she fought her way out of her gown. In a matter of seconds, they were down to bare skin.

She cried out when he pushed her knees high. His eyes held hers with an intensity that she could hardly sustain. Then he was on her, and in her, and rational thought slipped away. She didn't care about consequences; she didn't care about right and wrong. This was what she was made for. She could only feel.

She tried to hold back to prolong the pleasure, but he

wouldn't allow it. He wrapped her legs around his back and rode her to a fast and furious finish. She crested wave after wave and went soaring into a star burst of pleasure. He watched her eyes glaze over, then locking his body to hers, he gave himself up to his own violent release.

There had never been a silence like this one, thought Hugh, except perhaps the eerie silence that hung in the air after every battle. But this silence was a rebuke to him.

The last time they made love, she'd told him she loved him. He couldn't expect those words now. How had it come to this? He'd whisked her out of Vayle House with only one thought in his mind, to protect her. Yet here he was, naked, sprawled on top of her like some spent, conquering Viking.

Not quite spent. He could feel his sex hardening inside her, and that had never happened to him before. And, he reflected with a kind of guilty defiance, it felt damn good. In fact, she felt damn good. If she didn't like it, she had only to push him away.

When he flexed inside her, she lifted her hand limply in a half-hearted attempt to ward him off. She felt so shattered, she just wanted to go to sleep. Tomorrow, she would think of consequences, tomorrow in the clear light of day. Tonight, she was still dazed by her newfound knowledge that she could be as primitive as a cat in heat.

Her eyes flew open when he lunged deep in her body, and slowly withdrew. When he lunged again, a shivery breath caught in her throat, and her fingers curled like claws into the carpet. She looked up at him and saw that nothing had changed. His face was set in harshly sensual lines; his eyes were banked with emotions she could only guess at.

Don't ask for words, she warned herself. *He's incapable of giving you the words you want.*

When his body moved within hers again, she stifled a moan.

"Now tell me I'm not the man you want," he said.

Not want him? She was so unbearably aroused that it was like a pain. She reached for him, her arms twining around him, locking him to her, and he laughed softly into her mouth. Then he slowly brought her up to the edge again, until the pressure inside her exploded, and she went spiraling down, down, down.

They were still trying to recover their breath when they heard the tapping on the door to their suite. Hugh cursed and reached for his clothes. "Harper and Tom," he said.

Abbie wasn't nearly as calm as Hugh. Before he pulled on his shirt, she was on her feet, gathering up her clothes, and had bolted through the door, along the short corridor and into the bedchamber. She heard Hugh cursing as he went to answer the door.

Harper's voice, Tom's voice, then the tread of footsteps. With a squeal of alarm she dropped her clothes and dove for the bed. She pulled the bedclothes up to her nose and listened. Something heavy was deposited on the floor outside her door. They spoke in low tones for some minutes. Finally, their footsteps receded and there was silence.

A moment later, Hugh entered her bedchamber. He was carrying a box. "They've gone," he said and put the box on the floor. He left her and returned in a moment or two with her portmanteau.

Abbie said, "Aren't they going to share the suite with us?"

His look was enigmatic. "No. Their room is on the other side of the hall. So you see, we're quite alone."

She assimilated his words in silence. "But there's plenty of room here," she said.

"Yes, but it's not convenient."

Her brow puckered. "Convenient for whom?"

He opened his own box and removed a two-edged blade and a set of pistols. As he began to load one pistol, he said, "Convenient for us. I'm sharing your bed, Abbie. It doesn't matter to me if Harper and Tom know, but I thought it might matter to you."

She watched him wordlessly as he loaded the other pistol. When he was done, he moved around the room. The knife went under one of the pillows, one pistol went on the floor hard by the bed, and the other went on top of the dresser. He really did know what he was doing.

He was watching her with an expression that was challenging and angry at the same time. She was in no position to run from him like an outraged virgin. She couldn't cry "rape." If she was a fallen woman, it was as much her doing as his, more, in fact, because he hadn't been raised a Vayle.

"You want us to be lovers?"

"We *are* lovers," he stated.

There was another challenge there that she didn't feel up to answering. Why was he so still? Why was he staring at her with that shuttered expression?

"What, no arguments?" he asked lightly.

She shook her head. "No arguments."

She caught the glint of masculine satisfaction in his eyes, and that almost got her dander up. But he crossed to the bed and pressed a quick kiss to her lips before she could marshal her thoughts.

"I must talk to Tom and Harper," he said. "Try to get some sleep," and with another quick kiss, he left the room.

She snuggled under the bedclothes, but no sooner had she closed her eyes, than she began to feel guilty, not about Hugh, but about George. It didn't seem right that for the last half hour she'd been lost in a haze of sensual pleasure when the threat of death hung over her own brother. There must be something wrong with her, something depraved. Life shouldn't go on as though nothing had happened to George.

She dozed, dwelling on that thought, and when she awakened, she heard voices coming from the parlor. *Harper,* she thought, and smiled. They were all together again, and they made a good team.

It's all right, George, she whispered into the silence. *Hugh and Harper are modern-day gladiators. They'll save you.* She made a litany of it, and gently succumbed to sleep again.

She awakened to a rush of pleasure. There were no candles lit, and the fiery glow that cast odd flickering shadows on the walls and ceiling came from the red-hot embers in the grate. The covers had been pulled back, and Hugh was planted firmly between her legs, trailing random kisses along the inside of her thighs. Hot, wet random kisses that made her shiver in anticipation.

Whimpering, she pulled herself up and away from those tantalizing kisses and the brush of those beguiling hands.

"What's wrong, Abbie?" he asked softly. "Don't you want me to?"

Yes. No. She didn't know what was wrong except that she was in an erotic haze and couldn't think straight. The ripe flavor of their lovemaking clung to her skin, and her thighs were sticky. She was just beginning to discover what it meant to be a man's lover, and she didn't know if she was ready for it. They didn't talk. All they did was this.

When his warm hand palmed her breast, she jerked away from him.

"Abbie!" The sensual color in his voice had faded as had the caressing touch of his hands. "No, don't turn away from me. Talk to me. Tell me what's wrong."

That was the problem. They didn't talk. And it didn't flatter her ego to know that he had only one use for her.

She didn't want to quarrel with him, so she gave him a reason that was close to the truth. "Everything is happening too fast. I don't know what you expect from me."

Hugh knew he could have her very easily. He could sense her arousal. If he persisted, in another minute or two he could sheathe himself in her warm, willing flesh and take her on that wild ride to oblivion he'd been thinking about since he last took her there.

But he also sensed the resentment behind her confusion, and he understood that too. Since bringing her here, he'd made her spend most of her time on her back.

Maybe he wasn't as civilized as he thought.

The thought irritated him. Such things would never have occurred to him if Abbie hadn't called him a gladiator. Other women had called him worse, but other women didn't know him as Abbie did. Only Abbie's opinion counted; only Abbie could hurt him. And, by damn, how she could hurt him.

He pulled back from her. "I'm glad you brought that up," he said, "because there is something I want to say to you."

He swung out of bed, lit a taper from the embers in the grate, then put the flame to the candles on the mantelpiece. When he came back to her, she had the sheet drawn up to her chin. He reached for his shirt, not because he was cold, but because he thought she'd be more comfortable without the evidence of his arousal betraying where his thoughts were taking him.

"Abbie," he said, "I don't think it's such a good idea for us to be lovers. I mean, I want us to come to some arrangement where we both get what we want. Are you with me so far?"

"I think so," she said.

Her eyes were huge and steady on his. Her hair was a golden haze and fell around her shoulders in a sensual riot. She was more than beautiful, more than intelligent. So brave yet so fragile, his Abbie.

He chose his words with care. "You told me you wanted children. Is that true, Abbie?"

She tossed her hair back, draping it over her shoulders. In a prosaic voice he knew so well, she said, "We can't always have what we want."

"In this case, we can. You want children. I want you. Marriage, Abbie. It's the perfect solution for us."

She was afraid to believe him, afraid to hope. She said cautiously, "We don't have to get married. We can wait and see if I'm pregnant first."

He put the flat of his hand on her belly, over the sheet, and gently massaged it. "You're missing the point, Abbie. I want to make you pregnant. It pleasures me to think of my seed growing inside you."

She didn't know how such cold-blooded words could make her feel so hot. But when she looked up at him, she saw that he wasn't as unmoved as he pretended to be. He was watching her with eyes that were both heated and wary.

She leaned back on her elbows as she studied him. "You've really thought this out, haven't you, Hugh?"

More than she realized. "Is that yes or no?"

She felt a sudden shiver of apprehension as she pictured Hugh coming face-to-face with Nemo. Hugh was only one man and he was mortal. What did it matter if he wanted her for only one thing? Who knew what would happen tomorrow or next week?

"Yes," she said with a catch in her voice, and she held out her arms to him.

A slow smile spread across his face. He pulled back the sheet, climbed into bed, and spread her legs.

"Easy," he said, as she began to shudder. "This time let's savor the pleasure."

And he showed her what he meant, tormenting her with intimate, lingering caresses until her body ached for release. Her hands ran over his back, testing the hard muscles that rippled as he moved rhythmically inside her. He was lean, hard, and powerfully built. But he was just a man, and she was so terribly afraid of what could happen to him.

When her body convulsed under the driving pressure of his, she began to weep, and not all his frustrated entreaties could coax her into telling him what was the matter with her.

Hugh lay brooding for a long time after Abbie had tumbled into sleep.

CHAPTER 25

She slept well into the afternoon of the following day and was finishing her toilette, when she was startled by an almighty crash that came from the parlor. She was out the bedroom door in a flash, dashed into the parlor, and came to a sudden halt. Hugh was sitting at the table and had evidently been writing a letter. There was a young footman on his knees, gathering up broken china that lay scattered on the floor, and he was cursing furiously. The curses stopped when he saw Abbie.

"Bleedin' dishes slipped right out o' my 'ands," he said.

"Tom?" said Abbie. "Good grief, it is you! I hardly recognize you."

"That," said Hugh, "is because Tom is wearing a borrowed suit of livery—as a disguise. It's just a precaution."

She chanced a quick glance at Hugh, then looked away. She knew that her color was high but could do nothing about it. After the night they'd shared, she was surprised she could still walk. Her body was tender all over, and each movement brought some memory or other vividly to mind.

To cover her embarrassment, she concentrated on

Tom. "And very smart you look, too, Tom," she said, admiring the dark blue coat with silver buttons, the gray breeches, and the white silk stockings and gloves. "But what have you done to your hair?"

"It's powdered," he said, " 'cos I ain't 'aving no borrowed wig stuck on my 'ead. Who knows what's breeding in it? Them things is alive."

To give herself something to do, she bent down and began to help pick up the pieces of china.

"We're lucky," said Tom, "that I brung the dishes first. What if I'd brung in the servers of food? There'd be a right mess to clean up, that's wot." He tore off his white gloves. "That's it, then," he said. "You either sends me back to the stables where I belongs, Mr. Templar, sir, or I does my work without these confounded gloves."

"Gloves?" said Abbie.

"It appears," said Hugh, "that Tom's fingers are useless when he's wearing gloves. But footmen wear gloves, and not to do so would make him conspicuous."

"Wellington doesn't wear no gloves, not even at balls," Tom pointed out.

"You are not the Duke of Wellington."

Abbie intervened tactfully. "You wear gloves in the stables, don't you, Tom?"

"That's different. I'm not 'andling dainty dishes, or slippery silver servers. I'm not ladling out soup or pouring out wine or doling out dollops o' potatoes. Stable work ain't dainty. It's rough."

"Let me see your hands," said Hugh.

Tom held out his hands. The grime was ingrained, and there was dirt under the ragged fingernails.

"Wear the gloves," said Hugh, "and Miss Vayle and I will serve ourselves."

Tom sniffed. "As you wish," he said.

When the broken plates were gathered onto the tray and Hugh left to lock the door after Tom, Abbie wandered over to the table where there was a silver coffeepot and fresh cup and saucer. She was drinking coffee and looking out the window when Hugh returned. The scrape of his chair told her that he'd seated himself at the table.

"Abbie?"

Her cup jerked, and droplets of coffee spilled on her chin. She dabbed them with a handkerchief as she turned to face him. "Yes, Hugh?"

"Good. I thought you were never going to look at me. Now sit down."

She sat.

His brows were two dark slashes knit together. "I'm not apologizing for what happened last night, and I won't have you feeling guilty about it either. What we did was natural. It was bound to happen sooner or later. Maybe I was too ardent, but I would have stopped if you had asked me to. Always remember that: I'll stop if you ask me to."

She looked down at her hands. Apologize for those hours of joy in his arms? For the sweetest pleasure she had ever known? "I don't feel guilty and I don't want you to apologize."

"Look at me," he said softly.

She lifted her eyes to meet his. Whatever he saw there seemed to please him. With the back of his fingers, he lightly brushed her cheek. The gesture made her feel cherished.

"Abbie, why did you cry last night? Afterward, why did you cry?"

For any number of reasons. Because his proposal had

seemed so cold-blooded; because she wanted him to love her. But most of all, because she was so terribly afraid.

She leaned forward in her chair, her hands spread out on the table. "Tell me the truth, Hugh," she said. "Do you think George is still alive?"

"So that's it!" He studied her for a moment, then went on. "Yes, Abbie. Now that I've had time to reflect on it, I believe that George is alive. Think about it. If George were dead, there would be no point in concealing his body. Nemo would want us to know that he'd taken his revenge."

She'd used words like those to comfort her family, and to hear them on Hugh's lips calmed her a little. "Then where is George? And what does Nemo want with him?"

"I don't know, Abbie. But it isn't hopeless. I'll find Nemo, I promise you. And when I have him, I'll have your brother as well."

She felt anguish contract her heart. She didn't want Hugh to meet Nemo. Whatever happened, she wanted Hugh to be safe. She didn't want him to leave these rooms until someone else had dealt with Nemo. But there *was* no one else.

He saw the anguish and tried to distract her. "I've been making some notes," he said, indicating a sheet of paper on the table, "just some stray thoughts to fill the time until Harper gets here. But there are gaps in my knowledge. You can help by going back to the beginning, to Paris, and tell me all that you remember." When he saw the misery swimming in her eyes, he added, "This could be important, Abbie."

She took a sip of coffee, sniffed, and cast her mind back to the bookshop in the Palais Royal. "Little did I suspect," she said, "that when I entered Dessene's bookshop fate was lying in wait for me. It seems strange, now, that that meeting with Colette should have slipped from my mind. It certainly turned all our lives upside down. But at the time it was all so ordinary."

When she paused, he said, "You remember the girl?"

"Not very well. As I said, I wasn't really paying attention. I remember that she was young, younger than I am. And she was pretty. She tipped over my basket of books. That's when she must have passed me the book for Michael Lovatt. Almost immediately afterward, a group of Lifeguards entered the shop. One said, in French, 'I've never had an English girl before.' He was looking right at me and the others laughed. I was so frightened, I just wanted to get out of there. George hadn't heard, and I didn't tell him."

She found her handkerchief and blew her nose. "Do you know what I think, Hugh? I think Nemo was that soldier who spoke to me. I think he knew that Colette was hiding in the back of the shop, and he wanted to get rid of George and me. She must have known she'd been spotted, and that's why she put the book in my basket. Then Nemo murdered her. He told me so himself. He said he put a bullet in her brain."

Her voice cracked. "Why didn't she appeal to George and me for help? We could have done something if only we'd known."

"You would have been killed too. Colette knew that. And you did the one thing she wanted you to do. You left with the book."

"Only to have it impounded by British customs!" she said furiously. "A great help I turned out to be!"

"Then we owe Miss Fairbairn the credit, since if she hadn't written that letter, we wouldn't have known about Nemo."

His smile coaxed an answering smile from her, and

some of her tension drained away. Not long after, Tom returned with a laden tray, and as they ate she recounted everything she could remember, while Hugh took notes. When he stopped asking questions, she rose and moved restlessly around the room, then she stood by the window and looked out.

It had started to rain. In the street below, carriages were coming and going, and people were walking briskly, coat collars turned up, a few with umbrellas. Ordinary people, on an ordinary day. She wished with all her heart that she could be one of them.

She heard Hugh rise from his chair, then he was behind her, arms encircling her, hands slipping over her ribs to cup her breasts. She couldn't hide how he affected her. Her breathing became erratic, her breasts seemed to swell to fill his hands. She felt his mouth against the curve of her neck, and she shivered.

His voice was husky. "I need this," he said. "I need you. Will you come to bed with me, Abbie?"

She turned in his arms and kissed him. When she drew away, he rewarded her with one of his rare, unconsciously sweet smiles.

She led the way. He undressed them both and entered her almost immediately. It was what she wanted. Her body ached for him. At the end, his hands gripped her so strongly she knew that there would be bruises, but she needed that too.

They were still joined, still breathing hard, when he raised his head and looked down at her. His eyes were shaded with apology. "Abbie, I shouldn't have done that. I should have taken my time with you. I—"

She raised her head from the pillow, twined her arms around his neck, and set her mouth to his in a long, slow, sensual kiss.

"Thank God," he said, when he pulled himself from her. He began to dress. "I've never done that before."

She reached for her chemise. Her tone was dry. "Then all I can say is Desdemona, Catalina, and Mercedes don't know what they've missed."

His lips began to twitch. "I told you—those were the names of partisans. If you don't believe me, ask Harper."

"Maybe I've got the names wrong, but I'm sure there's quite a list."

He chuckled. "Abbie, I should have married you when—" He stopped and looked at her warily. "I never did explain about Estelle, did I?"

"No," she said. "You never did get around to telling me about your wife."

"Now, don't go giving me one of your clear-eyed stares." He raked his fingers through his hair. "I didn't tell you about her because she's not important."

"Maybe not to you, but she is to me." She sat on the bed and indicated a chair. "Sit down, Hugh. I'm all ears."

"I know how to get rid of that clear-eyed gaze," he said. "All-seeing, all-wise, and all-knowing Miss Abigail Vayle." He tilted her chin up and lowered his head. "All I have to do, Abbie, is make love to you. Then your eyes get misty as they're doing now, and your lids get heavy. I'll bet your heart is pounding like an athlete's after a race." He put his hand over her breast. "See? I was right."

"Hugh," she said weakly, "not again."

All amusement was gone from his face. "Then tell me no, Abbie."

But she couldn't say no to him, and he came down beside her on the bed.

• • • •

Abbie was in the parlor when Hugh unlocked the door to Tom. Her cheeks were pink, her hair was barely tamed, and her breath had yet to even. She picked up the newspaper that lay on the table and was studiously reading it when Tom entered and began to gather the remains of their meal.

"What kept you, Tom?" asked Hugh innocently. "Miss Vayle and I have been counting the seconds till your return. Isn't that right, Abbie?"

The look she sent Hugh would have burned him to a cinder if he'd seen it, but he wasn't looking at her. He'd gone back to working on the notes he'd made.

She snapped the paper open and stared at it blindly. What she'd learned about Estelle could have been written on the head of a pin. The man was totally exasperating. But she'd learned something important. Whether Hugh knew it or not, Estelle's betrayal still cast a shadow on his life. His trust was not given easily, and once lost was almost impossible to reclaim.

Now she understood why he'd been so hard on her. She'd betrayed him too, or so he thought, and she wondered how she could convince this difficult, complex, and wonderful man that she really loved him.

"Abbie?"

She snapped the paper again. "What?"

"I think I've found something interesting."

She lowered the paper. "What have you found, Hugh?"

"It was staring at us in the face all the time."

"What was?"

"Miss Fairbairn's letter. Colette passed the book to you, but nobody knew about it because Colette was murdered. Six weeks later, Miss Fairbairn writes that letter to

Michael Lovatt, and suddenly everyone is after the book, British intelligence, Nemo and his conspirators, and, I believe, Alex Ballard. What does that suggest to you?"

"I have no idea."

He looked at her somberly. "There's someone in the foreign office, or someone in government circles, who is passing information to the enemy—a traitor. How else would Nemo have known that the book had turned up? We're looking for a traitor."

"Maybe Alex Ballard was the traitor."

"I can't believe that. Alex came to see me in Bath to enlist my help. I was the one person he could trust because I was no longer attached to British intelligence. He must have suspected that there was a traitor passing information to our enemies. I believe Nemo murdered him."

Her eyes filled with misery. "A man like Nemo won't let my brother live, will he, Hugh?"

"I'll stop him, Abbie. This isn't over yet." When she was silent, he went on, "Just be patient. When Harper gets here with Giles's lists, we'll know more. Meanwhile, I'm going to write out a list of everyone remotely connected with that book and see if I can find some clue to who this traitor is."

"Giles's lists?"

"Didn't I tell you? I asked Giles to give me a calendar of the engagements of the Royal family and the Prime Minister and his cabinet. Nemo is an assassin. The book, well, the only reason he wanted to destroy it was to protect his mission. His real mission, I mean."

"To assassinate—? Who?"

"Someone important, someone whose death will profit Nemo and his master, Napoleon."

She couldn't hide her desperation. "We don't have

much time. He said he would be leaving England in a few days."

His eyes held hers. "I'll find him, Abbie. Trust me." He smiled whimsically. "I'm a gladiator, remember?"

Dark had fallen when they heard someone hammering on the door, then Harper's voice calling out, "I have the newspaper you ordered, sir."

This was another precaution, a code for "the coast is clear." It seemed rather silly to Abbie. She didn't see why Harper and Tom couldn't simply say "the coast is clear," but spies had their own way of doing things, and who was she to interfere?

Hugh never answered the door without his pistol in his hand. All these precautions made her realize just how dangerous he thought Nemo was.

Hugh entered the parlor first, and Harper was right behind him. Like Tom, he was all spruced up in his new livery, but unlike Tom, he was wearing a white wig, and his white gloves were immaculate.

"Did you get those lists?" asked Hugh.

"Right here," answered Harper. He slipped his hand into the inside of his jacket and produced a folded wad of papers.

"Help yourself to a glass of wine," said Hugh.

Abbie smiled when Harper removed his gloves before pouring out the wine. "I could take to a footman's life," he told her. "Do you know, they gets tipped for doing nothing? I captured one o' them lady's lapdogs in St. James's Street, as it scuppered from a carriage, and its mistress gave me a half sovereign for my trouble. Coachmen never gets tipped for nothing around here."

This was said in a baiting way for Hugh's benefit, but Hugh was already studying the lists and ignored him.

It was still raining outside. The room was warm. Abbie felt safe with Hugh and Harper here with her. She didn't think of these two men as master and servant. They were comrades, which explained why Harper overstepped the bounds of what was proper between a servant and his master.

Her gaze moved to Hugh when he threw down Giles's lists. "What is it, Hugh?" she asked.

"I've been a damned fool!" he said. "A stupid, prejudiced damned fool!" He stood up.

"Where are you going?"

"There's one piece of the puzzle that is still missing, but everything else has fallen into place. There's a dinner in the Prime Minister's honor tomorrow night at Lord Merkland's house. I think Nemo will be there, and George, too. I need to see the guest list for that dinner party."

Abbie's voice was shaking. "So you know where George is?"

"No, not yet. Harper, you stay here with Miss Vayle. I'll take Tom with me."

He gave Harper the key to the door. "Don't open the door until you hear me complaining about the weather. I'll be back in an hour or so."

She had risen, and her hands curled around the back of a chair. "And if you don't come back in an hour?"

"Harper will know what to do."

Then, with Harper looking on, he kissed her swiftly and left the room.

CHAPTER 26

When Harper locked the door behind him, Hugh felt the rush of blood through his veins. He'd felt like this many times in Spain. His mind was razor sharp, racing, teeming with impressions. Abbie had given him the map and everything was falling into place. One little piece was missing, and when he had that he'd know his way out of the maze.

Tom came out of the room opposite the suite with his pistol cradled in one arm. "Follow me," was all that Hugh said before descending the stairs.

The rain was coming down so thick and fast that it bounced off the pavement and ran in rivulets into the road. One of the hotel footmen held the doors for them and insisted on braving the elements to hail a hackney.

"I could 'ave done it," said Tom sullenly.

Hugh had more to think about than Tom's pique. "So you could, but then the footman wouldn't get his tip, would he?"

As they made to enter the coach, Hugh pressed a shilling into the footman's hand. Tom stuck out his bottom lip and glowered at the grinning lackey. Then Hugh shoved him into the coach and gave the driver directions to Vayle House.

When the hackney pulled away, the footman took the coin he'd been given and examined it under the light of the porch lantern. He'd keep it as a lucky piece, he decided, something El Centurion had given him before he, Nemo, had brought his world down around his ears. Templar was going to Vayle House on the other side of Mayfair. There was more than enough time to take care of the girl and disappear into the night.

When he entered the hotel, he kept his face expressionless. The landlord's wife was sitting in state in the little bar off the vestibule, and she wasn't pleased that her servant had come down with a fever and had sent his "cousin" to take his place. At the moment she was happy with him for hailing the hackney for her guests. He wanted to laugh out loud. He'd been playing a game with El Centurion. He'd wanted to look into his eyes and show his scorn for Templar's legendary reputation. He could have killed him there, on the spot, and his manservant with him. That he had not done so was a mark of his utter contempt. El Centurion was a nothing.

Nemo had had a few bad moments the night before when he watched them slip away from Vayle House in a boat. But he knew the value of patience. He'd taken a hackney to every spot on the river where they could have docked, and at the Blackfriars Inn, he'd been rewarded. One of the hackney drivers remembered a couple answering their description coming up from the river. He'd also overheard the directions the man had given his driver. They'd asked to be taken to a hotel in Gloucester Street, though he couldn't remember which one.

He'd been here since dawn. He'd decided to take Templar and the girl unawares, when they were sleeping. He had thought his best plan was to set a fire and get to the girl in the confusion. But this was better. Now there were only two of them to deal with.

The excitement of the chase began to hum in his blood. He could taste it, smell it. It was an aphrodisiac, hardening his body as no woman had ever done. It wasn't always this way. Only those kills that mattered to him personally affected him like this. It would pass as soon as the blood poured out of her veins. But in the future, when he was pounding into some stupid woman, reaching for his release, he would remember the chase and the kill, and his body would explode with excitement.

The landlady had come out of the bar and was watching him. He went to the kitchen, picked up the first tray he came to, and went upstairs with it.

Abbie turned from the window where she'd watched the lights of Hugh's hackney till they were swallowed up in the night. Harper was sitting at the table and was shuffling a deck of cards.

"It will help pass the time," he said, and he began to deal.

Abbie nodded absently and picked up the lists Hugh had been reading before he suddenly took off. The engagements of all the members of the royal family were there as well as those of Lord Liverpool and the leading lights of his cabinet.

"What made him suddenly decide that Lord Liverpool is Nemo's target? Why not the Prince Regent or Lord Castlereagh?" she asked.

"He didn't say, but when you thinks about it, it stands to reason. The Prime Minister practically runs the country."

"Does he? Much as my brother-in-law likes Lord Liverpool, he says that Castlereagh and Canning run the country."

"Yes, but them Frenchies don't know that, do they?"

She picked up the piece of paper with all Hugh's notes. "Why does he want the guest list to Lord Merkland's dinner party? Who does he expect to see on it?"

"He didn't tell me that either. Look, Mr. Templar said he'd be back in an hour. Why don't we have ourselves a nice rubber o' piquet to make the time pass quickly?"

She sat down and picked up her cards. "I don't know how to play."

"I'll teach you."

She shivered, but not unpleasantly. It was all coming together. All those threads that had been left hanging were beginning to weave themselves together. There was a coherency here that she'd missed because she hadn't tried to make connections. Things had happened and she had accepted them. But now she could see that they *were* connected. But she wasn't seeing clearly. She was groping for something that was just out of reach.

She glanced at the clock. In one hour, Hugh would return. "All right," she said, "let's play cards."

She had just taken the first rubber, much to Harper's disgruntlement, when they heard a scratching on the outside door. Abbie looked at Harper. He had half risen from his chair and his hand was raised in a silencing gesture. When the scratching came again, he reached for the pistol on the table and padded to the front door. Abbie went after him.

The sound that came from the other side of the door sounded like an animal in pain, then in a hoarse broken whisper, the sound of her name, "Abbie." Then there was a thud, as if someone had collapsed on the floor.

"Hugh," she cried out, and started forward.

Harper made a violent motion with one hand. "Get back!" he ordered.

"But it's Hugh!"

"Get back!"

He waited until she'd stepped into the doorway of one of the closet bedchambers, then he turned back to the door. "Mr. Templar," he said, "speak to me."

There was a long, sighing sound, then there was nothing.

Abbie cried, "Harper, he's badly hurt. He's fainted. Open the door!"

Harper hesitated, said Hugh's name again, and when there was no answer gently turned the key in the lock. In the next instant he was flung violently back against the wall as the door crashed open. Abbie saw one of the hotel footmen in gold livery and a white powdered wig. A knife flashed. He back-handed Harper in the face with the hilt, then drove it into his chest and Harper went down.

She was numb with horror, gulping air as she watched the dark stain appear on the front of Harper's coat. The footman stepped over Harper's body and kicked his pistol out of the way. Then he shut and locked the door. He was smiling.

"Miss Vayle," he said. "we meet again. May I call you Abbie? I think of you as Abbie. Don't you recognize me? Take a good look."

She knew, then, that this was Nemo, but he didn't look anything like the young man she'd encountered at the theater. This man was much heavier, and his face was lined. But he had light blue eyes, cold eyes, even when he was amused.

"No," she whispered.

"Let me refresh your memory. You danced with me at the Assembly Ball. Harry Norton? Does that help?"

"*You* are Harry Norton?"

His eyes danced with amusement. "And later that night, I had the pleasure of your company in your bed. I cannot believe that the woman who stands before me now was that sniveling, whining bitch who promised never to cross me. But you didn't keep your promise, did you, Abbie?"

Don't cower! her instincts screamed. *Don't show him you're afraid! That's what he wants, then he'll kill you.*

But she was afraid, deathly afraid. They were having an ordinary conversation like two ordinary people, and Harper was lying on the floor, bleeding to death—perhaps already dead. Nemo was going to kill her and she had no one to blame but herself. Hugh had told her never to open the door unless the code words were spoken, and she'd persuaded Harper, against his better judgment, to open the door. Hugh had told her to keep her pistol by her at all times, and she'd stupidly left it on the parlor table. If she'd done as Hugh had cautioned, she could have leveled her pistol right now and blown a hole through that grinning face.

But right behind her was the back door to the suite. She had Harper to thank for that. He'd made sure she was in a position to "fall back," as he would say, before he'd opened the door. But it didn't help. The back door was locked. She should have unlocked it the moment she knew there was trouble. Instead, she'd been frozen in place like a mesmerized rabbit before a striking cobra. By the time she opened the door, Nemo would be on her, and that would be that.

Why was he waiting? Why hadn't he finished her off? She was seized with a sudden fury. This was the man who had killed Colette. He'd boasted of it when he assaulted her in her own bed. He'd skinned Jerome alive, he'd told her, and put a bullet through Colette's brain. That poor French girl had chosen her to be the instrument of this monster's downfall. It wasn't going to end like this, not if she could help it.

Drawing more on instinct than logic, she straightened her shaking legs and threw back her head. "I can scarcely believe," she said, "that Napoleon's master spy would go to so much trouble to eliminate one worthless girl. Why are you afraid of me?"

"Afraid?" Something ugly moved in his eyes and was quickly subdued. In the same amused tone, he went on, "I fear no one and nothing. I have a reputation to keep up. You gave the book to British intelligence. You tried to trick me with a fraudulent book. What self-respecting spy could live with that? What if it were to get back to the Emperor? I would lose face."

She was as terrified of his smile and twinkling blue eyes as she was of the wicked-looking blade in his hand. "How did you know the book was fraudulent?" She didn't care how he knew. She just wanted to keep him talking so that she could edge toward the back door.

"Are you really so stupid? My agents were tracked down by British soldiers the same night you were released from prison. How else could British intelligence have known where to find them? Oh, don't look so crestfallen. You never stood a chance. You see, Abbie, I have sources in high places. I was always one step ahead of you."

"You killed Alex Ballard."

"But of course. We suspected that he knew too much. He signed his own death warrant when he went to your room that night."

"You were both looking for the book."

"Clever girl." He clicked his tongue. "What a wild life you lead, Abbie. Two gentlemen turned up in you hotel room in the middle of the night, and you were nowhere to be found. At the time, I was very angry. I thought we had an agreement, and you'd broken it. But later, when I learned the circumstances, I practically split my sides laughing. You really are hopeless, Abbie."

"Why didn't you kill Hugh when you had the chance?"

"Unlike Ballard, he didn't know anything, and too many dead spies would have caused an outcry in government circles. We would have disabled him, but that is all. We were afraid he might do exactly what he did do and take the book away from you. You're right, I should have killed him. It would have saved me a great deal of trouble later."

"And George?" she asked hoarsely.

"If it's any consolation, he'll live longer than you."

George was alive. The knowledge sank into her like rain in the desert. Not only did hope bloom, but so did her will to survive.

He removed his wig and tossed it on the floor. The dark hair that had curled so attractively when she saw him at the theater was plastered to his head.

"It's hot in here, Abbie, don't you think?"

Her time was up. She could either fight him or run.

When he began to shrug out of his jacket, she moved. She jumped back, slammed the door shut, and quickly turned the key in the lock. There was no light in the room and she was groping her way when she heard his laughter. It chilled her blood.

"Oh Abbie," he said, "I was hoping you would try something. I don't want an easy kill. Where's the pleasure in that? Run, Abbie, run, because when I catch you, I'm going to slice you into little pieces."

He was allowing her to escape! This was a game to him, a game of cat and mouse. Her fingers closed around the key as something heavy slammed into the door behind her. On a moan of terror, she opened the back door and hurled herself out of the room.

Hugh knocked on the roof of the hackney to attract the driver's attention. "Pull up, man," he cried, then with a roar, "Stop!"

The coach pulled to a halt just before the turn into Oxford Street.

"What is it?" asked Tom.

"I don't know," said Hugh. "I can't put my finger on it. The footman back there at the hotel? Why did he insist on hailing a hackney for me?"

" 'Cos," said Tom, " 'e knew you was an easy mark."

"But you were with me. Isn't that unusual? Wouldn't he have expected you to hail the cab for me?"

Tom snorted. "I've met 'is type before. Bold as brass, they is. But it worked. He was laughing at you when your back was turned."

"Laughing at me?"

" 'Cos he was too quick for you, and too quick for me, too. When I saw you put that shilling into 'is lily-white 'and, I wanted to spit on it. But that's footmen for you. They 'as an easy life, so they never gets their 'ands dirty."

Hugh frowned. "Hands? Wasn't he wearing gloves?"

"No."

Hugh stared at Tom with an appalled expression. Suddenly rising, he slammed the flat of his hand against the roof of the cab. "Driver," he roared, "get us back to the hotel at once! And I mean on the double. Now!"

She went down the stairs two at a time, and every step of the way he was right behind her. At any moment, she expected to feel his hand on her shoulder, dragging her back. Then it came to her that he was allowing her to outdistance him; that he was enjoying the chase, and when it suited him, and not before, the game would be over.

Cat and mouse.

Colette's face swam before her. She could see the French girl in vivid detail as she'd been that day in the bookshop when their hands had joined on the handle of her basket. Dark brown eyes shadowed with sadness; dark ringlets beneath a straw bonnet; and a sweet, sweet smile. She was so young.

Move! she told herself when she felt her legs buckling. *Think of Colette. You can't let her down.*

She pushed through the door at the bottom of the staircase and found herself in the kitchen. It was the dinner hour, and there were several footmen coming and going with loaded trays, and scullery maids bustling about, setting food on long tables.

"Help me, please!" She was panting, and could hardly get the words out. "He's going to kill me."

There was a sudden silence as everyone stared at her. When they looked over her shoulder, she whirled to face him. He was the same, and he was different. He'd removed his coat and waistcoat and was clad in only breeches and a white lawn shirt. He looked every inch the aristocrat. There was no sign of the knife.

His voice was cutting. "You slut! You slept with my

best friend. How many other lovers have you had, madam wife?"

"It's not true!" she cried out.

"I'm going to thrash you within an inch of your life."

As though on signal, all eyes were averted and everyone was suddenly busy. Was she the only one who could see the amusement in those pitiless eyes?

When he reached for her, she shoved one of the maids into his path, then sent trays of food toppling to the floor. On a sob of panic, she dashed through the corridor to the door that led to the courtyard.

The rain was driving down and the courtyard was deserted. It wouldn't have mattered. No one was going to help her. This was how Colette must have felt in the bookshop. There was no point in appealing to anyone. He was too clever. He could make people believe whatever he wanted. And if that failed, he would kill them.

She calculated that she had about ten seconds to hide herself. The stable block was too far away, and there would be ostlers and stableboys there who might tell him where she was hiding. Or if they got in his way, he would kill them.

There were several coaches in the yard, their traces empty of horses, and she ran to the one in the darkest corner where the lantern had gone out. She winced when the door creaked as she opened it. Quickly, silently, she slipped inside and pulled the door to without latching it. A moment later, a pool of light spilled onto the courtyard as he came out the back door.

She pressed her lips together to muffle the sound of her breathing, and when that didn't work she used her hand. She was trembling so hard, she had to grind her teeth together to try to stop their chattering.

"Abbie?"

She nudged the door open the merest crack. Now she knew why she'd had time to hide herself. He'd stopped to put on one of the coats that had been hanging on hooks in the corridor.

He put his hands on his hips. "I know you're here somewhere," he said. "I was watching from the window. You didn't go into the stable. So where are you, Abbie? In one of the coaches?"

Her fingers were gripping her mouth so tightly that her teeth were cutting into her lips. When she saw him open the door of the coach nearest to him, her whole body contracted.

She had to do something. She had to find a weapon to defend herself. Something. Anything.

Most coaches were equipped with pistols, but most pistols didn't work because their owners forgot to load them. An empty pistol was better than nothing. She hoisted herself slowly onto one of the banquettes and fumbled for the holster just under the coach lining. When her hand closed around the smooth, wooden pistol butt, she let out a shaken breath, and slowly pulled the gun free. She heard him slam the coach door, and she edged farther along the banquette.

Her fingers touched something and came away sticky. She stared down at her hand but could see little in that dim light. Slowly, she turned her head. A boneless heap was curled grotesquely in one corner of the banquette.

It was her imagination. Her nerves were playing tricks on her. It couldn't be what she thought it was.

She put out her hand and touched something cold and clammy. The boneless heap was a man, and he was dead.

A piercing scream tore from her throat.

Nemo was on her in moments. She didn't think of using the pistol. She was paralyzed with shock, and the pistol was clutched in her hand in a death grip. He yanked her from the coach, and with a back-handed slap to the face sent her flying against the wall.

He slammed the carriage door shut and knelt down beside her. It was too dark to see more than his outline, but she felt the point of his blade at her throat.

His voice was savage. "Say anything to anyone and it will be the last thing you do. Do you understand?"

She sobbed out. "You killed him."

"I needed his livery," he said carelessly. "Now keep your mouth shut."

Her thoughts were chaotic. No one killed for a suit of livery. He was mad. She had fallen into the hands of a monster. Colette. Poor Colette. She would be next. Then George.

People were running into the courtyard, maids, ostlers. He hauled her to her feet and dragged her into the light. "My errant wife," he told them, "has promised me that she won't stray again. All right, ladies and gentlemen, the show is over. Go back to your work. Now, if you don't mind, I'm taking my wife home."

There were a few titters, some low grumbles, but they were working folk who thought they were in the presence of gentry, and they backed off.

"Now move!" he told her, and he hustled her toward the arched carriage entrance that gave onto the main thoroughfare.

Hugh was in the suite upstairs when he heard Abbie's scream. They'd returned to the hotel only moments before, where they found Harper slumped on the floor, and beside him, a powdered wig and the gold jacket that distinguished the hotel's footmen. Harper had a nasty wound low on his shoulder, and he'd lost a great deal of blood, but it was the blow to his face that had disabled him. He was breathing; he would live. That's all Hugh wanted to know.

He ran to the window in one of the small bedchambers and flung it wide. In the courtyard below, lanterns flickered, but it was too dark to see clearly. The stable door was open and two ostlers had wandered outside. They were watching something, but Hugh couldn't make out what had attracted their attention.

"Take care of Harper," Hugh yelled to Tom, then he raced from the room.

As he hurtled down the stairs, he cursed himself for a fool. He'd underestimated Nemo. He should have kept one step ahead of him by switching hotels every night. He'd been out of the game too long. In his prime as a spy, he never would have missed the fact that the hotel footman had not worn gloves.

There could be no margin of error this time. If he hesitated or moved too quickly, Abbie would pay.

Abbie.

His lungs were burning when he burst into the courtyard. Two maids were standing in the porch, but there was no one else there.

"Where is the woman who screamed?" he asked harshly.

One maid pointed to the carriage entrance. " 'Er man took 'er away," she said. "She looked that terrified, didn't she, Maeve? I wouldn't like to be in 'er shoes when . . . "

Hugh ran back the way he'd come, through the front door and onto Gloucester Street. He had his pistol in one hand, and he reached into his boot and retrieved his knife. A pistol allowed a man only one shot before he had to reload it, and if that shot missed, it could be fatal.

He ran the length of the hotel and flattened himself against the wall at the entrance to the arch. He welcomed the rain. There were no pedestrians about and only a few hackneys. If they'd come through the arch, he would have seen them.

He held himself back from going into the tunnel. But his thoughts tortured him. Abbie could be dead or dying. Nemo could be slitting her throat at this very moment. He'd count to ten, and if they weren't out by then, he was going in.

Then he heard the shuffle of feet on cobblestones and he braced himself. Just before they came out of the arch, he charged. His target wasn't Nemo, but Abbie. The element of surprise was on his side, and his body slammed into hers, sending her staggering back before Nemo could react. But Hugh had left himself open, as he knew he would. He checked his momentum, but he was off balance. Nemo's knife flashed out and sliced into his arm, then he kicked Hugh in the ribs and Hugh went down.

Pain exploded through his body, but he rolled onto his back and tried to bring up his pistol. "Run, Abbie, run," he roared.

Just as he pulled the trigger, Nemo's booted foot connected with his hand and the shot went wild. The useless pistol clattered over cobblestones and came to rest beside Abbie. She got to her feet.

"Run, Abbie," Hugh roared again. "Run."

She was standing there in a daze. Didn't she see her danger? Why didn't she run?

Nemo laughed. "Yes, Abbie, run, because when I'm finished with—"

Hugh lunged with his knife and drove it deep.

Nemo stumbled back with the knife embedded in his thigh. A look of amazement crossed his face, but it quickly turned to fury. Hugh tried to rise. He made it onto one knee, but Nemo was faster. He got behind Hugh, grabbed him by the hair and dragged his head back exposing his throat. He raised his knife.

"No," said Abbie tonelessly. She came out of the shadows, and the pistol in her hand was aimed straight at Nemo's heart. She cocked it. "No," she said again.

Nemo smiled and shook his head. "You won't kill me, Abbie. I'm the only one who knows where your brother is. What will happen to George without me? He'll die."

He raised the knife, and without hesitation, Abbie pulled the trigger. The gun jerked up and the bullet blasted into Nemo's brain. He staggered back, hit the wall with a thud, and slid to the ground.

Abbie went down on her knees in front of Hugh and put her arms around him.

Hugh let out a shaken laugh. "I thought that was my pistol, Abbie. I thought it was useless."

"No. I found it in a carriage. I was waiting for the right moment to use it when you attacked me." Tears were streaming down her face. "It's not over yet, is it, Hugh? There's still one to go."

His head drooped on her shoulder. "We'll get him, Abbie. Then we'll get George."

CHAPTER 27

At Lord Merkland's stately home in Chelsea, all the gentlemen in his great dining room rose and gave the Prime Minister a standing ovation when he entered with his host. This was an all-male gathering of the Prime Minister's closest friends, old school chums and university cronies who, on this date every year, chose one of their own to whom they wished to pay tribute.

It just happened to be Lord Liverpool's turn, thought Richard Maitland cynically. It was the only thing that explained why they were honoring such a lackluster gentleman, even if he was the Prime Minister.

Bishop Ferrier gave the blessing, and when the amen was said and Maitland sat down, he realized he was sweating. He tried not to stare at any of the footmen; tried not to look at the glass door to the terrace that was slightly ajar to allow a breath of fresh air to enter that stuffy room. He had to appear natural. He couldn't give himself away. But he wished to hell it was all over.

He'd taken no more than a few sips of the turtle soup when Sir Giles stood and left with a footman. A few moments later the footman returned, and Colonel Langley left the room. Maitland's pulse started to race when, moments later, the footman returned for him.

They were in an anteroom, and Langley was looking grim. Wordlessly, he handed a note to Maitland. Maitland read it slowly. It was signed by Hugh Templar, and in a few, terse sentences stated that Nemo had been captured, that he was lodged in Newgate Prison and wanted to trade his life for information that would rock the British government.

"I'll get the Prime Minister," said Giles. "He should be told."

"No!" exclaimed Langley testily. "Let's think about this. This is Lord Liverpool's night, and I'll not have him disturbed without good reason. Richard, what do you make of this?"

Maitland said, "Templar must have used the girl as bait. He's a clever bastard. I'd better see to it."

This produced a dry laugh from Langley. "I know how much you dislike these dress-up affairs, Richard, but I want you to stay and make sure Lord Liverpool is well guarded. That goes for you, too, Sir Giles. Richard, how many men are patrolling the grounds?"

"Thirty."

"Keep them close to the house. I'll go to Newgate."

"Yes, sir."

"Sir Giles," said Langley, "give my regrets to Lord Liverpool. Tell him I shall save those school anecdotes for another occasion, and I won't spare his blushes."

Giles chuckled. "Yes, sir."

Maitland saw the colonel to his carriage. As soon as it pulled away, he looked at his watch. It was only eight o'clock.

•   •   •

Abbie squinted down at the watch that was pinned to her coat. "I can't see a thing," she said. "Daniel, do you know what time it is?"

"No. But I don't think we'll have long to wait."

"What if we're on the wrong track? What if George is not here?"

He patted her shoulder. "Let's wait and see if this plays out the way Tom said it would."

"Yes, but—"

"Shh!"

They were concealed in the shadows of an ivy-clad gazebo that overlooked the Thames on one side and a Palladian mansion on the other. Their eyes were trained on the house. Lights shone from the kitchen windows, but other than that, the house was in darkness. There were caretakers in the house, Tom had told them, but the gardeners who patrolled the grounds had been replaced by Hugh's men.

"How can Hugh be so sure that George is here?" she whispered. "And why didn't Hugh come for us himself? Why did he send Tom?"

"I don't know any more than you. Patience, Abbie. It will soon be over."

"Where did Tom go?"

"He's with Templar."

"Yes, but where is Hugh?"

"I don't know."

They'd been waiting here for an hour, and she was chilled to the morrow, but there was nowhere else she would rather be. Pray God, they would find George alive and the nightmare would be over.

Abbie clutched Daniel's arm. "Look," she breathed out.

A figure carrying a lantern had come round the side of the house. This is what they'd been waiting for, and

Abbie's breath caught in her throat as her excitement mounted. The figure did not enter the house as she'd anticipated, but turned aside and disappeared behind a clump of dense shrubbery. Her breath came out in a rush.

"Then . . . if George isn't in the house, where is he?"

Daniel said, "I hope to God Templar knows what's going on. Perhaps I should—"

He broke off when two other figures came round the side of the house. The one with a lantern lifted it high.

Daniel let out a relieved breath. "That's my cue," he said, then, "On no account are you to leave the gazebo, do you understand, Abbie? When we find George, I'll come for you."

"I understand."

"You're on your honor. This is no place for a woman!"

"I know."

"You have your pistol?"

She held up her pistol. "I never let it out of my sight now."

"Good girl!"

When Daniel slipped away, she leaned against a post and took several long breaths. The weight of the pistol in her hand was beginning to strain her wrist, so she cradled it in the opposite arm as Harper had taught her.

Tears pricked the back of her eyes. She would never forget her horror when Nemo had plunged that knife into Harper's chest. Thank God Harper was recovering. She wasn't sorry she'd killed Nemo—she, Abigail Vayle, who wouldn't allow the servants to lay mousetraps when the mice were eating her out of house and home. And if she had to do it over, she'd shoot him again.

She hoped Colette would somehow know that she hadn't let her down.

She began to tremble. It wasn't only Harper she was

thinking of. She remembered the line of Hugh's throat when Nemo had dragged his head back. Hugh had had a lucky escape. The arm that Nemo had knifed was practically useless. Then what was Hugh doing here, directing a dangerous operation, when he should be in his bed?

The minutes dragged by like hours. She grew restless and began to pace. Something was wrong, terribly wrong. Why hadn't Daniel come for her? What was keeping him?

The wave of terror that suddenly engulfed her made her body clench. "No," she whispered. George couldn't be dead, not now, not when they had such high hopes of finding him alive. It would be too cruel. She couldn't bear it.

Then what was keeping Daniel?

She stewed and fretted for a little while longer, then she went after Daniel.

Their quarry was easy to follow. He crashed through the underbrush like a panicked buffalo, and he held the lantern high to guide his steps. Hugh let him get well ahead before he cupped his hands and hooted like an owl. Silence. Then the others came out of the shrubbery and joined him.

"Douse the lantern," he said.

After this was done, they struck out along the path that was overgrown with ivy and bramble bushes, but not as overgrown as it had once been. This area had been used recently. All in all, it was a very clever setup. Lord Merkland's house, where the dinner had taken place that night, was practically next door, only half a mile along the road, and this was an ideal hiding place for an assassin who had to disappear in a hurry. After killing the Prime Minister, Nemo could have slipped away in the confusion and reached this place in a matter of minutes—long before a proper search could get underway. And no one would have given this property more than a cursory search. It was above suspicion, considering who owned it.

When their quarry halted, so did they. They had come out at the old, underground icehouse. At Hugh's signal, they silently fanned out.

There was a short flight of stairs down to the door to the icehouse, but they could still see the man with the lantern. He rapped on the door and gave the password.

It was Colonel Langley's voice, harsh, breathless, but unmistakable.

The door was opened a crack.

"Nemo has been taken," said Colonel Langley, "and he's squealing like a stuck pig. I want the boy out of here. I don't care where you take him, just get him out of here and get rid of him. Without him, they can't connect us to Nemo. What are you waiting for? Don't you understand? The game is up. Get the boy, and don't leave any evidence that will get us all hanged."

Hugh was sure that if there had been more light, he would see tears in Daniel's eyes and Giles's too. George was alive. By the same token, he knew he would see an expression of utter horror and grief on Richard Maitland's face. When Hugh had laid out all the facts for Maitland this morning, he refused to believe that Langley was a traitor until he'd seen the proof with his own eyes. Well, now he'd seen it.

Colonel Langley laboriously climbed the steps. He was limping now, and Hugh remembered that he'd got that limp years ago when he fell through a roof of a disused icehouse he'd forgotten was on his property. He'd found a horrifying use for it these last weeks.

Muffled sounds came from inside the icehouse, then

George was led out. His hands were bound behind his back and his mouth was gagged. Hugh waited until George and his jailer were clear of Langley before he took a step forward.

"Put your hands up," he barked out, "or I'll blow your brains out."

Langley's hands slowly rose.

The man who was guarding George said, "What took you so long, Mr. Templar, sir? It's bleeding cold in that there ice 'ouse. Our teeth is chattering like castanets."

At the sound of the unfamiliar voice, Langley jerked round. Hugh smiled. "Good job, Tom," he said. "Daniel, get George. Giles, get Langley's lantern and bring it over here, and don't get between Langley and me."

Daniel removed his brother's gag and bonds, then held him at arms' length. George was so weak, he could hardly support himself. His clothes hung on him loosely and were covered in filth. He smelled as though he'd bathed in a sewer. But he was grinning, and that grin was Daniel's undoing.

George squinted up at Daniel and his face puckered. "What's wrong with you, Daniel? Aren't you glad to see me?"

But Daniel couldn't speak. He embraced his brother and his shoulders began to heave. Giles came up and he enfolded both brothers in his arms. "Thank God! Thank God!"

It was a long time before they broke apart, and when they did, Daniel had found his voice. "If you ever again go off without telling anyone—" He broke off as George sagged against him. "Templar! There's something wrong with my brother! I think he's drunk."

"He's just weak," Hugh said. "They kept him sedated. A few days at home and he'll be his old self again. You did well, George. Without your help, we could never have caught Langley."

Langley lowered his hands. "So you were here earlier."

"I was, and in case you're wondering, your co-conspirators are already locked up in Newgate. You're the only one left."

"They're Nemo's co-conspirators, not mine."

"Nemo is dead," said Hugh.

Langley's head came up. "You've done well, Hugh."

"Miss Vayle killed him."

"I see." Langley paused. "Then who told you where to find young Vayle?"

"No one told me. When I finally figured out that you were Nemo's accomplice, I decided to take a look around your house. When I got here, I noticed something strange—your gardeners were armed. One of them took the path to the old icehouse. It struck me that that would be the perfect place to hide a hostage. Maitland and I came back later with a detail of soldiers and we found George."

"Then why didn't you arrest me at once? Why go through that charade at Merkland's house?"

"Because the evidence against you was circumstantial. George had never heard of you and didn't recognize your description. We had to catch you red-handed."

George said, "I did my part, too, Daniel. Tom was going to take my place, but I wouldn't let him. No, don't look like that. It was all right, really. Tom's been feeding me bread and hot soup, and I . . . I . . ." His head slowly sank down on Daniel's breast.

Maitland, who had been standing quietly with his pistol trained on Langley, suddenly exploded. "Do you know what I told Templar when he came to see me this morning? I scoffed at his suspicions. I told him that Nemo had set you up. I said that unless I caught you in the act, I would never believe you were a traitor. *Why,* in God's name, why?"

When Langley was silent, Hugh said, "The usual reasons. Money. There was no legacy. That was just a pretext to explain how he could afford to refurbish his house and launch young Hetty in style."

"Money!" Maitland's tone was scathing.

Langley's face turned a fiery red. His tone was just as cutting as Maitland's. "Do you know what my income is? Do you know how much a colonel in the British army makes? I have a daughter to launch in society. I had a stately home that was crumbling around my ears. But we managed; by scrimping and cutting corners, we managed to get by, until the minister decided to get rid of me. I gave my life to my country, and this was to be my reward. They said I was too old. They were going to pension me off, force me into retirement and let a younger man take my place. Oh, yes, and as a sop to my pride, they allowed everyone to think the idea had come from me.

"Who betrayed whom? What I did, I did for my wife and daughter. They deserved better than this. So don't try to make me feel guilty."

Maitland said bitterly, "And you think that makes it all right? Because you were slighted, four of my agents had to die? And Ballard—how could you have turned on one of your own?"

"Because he suspected me! He was asking awkward questions. I had the letter from Miss Vayle long before it reached your desk. I knew you'd find out about it soon enough from the Paris office, but I wanted to give Nemo time to get to England and get the book first.

"Somehow, Alex found out about the letter. If he had found the book he would have gone over my head and given it to the minister. I couldn't let that happen."

Maitland tried to control his anger, failed, and burst out, "So when Alex turned up in Miss Vayle's room in Marlborough, Nemo was waiting for him! There are no words base enough to describe a man like you."

Daniel said urgently, "Can't this wait? George is shaking. He's not well. It's all right, George. We're going to get you home right away."

But George resisted and fought his way out of his brother's arms. He pressed a hand to his eyes.

"George—"

"No, Daniel! No! I want to hear what that man has to say. I want to look into his eyes and ask him *why*. They were going to kill me and leave my body in the grounds of Merkland House so that everyone would think I had murdered the Prime Minister. I was to be the scapegoat. But I never understood why they were doing all this."

Hugh and Maitland had already heard George's story so it came as no surprise to them. But Daniel's face went parchment white and he crouched as though he would spring at Langley. Giles prevented it by clasping Daniel in a bear hug and subduing his struggles.

"I'll kill him," Daniel ground out. "Damn you, Giles, let me go. I'll kill him! I swear it!"

"No, Daniel!" Giles tightened his arms, holding Daniel in a vice-like grip. "He's not worth it. And he'll hang for his crimes."

"I think not."

At Langley's sharp retort, there was a sudden and profound silence. Everyone looked at him, and under that intense scrutiny, a transformation took place. He squared his stooped shoulders; he lifted his chin proudly and gave back stare for stare. He was every inch the commander.

Hugh experienced the oddest sensation. Fragments of

memories flashed through his mind with the speed of lightning: Langley, grim-faced and pacing when an agent was late in reporting back; Langley, roaring like a lion when someone took foolish risks; his face ravaged with grief when one of his men didn't return from a mission.

And his men had worshiped him.

He'll hang for his crimes.

"First of all," said Langley, "in answer to that young man's question, I'll say only this. It was Nemo's idea to use him as the scapegoat, not mine. Nemo was out of control. He was using the boy to punish Miss Vayle because she didn't follow orders. He wouldn't listen to reason, and I had gone too far at that point to turn back.

"As for why we were doing it, I think that must be obvious by now. With Lord Liverpool out of the way, there would be no one in charge until Parliament could agree on someone to replace him, and that could take weeks. It would be a good time for our enemies to strike."

Giles said, "What enemies? What are you talking about?"

Langley smiled. "And I thought you were all so clever."

"It must be Napoleon," said Hugh. "Nemo is Napoleon's man. He wouldn't kill for anyone else."

Maitland shook his head. "No," he said. "Napoleon is locked up on Elba. Langley wouldn't go that far. He despises Napoleon." Then, as the truth dawned on him, "My God, we'd better alert the Prime Minister at once."

"You're too late." Langley made a sudden movement with his hand, silencing everyone. "If everything has gone to plan, Napoleon has already broken out of Elba. I expect the news will reach England in a few days."

Giles suddenly exclaimed, "The two events would

have occurred simultaneously! That's it, isn't it? Lord Liverpool's assassination and Napoleon's escape from Elba were meant to coincide. And with the Prime Minister out of the way, there would be chaos in Parliament, no one at the helm to stop Napoleon."

Langley gave a dry laugh. "Don't look so aghast, all of you. Nothing will come of it. Let Napoleon raise his standard. No one will join him. His generals are loyal to the French crown now. There will be no war between England and France."

Giles said quietly, "You're a fool if you believe that."

"But I do believe it, otherwise I would never have embarked on this scheme. Good God! You can't believe I would have seen my country go down to defeat. Napoleon is finished I tell you. I used Nemo. He didn't use me."

"You—"

Langley said testily, "I've said my piece and that's all I'm going to say. Well, Richard, what are you waiting for? Do your duty and act like an agent."

Maitland shook his head. "I don't have the stomach for it."

"I do," said Hugh.

Langley's eyes locked on Hugh. "My pistol is in my pocket. You deliberately allowed me to keep it, didn't you, Hugh?"

Hugh was silent.

"Thank you for that," said Langley softly. Then, brusquely, "You'd be a fool to take chances. I'm going to shoot to kill."

"I'm counting on it."

Langley reached for his pistol.

There was a movement on the path, and Abbie came into the light. "No!" she screamed. "No, Hugh!"

"Abbie, get back!" Hugh roared.

Langley aimed his pistol at Abbie. It was Maitland who shot him dead.

Hugh closed his eyes and rested his neck on the back of the banquette. He and Maitland were the only two people in the carriage, and neither of them had spoken since they'd dumped Langley's body in his luxuriously appointed mansion. Hugh guessed that Langley's plan had been to move his family into it in another week or so, after things had quieted down and he'd obliterated all traces of the old icehouse. Instead, he was lying in a heap, growing colder by the minute, in front of the white marble fireplace in his formal drawing room. Nemo had fared no better. He would be buried on the morrow in a pauper's grave, just an unfortunate, nameless footpad who had come to a bad end. Giles was going to take care of everything.

He should be feeling elated now that George was safe, but he couldn't seem to muster any emotion at all. Not even the thought of Napoleon could jog him from his inertia. Giles would have informed the Prime Minister by now, but really, he wasn't interested. That would come later, he supposed. For now, he was still trying to come to terms with the fact that one of the best damn commanders in the British army had turned traitor.

There had been no piece of brilliant deduction on his part to unmask Langley. He'd put his chief's name on his list of suspects simply because Langley was a member of British intelligence. He'd even put Giles's name on his list because Abbie's brother-in-law seemed to have inside knowledge of everything that went on at Whitehall. At the top of that list, of course, was Richard Maitland's name.

He'd wanted it to be Maitland because he couldn't stand the man. But it just didn't wash. If it hadn't been for Maitland, the men who attacked him at the Black Boar wouldn't have been frightened off. So Maitland couldn't be one of Nemo's men. He had to be in the clear.

By a process of elimination, he was left with Langley's name. But he trusted the colonel so much that he hadn't even bothered to think things through. It was only when Harper had brought him the calendar of the Prime Minister's engagements that doubt began to set in. He knew that Lord Merkland and Langley were neighbors, and he knew that Langley's house was lying empty. It would be the ideal place to hide a hostage or an assassin who, having completed his mission, needed a safe place to stay. That started another train of thought: the expense, as Abbie eloquently described it, of launching a young woman in society; the expense of refurbishing a house for a come-out ball. Where had the money come from?

A legacy, Langley had told everyone. But was it true?

And in the early hours of this morning, Giles had used his influence and connections to discover that there was no legacy. Langley was paying for everything in gold coin, but where the money was coming from was anyone's guess.

Maitland said, "That's the trouble with having a traitor in our midst. You don't know who you can trust."

"What?" Hugh sat up.

"I was thinking of Ballard, not knowing who to trust, not knowing what he was up against. He wouldn't have known about Nemo. None of us did until the book was decoded. Except Langley, of course. When I think of Ballard, I wish to God I'd let that bastard hang."

"Why didn't you?"

"You know why. Because Langley trained us."

Maitland lapsed into silence, leaving Hugh to his own thoughts. He was thinking of Abbie and how she'd witnessed Langley's last moments. She'd walked in on an execution. Though he and Maitland hadn't talked about it beforehand, they'd both known they would never allow Langley to go to trial. And Langley had known it too. He'd taught his agents to clean up their own messes. And that's exactly what they'd done.

If that made him barely civilized, so be it.

Abbie seemed to think so. She hadn't said a word to him when she left with George.

It had been a mistake to allow her to go out to Langley's place. But he'd thought it only right that she should be one of the first to greet George. She'd risked so much for her brother. He should have known she wouldn't do as she was told and remain in the gazebo.

And she'd seen him in the worst possible light.

El Centurion. Gladiator. Barely civilized. Maybe he was all these things, but couldn't she see that he'd had no choice?

She would be home by now. He could imagine the joy at Vayle House. And so there should be. They'd lived through hell, and George most of all. He'd spent weeks in a windowless cellar that was heated only at night so that the smoke escaping through the makeshift chimney could not be detected by outsiders. There had been a straw pallet on the earth floor, a table and chair, a commode, and that was all. Most men would have gone mad. What had kept George sane was hope. He'd known that his family wouldn't let him down.

Good had triumphed over evil and that didn't happen very often. Then why the hell was he so glum?

He thought of his own house and how Harper would growl at him again because he'd missed the action. He'd been in no shape to dress himself, let alone take part in anything. He would be waiting up for him, wanting to know how everything had turned out. They would commiserate, and maybe get drunk together, but they would both know that there wasn't enough whiskey in the whole of England to blot out the memory of what Langley had done.

He wondered what Richard Maitland had to go home to.

He opened his eyes. "Why don't you come home with me and we'll crack open a bottle or two? This has been a god-awful night, and I feel like drowning my sorrows. And Harper will be there."

"How is Harper?"

"Cantankerous, but he'll live."

They both smiled.

Maitland said, "I've always envied you Harper. Loyalty like that is priceless." He laughed mirthlessly. "That's where I went wrong with Langley."

"Then you'll come?"

"Won't you be going to Vayle House?"

"I'm not in the mood for it. They didn't know Langley. They won't understand how I feel. Hell, even I don't know how I feel, and I'd only be a damper on their high spirits. I'll wait a day or two before I drop in on them."

"In that case, I accept your invitation. There's nothing and no one waiting for me at home." Maitland stretched out his long legs. "He was the best, wasn't he? I mean, before this happened. He was an excellent commander."

"None better. He trained us well."

"They shouldn't have forced him into retirement.

That was not well done." He sighed. "But that doesn't excuse what he did."

"No," said Hugh.

"I had to be the one to put him down."

"I never doubted for a moment that you would do it."

"I had a dog when I was a boy. We were inseparable. I even took him to church with me. Then he got rabies. I didn't want to kill him, but I had no choice. It was the hardest thing I've ever done."

"I understand."

After a long interval of silence, Maitland said, "I hope you will accept my apology for being such a jackass."

"You mean for suspecting me? Well, if it's any consolation, I suspected you too. So our apologies cancel each other out."

"I hope Miss Vayle is as forgiving as you."

"Miss Vayle is more forgiving than I am. Which puts me in mind of something. She said that you showed her my record as an agent, but there are no records, so what exactly did you show her?"

"When I began to suspect you, I made up my own file, tracing your career from the beginning, trying to spot when you had turned bad. There was nothing, of course. You were an exemplary agent, one of the best."

"An exemplary agent? I can't believe I'm hearing this. You've always made it clear that you dislike me intensely."

Maitland's Scottish brogue rolled off his tongue. "That was on a superficial level. I knew you were good at your job. That's why I was so bloody minded when I began to suspect you were a traitor."

Hugh let out a laugh. Maitland folded his arms across his chest and glowered at Hugh.

Hugh said, "Richard, you've just restored my faith in human nature. No, I mean it. I was more prejudiced than you. I allowed my superficial dislike of you to cloud my judgment of your abilities, and in an agent, that is inexcusable."

He held out his hand. Maitland looked at it suspiciously, but after a moment put his own hand in Hugh's and gripped it.

Hugh said quietly, "Friends?"

Maitland stopped glowering. "Friends," he said at last. "Now take that silver spoon out of your mouth, Templar, so we can get drunk together."

CHAPTER 28

On the day after George's rescue, the papers carried the shocking news of Napoleon's escape from Elba and his subsequent landing on the coast of France. On the second day after George's rescue, it was reported that Colonel Langley had been tragically shot dead by housebreakers whom he had surprised in his magnificently refurbished house in Chelsea. On the third day, Hugh and Maitland called at Vayle House.

They were shown at once into the family's private sanctum, the upstairs parlor overlooking the Thames. Harriet and Giles were out walking in Hyde Park with their two infant daughters, but everyone else was there.

George was the focus of attention. With his calm gray eyes, light blond hair, and slightly squared chin, he closely resembled Abbie. His clothes were hanging on him but he looked relaxed and happy.

As the conversation went on around him, Hugh's eyes frequently strayed to Abbie. She didn't appear to notice. She had eyes only for George. Every once in a while, she would touch him, not obviously, but as if by accident.

Then her eyes would fill with tears and she would look away, but she would not look at Hugh.

George said, "I never really thanked you for rescuing me, Mr. Templar, and you, too, Mr. Maitland. I never completely gave up hope, but I knew that my life was hanging by a thread. Bea has told me how much I owe you both, and I shall be forever in your debt."

"As we are in yours," said Maitland. "It was a brave thing you did, a very brave thing, returning to that hole in the ground so that we could catch Langley red-handed."

Everyone in the room knew what part Colonel Langley had played in things, and everyone knew they could never speak of it outside these walls.

George said, "I never saw him. It was the other one who would visit me from time to time."

"Nemo?" said Hugh.

"I think so. When I first met him, he said his name was Ashton. He was supposed to be taking me to Chatsworth to talk to the duke's gardener. He drugged me, and when I awakened, I was in that hole." He looked at Abbie. "I didn't want to write those letters, Bea, but he told me if I didn't, he would kill you."

"It's all right," she soothed. "I understand."

"He told me he'd killed Colette. She was the girl in the bookshop, wasn't she? The one who passed you the book?"

"Yes."

"Then," he said fiercely, "I'm glad you and I did our part to bring Nemo and Langley to justice. I've thought about it constantly, and it feels right to me that we completed what Colette started. She chose us, and we didn't let her down."

Lady Clivendon began to weep, and to cover the awkwardness, Daniel began to pass around glasses of sherry. "We've been reading the papers," he said. "I can't say we were surprised to hear that Napoleon has landed in France. But the question that everyone is asking is, Does this mean war? Maitland, Templar, what do you think?"

Maitland looked at Hugh, and when he saw that Hugh was looking at Abbie, he answered the question. "I don't think there's any doubt of that."

"Then I suppose you'll both be rejoining Wellington?"

Again Maitland looked at Hugh, with the same result. "I think I can speak for us both when I say that if the call goes out, of course, we'll rejoin Wellington's staff."

"You mean," said Abbie, "behind enemy lines as spies?"

Maitland smiled as he shook his head. "I'm afraid, Miss Vayle, I'm not at liberty to answer that question."

Abbie jumped to her feet and ran from the room. Hugh went after her.

He caught her on the landing. There was a brief struggle, then he grabbed her arm and half dragged, half propelled her into a small book room. When he shut the door and let her go, she rubbed her arm and backed away from him.

"Abbie," he said, "I want to apologize for what happened at Langley's place." When there was no response, he exhaled a long breath. "I don't know how much you saw or heard outside the icehouse—"

"Plenty!" she retorted.

This time, he *inhaled* a long breath. "I know I must

seem hard to you, but we couldn't refuse George's offer. We had to make Langley show his hand. It was the only way to prove his guilt. And George was willing. He understood.

"As for Langley—" He was forced to clear his throat. "I'm sorry you had to witness that scene. But try to see it from my point of view and Maitland's. Langley had recruited us; he'd trained us. He was our mentor. We trusted him implicitly. And he betrayed us. We did no more than Langley had trained us to do. He deserved what he got." He paused. "Did we seem brutal to you? Well, this is war, and war makes brutes of men. Sometimes only brutal methods will do. But I'm sorry you had to witness that scene."

He had rehearsed in his mind how he would defend himself. All the same, he was taken aback when she walked to the window and stood staring out with her back to him.

"It's all a game to you, isn't it, Hugh?" she asked tonelessly.

"What is?"

"Chasing down spies; gladiator fights to the death."

"You ought to know me better than that."

"Oh, I think I know you." She gave him one swift glance over her shoulder, then looked out the window again. "I've read your file, remember?"

"So we're back to that, are we?"

He stared at the rigid line of her back, and he felt utterly defeated. This was one battle that would never end, one battle he did not think he could win. She had seen him in the worst possible light, and he did not know how he could erase the memory from her mind.

As hope died, anger began to rise in him. He had waited for three days and had received not one word from her. A fool would have known what to make of it. He'd made excuses, told himself that she deserved time alone with her family and George. But he'd known, deep down he'd known, that she'd shut him out of her life.

Mortified pride ripped through him, savaging his control. He tried to hang on to it, but she turned to look at him, and her cool-eyed stare snapped the last shreds.

"There is never any pleasing you, is there, Abbie? You wanted a gladiator to save your brother, but now that George is safe, I'm not fit to kiss the hem of your gown. You read the file that Maitland kept on me, and now I can do nothing right in your eyes. Well, I am more than the man in that file, and if you can't see it, there is no hope for us."

She swiveled to face him, shock and disbelief mirrored in her eyes. He did not see them. He was riding the wave of all the pent-up doubts that had made him writhe since she walked in on Langley's execution.

"Yes, I became a gladiator again, but with the best reason in the world. I would have done anything to protect the woman I love. Do you think that anything less than fear for your welfare could have dragged me back to the kind of life I loathe? I don't deny that I handed you over to Maitland. But I wasn't thinking like an agent. I wasn't doing my job. I was thinking like a man. I loved you, and you had betrayed me. What did you expect me to do? I was bitter. I wanted to punish you. I tried to apologize, to make amends. But you wouldn't listen, not until you needed me again—to save your brother.

"Now, I begin to comprehend." His eyes moved over her in a slow, insulting appraisal. "That's why you gave yourself to me, isn't it? It was in payment for services rendered. My God, what kind of man do you think I am?" He strove to control his breathing. "That's a stupid question! You've made it abundantly clear what you think of me. By damn, no woman will ever have such power to hurt me again."

She stood stock-still, incapable of movement or speech. Tears of contrition blinded her eyes, and she covered her face with her hands. One of those horrible aching lumps was lodged in her throat. How could she have hurt him like this? But he had misunderstood. She wasn't looking down on him because he was a gladiator. She was mortally afraid that he wasn't enough of a gladiator to stand up against someone like Nemo. It was fear that had made her lash out at him. She wanted to keep him safe. She loved him.

And it seemed that Hugh loved her too.

"Hugh, forgive me," she whispered brokenly, and blinking away tears, she reached for him.

But Hugh was no longer there.

She picked up her skirts and dashed through the open door. Down the stairs she raced, taking them two at a time, screeching his name like a banshee. She caught up with him in the front gardens. She grabbed for his wrist and tugged with all her might. Though he shook her off, he turned to face her.

Her words were punctuated by the harsh sound of her breathing. "Just where do you think you're going, Hugh?"

The sneer on his face shook her confidence, then she saw the pain in his eyes, and her heart seemed to break open.

"Don't worry, Abbie," he said. "I realize Bath is too small for both of us. I thought I might retire to Oxford, or maybe Endicote. I'm thinking of buying Mrs. Deane's house. And there are plenty of Roman ruins around both areas to keep me out of your way for years to come."

"But . . . I thought you were going to rejoin Wellington. It's what Maitland said."

"Contrary to what you think, I don't burn with the lust to kill my fellow man. I never did. All it ever was to me was a job that someone had to do. When I got out of the service, I promised myself that I was never going back, and nothing has made me change my mind."

He turned and walked away from her.

She held up her arms, hands fisted, as though beseeching the heavens to help her with this stubborn man. "Hugh Templar," she cried out. "Don't turn your back on me now. I love you, Hugh. I love you with my whole heart."

He stopped walking, but he kept his back to her.

She cried despairingly, "As God is my witness, I love you, Hugh."

It was only a coincidence, Hugh told himself, but as Abbie's words died away, the heavens blazed with an explosion of warring thunderbolts and the earth shook. Before he had captured her in his arms, the rains came down like a river in spate.

He hustled her up the front steps and into the house. "I shall never understand the mind of a woman," he growled. "If you love me, why did you look at me as though I were beneath contempt? Why did you say what you did?"

"Because I was scared out of my wits; because I thought you were going to become a spy again. I couldn't help thinking what happens to gladiators. They're never allowed to retire or give up. They don't grow old. They just keep on going until they meet someone who is stronger, faster, more ruthless than they are.

"Do you think," she cried softly, reaching her arms

around his neck and burying her face in his coat, "that I shall ever forget these last few days? Nemo with a knife at your throat? And you, inviting Langley to shoot you when you could barely hold your pistol straight?"

She began to shiver, and he opened his coat, drawing her into the warmth of his body. She looked up at him with huge, tortured eyes. "If you ever go back to that kind of life, how shall I endure it? Every day you were away from me, I would die inside. I never knew how fragile gladiators could be."

He closed his eyes as the balm of her words healed every festering sore. With shaking fingers, he framed her face. He whispered hoarsely, "And I never knew how fragile I was until I met you. I love you, Abbie. As God is my witness, I love you."

They didn't hear the clash of thunderbolts or the raging tempest outside. They were locked in each other's arms, and nothing existed beyond themselves.

Several weeks later, on their prolonged honeymoon in Endicote, Abbie was sitting up in bed, reading a letter from her sister, while Hugh snuggled close to her warmth with a big smile on his face. When his hand brushed an intimate part of her anatomy, she slapped it away. Hugh frowned. That had never happened before.

He propped himself up on one elbow and studied his beautiful wife. A frown marred her brow, and she was chewing on her bottom lip.

"Not bad news, I hope?" said Hugh.

"Harriet," said Abbie fretfully, "is spending money like water." She waved the letter under his nose. "This is nothing but a list of her most recent purchases. She has even pursuaded Giles to buy her a phaeton so that she can drive in Hyde Park."

"Why should that surprise you? Harriet loves to shop and Giles loves to indulge her."

"The point is, she told me that after what had happened with George, she took no pleasure in things and that she would devote herself to people."

"People will say anything in a crisis, and once the crisis is over, they go back to their old ways. There's nothing unusual in that." When Abbie's frown did not fade, he said reflectively, "Quite frankly, I don't relish the thought of Harriet doting on me, and I don't think Giles would either. Men hate women who fuss. And now that I know Harriet better, I realize she's a good sort. No really, I mean that. I like her just the way she is."

"I suppose . . . but . . ."

"But what?"

She tossed the letter aside and snuggled down beside him. "When George was abducted, we all went through such soul-searching. And now look at us. Nothing has changed. We're just the same old people we always were."

"I don't want you to change," said Hugh. "Do you want me to change?"

"No. I just want us to cherish each other."

"And that's how it will be. It's drawn us all closer together. That's what matters."

After several minutes of pleasurable activity, Abbie sighed into his mouth. "Hugh, will you still love me when I'm ugly and fat and swollen with child?"

"What do you think?"

She shook her head at his glowering expression. "I've said it before and I'll say it again: for someone as clever as you, you can be incredibly dense. Give me your hand."

He gave her his hand, and she placed it with fingers splayed out against her flat stomach, then she watched the daze creep into his eyes as enlightenment dawned. She didn't need words. In his eyes she read everything she'd hoped to see and more besides, and her heart sang.

But he gave her the words anyway.

AUTHOR'S NOTE

Napoleon broke out of Elba in March 1815. Contrary to what many people expected, including the fictitious Colonel Langley, Frenchmen everywhere flocked to join their former Emperor. Three months later, on June 18, two of the most brilliant generals the world has ever seen, Napoleon and the Duke of Wellington, finally came face-to-face in the battle of Waterloo. Napoleon was defeated and spent the rest of his life in exile on the island of St. Helena.

Hugh and Abbie's story is not quite finished. Though Hugh never returned to British intelligence, after much soul-searching, and with Abbie's blessing, he rejoined his regiment to fight as an ordinary soldier at Waterloo. Harper went with him when the Prime Minister, in gratitude for Harper's part in uncovering the plot to assassinate him, used his influence to reinstate Harper in the British army.

Hugh and Harper survived the battle. On returning to England, Hugh took up his life with Abbie, and they divided their time between Oxford and Bath. Harper, meanwhile, joined Richard Maitland's staff when Maitland took over Langley's job as chief of intelligence.

If you want to read the epilogue to Hugh and Abbie's story, e-mail me [thornton@pangea.ca] and I'll send you a copy.

Now, it's more than time that I let these characters go. . . .

ABOUT THE AUTHOR

ELIZABETH THORNTON holds a diploma in education and a degree in Classics. Before writing women's fiction she was a school teacher and a lay minister in the Presbyterian Church. *Whisper His Name* is her eleventh historical novel. Ms. Thornton has been nominated for and received numerous awards, among them the Romantic Times Trophy Award for Best New Historical Regency Author, and Best Historical Regency. She has been a finalist in the Romance Writers of America Rita Contest for Best Historical Romance of the year. Though she was born and educated in Scotland, she now lives in Canada with her husband. They have three sons and five grandchildren.

Ms. Thornton enjoys hearing from her readers. Her e-mail address is <thornton@pangea.ca> or visit her at her home page:

http://www.pangea.ca/-thornton

or write to her:

P.O. Box 69001 RPO Tuxedo Park
Winnipeg MB R3P 2G9
Canada

Read on for a preview
of Elizabeth Thornton's next
thrilling historical romance. . . .

ALMOST A PRINCESS

On sale in
January 2003

Chapter 1

*I*t was moving day for the members of the Ladies' Library in Soho Square. Their lease had run out, and one of their staunchest supporters, Lady Mary Gerrard, had offered her mansion in the Strand. The house was buzzing as an army of ladies and their helpers set to work to transform their new quarters, room by room, from a palatial residence to a library with lecture rooms, reading rooms, and a bright and airy tearoom.

Lord Caspar Devere stood just inside the marble entrance hall, taking it all in. He was a harshly handsome man, thirtyish, well above average height, with dark hair and gray, gray eyes that, for the moment, were distinctly amused.

He left his hat and gloves on a hall table and wandered into the main salon. Some of the men who were helping the ladies were known to him, and that brought a smile to his lips. Not many gentlemen wanted it known that their wives or sisters were members here.

As the Viscount Latham passed close by, carrying a chair, Caspar called out, "Freddie, where can I find Lady Octavia?"

On seeing Caspar, the viscount registered surprise, quickly followed by amusement. In a stage whisper, he replied, "I won't tell anyone I saw you here if you don't tell anyone about me." Then in a normal voice, "Try next door. That's where she has set up her headquarters."

Caspar wandered into another salon, and there she was, the library's founder and driving force, Lady Octavia Burrel. Dressed all in white in something that closely resembled a toga with a matching turban, she directed her small army as they came to her for their orders. Though there was much coming and going, there was very little confusion.

Caspar was not there to help but to gather information, and when the crush around Lady Octavia thinned, he quickly crossed to her. He was sure of his welcome because he'd known her for as long as he could remember. She and his aunt were close friends.

When she saw him, her chubby face lit up with pleasure. "Lord Caspar," she said. "This is a surprise! I had no idea you were interested in our cause."

As Caspar well knew, there was a lot more to the Ladies' Library than its innocent name implied. The cause to which Lady Octavia referred was improving the lot of women by changing the antiquated marriage and property laws of England. The Library was also involved, so rumor went, in helping runaway wives evade their husbands. In some circles, Lady Octavia and her volunteers were seen as subversives. In the clubs he attended, they were frequently the butt of masculine laughter. But there were others who supported the aims of Lady Octavia and her League of Ladies. His aunt was one of them. He had never given the matter much thought.

"I suppose," said Lady Octavia, "I have your aunt to thank for sending you to help us?"

He avoided a direct answer. "I left her in Soho Square, directing things there. I'm looking for Miss Mayberry. My aunt told me she might be here."

"She's in the pantry. Turn left and go past the green baize door at the end of the hall."

As Caspar walked away, Lady Octavia's gaze trailed him. He was easy to look upon, she reflected, this young man who appeared to have everything. His aunt, Lady Sophy Devere, had kept her informed from the day he was born. As heir to his father, the Duke of Romsey, wealth, privilege, and position were already his, and it showed, not in arrogance exactly, but in something close to it. But it wasn't unattractive—just the opposite, especially to women.

There wasn't a woman born, his aunt said, who could resist Caspar, more's the pity. It would do him a world of good to taste rejection. Lady Octavia wondered how Lord Caspar had come to meet Jane Mayberry. Jane didn't go into society.

She frowned when another thought occurred to her: Lord Caspar and his volatile mistress, La Contessa, had recently parted company.

She dithered, debating with herself whether she should go after him, just to make sure that he did not have designs on Jane, when Mrs. Bradley came up and said that she was wanted in the old earl's library.

This request cleared Lady Octavia's brain. She was letting her imagination run away with her. The poor man was just trying to help.

≥

He found her in the first room past the green baize door. She hadn't heard him enter, so he took a moment to study her. She was perched on a chair, on tiptoe, fiddling with crockery on the top shelf of the cupboard. The first thing he noticed was a pair of nicely turned ankles. Unfortunately, they were encased in blue woolen stockings. He should have guessed. He'd made a few enquiries about Jane Mayberry and had learned, among other things, that she was a very clever young woman. Clever women, Lady Octavia and his Aunt Sophy among them, wore blue stockings as a badge of honor, a kind of declaration that their minds were set on higher things. "Bluestocking" was a derogatory term that had been coined to describe such women, and they wore that like a badge of honor, too.

With Caspar, it was silk stockings or he wasn't interested.

Her fine woolen gown was a muddy green, "olive" his mistress would have called it, but it was not a color he particularly liked. All the same, it suited the honey-gold hair streaked blond by the sun. The gown was well cut and revealed a slender waist and the long, graceful line of her throat.

He coughed to warn her of his presence, then shifted his gaze when a tawny, bristling mass rose from the floor and positioned itself in front of him with bared fangs.

As she turned from the cupboard, Caspar said softly, "Call off your dog or I shall be forced to shoot it."

"If you do," she said coolly, "it will be the last thing you do." Then to the dog, "Lance, down."

The dog, of indeterminate pedigree with perhaps a touch of wolf thrown in—and that didn't seem right to Caspar because there hadn't been wolves in England for three hundred years—sank to the floor and rested its jowls on its immense paws. Its gaze never wavered from Caspar.

"He doesn't like men," said Miss Mayberry, stepping down from her chair. "Lady Octavia should have warned you. I'm Jane Mayberry, by the way."